THE MEMORY COLLECTOR

Meg Gardiner is originally from Southern California, where she practised law and taught at the University of California, Santa Barbara. She is the author of five Evan Delaney novels as well as the first Jo Beckett thriller, *The Dirty Secrets Club*, described by Jeffery Deaver as 'A winner all the way.' She lives with her family near London.

Praise for Meg Gardiner and *The Memory Collector*:

She is up there with Michael Connelly and Lee Child.
Stephen King

Meg Gardiner is an astonishing writer. *Tess Gerritsen*

Author Gardiner makes every one of her characters leap alive off the page, and I personally am in love with the most compelling of them all, Jo Beckett.
Jeffery Deaver

Riveting . . . a book you just can't put down . . . *The Memory Collector* is a first-class thriller with non-stop action.
Chicago Sun-Times

Meg Gardiner captivates . . . an exceptional follow up to her first Beckett novel, *The Dirty Secrets Club*.
Carolyn Lessard, Associated Press

Gardiner skilfully balances cutting-edge science and gripping suspense in this believable thriller about a technology that is capable of destroying the brain's ability to store short-term memories.
Minneapolis Star-Tribune

Also by Meg Gardiner

Jo Beckett series

The Dirty Secrets Club

Evan Delaney series

China Lake
Mission Canyon
Jericho Point
Crosscut
Kill Chain

MEG GARDINER

The Memory Collector

blue door

Blue Door
An imprint of HarperCollins*Publishers*
77–85 Fulham Palace Road,
Hammersmith, London W6 8JB

www.harpercollins.co.uk

Special overseas edition 2010
1

First published in Great Britain by
Blue Door 2009

ISBN: 978-0-00-735256-2

Set in Sabon by Palimpsest Book Production Limited,
Grangemouth, Stirlingshire

Printed and bound in Great Britain by
Clays Ltd, St Ives plc

Mixed Sources
Product group from well-managed
forests and other controlled sources
www.fsc.org Cert no. SW-COC-1806
© 1996 Forest Stewardship Council

FSC

FSC is a non-profit international organization established
to promote the responsible management of the world's forests.
Products carrying the FSC label are independently certified
to assure consumers that they come from forests that are managed
to meet the social, economic and ecological needs
of present and future generations.

Find out more about HarperCollins and the environment at
www.harpercollins.co.uk/green

Acknowledgments

For their encouragement and their help with this novel, I thank Ben Sevier; Deborah Schneider; Sheila Crowley; Sara Gardiner, M.D.; John Plombon, Ph.D.; Kelly Gerrard; Adrienne Dines; Mary Albanese; Luigge Romanillo; Lejon Boudreaux; Leif Eiriksson; and Paul Shreve.

1

Later, Seth remembered cold air and red light streaking the western sky, music in his ears, and his own hard breathing. Later, he understood, and the understanding stuck in his memory like a thorn. He never heard them coming.

The trail through Golden Gate Park was rutted and he was riding with his earbuds in, tunes cranked high. His guitar was in a backpack case slung around his shoulders. Crimson sunset strobed between the eucalyptus trees. When he reached Kennedy Drive, he jumped the curb, crossed the road, and aimed his bike into the shortcut through the woods. He was a quarter mile from home.

He was late. But if he rode hard he could still beat his mom back from work. His breath frosted the air. The music thrashed in his ears. He barely heard Whiskey bark.

He glanced over his shoulder. The dog was at a stand-still on the path fifty yards behind him. Seth skidded to a stop. He pushed his glasses up his nose, but the trail lay in shadow and he couldn't see what Whiskey was barking at.

He whistled and waved. 'Hey, doofus.'

Whiskey was a big dog, part Irish setter, part golden retriever. Part sofa cushion. And all heart, every dumb inch of him. His hackles were up.

If Whiskey ran off, chasing him down could take forever. Then he'd totally be late. But Seth was fifteen – in a month, anyhow – and Whiskey was his responsibility.

He whistled again. Whiskey glanced at him. He could swear the dog looked worried.

He pulled out his earbuds. 'Whiskey, come.'

The dog stayed, fur bristling. Seth heard traffic outside the park on Fulton. He heard birds singing in the trees and a jet overhead. He heard Whiskey growl.

Seth rode toward him. It might be a raccoon, and even in San Francisco raccoons could have rabies.

He stopped beside the dog. 'Hey, boy. Stay.'

He heard a car door close, back on Kennedy. Boots crunched on leaves and pine needles. Whiskey's ears went back. Seth grabbed his collar. Tension was vibrating from the dog.

The birds weren't singing anymore.

'Come. Heel,' Seth said and turned around.

A man stood on the trail in the dusk, ten feet ahead. Surprise fizzed through Seth all the way to his hair.

The man's shaved head ran straight down to his

shoulders without stopping for a neck. His arms hung by his sides. He looked like a ball-park frank that had been boiled all day.

He nodded at Whiskey. 'He's a handful. What's his name?'

The sun was almost down. Why was the guy wearing sunglasses?

He snapped his fingers. 'Here, dog.'

Seth held Whiskey's collar. The fizzing covered his skin, and he had a bright, thumping feeling behind his eyes. What was this guy after?

The hot dog in shades tilted his head. 'I said, what's his name, Seth?'

The brightness pounded behind Seth's eyes. The man knew who he was.

Of course the man did. Seth was lanky and had coppery hair that stuck up like straw and pale blue eyes that could shoot people the look, the one his mom called the thousand-yard stare. *Just my luck*, she said sometimes. *You look exactly like your father*.

Seth gripped Whiskey's collar. Just *his* luck. His bad luck. His bad, bad, oh, *shit* – this had to do with his dad.

What was this guy after? This guy was after *him*.

He took off. He jumped on the pedals and bolted like a greyhound, ninety degrees away from Oscar Mayer man, riding like a maniac into the woods.

'Whiskey, *come*,' he yelled.

There was no trail, just bumpy ground covered with brown grass and dead leaves. He gripped the handlebars

3

and pedaled harder than he thought his legs could turn. His glasses bounced on his nose. His earbuds swung down and bucked against the bike. Tunes dribbled out.

Behind him, Whiskey barked. Seth felt too scared to look back.

Oscar Mayer wasn't the only one. Whiskey had been growling at something on Kennedy Drive, and Seth had heard a car door slam and footsteps on the trail. His throat felt like it had an apple jammed down it. Two guys were here to get him.

He had to warn his mom.

His cell phone was in his jeans pocket, but riding like a psycho, he couldn't reach it. A moan rose in his throat. He fought it down. He couldn't cry. The trees had darkened from green to black. Ahead, a hundred yards away through the branches, he glimpsed headlights passing on Fulton Street.

He had to get home. His mom – God, what if these guys went after her, too?

Ninety yards to Fulton. Headlights glared white through the trees. Seth's hands were cramping on the handlebars, his legs burning. The guitar bounced in the backpack case. The bike slammed over a rut. He held it, straightened out, and kept going. There'd be people on Fulton. The headlights drew closer.

Behind him, Whiskey yelped.

He looked over his shoulder. His dog was bounding after him through the brush. Behind the dog came Oscar Mayer.

'Whiskey, *run*,' Seth yelled.

4

His legs felt shaky but he dug in again, flying toward the street past an old oak tree.

The second man was waiting behind it.

He shot out an arm as Seth rode past and grabbed the neck of the guitar, yanking Seth off the bike. Seth's feet swung up and his arms flew wide. He crashed to the ground on top of the guitar. Heard the strings sproing and the body crack. The breath slammed out of him.

The man grabbed him. This guy was square with a gray buzz cut, like a concrete brick. He was old but covered with acne. He dragged Seth to his feet.

Seth kicked at him. 'Let me *go*.'

It came out as a scream. Seth swung a fist and kicked for the man's knees.

'Jesus.' The man twisted Seth's arm behind his back.

A sharp pain wracked Seth's elbow. The man shoved him toward the bushes.

Then, in a rush of muscle and power and furious barking, Whiskey attacked. The dog lunged and sank his teeth into the man's wrist. The brick reeled and let go of Seth.

Seth staggered, glasses crooked, through the trees toward Fulton Street. Behind him he heard crazy barking. The brick shouting. A horrible yelp from Whiskey.

Forty yards to Fulton. Whiskey's whimper fell to a moan of pain. Seth kept running. Twenty yards. He could hear his dad: *Don't swerve for an animal. If it's between you and a dog in the road, you need to be the one who lives.*

But this was happening because of his dad, and he

had to get out of it or he and his mother were going to be in a whole huge world of pain and fear.

Fifteen yards. He could see the street, cars, the sidewalk, the cross street that led off Fulton. *His* street – his house was a block up the road. He squinted, trying to tell if his mom's car was parked there.

Somebody was standing on the driveway. A woman – he saw pale legs in a skirt. Long light-brown hair.

His strength flooded back in a vivid burst. '*Mom!*'

Whiskey wailed.

Seth faltered. Whiskey had rescued him – he couldn't abandon the dog. He spotted a rock, picked it up, and turned around.

Oscar Mayer was barreling straight at him. Before Seth could jump the man hunkered low, like a linebacker, and tackled him.

Seth hit the ground so hard his glasses flew, but he kept hold of the rock. He bashed it against the guy's head.

'Let me fucking *go*.'

The man grabbed Seth's hand and pinned it to the ground. The brick ran up, jerking Whiskey by the collar.

'Really is his old man's kid, isn't he?' The brick turned his arm, looking at a bloody bite. 'Bastard mutt.'

Seth threw his head back. 'Mom!'

Oscar Mayer grabbed Seth's face and tried to force his mouth open and shove a handkerchief inside to gag him. The man had blood on his forehead where the rock had hit. Seth locked his jaw. Whiskey surged, trying to reach him. The man pinched his nose. Seth kicked, trying to get the guy's knees, but next to the human hot dog he was just a stick insect. He opened his mouth to gulp a breath and got the handkerchief jammed past his teeth.

The man grabbed Seth's hair, leaned down, and put his lips next to Seth's ear. 'I'll hurt you.' His voice, so close, made wet noises against Seth's skin. 'But first I'll hurt your dog. With a screwdriver.'

All Seth's strength turned to water. A dark weight pressed on his chest, and tears rose uncontrollably toward his eyes.

Oscar Mayer smiled behind his shades. His gums looked pink and glistening. He turned to the brick. 'Call.'

Without his glasses the twilight looked blurred and murky. Seth heard the brick on a cell phone.

'Come on.'

Oscar Mayer wiped the back of his forearm over his brow. 'You know what this is about?'

On the street, a black van screeched to a stop. A man hopped out and strutted toward the woods. He was a skinny white guy, but he looked like a gangbanger. Or like one Seth had seen on MTV. Blue bandanna tied around his forehead, chain hanging from the pocket of his saggy jeans, shoulders rolling. He was like the *Mickey Mouse Club* version of a lowrider.

Oscar Mayer eyed the man like he was dressed for a parade. Marking him down as a moron. A scary one.

Then he turned his hot dog head back to Seth. 'You know where your dad is? What he's doing?'

Seth clamped his mouth shut.

'You got a choice. You want to get hurt or disappear?' He scanned Seth's face and let his wet mouth smile again. 'Didn't think so.' He looked at the other men. 'Get him up.'

2

The wind grated across the water. Chuck Lesniak ran a handkerchief over the back of his neck. Along the riverbank the green grass was shoulder-high. It swayed under the breeze, whispering to him. *Brass ring.*

The first mate walked past, carrying a beer cooler down the dock to the jet boat. It was a humid March evening, and the first mate's faded Manchester United shirt clung to his back. The skipper of the jet boat wore epaulets and a sea captain's hat with gold braid, even though they were a thousand miles inland. He was a compact Zambian with a smile the size of an ostrich egg.

He waved to Lesniak. 'Please, come aboard.'

His Tonga accent was heavy. His warmth seemed genuine. His name tag read WALLY. He sensed Lesniak's nervousness. Chuck was the only passenger on tonight's cocktail-hour tour of the Zambezi River. He'd paid for a private ride.

'Please. The boat is thoroughly sound. I will show you. Her engine is three hundred fifty horsepower and built by Chevrolet.'

Captain Wally was misreading Lesniak's apprehension, but that suited him. He nodded. 'Made in the USA. Then it's A-okay with me.'

Lesniak climbed aboard. The boat rocked and his binoculars swung from the strap around his neck. It was a whomping big speedboat, called a jet boat to convince tourists they were having an extreme-sports experience along with their wine coolers. He touched his pants pocket to check that the flask was secure. The flask was the only bottle he needed tonight. The wind hissed through the grass again. *Not long now.*

The first mate cast off from the dock. Captain Wally started the engine. It rumbled awake, spewing exhaust. He goosed the throttles and slid smoothly away from the dock. White water churned behind the boat.

Over the gargle of the engine, the captain called to him. 'Please, have a seat in the bow. It is cooler there. Enjoy a beverage.'

Lesniak edged to the front of the boat, grabbing a beer from the cooler. A beer couldn't hurt. Could steady his nerves. *Brass ring. Last chance to grab it.*

He had to keep calm. If he could do this, he'd be set for life. Then he could split to California. Forget South Africa – he was never going back. He'd only moved to Johannesburg to work for the company, and that job was gone. He snorted. *It's not a job, it's a malaria-ridden adventure.* Screw Chira-Sayf and all its shiny promises.

10

He'd never adapted to South Africa, even though Jo'burg looked like Dallas, and everybody spoke some kind of English, and he had a Porsche and a house with a maid and a cook and guard dogs and CCTV mounted behind the razor wire on the walls that surrounded his lush garden. And he'd had money, boo-coo bucks compared to what a materials technician made in the U.S. Until the boss pulled the plug.

The boat accelerated through thick air. The sun hung fat and red above the water. Lesniak uncapped his Castle lager, tilted his head back, and drank.

The beer was icy. Yes, he deserved this. This drink, this chance. The flask felt warm in his pocket. *Brass ring*.

Why had the boss shut the project down? Only one answer made sense: He was getting rich out of it. Screw the employees, lay everybody off, while the fat cats slurped the cream.

Yeah, Alec Shepard was keeping the technology, keeping the product for himself, and planning to sell it to God knows who. That's how the rich operated.

The river was huge – sinuous, half a mile wide, and running high. In the ripening sunset the water looked darker than blue, almost purple. He checked his watch. Ten minutes to rendezvous.

He'd been here less than a day, taken a flight from Jo'burg to Lusaka and then a commuter hop down to Livingstone, Zambia's tourist hot spot. He'd spent the night in a five-star lodge beside the river. Ignored all the activities on offer – wildlife safaris, African dance performances, whitewater rafting below Victoria Falls.

11

Sat in his air-conditioned room watching ESPN on cable. March Madness, Kentucky vs. UCLA. He'd kept the blinds closed. Even ten thousand miles from California, smack in the center of southern Africa, he felt paranoid.

When you renegotiate a deal to cut out the middleman, you'd better look over your shoulder.

His contacts had chosen this spot for two reasons. First, because Livingstone and Mosi-O-Tunya National Park were full of European tourists, so a couple more white faces wouldn't draw attention. Second, because this was a great place to smuggle something across a border.

He'd come this far. He'd gotten the flask out of the lab and out of South Africa. Now he was about to make the transfer. He couldn't mess this up.

Sweat broke on his forehead. He was a big man, and the heat got to him. He wiped the handkerchief over his brow and drank the rest of the Castle in one go. *Relax.* When the meet went down he couldn't look half-crazed. Looking jumpy would unmask him not only as an amateur, but as an easy mark.

The breeze rippled the surface of the river, turning it silver. He raised the binoculars and scanned the southern shoreline. Near the high grass of the riverbank a canoe bobbed on the water. Locals, fishing. A pontoon boat was motoring upriver, a sunset booze cruise carrying sunburned Dutch and Japanese tourists, wealthy folks who were probably staying at the Victoria Falls Hotel over there in Zimbabwe. Beautiful, awful, fucked-up Zimbabwe, ruined by greed and egomaniacal cruelty. Screwed by – what did you call it? Politics.

12

Politics, that's what was close to ruining his future. He was a smart guy, everybody said so. He said it to himself every morning in the mirror: *You're smart. You matter*. The project mattered. Killing it was criminal.

But he was about to fix that. The company's work wasn't going to disappear down some black hole. He was going to make sure it got to people who could put it to good use. His payday would be a thank-you for services rendered.

And handing it over in a broken country would ensure that nobody in the wider world took any notice.

The sun glittered on the water. The river looked like a trail of mercury pouring across the vast green plain. What had the hotel brochure said – when the river was high like this, 150 million gallons of water spilled over the falls every minute? Incredible.

He pulled another beer from the cooler. He had to stay chilled and show he had the balls for this. He tried to uncap the beer but the bottle opener chattered against the glass. Maybe the big Chevy engine was making it rattle, but he didn't think so.

Captain Wally put the boat into a sweeping turn toward the center of the river. Ahead, egrets flew from an island, blindingly white against the purple water and green shoreline. The sky above was the blue of glazed pottery.

This was when most folks got the travelogue. *Look, there's a hippo. See that log? It's no log, it's a crocodile.* But Lesniak had been specific: No talk. He'd paid for the ride.

He'd paid extra for the stop they were going to make. He glanced again at his watch. In two minutes they should cross to the Zimbabwean side. He drank half the beer, getting ready.

He was doing the right thing. This was important. *Brass ring.*

As they skipped across the water he scanned the shore-line, seeing thick grass, acacia trees, a thin sandy beach. Downriver, another jet boat was racing in their direction.

Straight at them, actually. Captain Wally eased back on the throttle.

Lesniak frowned over his shoulder. 'What's going on?'

Captain Wally smiled. 'My cousin. Last week he borrowed sixty liters of fuel. Now he is repaying me.'

The other boat turned in a broad arc, cutting a white wake across the river. Then it dropped to a crawl and settled low in the water. The skipper gave a languid wave. In the bow a passenger slouched beneath a baseball cap, arms crossed, a fishing rod at his side. He gazed at the southern shore, seemingly unperturbed by this time-out for family business. As if thinking: *It's Africa. Go with it.* The boat pulled alongside and its skipper called out in Tonga. Captain Wally laughed. Lesniak raised the binoculars and scanned the shoreline again. Where was his contact?

The boat rocked, and from the corner of his eye he saw Captain Wally's first mate hop to the other boat to grab the fuel cans. He refocused the binoculars. There – ahead, a Nissan Pathfinder edged through the tall grass down to the beach. His heart began ringing like an alarm clock.

The Pathfinder was muddy and had Zim tags. He felt

14

a pang of disappointment. But what had he been expecting, diplomatic plates? Or fuzzy dice with an intelligence service logo hanging from the mirror?

Something. He'd been hoping for some clue that told him who his contact really worked for. A U.S. or European agency, or the Israelis, or maybe some group farther east.

The boat rocked again, and the hull reverberated as feet landed on the deck. More conversation in Tonga behind him. *Forget the family gossip, skipper. Get going.*

The engine revved and the boat rose at the bow, moving sharply away from Captain Wally's cousin. It headed straight down the center of the vast river.

Lesniak turned. 'Head for shore, that's the guy . . .'

The wind chattered against Lesniak's shirt. The engine growled, deep and dirty. The boat bounded across the water.

Captain Wally was no longer at the wheel. Captain Wally was no longer aboard. He and his crewman were on the cousin's jet boat, which was fast receding into the distance.

Standing at the wheel was the cousin's passenger.

Lesniak gripped his beer. It felt clammy. *He* felt clammy. 'You?' he said.

The man at the wheel wore jeans and a black T-shirt and even blacker sunglasses. With the sunset glaring behind him, it was impossible to tell what he was looking at. Or whether he had eyes. He was lean and taut, his mouth grim in a sunburned face. He had removed his baseball cap. His copper-colored hair caught the sunlight.

The boat cut smoothly through the swollen river. The wind and spray turned the sweat cold on Lesniak's back.

He saw the southern shore recede. He saw the Nissan Pathfinder flash past. *Brass ring . . .*

'Where are you going?' Lesniak said.

The man held the throttles steady. Slowly his head clocked around until his sunglasses seemed to center on a spot between Lesniak's eyes. The beer bottle slipped from Lesniak's fingers, hit the deck, and rolled around, clinking.

'I can explain,' he said.

The man spun the wheel and drove the boat toward a cluster of tiny islands. They left the open flow of violet water and swept into a narrow channel between islets knotted with trees. Egrets carpeted the branches like huge blossoms. The man cut the throttles back to idle. The boat settled lower in the water.

The man stared at Lesniak. 'Give it to me.'

Lesniak's chest rose and fell. White wings loomed all around. The smell of bird shit hit him so hard he gagged.

'I don't know what you're talking about.'

'We both know that's not true. Give it to me.'

Lesniak put the back of a hand to his nose. He felt his courage and self-assurance shrivel.

He had never bothered to learn this man's name.

He knew him only as Rusty. That's what they all called him – Rusty, the sheepdog. The herder. The babysitter. The hired hand, a glorified gofer, a guy who showed up when the bigwigs came to town. Somebody's ne'er-do-well relative, he'd heard, who landed himself a cushy job nannying execs and tech geeks on corporate road trips.

Wrong. This guy was no nanny. Why had Lesniak never noticed he was a mean and cold son of a bitch?

'I don't have it,' he said.

'The guard at the lab talked. I know you took it.'

The boat swayed with the current. Rusty the sheepdog turned the wheel to keep it pointing downriver. 'Who got to you?'

Birds fluffed themselves in the trees. White wings everywhere, blank eyes, all watching, none seeing him. Lesniak's lips pulled back, and he knew, horribly, he was smiling. *Stop it*, he told himself. *You look like a fool.* His left hand went reflexively to the pocket of his chinos, felt the contours of the flask. He couldn't stop grinning. If he stopped, he'd burst into tears.

This was *his* chance. He'd managed to get here with the product because of *his* sweat and ingenuity and willingness to take the risk. This was *his* brass ring.

The boat slid beneath grasping branches. The air was thick and stinking. Beneath the rumble of the Chevy engine Lesniak heard a rushing sound. Maybe it was his own blood, trying to flee his veins.

'Who hired you?' the sheepdog said.

He had to play this carefully. He cleared his throat. 'Make me an offer.'

Rusty's sunglasses didn't reflect the sunset. They were pure dark, carbon black, nothing there. He spoke slowly.

'You have rained down grief on my head. So tell me who hired you, and then give it to me.'

'What?' Lesniak blinked. Grief? That wasn't how you negotiated. 'Seriously, make me an offer. I'm flexible.'

Rusty goosed the throttles and lazed the wheel to the right. They cleared the bird islands and rejoined the main

17

channel of the river. *My God*. The tourist brochures had said the Zambezi was a mile wide at this point, but he hadn't pictured what that meant. The rushing sound was louder. Not his blood, but millions of tons of water roaring over rocks around another bend downriver.

The wind felt like a cheese grater on Lesniak's face. He wiped his hand across his upper lip. 'An offer. I'm open. What I have, it's uncut. Pure. Perfect clarity . . .'

Rusty leaned down. Maybe he was grabbing a beer. Maybe this was all a joke.

He came up with a hunting rifle.

Of course he did. Back at the hotel, girls in bikinis were lounging poolside while waiters served them frosty drinks with pink umbrellas. But out here, every tour guide and his grandmother carried a hunting rifle, because they were cruising through the African bush along the shores of a goddamned game park.

How could this be happening to him? He was a top-notch technician. He had an A.A. from DeVry. He played on the company softball team. He was a normal California guy who just wanted his BMW and a nice house in Los Gatos and some recognition and his freaking *brass ring*.

Rusty pointed the barrel of the rifle at Lesniak's chest. 'You'll give it to me right now, and then you'll tell me who's behind this.'

The sheepdog had turned on his flock.

Lesniak felt itchy. Felt naked. Saw the muzzle aimed at his heavy, sweating stomach. *Say something. Be a man.* 'Or?'

'Or you'll give it to me.' Rusty's face was expression-less. '"Give" being loosely defined. Maybe involving free will on your part, maybe not. Your choice.'

'You can't kill me. Captain Wally saw you, and his first mate, and his cousin. They're witnesses.'

The barrel stayed level on his chest.

The first hint of a whimper floated up Lesniak's throat. Rusty had paid them off. Of course he had. The Zambians were men who made, what, two dollars a day? He'd probably bought them for the price of a Big Mac.

And nobody knew Lesniak was here. He'd told people at work that he was flying to London for R&R before heading home to the Bay Area. At the hotel today he had told nobody he was taking a boat ride. And he'd given Captain Wally a fake name.

Nobody would miss him for weeks.

In the distance, the sound of rushing water rose to thunder. Lesniak glanced downriver. Beyond a tree-lined bend, mist boiled into the air, so thick it obscured the view. But his thoughts turned as clear as glass.

Rusty the sheepdog had come here to take the flask. Maybe for himself, maybe for the CEO, maybe for one of the groups that would beggar themselves to buy what was in it.

Whether Rusty shot Lesniak before he took it or after didn't matter. The man was going to kill him.

Lesniak lurched to the side of the boat and jumped.

He belly-flopped, hard. The water engulfed him as if he'd been swallowed by a dragon. The current surged, hauling him along faster than he could have believed possible. Reflexively he opened his eyes and saw blue gloom. He flailed upward and broke the surface, gasping.

The river, swollen from the summer's rains, rolled him up and down as if he were a thorn stuck in the dragon's chilly skin. The shore was a distant strip of green grass. He thrashed, struggling to keep his head above water as it swept him along.

Ten yards to his left the boat was keeping pace with him.

Oh, sweet Jesus. He kicked, feeling the flask bump his leg. His clothes and shoes dragged him down. The boat pulled alongside.

'Give me your hand,' Rusty said.

'Don't shoot me.' A swell lifted him, and he saw a cluster of tiny islands ahead. Trees grew densely along their edges, branches dragging in the river.

'Your hand,' Rusty shouted.

If he could get under the low-hanging branches, Rusty wouldn't be able to reach him. Lesniak swam for it. He choked, 'Shoot and the flask goes down with me.'

'If you die, you'll float. Long enough for me to retrieve your body,' Rusty said. 'Alive or dead, you'll give me the stuff. It's your choice.'

A sob broke from Lesniak's mouth.

'Listen to me. I'll swap. You give me the stuff, and I'll give you the jet boat.'

Lesniak windmilled his arms. In the fast-flowing water, the islands bobbed in and out of sight. If he could get in beneath the trees, he could hide.

His arms were leaden, his lungs burning, water sloshing

20

in his mouth. He coughed, looked ahead, saw waves, branches, a log. The islands drew closer.

The log twitched its tail.

He screamed. So much adrenaline dumped into his system that the sunset turned white. The tail switched back. The crocodile was floating directly ahead of him. *Oh Jesus oh Jesus . . .*

He turned, wailing. The river poured him toward the croc.

The boat pulled alongside. Rusty yelled, 'Get aboard. Hurry.'

Lesniak slapped at the fiberglass hull and his hands slid off. Hysteria rose in his chest. The sound in his ears was Chevy engine and rushing water and his own panicked sobs. He clawed at the slick fiber-glass. He tried to dig his fingernails into the wet side of the boat.

A hand clamped around his wrist. Rusty began to haul him up.

Lesniak's legs dragged in the water. He grabbed Rusty's forearm. 'Pull me out. Pull me out.'

Rusty grunted with effort. 'Grab the lip of the hull, not me.'

Kicking wildly, Lesniak dug his nails into Rusty's forearm. 'Don't drop me. The croc . . .'

Straining, Rusty pulled Lesniak halfway out of the water. Lesniak's feet propellered. He looked up, frantic, and saw blood running from Rusty's forearm where his fingernails were clawing the man's flesh.

Oh, God. Rusty wasn't big enough to pull him aboard. Lesniak outweighed him by forty pounds, easy. His panting increased. His feet were still in the water and *oh God, the croc, the croc . . .*

The boat rolled and began to spin. Rusty slid toward him on the slippery deck. Lesniak screamed and tried to climb up Rusty's arm.

Rusty gasped, 'Let go of my arm, grab the hull, and let me pull you –'

'Help me!' Lesniak screamed.

Rusty grabbed Lesniak's belt. Lesniak felt himself being pulled up – shoulders above the side, gut bumping the lip of the hull. He kicked helplessly, trying to worm both feet out of the water. The boat swung lazily around, rising and falling on the flow of the river. He grabbed at Rusty, clawed for his shirt, swiped a hand, and knocked the man's sunglasses off his face. He had to get out of the water. He was crying, he heard himself, he couldn't stop.

Rusty groaned with effort. 'Stop fighting me. You'll pull me over and we'll both drown.'

Lesniak wriggled a knee over the top. His shoulders drooped back toward the waterline. They were spinning in a circle. His right foot was tingling. *The croc, oh Christ, the jaws the teeth the hideous pain . . .* He slid back down the hull. Rusty grabbed for him and got a hand on his pants pocket.

The pocket ripped open. The flask fell out and landed on the deck.

Lesniak stared at it. The boat continued its lazy spin. The flask glinted in the sun. Around the screw-top lid, he saw bubbles.

22

Oh, shit.

Bubbles were foaming from under the lid of the flask. The seal had broken.

The boat rolled. The flask slid across the deck. No, no – if a wave swamped the boat the flask could be swept overboard. Lesniak let go of Rusty's arm and reached for it. The flask was his future, everything important and good and brass fucking ring and –

'I can't hold you,' Rusty shouted at him. 'Hang on to the hull.'

No way, not in a million years. Hang on and Rusty would grab it and he'd never get it back and everybody would find out and . . .

The flask gleamed. He stretched, fingers grasping.

The boat snapped into a roll. Lesniak lost his grip and fell like a punching bag back into the water.

The current took him. He surfaced and spun around, frantic. He was moving fast again, clear of the little chain of islands. A huge roar rose in his ears. It wasn't the engine anymore, but the water, the sound of water coursing over rocks in massive amounts.

On the boat, Rusty had the flask. Struggling for balance as the boat spun, he tightened down the bubbling top and shoved it in the back pocket of his jeans.

Lesniak stared, stunned. Rusty fought his way back to the controls of the speedboat. He wiped his bloody arm against his shirt, turned the wheel, and headed downriver. Fast. Straight at him.

Hell, oh, no. With that huge Chevy engine and a fiberglass hull that would crack his head like a teacup. Lesniak turned and began a final, thrashing attempt to outswim it. The water swept him forward.

He heard Rusty shouting at him. Heard 'Stop,' and 'Don't . . .'

Terrified, he looked back over his shoulder. Without his sunglasses, Rusty's eyes looked freakishly pale in the sunset. A flock of egrets sped low across the river behind him, white and graceful.

The jet boat bore at him. Then Rusty spun the wheel. The boat went into a tight, arcing turn. It passed ten yards behind him, spewing white water in its wake, and turned upriver.

Bobbing on the swift current, exhausted, Lesniak felt a knot in his throat. The guy was leaving. Thank God.

Thank God, *hell*.

Rusty had the flask. He had the stuff. Slick, all of it.

The boat receded slowly, motor roaring. This was why it had the huge Chevy engine – it needed every single horsepower to fight the current here. The growl of the engine was hard to hear above the ever-louder rush of water over rocks.

His heart leaped into overdrive. He spun. He was in the center of the river, coming around a broad bend at great speed, into the dusk, islands far away, riverbanks just a hint at either edge of his vision.

He rose on a swell, like a body surfer, and saw ahead. His mouth opened.

Riding like a fly on one hundred fifty million gallons of water, sweeping into a trough, he turned and started swimming upriver. Mouth open, eyes open, lungs busting.

Feet heavy in his shoes, arms weak, he swam desperately, hearing the roar behind him. He saw the shore, low and green and immensely distant. He saw the red sunset shimmering on the slate surface of the water. He saw the mist rise overhead. Mosi-O-Tunya, they called it, the smoke that thunders, Victoria Falls. He felt himself pulled backward as the mighty Zambezi turned into a high dive, a mile-wide thrill ride, a blue dragon taking to the air and leaping off the cliff into the gorge. He tried to grab the water itself, to hold himself up, to stay here and not plunge toward the rocks three hundred fifty feet below. But though he screamed out to the river gods, nobody could stop him as he swept toward the edge.

3

Jo Beckett held her arms away from her sides and spread her feet. People eddied around her, staring briefly before they hurried on. Ten feet ahead, a cop stood with arms crossed. His radio scritched. Behind her she heard the snap of latex.

'Don't worry, these gloves are clean,' the woman said. 'Wider stance.'

Jo complied. The woman pressed her spidery fingers up the inside of Jo's thighs.

The cop shifted his weight. 'Come on, it's an emergency.'

Hands ran around Jo's ribs, down her back, and across her rump.

She forced herself not to flinch. 'Just don't tuck a dollar bill down the waistband of my jeans.'

The woman's hands paused, and she glared.

Jo offered a contrite look. 'Never mind – I'm a lousy dancer. I'd fall off the pole. Can I –'

'A terrorist isn't getting past me just because somebody claims to be in a hurry.'

'She's not a terrorist,' the cop said. 'She's a doctor with the mobile crisis team.'

Damn right, Jo wanted to tell the screener – maybe using one of the curses her grandfather had picked up in the Cairo backstreets of his childhood. But that, she decided, was a rotten idea.

Airports, she thought, sucked like a bilge pump.

San Francisco International was packed and noisy. The crowd bumped through the security line like cattle being prodded toward the chute at a stockyard. The checkpoint's plastic bins banged against each other, sounding like a discordant drum line. A posse of screeners waved people forward, saying, *Hurry up, move along.* Show your boarding pass. Now show it again. Now show it to *that* screener. Jo knew redundant checks prevented slip-ups. But if this checkpoint had been a person, it would have obsessive-compulsive disorder. Defending against a previous threat, not anticipating the next one.

Such as the possible situation at gate 94.

Outside, a March storm pounded the Bay Area. Rain clouds rolled overhead, a nasty jumble of gray and black. A cold wind scoured the runways.

The screener lowered her hands. 'You're clear.' Her tone implied, *For now, girly*.

Jo hurriedly reclaimed her earrings, and belt, and Doc Martens, and her necklace with the Coptic cross, and her satchel, and her dignity. She suspected that airports were either a psych experiment in mass humiliation or a conspiracy to drive the traveling public insane. Possibly both. *Shoes off, lab rats. Aggravating, isn't it? Here, have some Xanax.*

The airport cop, Darren Paterson, wore an apologetic look. He was baby-faced African-American, wearing a uniform that fit him like Glad Wrap.

'Sorry about that,' he said.

She tied her Doc Martens. 'No problem. My service said you're looking for a psych eval on a passenger who came in on a flight from London. You think he needs to be fifty-one fiftied?'

'That's what you need to tell us.'

Section 5150: involuntary commitment. As a psychiatrist, Jo had the authority to send people to a custodial psychiatric facility for seventy-two hours.

She only got calls like this if the police thought someone was dangerous to himself or others. But usually the cops themselves took people into custody under section 5150 and transported them to an E.R. for psychiatric evaluation. Maybe the airline had requested medical personnel. Maybe Paterson wanted experienced backup – he looked so young that she suspected he was a rookie. Maybe something truly bizarre was going on. In any case, when her service buzzed her she'd been two minutes from the terminal, and the authorities had decided against waiting for the rest of the crisis team to arrive.

'Glad you were in the vicinity,' Paterson said.

'You lucked out. I was dropping my brother off for a flight to Los Angeles.' She walked with Paterson along the concourse. 'What happened?'

28

'Ian Kanan arrived on a Virgin Atlantic flight from Heathrow. Became confused and combative when the plane landed. He's barricaded himself aboard.'

The terminal echoed with the roar of jet engines. Rain slashed against the plate-glass windows.

'"Confused and combative," but you didn't arrest him. What exactly did Kanan do?' Jo said.

'When they touched down he jumped out of his seat and tried to open the emergency exit.'

'With the plane still rolling?'

'Two male passengers tackled him. Flight attendants say Kanan threw them off like they were made of papier-mâché. Apparently he fought like a maniac.'

'In what way?'

He glanced at her. 'As in crazy.'

She smiled briefly. 'Most people see bizarre behavior and think, *Nuts, or not nuts?* Psychiatrists think, *How nuts, and what kind?*'

They reached the gate. Down the Jetway, a clot of airline personnel huddled inside the open door of the airliner. They looked at Jo with a mixture of relief and bemusement, as if thinking, *A shrink? Talk him off the plane – yeah, that'll do it.*

The captain stood in the cockpit doorway. 'Get him off my aircraft.'

Officer Paterson pointed down the aisle. 'He's in economy.'

Jo said, 'No wonder he went berserk.'

The flight attendants turned to her. Jo put up a hand. 'Kidding.'

29

She looked down the empty length of the jet. More airline staff and another police officer hovered near the galley.

You never knew what you were going to get in these situations. Catatonia. Religious mania. A bad drug trip. Drunkenness or a violent psychotic episode. A guy trying to detonate his shoes.

She had no time to take a complete history on Ian Kanan. But the two passengers who subdued him had remained aboard the plane. Ron Gingrich was a tough-looking fifty-five with a gray ponytail and Grateful Dead shirt. Jared Ely was in his twenties, wearing a black T-shirt, green Crocs, and a surfeit of nervous energy.

'Tell me what happened,' Jo said.

Gingrich smoothed his goatee. 'We landed hard. Crosswind; it felt like we were coming in sideways. Hit with a whump, and people were like, *Whoa*. The plane was rattling real loud. Couple overhead compartments fell open. Then this guy' – he pointed toward the back of the plane – 'comes tearing up the aisle. He jumps over the woman sitting in the exit row and starts ripping open the emergency door.'

Ely nodded. 'It looked like he knew exactly what he was doing.'

'What do you mean?' Jo said.

Ely's gaze was sharp and thoughtful. 'He didn't hesitate. Didn't stop to read the instructions on the door. He got straight to business, like he'd done it before.'

Jo nodded. 'Then what?'

'We grabbed him.'

'Spur of the moment,' Gingrich said. 'We just moved. I tell you, the guy fought like a demon. But two against one, we overpowered him.'

'Did he say anything?' Jo said.

Gingrich nodded. 'Oh, yeah. Crystal clear.'

Ely said, 'He kept telling us we were crazy.'

Jo turned to the flight attendants. 'How was Kanan during the flight?'

'A zombie,' said a young blonde. 'He didn't read, didn't watch the movies, didn't even watch the air map. Didn't eat. He sat there.'

'Did he drink?' Jo said.

'No.'

'You sure?'

The young woman's name tag read STEF NIVESEN. Her face turned wry. 'We flew in from the U.K. Everybody drank. Except him.'

'Did you see him take any medication?'

'No.'

'Where's his carry-on?'

The flight attendants had taken Kanan's backpack to the first-class galley. Jo poked through it, seeing a laptop, finding no drugs or alcohol. She did find Kanan's passport and itinerary. She scanned them and handed both to Paterson.

'He didn't come from London. He came from South Africa and changed planes at Heathrow.'

'Does that matter?' Paterson said.

'Maybe.' Jo looked down the length of the plane. 'Come on.'

Paterson led her down the aisle. The crowd near the galley stepped aside. The second cop, Chad Weigel, was standing outside the door of the lav.

He raised his hand to knock but Jo said, 'Hang on.'

She turned to the flight attendants. 'Did you unlock the door yourselves and try to get him out?'

'Twice,' said a British flight attendant whose name tag read CHARLOTTE THORNE. 'The first time, he braced himself against the door so we couldn't push it inward. He also told us to get the hell back. The second time, he didn't say anything. It seemed he was slumped against the door.'

'Unconscious?' Jo said, thinking, *Drugs, drunk, sick?*

The flight attendant shrugged. 'He didn't respond.'

Officer Paterson said, 'What do you think?'

'Let's find out.' Jo knocked on the door. 'Mr Kanan?'

She heard water running in the sink. She and Paterson exchanged a look.

The door opened. The man inside turned to step out, saw her, and stopped dead.

Ian Kanan was in his midthirties, five-ten, white. From the back, wearing a coat, he would have seemed unexceptional. Face-to-face with him, Jo saw the way his denim shirt ran tight across his shoulders. She saw the self-awareness that ran head to toe. She saw scratches, deep ones, on his left wrist. He was lean and whippy. His hair was short and rusty brown, the color of iron ore. His eyes were the palest blue she had ever seen.

32

Almost colorless, and bright, like a seam of ancient ice. Jo felt as though she were staring into a crevasse.

'Excuse me,' he said and stepped out the door.

He saw the people gathered in the aisle, all staring at him. His eyes went to Officer Paterson and to the gun holstered on Paterson's belt.

'What's going on?' he said.

'Mr Kanan, are you all right?' Jo said.

He glanced out the windows. The gray sky churned and rain blew across the view. His eyes clicked to the aisle. The empty jet. The term *escape plan* ran through Jo's mind.

His eyes clicked back to her. 'I wasn't feeling well.'

A fully formed sentence, pronounced clearly, in response to her question. That was promising. His gaze was acute, but Jo sensed something else behind it – tightly controlled confusion. Paterson's hand hovered near his weapon.

'I'm Dr Beckett. Can you tell me why you don't want to get off the plane?'

'I'll get off the plane. Why wouldn't I?' he said.

Everybody stared at him.

'Is there a problem?' he said. His eyes said something else entirely. His eyes said, *Big problem*.

'I'd like to talk to you. Shall we do that in the terminal?' Jo said.

'Talk? Why?' Kanan said.

In her peripheral vision, Jo saw Officer Weigel shake his head. He said, 'Because you blockaded yourself in the bathroom for an hour and –'

Jo put up a hand. Kanan's face was dead still. His pupils looked normal size, equal and reactive. She couldn't smell alcohol on him. He wasn't weaving, shaking, or slurring his words. And yet she sensed that something was very wrong. Again he glanced around the jet. He seemed unsettled by the fact that it was empty.

'You're the last off,' she said. 'The crew needs to shut down the plane. Let's talk in the terminal.'

He looked her up and down, a slow glance. 'Sure.'

The police officers bracketed him up the aisle, Weigel ahead, Paterson behind. Following a few yards back, Jo saw how Kanan's hands hung loose at his sides. It seemed casual, but the way he held himself reminded her of a gunslinger. When they passed the emergency exit row, he saw the partially opened door. He frowned at it, his head clocking around as he walked.

'Why's the exit open?' he said.

Jo could have sworn the temperature dropped ten degrees. Kanan kept walking. Ahead stood the two men who had tackled him. Kanan picked up his pace. Abruptly he reached into his back pocket.

Officer Paterson said, 'Hey.'

Kanan ignored him, and then it was too late. By the time he pulled out a cell phone, Paterson was on him.

Paterson was fast. Kanan was faster. He spun, grabbed Paterson's hand, smashed his elbow, and drove the cop to his knees.

Paterson cried out. The British flight attendant said, 'Bloody hell.' Up the aisle, Officer Weigel turned around.

For a fraction of a second Kanan's face was ferocious.

34

He stared down at Paterson. Then confusion seemed to sweep over him again.

'What . . . ?'

Kanan gazed at Paterson with horror. Behind him, Officer Weigel unsnapped a holster and charged.

Jo put out her hands. 'Wait –'

Weigel drew a Taser. 'Doc, get back.'

He fired. The darts hit. Kanan jerked rigid.

Paterson broke free. Kanan stood motionless. And, so quick Jo barely sensed what was coming, Kanan's hands drew upward and turned in, as if he were cringing. They drew into balls against his chest. His eyes blanked. His gaze rolled sideways, and then his head followed, slowly, turning to the left as though pulled in a circle by a weird magnet. Paterson stumbled to his feet and charged.

'Don't!' Jo shouted.

She was too late. Paterson tackled Kanan, who went down like a tree.

Jo ran toward them. 'Officer, stop. No.'

Paterson was wrestling Kanan. 'Face down.'

Kanan didn't respond. He continued rolling leftward, hands clenched to his chest, face pressed against the floor.

'Hands behind your back,' Paterson said breathlessly.

Jo grabbed Paterson by the shoulders. 'Stop. He's having a seizure.'

'He's resisting.' Paterson grunted, straining to pull Kanan's hands down.

'Officer, he's seizing,' Jo said. 'Get off. Move.'

Kanan wasn't jerking or flailing or beating his head

35

against the floor. He was simply gone, into a realm where bright lines flared at the corners of his vision and a panoply of color spun across the mind. He kept turning.

'Partial seizure,' Jo said. 'Get off him. *Now*.'

4

Kanan lay in the aisle of the jet, turning as if on a rotisserie. Jo tried to pull Paterson away from him.

'Call the paramedics,' she said.

Officer Weigel loomed over them, Taser in his hand. 'He got a hundred thousand volts. He'll come out of it.'

'The Taser may have triggered the seizure, but something else is wrong with him. Officer Paterson, let go.'

Paterson relented. Jo knelt at Kanan's side, fear pouring down her back like cold water. She wasn't a trauma doc. She was a forensic psychiatrist. In her line of work the crisis cases never presented medical emergencies. Her crisis cases were already dead.

She shook it off, telling herself: *Go through it step by step. First, ABC. Airway, breathing, circulation.* She checked that Kanan was breathing and had a pulse. Then she stripped off her sweater, rolled it up, and tucked it under his head. Heat was pouring off his skin.

'Paramedics and an ambulance. Call them,' she said.

'You're not going to section him?' Paterson said.

'No. I'm getting him to an E.R.'

Paterson got on the radio. Jo checked Kanan's face and head for fractures and lacerations. The only cuts she could see were the gouges on his forearm. She avoided touching them and began to wish she'd brought latex gloves. In the aisle she spied his cell phone. She picked it up. Looked at dialed calls – an area code 415 number, about forty-seven times.

Like an ebbing wave, the seizure subsided. Kanan stopped turning and lay limp on the floor. His eyes closed and opened again. Above Jo, Paterson's radio leaked static.

She put a hand on Kanan's shoulder. 'Mr Kanan? Ian?'

She heard the clink of handcuffs being removed from a utility belt.

'Don't,' she said. 'He has a head injury. Where are the paramedics?'

'On their way,' Paterson said. 'He assaulted a police officer. He needs to be restrained.'

'You're not going to arrest him.'

'That's not your call. Sectioning him is. You going to do that?'

Kanan shifted. 'What's . . . am – river's too . . .'

'Ian,' Jo said.

'All wrong it's . . .' He looked at her as though seeing her through a distorted video link. 'Slick it's too . . . falls – misty it's . . .' He blinked and grabbed Jo's arm. 'Get you.'

38

He began breathing rapidly. Jo took his pulse. One forty-eight.

'Is anybody here to meet you?' she said. He was wearing a wedding ring. 'Is your wife picking you up?'

His gaze sparked, as though her voice had lit a fuse in his brain. His eyes rolled back to whites and his lips parted. Beneath Jo's hand his body tensed.

He convulsed. This time the seizure was grand mal.

The ambulance rolled north through the rain on 101, its siren shooing traffic out of its way. Kanan lay strapped to a gurney, unresponsive. Jo sat by his shoulder. The paramedic kept her balance as the vehicle took a curve. She called Kanan's name and flashed a penlight in his eyes.

Officer Paterson lurked by the back doors, baby face puckering with suspicion. His left hand ran back and forth over the handcuffs on his utility belt.

Jo shook her head at him. 'You can't cuff a seizure patient.'

'One hand to the stretcher.'

'No. We need to be able to maneuver him. If he vomits we have to keep him from inhaling it, or he could die.'

'He's a loose cannon. And he's going to be under arrest,' Paterson said.

'If you think you can Mirandize him in this condition, you're the one who needs sectioning.'

Kanan groaned. The paramedic said, 'Ian, can you hear me?'

A gust of wind whistled over the ambulance and flung rain across the windows. Kanan's eyes woozed open.

Jo took his hand. 'What's your name?'

He blinked as though trying to focus. 'Ian Kanan.'

His gaze cleared. His pupils were equal, reactive to light, and had a wolfish glow. Jo felt a prickle along the back of her neck.

On the jetliner, Kanan had dropped Paterson to his knees with the speed of a train wreck. Despite her spirited defense of him, Jo didn't want Kanan to do worse to anybody in the ambulance.

'You had a seizure. Lie still,' she said.

'I what?'

'Do you have epilepsy?'

He frowned. 'That's a crazy question.'

Jo was board-certified in both psychiatry and neurology, but as a forensic psychiatrist, her work dealt almost exclusively with history. When the police or medical examiner couldn't determine why somebody had died, they called her to perform a psychological autopsy on the victim. She spent her days deciphering the countless ways the pressures of the world could end a person's life.

Now she had a live case, a man with a huge and unidentified problem, who she sensed might turn on her at any moment.

'Do you recall hitting your head?' she said.

'No.' Hands on his jeans pockets. 'Where's my phone?'

'I have it.'

'I need to make a call.' His gaze zinged to Jo. 'You're American? Did the embassy send you?' He looked around the ambulance and his face tightened with alarm. 'Where am I?'

40

'On your way to San Francisco General Hospital. Are you on medication?'

'No. San Francisco?' He tried to sit up. 'Who are you?'

'Dr Beckett.' She pressed a hand on his chest. 'You were in southern Africa. Are you taking antimalarial drugs?'

'Quinine? Sure – Tanqueray and tonic.'

'Lariam?'

Lariam could have severe side effects, including seizures and psychosis.

'No,' he said.

'What were you doing in South Africa?'

His pale eyes looked eerie. She couldn't tell why he hesitated. But whether he was confused or calculating, it took him ten full seconds to say, 'Business trip.'

The wind rattled the ambulance and a burst of rain sprayed the window. Jo didn't tell Kanan the two reasons they were heading to San Francisco General – it was the area's only level-one trauma center and San Francisco's designated evaluation facility for patients placed on psychiatric hold. Kanan glanced around. His gaze reached Officer Paterson and stuck.

Jaw tightening, he lurched against the straps on the gurney. 'My family. Did something –'

'Hey.' Paterson moved instantly to Kanan's side. The paramedic pressed Kanan back against the pillow.

Jo put a hand on his arm. 'What about your family, Mr Kanan?'

For a second he looked fearfully bewildered. Then he blinked and forcibly slowed his breathing. 'What happened to me?' He looked at Paterson. 'Am I under arrest?'

41

Paterson said, 'Not yet. But you wanted to get off your flight so bad, you tried to jump out while the plane was rolling.'

'Did we crash?' He looked around the ambulance. 'Did the plane go down?'

Jo gazed at him, puzzled. In the space of two minutes Kanan had gone from unconscious to intensely alert, articulate, strong, and confused.

'Mr Kanan –'

'Ian.'

'Ian, I'm a psychiatrist. The police called me to the airport to evaluate you because –'

'You think I'm nuts?'

'I think you have a head injury.'

He stared at her for a long moment. A look of pain, and understanding, seemed to jolt him. His breathing became choppy. 'They'll say it's self-inflicted.'

The cold trickle ran down Jo's back again. 'Your injury?'

'It's over, isn't it? I failed.'

'Failed at what?'

He squeezed his eyes shut. For a second, Jo thought he was fighting back tears. Paterson's radio guttered. The sound caught Kanan's ear. He opened his eyes and looked at the young cop. And as Jo watched, Kanan's face relaxed. He blinked, breathed deeply, and turned to her, eyes shining and untroubled.

'Hey. What's going on?'

'We're taking you to the hospital.'

Puzzlement. 'Why?'

Slowly, Jo said, 'Do you recall what I told you a minute ago?'

'No. Who are you?'

The paramedic wrapped her stethoscope around her neck. 'Man.'

Paterson braced his hand against the wall of the ambulance. 'What is it?'

Jo felt grim. 'Amnesia.'

She looked at Kanan, thinking, *And not the good kind.*

Seth sat on the floor with his back against the frame of his bed. He was quiet. He'd been quiet for days. The men had told him to keep his mouth shut.

But inside, his mind was full of noise, like feedback from an amplifier. Because he hadn't kept his mouth shut when the men dragged him into the park. He had talked. He'd told them about his dad.

His stomach hurt. It hurt like a fist was squeezing it, a fist made of wire. He wrapped his arms around his shins and put his head down on his knees.

My dad's gone and you'll never catch up with him. He's in the Middle fucking East and if you think you . . .

He'd said it to scare them. So they'd know his dad wasn't like some tour guide who herded people around on vacation. He was a mean mofo who could take on the Middle East, *alone.* But why had he said it? Why why why . . .

The room was dim and the floor was hard. That was okay – he wanted it that way, preferred the hard floor to the creaking bed. The hard floor forced him to stay alert, kept him thinking.

What was he going to do? The men – the human hot dog and the brick with acne and the Mickey Mouse rapper – had told him the consequences of not keeping his mouth shut. Of trying to tell anybody at all. They'd been specific and elaborate. *We'll demonstrate on your dog. Then we'll do it to your mom.*

He squeezed his eyes closed and put his hands over his ears, trying to shut out the memory.

Whiskey was okay for now. Seth heard the dog in the kitchen, lapping water from the bowl. But Whiskey wasn't safe, and neither was Seth's mom. The men had Seth where they wanted him. And they could get to him without warning, at any moment.

The wire fist tightened around his stomach and then grabbed his throat. He had to do something. He had to figure a way out. But how? He was trapped.

Neurologist Rick Simioni found Jo in the hospital hallway. His face was a beacon of alarm.

'Was I right?' Jo said.

'Anterograde amnesia. Unquestionably.'

Simioni's dress shirt and lab coat were swan white. He smoothed his tie. 'Kanan knows who he is. Remembers everything about himself, his life, and the world, right up till the beginning of the flight today.'

'Then?' Jo said.

'Blank.'

Mild amnesia was common following a head injury. But it was often limited and transient – as patients improve, so could their memories. Not, however, in Ian Kanan's case.

'Nothing new sinks in?' Jo said.

'It hits, sticks for a while, and slides off. His brain receives new information but isn't absorbing it.'

'How long can he retain information before he forgets it?'

'Five, six minutes.'

'What happens?'

'He doesn't lose consciousness. Doesn't have a seizure – EEG shows no ictal patterns. But if his attention wanders for very long, all the information he's gathered simply evaporates.'

'Short-term memory loss,' Jo said.

'His vision, hearing, and speech are perfect. You tested him and noticed no muscle weakness . . .'

'He was post-ictal with a Glasgow Coma Score of eleven. He'd suffered one partial complex seizure, one grand mal.'

The news was grim. Short-term memory loss – anterograde amnesia – didn't mean you forgot things for a short while. It meant you couldn't form new memories. And it was both a symptom and a result of catastrophic brain injury.

'What's causing it?'

'You need to see the MRI,' Simioni said.

In the radiology suite, light boxes hummed on the walls. A PET scan glowed on a cinema-display computer screen, somebody's lungs and liver imaged as Timothy Leary might have hallucinated them, rendered in crimson, cobalt, and screaming yellow.

By contrast, the black-and-white MRI scan of Kanan's brain looked dull. And devastating.

45

The radiologist was a precise man from Hyderabad named Chakrabarti who had little hair and expressed less emotion. He acknowledged Jo with an economical nod.

Jo approached the screen and examined the cross-sectional slice of Ian Kanan's head. Slowly, quietly, she said, 'What *is* that?'

Chakrabarti touched the image with his index finger. 'A lesion.'

'Of the medial temporal lobes. I see. What's *that*?'

Deep within Kanan's brain, where the gray matter of the medial temporal lobes should have been, was a dark fuzzy space.

'There's more on the next cross section,' Chakrabarti said.

'More sounds bad,' Jo said.

'It is.' He typed on the keyboard. 'Mr Kanan had difficulty staying still in the scanner. He was quite agitated. He would lie calmly for a minute, then forget where he was and try to climb out, yelling, "What the hell is this?"'

'Like his brain kept resetting to Start?' Jo said.

'*Groundhog Day*,' Simioni said.

Chakrabarti brought up a new image. Simioni took a breath. Jo felt a flicker of nausea.

Kanan's medial temporal lobes seemed to be etched with black strands. It looked as though somebody had scratched lines in the image with a rusty needle.

'Those . . . tendrils – are they causing the memory loss?' Jo said.

Simioni pointed with a pen. 'The medial temporal lobe,

and particularly the hippocampus, is the part of the brain that encodes facts and events into memory. So I'd say yes.'

'What is it?'

Chakrabarti said, 'I don't know. It's not a bleed. Does he remember suffering head trauma?'

'He says no,' Jo said. 'Is that viral? Bacterial?'

The two men stared at the screen but had no answers. Simioni said, 'Have you reached his wife?'

'No answer. Left messages,' Jo said.

They stared some more. Simioni turned. 'Let's tell him.'

5

The black van idled on the driveway, waiting while the garage door opened. Rain sliced across the windshield. The door droned up and the van pulled in.

Alan Murdock shut off the engine. 'Unload the supplies.'

Vance Whittleburg hopped out, hitched up the saggy jeans that hung halfway down his behind, and began shifting grocery bags and boxes of ammunition into the house. Even carrying sodas and ketchup, he made sure to strut like the gangbanger he dreamed of being.

Murdock put the garage door back down. This was a neglected rental house in Mountain View, off San Antonio Road. It was hard by the railroad tracks and hardly the only home on the street with a weedy lawn and garbage cans in which stray dogs foraged. The street didn't have a neighborhood watch. It was a place where nobody cared. And nobody would take notice of temporary tenants coming and going.

The door from the house opened and Ken Meiring pushed into the garage. Gauze circled his overmuscled forearm, covering the bloody bite Seth Kanan's dog had inflicted. Ken's face was red, all the way into his crew cut. The acne that ringed his neck stood out like plague buboes. If the guy didn't lose some weight and cut down his steroid dosage, he was going to give himself a stroke.

Murdock walked to a cabinet along the wall. 'Got news that'll lower your blood pressure.'

'Go ahead, Dirty Harry – make my goddamned day.'

Murdock ignored the mockery. So he wasn't a San Francisco cop anymore – he was entitled to wear the SFPD T-shirt until it fell apart.

'You don't complain about the parting gifts I brought with me from the department,' he said.

He opened the cabinet. It was stocked with goodies he had liberated from police custody, including plastic handcuffs, CS gas, and a handy nightstick. He set a box of nine-millimeter ammunition inside, next to his pistol.

Ken grunted. 'Fine, sprinkle pixie dust on my mood.'

'He's here.'

Ken's eyebrows rose.

'Came in on a Virgin Atlantic flight this morning.' Murdock smiled, exposing his small teeth. 'We're back in business.'

'You positive?'

Outside, the Caltrain lumbered down the tracks. The bare lightbulb that hung from the roof of the garage jittered. Ken stared at Murdock like he was watching the light reflect off Murdock's shaven head.

49

Murdock's smile receded. 'You should really have more faith in me, Ken. The deal is back on track.'

'When?'

Murdock locked the cabinet. 'Patience.'

'Patience is dangerous. Kanan is a wild card.'

Murdock turned, stepped close, and lowered his voice. 'But we hold all the aces.'

Ken slowly, gradually, nodded. Murdock stepped back.

'You need to expand your horizons,' he said. 'This isn't like hijacking a truck full of restricted electronic gear. This is the big leagues. Mergers and acquisitions, Ken.'

Ken looked unconvinced.

'Acquisition, anyhow,' Murdock said. He took out his phone. 'And we have a monetary wizard setting up the next phase.'

'That who you calling?'

Murdock smiled again. His gums made a wet sound. 'The sales department.'

As he listened to the phone ring, he slapped Ken on the back. 'Get yourself geared up. Kanan's bringing back liquid lightning. Enough to shock the whole world.'

Ken eyed him. 'Maybe. But we have to get it from him.'

Jo walked toward the E.R. with Simioni, flipping through Ian Kanan's passport and wallet. The passport showed visits to Jordan, Israel, South Africa, Zimbabwe, and Zambia, all stamped within the past two weeks. His driver's license listed a home address near Golden Gate Park.

A corporate photo I.D. said IAN KANAN, CHIRA-SAYF IN-CORPORATED, SANTA CLARA. Silicon Valley, she suspected.

Simioni had a printout of Kanan's MRI. Jo knew it would hit Kanan like a hammer blow.

As a forensic psychiatrist, she mercifully avoided dropping doom on people. She analyzed the dead for the police – she didn't break bad news. Not anymore. Not since the moment she'd told her mother- and father-in-law their son was dead.

She knocked and went through the door into the E.R. room. Kanan was pacing by the window, phone pressed to his ear. He was dressed in his street clothes. He looked like a penned animal.

'Misty, I'm back, babe. I'm on my way.'

The door clicked shut. Kanan turned, saw Jo and Simioni, and hung up. He extended his hand. 'Ian Kanan. Doc, give me the word – what's happening? Because I need to leave.'

Simioni hesitated, comprehended that Kanan didn't remember him, and shook. 'Rick Simioni. I'm the neurologist who sent you for the MRI.'

Kanan frowned. 'MRI?'

Jo offered her hand. 'I'm Dr Beckett. You suffered two seizures and have a severe head injury. It's affecting your memory.'

'What are you talking about? My memory's fine.'

'Do you recognize me?'

His gaze slid smoothly up her body. It took in her athletic physique, her dark eyes, her long brown curls. It stopped at the laminated hospital I.D. clipped to her sweater.

51

'No. Should I?' he said.

'I'm a psychiatrist. I brought you here from the airport. I've been with you for nearly two hours.'

'I don't remem –' His face dropped. In the sudden quiet, a lash of rain hit the window. 'I have amnesia?'

'Yes.'

Simioni said, 'A particular kind called anterograde amnesia. You haven't lost old memories. But something has damaged the part of your brain that forms new ones.'

'"Something." What?'

'We're investigating that.'

'Don't you know?'

'Not yet. We need your history. Talk us through what you were doing in Africa and the Middle East.'

Kanan held back, his face registering disbelief at *not yet*. Finally he said, 'Business trip.'

'What do you do, Mr Kanan?'

'Ian. I'm a security consultant for a tech company in Santa Clara.'

Jo had guessed right. 'What does your job involve?'

'I help the company keep hold of its equipment and its people.'

'How?'

He raised a hand. 'Stop. You're saying I have a head injury and keep forgetting everything?'

'Yes. And help us. You just came back from the developing world. What does your job involve?'

He hesitated and then seemed to calm himself. 'When company personnel head overseas, I go along to scout dicey situations. I ride herd on engineers and executives.

52

Make sure absentminded programmers don't leave their laptops on a train and that nobody plays away from home in a way that could get them hurt.'

'Excuse me?' Simioni said.

'I keep executives from getting so drunk they get rolled by prostitutes or reveal trade secrets to foreign competitors.'

Simioni crossed his arms. 'You do any industrial health and safety work?'

Kanan's smile was brief and wry. 'I'm a babysitter.'

Jo and Simioni exchanged a glance, puzzled. The possibilities were numerous and awful and none of them made immediate sense. A blow to the head. Viral encephalitis. Brain surgery performed with a Black & Decker drill. Tapeworm larvae burrowing into Kanan's brain.

Jo forcibly ignored that image. Kanan's eyes were bright. He was handsome and lucid and in deep trouble.

'You're saying something's wrong with me?' he said.

'Something serious, yes,' Jo said.

Simioni held out the MRI photos. As Kanan examined them, his face paled.

There was little point breaking it to him gently. There would never be a good time to explain things to him – anything – ever again. Whatever he learned, he could never assimilate. He could only be reminded of it, endlessly. A melody poured through Jo's thoughts. Red Hot Chili Peppers, 'Strip My Mind.'

Simioni asked Kanan a list of questions. Fever? Drinking unfiltered water or eating suspect food from a Zimbabwean food stall? No, no, and no.

Kanan stared relentlessly at the images. 'I've never heard of this.'

'It's extremely rare,' Jo said. 'Did anything strange happen on your business trip? Anything at all out of the ordinary?'

'No.' He looked up. 'What's the treatment?'

'We're working on that,' Simioni said.

Kanan's voice sharpened. 'Don't you know?'

'We won't even have a chance to treat it unless we can figure out what's causing it.'

Kanan looked rigid, like a spring pressed down, ready to blow. 'Prognosis?'

'The part of your brain that processes information and sends it to long-term storage is damaged,' Jo said. 'It means information won't be transferred to memory. It will slough off.'

He jabbed a finger at the MRI printout. 'You're saying this part of my brain is being scratched out.' He drew a breath. 'Erased.'

'In a way, yes.'

'Like I'm looking through a camera viewfinder but can't click the shutter,' Kanan said. 'Am I going to become a vegetable?'

She held on to his gaze. 'No.'

'I'm gonna end up staring out the window drooling?'

'Not at all,' Simioni said.

Kanan's gaze lengthened. Simioni continued explaining things, but Jo knew that Kanan heard none of it. His head and heart were stuck at the screeching red letters that had just been scrawled across his life. *Mind wipe.*

Jo touched Kanan's hand. 'You have some kind of brain trauma. That's all we know.'

She gauged his pulse. It was fast and strong. He was wearing a denim shirt over a brown T-shirt. The logo on the T-shirt said FADE TO CLEAR. Kanan saw her reading it.

'My kid's garage band. They got a dozen shirts made in the Haight.' He blinked. Though he looked calm, he was breathing rapidly. 'Find out what's wrong with me. Fix it.'

'We're trying,' Jo said. 'But it's doing damage right now, and that damage is not the kind that can be repaired.'

Simioni's pager went off. 'Have to go.' He crossed his arms. 'Mr Kanan, we're doing everything we can. Hang in there.'

He left. Kanan watched the door close.

'None of this makes sense. I remember everything. Ian David Kanan. Age thirty-five. Blood type A-positive.'

He reeled off his address, date of birth, driver's license and Social Security numbers. 'I broke my arm at summer camp when I was eight. I took Misty to the senior prom. I work at Chira-Sayf. I can recite the security code to open the door to the lab there.'

'What time is it?' Jo said.

He looked bemused. 'I don't know, dinnertime?'

'Twelve thirty P.M.'

Kanan looked out the window. The noon sun was fighting the rain clouds. The sight took him aback.

'How did you get here?' Jo said.

'I guess – I drove.'

'Ambulance.'

He frowned in confusion and surprise.

Jo lowered her voice. 'In the ambulance, I told you about the head injury. You said, "They'll say it was self-inflicted."'

He didn't reply, but instead took out his phone. 'Excuse me. I need to call my wife.'

'Look at your dialed calls register.'

He thumbed the keypad. He saw the dozens of calls he'd made and looked for a second like he'd been hit between the eyes with a rock. Jo let silence settle on the room.

'Who's going to say your injury is self-inflicted, Ian? And why?'

He stuck his phone in his pocket and turned toward the door. 'I need to leave.'

Jo stepped firmly into his path. 'What happened to you?'

He stopped, but just barely. 'Please excuse me. But I'm going now.'

'What happened overseas? How did you get those gouges in your arm? Tell me. Because I can still section you. And the cops won't hesitate to arrest you.'

He raised an eyebrow. 'You're a spitfire. Ever been a drill sergeant?'

'I didn't need to be. I'm mean enough to keep soldiers in line without having to pull rank.' She hoped that never got back to the man in her life. 'Now tell me – what happened to you?'

Kanan's face tightened, and for a moment she thought he was going to bat her aside. Then the sad mixture of pain and irony spread across his face. 'The real question is, what's *going* to happen to me?'

Her shoulders inched down. 'You're going to stay the same person. This won't affect your intelligence or personality. It won't affect your existing memories. It won't erase any of the knowledge and skills you have.'

'I'll still be able to drive a car and skin a deer.'

'Yes.'

'I'll know everybody? I'll still recognize them?'

'Yes. This isn't dementia. It's not Alzheimer's.'

'But my brain won't record.'

'In essence, no.'

'So it's all live performance. Nothing goes into long-term storage. I have no hard drive.'

He didn't cry. He merely put his phone away. 'That other doctor' – he glanced at the door, indicating the departed Simioni – 'he split so you'd stay and have to explain it to me.'

'I'm a shrink. I'm supposed to be good at handling –'

'People whose lives have been destroyed?'

'Yes.'

He held still for a moment and let out a low nonlaugh. 'Thumbs-up for honesty. What do you do – you're a lone ranger, riding around committing wackos on the fly?'

'I'm a forensic psychiatrist. And I'm on call for emergencies, such as the one you had at the airport today.'

'Forensic . . .'

'That doesn't mean I work CSI. It means psychiatric work that intersects with the law.'

'Did I break any laws today?' he said.

'The cops think so.'

She told him about tackling Officer Paterson on the plane and being Tasered. It was all news to him.

'They out there waiting to arrest me?' he said.

'They're out there. I've deterred them from arresting you for now.'

'I don't feel like I'm forgetting anything.'

'What do you feel is happening?'

He eased a glance at her. 'You sure sound like a shrink.'

She spread her hands and shrugged.

He exhaled. 'It's just going to dissolve, isn't it? Everything I see and hear. This conversation. The future.' He looked out the window. A splinter of sunlight cut silver across his face. 'I'm going to live in a continuous present.'

Jo thought about it. 'I guess that's one way to look at it.'

'Will I remember big things? Who's president? An asteroid smashing into the earth?'

He wouldn't remember being *elected* president. Every moment would be fresh, every experience new, every person he met a stranger.

'What do I do? How do I cope?'

'You'll need to work out strategies to help remind yourself where you are, where you're going, where you've just been. Notes. Photos. A PDA. Keep a camera, pen, and paper with you.'

'I won't be able to work, will I? Or be by myself. I'll need . . . a babysitter.' He ran a hand across his forehead. 'To tell me if I've brushed my teeth and wiped my own goddamned ass.'

58

Quick as a whip, he swung an arm and upended the bedside table. The phone crashed to the floor with a sick ringing sound. Jo held still. Her hearing felt all at once ten times more acute. She seemed to hear dust swirling on the air and Kanan's heart thundering in his chest. The door was six feet to her left. She got ready to jump if he turned on her.

Tentatively she raised a hand. 'Ian, your wife isn't home. Does she –'

'How do you know she's not home?'

He pulled out his phone and yet again speed-dialed his home number. Jo crossed to him, hands up, and gestured for him to hand the phone to her.

It was ringing. She took it and showed him the call register. His face fell.

He was quiet a moment. 'I need to go.'

'Not yet. Does your wife have a cell phone? Can you call her at work? How about family, friends?'

Instead of answering, Kanan looked out the window. In the sunlight his pale eyes seemed to shine white.

'I'm going to die, aren't I?'

Ain't we all, honey. 'There's no evidence this condition is terminal.'

'Spare me, doc. Even if I keep breathing, it doesn't matter.' He touched two fingers to the side of his head and tapped, like he was pointing a gun at himself. 'I'm over. Five minutes at a stretch, that's all I'll remember, isn't it?'

'Likely.'

'You're really gonna be shrinky about this, aren't you?

Stand there waiting for me to unload. Fine – I've been shrunk before, several times, and I'm not crazy. So listen to me,' he said. 'Even if I'm not cold in the ground, I'm losing myself. The Reaper's here to collect, while I'm still walking. It's a harvest.'

Stormy light angled across the hospital room. Jo held still, taking in Kanan's body language. He seemed calm – but calm like a high-running river, where smooth water covered nasty rocks below. His composure was covering rage. It was covering confusion and fear, and more. He was holding something back.

'Ian, tell me what happened in Africa.'

'That's not important.'

'Do you know what's wrong with you?'

White gaze. It was like looking into the heart of a diamond. Clear, hard, and absolutely lifeless.

'What's causing this problem?' she said.

He held absolutely still for a long beat. 'I've been poisoned.'

'With what?'

'Get me a piece of paper and a pen.'

She opened her backpack, took out a notebook and tossed it to him. 'Pen's in the spiral binding. Start writing.'

He did.

'How were you poisoned? Accident?' Jo said.

'Maybe.'

'Maybe not?'

He looked up at her. For a second his eyes dimmed, as though a crack of pain had gone through him. 'Maybe not.'

'List all the people who might even conceivably wish you harm.'

'I don't need to.'

'Why not?' She raised an eyebrow. 'Because you know who poisoned you? Or because you poisoned yourself?'

In the hall outside, two paramedics strode past, pushing a stretcher on which a patient lay screaming. Kanan turned at the sound, pen poised above the notebook.

'Ian?'

He turned back to her, eyes clear. 'Is this an E.R.? Did something happen, Doctor . . .' He read her I.D. 'Beckett?'

6

The light was patchy, silver through clouds. The shadows in the room deepened and stretched, like the moment. Jo took the notebook from Kanan and showed him what he had written. *Jo Beckett. Forensic shrink.*

'What's going on?' he said.

She found an indelible marker in her satchel. 'Let me see your arm. Unbutton your sleeve.'

He rolled up his right sleeve and held out his forearm. She turned it palm-up and wrote *Severe memory loss. I cannot form new memories*. 'You're going to need a medic alert bracelet, but this will do for now.' She handed him the pen. 'If there's anything else you need urgently to remember, write it now.'

He was going to need a lot more. A camera. A constant companion. He stared at the words, stunned.

'You have a brain injury. You told me you might have

been poisoned. I need to know how, and with what,' Jo said.

He put a hand against the side of his head. Closed his eyes and doubled over.

'Ian?'

He bolted for the trash can. He grabbed it, bent over, and vomited.

Behind her the door opened and Rick Simioni came in. He saw Kanan hunched over the trash can and headed toward him.

Kanan straightened. Catching sight of Simioni, he whirled. 'Who are you?'

'Dr Simioni, the neurologist.'

In the open doorway, a woman stood watching. She had the shine of varnished wood. A willow, hewn and bright. Her limbs were tan and sinewy, her hair a sleek caramel flow. Her eyes, hot with shock, were pinned on Kanan.

'Ian.' Her voice was choked.

Kanan straightened and put his hand against the wall, bracing himself. Though his head hung low and he looked pale with nausea, his colorless eyes met hers.

Simioni put a hand on Kanan's elbow. 'Sit down. Come on.'

'In a minute,' Kanan said.

The woman crossed the room to him. She raised a hand and tentatively, tenderly, touched his chest.

Simioni waved Jo out of the room. 'Give them a minute.'

Jo stepped into the hallway with Simioni. The door

to the room slowly swung shut. The young woman stepped close to Kanan and touched his cheek. Kanan's eyes were unreadable. Relief, confusion, joy, despair – Jo couldn't decipher his gaze. He took her hand from his face, clutching it tightly. The door clicked shut.

Jo looked at Simioni quizzically.

'That's his wife,' he said. 'She took the news badly.'

'Where has she been for the past two hours?' Jo said.

'I didn't ask. You look like you've been jumped by the boogie man. Something new going on with Mr Kanan?'

'Bunch of somethings. Very weird.'

Simioni looked at the closed door. He hesitated, and when he turned back to Jo he was frowning.

'Add something to the weird list,' he said. 'The airport cops collected his luggage and sent it over. He was traveling with some unusual souvenirs – a sword and a couple of daggers.'

'What kind of sword?'

He looked bemused. 'That's an odd question.'

'Is it ceremonial, or an Olympic-sanctioned epee, or a broadsword he jousts with when he dresses up and goes to the Renaissance fair?'

'It's not covered in blood. And it's old. Very. The . . . what do you call it, the handle –'

'Hilt.'

'– is elaborate. It has writing on it, old and worn down. In Arabic. Why do you want to know?'

'He's been in Africa and the Middle East. He says he's a corporate babysitter, but he comes home with weaponry. He tells me he's been poisoned and may have tried to

64

commit suicide. And I have a four-hundred-year-old Japanese *katana* in my living room. If I hear somebody's importing sharp objects, particularly a knife-and-sword combination, I want to make sure he's not going to use them to commit hara-kiri.'

The door to the E.R. room opened and Kanan's wife walked out. She looked pale.

Simioni walked over. 'Mrs Kanan –'

'I can't.' She raised a hand. 'Can't talk about . . .' Her face crimped and she put the back of her hand to her mouth, as if suppressing a scream.

Ian Kanan's wife was petite. Even wearing stack-heeled boots she was an inch shorter than Jo, and Jo wasn't a giant. Her sleek flow of caramel hair conveyed athleticism and self-confidence. Her coat was white wool, fitted, stylish. Beneath it her black sweater was tight and her blue tartan skirt hugged her rear end. Aside from the corporate hair she looked like a high-fashion Glasgow punk.

Voice shaking, she said, 'Help him.'

She turned and rushed down the hall.

Jo and Simioni gave each other a look. The neurologist shook his head, indicating, *Don't make me be the one . . .* as if he would play rock-paper-scissors with Jo to see who calmed her down.

Jo went after her. 'Mrs Kanan.'

Her voice seemed to hit the woman like a horsewhip. She broke into a jog and kept going.

'Please wait,' Jo said. 'We need your help.'

The woman turned the corner. Jo followed and saw

her at the junction of two hallways, looking around in confusion. She couldn't tell whether the woman was shocked, horrified, or simply trying to hang on to her final seconds of normality before her organized and happy life disintegrated like wet paper.

Jo put out her hand. 'Jo Beckett, M.D.'

Kanan's wife hesitated a long second before she relented and shook. 'Misty Kanan. Is it true? In five minutes he'll forget I was here?'

'Yes.'

'It's crazy. He's crazy. That's what you're saying. He's losing his mind.'

'That's not what I'm saying.'

'His brain is shot full of holes. How does that not equal going insane?' She ran both hands over her cheeks. 'Stop this thing. Fix it.'

'We don't know what it is.'

'Give him drugs. Operate. Do something. Electric shock treatment. For God's sake, *something*.'

'We're trying to get to the bottom of it. We need your help. We need you to get him to talk.'

'He doesn't want my help. He's . . . God, that man. He wants to be strong. He'll never admit to weakness.' She pressed her hands to the corners of her eyes. 'Hypnotize him. You're a psychiatrist – snap him out of it. Turn his memory back on.'

'His memories are not being misplaced. They're being destroyed before they can become permanent. We can't reboot his system and call them up. It's not like flipping a breaker switch and restoring power.'

Misty looked at Jo and past her shoulder, antsy. She seemed as tense and jagged as a spool of concertina wire. She ran her hands up and down her arms, scratching like she itched.

'I need air.' She began walking down the hallway.

'Wait – give me your phone number,' Jo said.

Misty stopped, found a piece of scratch paper, and scribbled on it. 'My new cell number. Call me anytime. Day or night.'

She turned and rushed down the hall, swerving around an orderly pushing an elderly man in a wheelchair. Jo heard her break into tears.

She watched her flee, thinking, *What the hell?* She ran a hand through her hair. Exhaling, she walked back around the corner.

Simioni was nowhere in sight, but Officer Paterson was at the nurses' station. She walked over and offered an apologetic smile.

'On the plane, I may have seemed more concerned about Kanan than about you. Is your elbow all right?' she said.

'Fine. Thanks.' His baby face looked tired. 'It's time to read Kanan his rights.'

'You can read him his rights. He'll understand them. And five minutes later he won't remember that you've done it.'

'Head injuries can make people violent. He may lash out again. He should be restrained.'

Next verse, same as the first. 'Give me some time –'

'You've had time.'

She put up her hands, knowing she'd pushed it as far as she could. Beyond Paterson she saw Simioni walking up the hallway. He was carrying a backpack and a package wrapped in bubble wrap.

He set them on the counter. 'Kanan's carry-on, plus one of the daggers he brought back. Recognize the type?'

Paterson's face took on a look of utter incredulity. He shook his head at Jo. 'What did you say to me back at the airport – "How nuts, and what kind?" Wrong question. It's *who's* nuts. And the answer is you doctors. Kanan should be in a straitjacket.'

Jo opened her mouth to snark back, and her phone rang. The ringtone consisted of a death-metal lick and a singer screaming, '*Psychosocial.*' She grabbed it and turned away from Paterson and Simioni's horrified faces.

She saw the display, and her face flushed. She answered quietly. 'Call you back?'

Gabe Quintana said, 'Day or night. You know how to find me.'

'Great.' She hung up, heart kicking, and turned back around. 'Sorry.'

Paterson huffed a breath from beneath his form-fitting uniform shirt. 'Is Kanan stable?'

'That's a relative term,' Simioni said. 'But his life is not at risk right now.'

'I need to place him under arrest.'

Jo acquiesced. Kanan would have to deal with it. 'You're not taking him to the jail tonight. He's been admitted to the hospital.'

68

'Understood. But I need to go through the formalities.'

Reluctantly, Jo and Simioni accompanied Paterson to Kanan's E.R. room. Paterson opened the door.

Kanan was gone.

7

'Damn it.' Paterson grabbed his radio and stalked down the hall.

Kanan was gone, along with the things that had been on the bedside chair: his jacket, wallet, and passport. Crumpled on the floor by the bed was a blue tartan scarf that matched Misty Kanan's skirt. Jo picked it up. A bubble-wrapped package sat on the visitors' chair, ripped open. Simioni hurriedly checked inside.

'Sword's here,' he said. 'Dagger . . .'

In the hallway an orderly was passing by. Jo caught him. 'Did you see a man leave this room? Rusty hair, pale blue eyes?'

'Couple minutes ago. He came out, asked me if I'd seen the woman who was here before.'

'His wife?'

'Tartan skirt, nice looking?'

'Yes.'

'Told him I saw her head that way.' He nodded down the hall.

The cop had gone the opposite direction. Jo turned to Simioni. 'Get Paterson.'

She rushed down the hall in the direction the orderly had indicated. Kanan couldn't have gotten far. She silently berated herself. Kanan had repeatedly insisted that he wanted to leave. She shouldn't have presumed that Simioni and Paterson were watching him.

What was driving Kanan to split?

Pop quiz: Business trip, poison, and weaponry – which ones don't go with 'corporate babysitter'?

She reached the end of the hall and pushed through the double doors. If Kanan got outside, would he wander aimlessly? Did he know the neighborhood?

She rounded a corner into another hallway. At the far end, near a bank of elevators, she saw him.

He was walking away from her, his stride measured, his head turning as his gaze swept the hallway.

Jo headed toward him. 'Ian, wait.'

He turned. His eyes locked onto her like targeting radar, without recognition.

Where was Officer Paterson? She glanced over her shoulder. No sign of the cop. She approached Kanan slowly, hands out.

'I'm Dr Beckett. Please don't leave. You have a severe brain injury.'

His gaze ran across her, bit by bit, until he saw the tartan scarf in her hand. His expression tightened as though he'd stepped on a nail.

71

'Misty left this in the E.R.,' Jo said. 'I found it.'

He lunged at her.

She dodged but he was fast. He grabbed her and with shocking ease pulled her through the open door of an elevator. She inhaled to shout and he swung her off her feet, spun her around, and clapped a hand over her mouth.

She squirmed and raised her knees and tried to kick him. She saw the doors sliding closed, the bright waxed floor and clinical walls and heartless fluorescent lighting in the hallway disappear into a slit, and then gone.

With his knee, Kanan pressed the stop button.

'What are you doing with Misty's scarf?' he said.

He was lithe and strong, his balance superb, his words clear. Jo raised her foot and tried to kick the alarm button. Kanan lifted her off her feet and carried her to the far corner of the elevator. Her claustrophobia screeched at her. *Tight space, violent paranoid.*

'Who are you working for?' Kanan said.

Writhing, she tried to kick him in the instep.

'Who?' He pinned her flat against the wall. 'If I take my hand off your mouth, will you scream?'

Abso-frackin-lutely. She shook her head.

'You're right, you won't.' His right hand came up. It held one of the ancient daggers. 'You'll answer me, very quietly.'

The blade shone under the lights. Within its gleaming steel were weird patterns. Kinked lines, dark, not quite twisting – almost like a circuit board. As the angle of the blade altered, they shimmered like oil.

It wasn't a ceremonial seppuku knife. Not Japanese.

But old – so old that it had almost certainly done the job before, and more than once.

She wasn't going to scream.

Yet.

He took his hand off her mouth. 'What do you want? Do you have it?'

'Misty came to see you in the emergency room not fifteen minutes ago. I spoke to her.'

'Bullshit.'

'You can't remember. Come back to the E.R. and –'

'Stop lying to me.'

Convincing him she was telling the truth was out of the question. Misty hadn't had to sign in when she came to the hospital. Maybe the cops could tell Kanan that his wife had been there, right after they cuffed him, and holy flaming crap, that blade looked sharp.

'I'm a psychiatrist. I brought you here in an ambulance from your London flight. You told me you'd been poisoned on your business trip to Africa. You said, "They'll say it was self-inflicted."'

Instead of confusion, disbelief and anger rolled across Kanan's face. 'Self-inflicted? You don't get so lucky. And not poisoned. Contaminated.'

That was something different altogether. Despite her fear, she said, 'What with?'

He put his ear close to hers. 'Listen to me.'

He was breathing hard, thrumming with tension. Jo sensed that he was close to breaking down. If she hadn't been terrified, she would have felt sorry for him. But she felt like she'd fallen into a pit with a wounded animal.

'If you're a shrink, you can be quiet and listen for one minute. Isn't that what you're trained to do?'

The elevator felt like a tin can that could easily crush her. *Don't hyperventilate*, she told herself. *Just breathe.*

And don't point that knife at me. She didn't have a weapon, or a shield, or anything to defend herself with. Her belt, maybe. Her hands.

'You saying you don't know what got to me?' he said.

'That's right.'

'And you want to know why?'

'Yes.'

His lips drew back, revealing white teeth. 'Slick. Really. Slick.'

Her heart sank. 'I'm not trying to trick you. You have a serious brain injury. You need help. What were you contaminated with?'

'Be quiet. I'm going to get them. Where are they?'

'Who?'

He knocked her against the wall. 'I'm on the job. I'm doing it. But I will get them.'

On his left arm, just below his elbow, Jo saw black lines on his skin. It was writing. And though she had written *memory loss* on his right arm, this was something different. These were words she hadn't written.

She hated it when words were written on people's bodies.

'Are you looking at me?' he said.

Jo looked. In his ice-chip eyes she saw fury. Behind the fury, the great engine for it, was entropy: chaos, fear, grief. The knife hung in his hand.

'I know I can't remember everything. But I'm not crazy.

I will finish the job.' He watched her, seemingly to see if she believed him. 'You believe that?'

Of course not. 'Of course.'

'Dig this. I don't care about the consequences to myself. You've already poured down grief on me. And when I rain it back on you, nobody's going to punish a guy in my shape. What can anybody do to me that's worse?'

He held her gaze, eyes no longer diamond-dead but swimming with light. His chest rose and fell against hers. His lips were inches from her ear. He stared at her, maybe searching for confirmation, and relaxed his grip.

It gave her four inches and a brief second. She threw herself forward against him, brought up her left leg, and kicked at the control panel. She hit the red alarm button.

A siren scorched the elevator. Angrily, Kanan shoved her away from him. Shaking his head, he punched the open button. The knife hung loose in his hand, seemingly forgotten.

The door began inching open. Kanan's gaze fell to the laminated hospital I.D. clipped to Jo's sweater. He yanked it off.

Held it up. 'I'll find you.'

The doors opened. He turned and ran.

Jo put a hand on the wall. The light seemed intensely bright. Her heart drummed in her ears.

The doors of the elevator began to slide closed again. She skittered out like a hockey puck, straight past a couple of interns in scrubs. She looked up and down the hall, but Kanan was gone.

She grabbed one of the interns. 'Call security.'

That message on Kanan's arm. She didn't know whether it had been written there when he got off the plane, or whether it had been added at the hospital. Each time she'd seen him, he'd had on his longsleeved shirt.

The humming in her head increased: joy, anger, relief, an almost giddy sense of excitement at making it out unscathed.

One of the interns said, 'Everything all right?'

'Elevators,' she said. 'Nightmare.'

The ringing of the alarm bell filled the hallway. But it couldn't overcome the echo of Kanan's voice. *I'm going to get them.* Jo feared what he meant. Because she knew what she'd seen on Kanan's skin: names. And two words written in ink, running up his arm like a shot of fatality straight into the vein.

They die.

8

Jo downshifted as traffic ahead of her slowed on the rain-slick freeway. Her hair flew around her. She hit the hands-free phone and redialed.

This time, the call was answered on the first ring. 'Jo Beckett. You're bringing cases with you to the department when you call now?'

'Wonderful to hear your voice too, Lieutenant.'

In reply, Jo heard Amy Tang flick her lighter. 'No, you light up my days. I sit at my desk reading women's magazines, waiting for you to call. What wardrobe should I go with this spring – Hollywood elegance or fairy princess?'

'Black, Amy. Or black.'

Tang laughed, a brief *ha* that slipped out despite her best efforts. 'Please, doctor. I'm at your disposal. Meet me at that coffee place down the hill from your house. I can give you ten minutes, because I'm a living doll.'

Tang sounded as though she didn't need any more caffeine, but Jo said, 'I'm on my way.'

Fifteen minutes later, she managed to find a parking spot two blocks from Java Jones. The coffeehouse sat on a funky side street at the bottom of Russian Hill near Fisherman's Wharf. Jo wrangled her scarf over her head, turned up the collar on her jean jacket, fed quarters into the meter, and dashed along the sidewalk. The plate-glass windows at Java Jones were steamed over. The lights inside had the amber glow of a fogged-in Parisian café, circa 1870. It looked like a Monet painting. She pushed through the door, half-drenched.

The come-and-get-it smell of espresso welcomed her. Fall Out Boy was playing on the stereo, 'Hum Hallelujah.' Lieutenant Amy Tang stood at the counter, fingers tapping double-time, waiting for her order.

Tang was a sea urchin, small and prickly. She wore a black peacoat, black slacks, black boots. Spiky black hair. Jo knew that beneath the barbs, she had a heart – a cautious, well-guarded heart. But reaching it could result in cuts and bruises. She liked Tang enormously.

With chilled fingers, Jo fumbled to remove her sodden scarf. It had gotten wrapped over her hair and half her face.

Tang eyed her. 'You trying out for ninja school?'

'You auditioning for *The Matrix*?' Jo unwound the scarf like a mummy removing its wrappings and shook water from her brown curls.

Behind the counter, Jo's sister Tina was pouring Tang's order. 'Jo's into the whole woman warrior, Bushido,

78

take-no-psychic-prisoners thing. Me, I take after our Irish ancestors. We're poets and musicians.'

'More like pranksters and subversives.' Jo held up her phone. 'You hijacked this. Please delete the ringtone you installed.'

'But "Psychosocial' is a *sick* ringtone."

'Ironic, I got it. But the screaming scares small children and grown police officers.'

The ratty day wasn't denting Tina's mood. She resembled Jo, minus ten years and a couple of inches, plus enough silver in her ears and on her fingers to be confused for a magnet. She was so effervescent that Jo wondered what would happen if she walked past an open drawer of cutlery on a particularly dynamic day.

Tina took the phone. 'I'll change it on one condition. Tomorrow night – Jo, don't give me that look, you've been promising for months, and you back out every time. Come on.'

'If you want me to go on a girls' night out, you have to give me a hint. What will we be doing? Popsicle-stick crafts? Krav Maga?'

Tina stuck out her bottom lip and made puppy eyes.

Jo raised her hands. 'Fine, I give up.'

Tina clapped her fists together like a delighted kid. She handed over Jo's coffee with a grin.

Jo laughed. 'I just walked into a trap, didn't I?' She took her coffee. 'Thanks. I think.'

Tang led her to a table. 'I talked to the officers from the airport division. Nasty run-in you had with this Kanan character. You okay?'

'No harm, no foul. But he said he's going to find me,' Jo said.

'How would he do that?'

'He grabbed my hospital I.D. Let's say he could take it from there. He seems resourceful.'

'So he's a possible stalker. With brain damage. What else?'

'I think he's gone out to kill somebody.'

'How'd you reach that conclusion?'

'He has a list of names and the words *They die* scrawled on his forearm.'

Tang set down her mug. 'From the top, please.'

Jo told Tang the story: the siege on the 747, the Tasering, the seizures. The bizarre MRI results, Kanan's rage and determination to leave the hospital. His aggression against her in the elevator.

'He said he's on the job, and he'll finish it, and he's "going to get them." And he said he has nothing to lose. Add in *They die* and you've got a hit list.'

'Is he the type to go nuts?' Tang said.

'Who knows? His brain is being cored like an apple.'

'What do you think is going on?'

Jo took a breath. 'I hesitate to speculate without more evidence.'

'SWAG, Beckett.'

Scientific Wild-Ass Guess. Jo leaned back, tapping her fingers on the wooden tabletop. 'Okay. Here's a working hypothesis.'

'You mean a hypothesis we should work from. Playing defense.'

'You got it. Kanan went to southern Africa, supposedly on a business trip. While he was there he was contaminated with a highly dangerous substance that is causing irreparable damage to his short-term memory. He may have been engaged in illegal activity.'

'Such as?'

'Stealing something.'

'Because, if he knows what caused his brain injury, why else would he hold back?'

'Exactly,' Jo said.

'You think he was involved in a heist?'

'Working hypothesis.'

'So, he stole something dangerous. But it went wrong, and he got contaminated.'

'Which might be why he asked me if I "have it" and swore he was still on the job.'

'A falling-out among thieves? Is he after his co-conspirators?' Tang said.

'Revenge is a plausible motive.' Jo leaned forward. 'Something's tormenting him. Beyond the head injury, I mean. Pain and fear are driving him.'

'You sound sympathetic.'

'Empathic. I am. I can sense his pain, and it's awful.' She picked up her mug. 'Doesn't mean I'm a sucker. If we don't find Kanan, people are going to die.'

Tang took a notebook from her coat pocket. 'Did you see any of the names on his hit parade?'

'One. Alec.'

'No last name?'

'Sorry.'

'This anterograde amnesia. It won't gradually improve?'

'Unfortunately, no. It's rare but devastating,' Jo said.

'Why does he remember things for five minutes and then forget it all?'

'Memory formation doesn't happen instantaneously. It's a process, not an event. And it occurs in several parts of the brain. When new information comes in, it's held in working memory for a few minutes. Then the medial temporal lobes encode the information and send it to the parts of the brain where it's stored permanently as long-term memory.'

'But Kanan's encoding equipment is damaged. And it won't recover?' Tang said.

'Not given the way his brain looks on the MRI. That brain matter's been eaten away from the inside. It's gone.'

'What caused it?'

'Kanan first told me he'd been poisoned. Then he said "contaminated."'

'With what?'

'No idea. And I don't know whether it's accidental or deliberate. He was either confused or being cagey. Did somebody try to kill him? Did he try to kill himself? He wouldn't clarify.'

'What do you want to do?'

'Attack it the same way I do a psychological autopsy.'

'He isn't dead.'

'But the cause and manner of his injury are equivocal.'

Jo performed psychological autopsies in cases of equivocal death, when neither police nor the medical examiner could determine whether a victim's death was natural, accidental, suicide, or homicide. She consulted on the sneaky cases, the ones lying in the tall grass so they couldn't be clearly seen. The cases the people who liked confessions and hard evidence couldn't unravel.

'Branching out?' Tang said.

'Yeah, expanding my résumé beyond Lifestyles of the Dead and Infamous.' She gave Tang a tart smile. 'I can dig into Kanan's history and try to find out how he got this . . .' *infestation*, she almost said. 'Contamination, or whatever it is. Then maybe I can find out what the hell it is. And figure out who he's after.'

Tang cupped her hands around her mug. 'The department called you in, correct?'

'For a possible fifty-one fifty. So I'm not on board as a consultant, just as a member of the mobile crisis team. However, your general works detail has a psych liaison.'

'Social workers charge a lot less per hour than a shrink.'

'Great. Get yourself one. I'll head to Maui until the social worker brings Kanan in and convinces him not to hunt me down.'

Tang put up her hands. 'I'm just ragging you, on behalf of the taxpayers. Listen. Kanan battered passengers on the jet, assaulted a police officer, and grabbed you at knifepoint. That's kidnapping, false imprisonment, and assault with a deadly weapon. I want you to consult as psych liaison on this case. Evaluate Kanan and help us find him.'

'Good. Thanks.'

'Get to it,' Tang said. 'Find out who he's after.'

Before he finds me, Jo thought. 'You've got it.'

Tang downed the rest of her coffee and got to her feet.

'There's something else,' Jo said.

'I hate hearing "else." It sounds like "worse."'

'It is. Kanan can't be called off,' she said. 'If he's determined to kill, he will not stop. Because even if I convince him to back down, within five minutes he'll forget. Then he'll be gone again,' she said. 'We have to get him in custody before somebody dies.'

Tang looked pensive. 'Let me know when you get hold of Kanan's wife. We'll pay her a visit.'

Jo dropped her keys on her hallway table and headed for the kitchen. The house was cold. She kept her jean jacket on, turned up the heat, and turned on some lights. Her hardwood floors gleamed. Her reflection followed her from the hallway mirror.

The morning's events felt almost viscerally fresh. Kanan's scent lingered in her sweater. She wanted to rid herself of it but forced herself to sit down at the kitchen table while her memories were vivid and write her initial notes on Kanan's case, starting with everything he had said to her.

The Reaper's here to collect, while I'm still walking.

It was an awful thought. Living, but without memory, without the ability to learn and remember. To have life flicker into brightness only to pass from sight, forever out of reach, like a scene glimpsed from a car window at high speed – it was a nightmare.

She touched the Coptic cross that hung from a chain around her neck. It encouraged her to believe that death might not mean dissolution, but instead radical change.

For a brief second she saw her husband, Daniel, alive,

then dead. The memory clawed at her around the throat. Daniel was gone, their life together erased. But mental erasure – having one's experiences collected, swept away – that idea frightened her in a different way. The mind was intelligence and humor and soul. Without memory, what was left?

She put down her pen and went upstairs to shower.

In a frame on the dresser in the bedroom she kept Daniel's photo. It was a snapshot from one of their last climbing trips to Yosemite. Daniel was standing behind her, arms around her shoulders, an amused look on his face. Jo was laughing. Behind them, Half Dome glowed with the golden light of sunset.

Miss you, dawg, she thought.

Daniel had been a trauma doc, driven and talented and curious about the world. In the E.R. he had been like a Buddha at the eye of a storm. But though he was outwardly calm, he had burned with fires that he locked inside and only let her glimpse at moments of tension. When he got in those moods and wouldn't talk, but would go for a ten-K run or sit on the front porch watching neighborhood kids playing basketball in the park across the street, she finally learned to knock him back to the present.

'Don't make me get the skillet,' she would tell him. 'It rings like a gong when I hit it against your thick skull, but I want to cook with it later.'

And nine times out of ten, he'd smile and swing her around to sit beside him on the steps. When he smiled, he looked transformed.

And when he woke her before dawn, because he'd

been paged, or had battled the covers to a draw, sometimes she just said, 'Skillet,' and he would ignore her objections and laugh and ruin the rest of her night's sleep.

These days she woke alone. At first it had been with a shock, every time – moments of confusion before the memories and reality rolled back in like slag, like the shipwrecked remains of their journey together. Like the ruined medical supplies that had sloshed through the wrecked medevac chopper in which Daniel had died. On those first mornings, merely opening her eyes, seeing the morning light, had lit a fuse that made her relive the event.

Time had softened that pain. When she woke, the thick rope of grief no longer tightened around her throat as she looked out at the endless horizon of the day and a world where Daniel wasn't. Where he would never be, where she could not conjure him. The vast, busy, roiling world, which demanded that she fight her way through it, where she had felt lost, wanting to share, to question, to lean on him and prod and laugh and wrap her arms around him and fall into his embrace, to hear him once, just once more, even for a snap of time that was like a door blowing shut, just to hear him say, 'Johanna,' and know she was his anchor, and he the star in the night sky she hung her hopes on, everything she aimed for and chased after and watched with diamond-bright love.

Memory. She had learned, over the previous two and a half years, how to remember her husband without being hooked and yanked into the realm of tears. She'd learned to recall him, and even his death, without reliving the experience; to avoid becoming transfixed by the image, to prevent adrenaline from jacking through her veins until she wanted to scream. She'd learned that in the bereavement group at UCSF, which she now ran. She'd learned how to step back, to empathize without breaking down, to throw a rope across the chasm of grief and be there for others crossing the gulf.

She could look at the photo on the dresser now with fondness. Most of the time. She could wake eager to face the day. Most of the time.

And these days, she could wake with a smile and a rush in her pulse and a silly, moony feeling that she hadn't known since she was a teenager. The feeling of a crush.

She threw her clothes in the hamper, pulled on a black and white kimono, and tiptoed fast across the cold wood floor to turn on the shower. She stood under the hot water and let it wash away the morning's anxieties and Ian Kanan's aggression. Then she dried her hair until the curls lay loose and confused down her back, pulled on an ivory fisherman's sweater and green combats and wool socks, and opened the shutters. The day outside had turned from gloomy to *Hell, yeah*.

Her house peered out across rooftops from the top of the hill, past the slick green of the magnolia in her back yard, over Victorian apartment buildings and houses painted Matchbox car colors. Beyond a neighbor's Monterey pine, past neighborhoods that rode the hills and valleys like homes on a rolling sea, past the dark forests the Presidio, was the Golden Gate Bridge, pulsing red in the stormy afternoon light. She twisted her hair up into a swirl and captured it in a claw clip.

She was halfway down the stairs when the doorbell rang. Her heart gave a kick. Probably FedEx, or Wendell the mailman on an amphetamine bender, doing his rounds five times faster than his colleagues. And five times worse. Probably delivering the wrong mail to everybody on the hill again.

But if it wasn't Wired Wendell, the possibilities distilled to *Oh, crap* and *Should have put on lipstick*. Jo crossed the front hall and opened the door.

Gabriel Quintana stood on the porch. He was holding a sack of doughnuts and two cups of coffee large enough to power a top fuel dragster.

'Can I corrupt your day?' he said.

She smiled.

Taking the doughnuts, she let him in. 'Bring me sugar, butter, and caffeine, and you can take my soul.' They walked down the hall to the kitchen. She looked in the sack. 'Oh, yeah. What do you want me to do? Name it. Rob a bank? Toss one of those chocolate puppies on the counter and point me at a teller.'

'That's not what I want.'

He set the coffee cups on the counter. He wrapped an arm around her waist, pulled her against him, and kissed her.

She didn't need lipstick after all.

She slid her arms over his shoulders. He was wearing a blue plaid flannel shirt over a black T-shirt and jeans. Old Caterpillar boots. He looked like he'd dressed out of the *My Name Is Earl* handbook.

'Happy Thursday,' he said.

She felt like she was cresting the rise on a roller coaster, heart galloping before the plunge, arms tingling, brain stutter-stepping like it was about to trip. *Golly. Hee. Hot shit.* Other thoughts came to her and she brushed them away. *Transitional man. Chemical reaction. Careful, doctor.*

She had circled away from Gabe Quintana for ages before finally giving herself permission to jump in, feet first. She looked at this like tackling a rock face for the first time. *Just breathe. Go for it.*

He released her and took the coffee, a smile lurking at the corners of his mouth. 'You free for dinner tomorrow?'

'I'll need more than doughnuts.'

'Eight o'clock? I'll make a reservation at the North Beach Restaurant.'

The North Beach Restaurant was San Francisco Italian honed to an edge that folks back in Tuscany could only aspire to. And it wasn't cheap.

'Any occasion?' she said.

'Do I need one, *chica*?'

'No,' she said, thinking, *Something's up.* Something had been up for a while, but Gabe played his cards close to the vest.

Gabe was in his third year of a graduate program in theology at the University of San Francisco. It was a mystery she hadn't yet solved: Why had a former air force enlisted man and single father thrown himself into studying Catholic moral theology?

'Will Sophie be able to join us?' she said.

'She's going to her cousin's birthday party. It's a sleepover.' He smiled and drank his coffee.

She smiled back. The house all at once felt overheated. 'You on your way to Moffett?'

'Yeah.'

He looked out the French patio doors at the mix of storm clouds and sunshine. Storms meant a greater chance that he'd spend the day rescuing crewmen from capsized ships, or drivers whose cars had spun off rain-slick roads into a mountain ravine. Gabe was a P.J., a pararescueman, with the 129th Rescue Wing of the California Air National Guard. He was a former tech sergeant who had spent years on active duty with the air force as a combat medic and now worked as a civilian reservist with the squadron out of its base at Moffett Federal Airfield in Mountain View. He was a search and rescue expert for the unit who had more expertise than nearly anybody in the world at pulling people out of horrible situations, anytime, night or day, on land, at sea, or underwater.

'You on your way right this minute?' she said.

'Unless you've got a better idea.' His mouth turned up at the edges. 'If it's quiet today we're going to hit the fight room. Before I go, I can show you some moves.'

'I'm a climber, not a fighter. I can show you some holds.'

She grabbed his shirt and hauled him to her. As she pressed her mouth to his, he picked her up and popped her onto the kitchen counter. She wrapped her legs around his waist. She was ringing like a railroad crossing alarm.

He breathed. 'Damn. These holds of yours, can they

90

kill a man? 'Cause when you rob that bank, I want to be alive to enjoy the loot. And –' He glanced out the back doors. Frowned. 'Is that . . . ?'

Jo looked toward the back yard. 'Shoot.'

At the fence, peeping over, was her neighbor.

She let go of Gabe and hopped off the counter. 'For Pete's sake.'

Ferd Bismuth's hair was slicked down with so much Brylcreem that it was the color of a greasy hamster. His eyes were bright and hopeful. He waved.

She went to the French doors to close the shutters. As soon as she extended her arm toward the glass, Ferd held up a finger and nodded, as though she had just beckoned to him. He began walking along the fence line toward the street.

'No,' she said. 'Agh.'

Ferd's head bobbed along, half-visible, his eyes never leaving her. He tripped. Dropped from sight. Popped back up and kept walking. He had holly in his hair.

Gabe said, 'Want me to stand behind the door and growl like a rabid poodle when he knocks?'

'Thanks, but I can handle it.'

'In that case, I'm out of here.' He grabbed his coffee, pulled his keys from his jeans pocket, and headed for the front door.

'Chicken,' Jo said.

He turned around. His hair was the color of a coal seam. He was as lean as a jaguar and walked with the self-possession of a big cat as well. He had an unself-conscious and steady grace.

He was giving her time, she knew. They'd been seeing each other since November – sporadically, because he'd been away, she'd been away, and because he didn't want to rush her.

Gabe knew only too well how grief had torn through her life. He was the one who had told her that Daniel was dead. But she wondered if he knew how strongly he affected her. That if he stepped toward her again, she might detonate like an unstable stick of dynamite.

Ferd knocked on the front door. Urgently and repeatedly.

'You dare me to stay?' Gabe said.

She didn't care for the gleam in his eye. 'No.'

His smile widened. 'I'll just stay a few minutes.'

'You're evil, aren't you? Inherently, I mean.'

'I bought your soul with a doughnut. What do you think?'

The knocker clacked again. Capitulating, Jo went and answered it.

Ferd filled the doorway, bouncing on his toes. 'Have you seen the news?'

Talking to Ferd was like containing weasels in a box. If she didn't mind her words, his anxieties could slip free, sending him on flights of misery or hypochondria.

'I'm avoiding the news. I don't want to spoil my day,' she said.

He bounced. He wasn't overweight, but he dressed in such baggy clothing that Jo suspected he'd been heavy as a teenager. The computer-store name tag pinned to his shirt said HI, I'M FERD.

'Monkey virus,' he said.

Ferd was a long-term house sitter at the faux mansion next door. The owners were away in Italy, and Jo doubted they knew about Ferd's little housemate, Mr Peebles – a capuchin but not a friar.

'Hadn't heard anything about it,' she said.

He glanced surreptitiously down the steps. 'Can I come in? I don't want the neighbors overhearing.'

Despite her training as a therapist and her talk about maintaining boundaries, she didn't tell him to get lost. He was a cast-iron pain, a spectacular neurotic, but he was a watchful neighbor and had helped her out when her house was damaged in an earthquake the previous October. She let her good mood and the strong coffee and the memory of Gabe's kisses overwhelm her urge to send him away.

He walked straight down the hall and into the kitchen. He saw Gabe, stopped, and stood rubbing his hands together like a mad scientist.

'Ferd,' Gabe said, holding out the doughnut sack.

'No, thank you,' Ferd said.

Jo came in behind him. Gabe sipped his coffee, looking like he had all the time in the world. For a man qualified far beyond paramedic level, a man trained for trauma evac under battlefield conditions and who had more parachute jumps under his belt than some members of the 101st Airborne, he knew how to project the image that life's a beach. Nothing but flip-flops and good surf and a cold bottle of beer. But Jo had spent enough time with him in the past few months, and before that, in the direst of circumstances, to know that his passions and his pride and a fierce killer instinct ran deep.

He was staring at her notes on Ian Kanan.

Ferd stepped between them. 'This virus has been documented in the Congo. I read about it on the World Veterinary Association website. Several species in the interior highlands have been affected.'

Jo slid past him. 'Glad the vets are on the case.'

A pebble of annoyance lodged in her mind. Gabe was reading her notes and looking at the photocopies of Kanan's passport and driver's license. She gathered them up and closed her laptop.

'I'm monitoring the situation,' Ferd said. 'But I don't know the latency period for the virus.'

'Sure you don't want a doughnut?' she said.

'How long can these diseases incubate?'

Jo put her hands on her hips. 'Dude. Mr Peebles didn't come from the Congo. He came from a pet shop in San Mateo.'

Mr Peebles was the monkey Ferd had managed to obtain as an emotional assistance animal. But the little creature was every bit as suspicious and overanxious as Ferd and acted out its compulsions without inhibition. It escaped from his house with semi-regular efficiency. It had a look in its eye like it was getting instructions via a Secret Service earpiece – for a hit. And it knew how to fling shit with deadly accuracy.

With his miniature doppelgänger living in the mansion, Ferd seemed closer to panic than ever.

He eyed Gabe. 'These viruses can rage like wildfire.

It could make *Outbreak* look like a picnic.' He turned to Jo. 'Don't worry, I'm on top of things.'

'Good to know.'

He stood smiling at her, head slightly tilted, eyes defocusing.

'Ferd.' She didn't want him daydreaming that he had rescued the Elf Princess Johanna and saved the hobbits from doom.

His head snapped back up. 'I'm wondering. You know, about the symptoms.'

'A vet would know,' Jo said.

God exists and will punish you for ruining the life of a local veterinarian, her conscience muttered.

'The abstracts only mention physical signs,' Ferd said. 'Not psychological symptoms.'

Jo shook her head. 'Nope.'

'But –'

'Mr Peebles is eighteen inches tall and weighs four pounds. He's small enough. He doesn't need a shrink.' And especially not her.

'He's . . .'

Gabe looked up from his coffee. 'Write it all down. Keep a log.'

Ferd nodded. 'That's not a bad idea. I'm just worried that –'

'Keep it quiet for now. You don't want to start a panic.'

Ferd frowned. Venting his worries aloud was his modus operandi.

'Picture driving down Geary Boulevard with Mr Peebles in the passenger seat, when the city's scared witless

95

about infected monkeys,' Gabe said. 'A mob would put a trash can through your windshield.'

Ferd put a hand to his stomach. 'But . . . I just can't help worrying about the way he's acting. He –'

'You'd be lucky to get out with anything besides your socks on.'

Jo said, 'Just keep an eye on things.'

Ferd straightened and nodded sternly. 'If he shows symptoms, I'll alert you.'

'Please.' Jo began inching him toward the door.

He called over his shoulder. 'Have a good day at school, Gabe. I'm going to work.'

Jo got the door closed and walked back to the kitchen. Gabe was pacing near the kitchen table, arms crossed. She gave him a look.

He nodded at her notes. 'That a new case you're working on?'

She stuck her hands in her back pockets and waited for him to apologize. He didn't.

'That's confidential information,' she said.

'The notes were open on the table. I didn't mean to pry.' His eyes were a warm brown, but his gaze was cool. 'The man involved, Kanan – he grabbed you and threatened you?'

'I'm fine. The police are looking for him.'

'Kanan's a security consultant for an outfit in Silicon Valley?'

'Gabe, you don't need to worry about this.'

His shoulders tightened. 'Is he?'

She relented. 'Yes.'

'He doesn't sound like a corporate sheepdog. He sounds like a security contractor.'

She didn't think she was hearing him right. 'You think he's a mercenary?'

'Describe the guy for me,' Gabe said.

'You saw his photo.'

'Passport head shot. It's not enough.'

'Midthirties. Your height. Dressed casually, but obviously in shape. Lean. Carries himself . . . alertly.'

'Ripped?'

'Yes,' she said.

'"Alertly." You mean high-level situational awareness?'

'Aside from his memory loss, yes.' She recalled thinking that Kanan held himself like a gunslinger. 'Go on.'

'It's just a suspicion. But the kind of people corporations hire to shepherd their employees on trips to third world countries aren't school crossing guards.'

His seriousness shook her. 'I'll check it out,' she said.

'Good. Mind if I do as well?'

'You don't need to.'

'Do you mind?'

'You're not involved.' She saw no change in his expression. 'No, I don't mind. Depending on what you plan to do.'

'Find out who he worked for before signing on as in-house security for Chira-Sayf. I can ask people I know. See if he worked for a security contractor with military ties.'

'Okay.' She felt uncomfortable accepting his offer of help. She wasn't a damsel in distress. 'Gabe, this is generous of you, but overcautious. Kanan doesn't scare me.'

Even then, his face didn't change. She saw only a flicker in his eyes before he stepped forward and put his hand on her hip.

'He should.' He kissed her again. 'I'll call you.'

9

Seth had lost track of time again. He couldn't keep his mind focused. He tried to think about school, about algebra, but couldn't concentrate. Today was one more day when he hadn't turned in any homework. He tried to think about the band but kept hearing his guitar crack and sproing when he fell off his bike and landed on it. The fear swallowed everything.

He looked at his plate. It was chipped. His hot dog sat there, lukewarm.

He knew the men were out there. He was being watched. The whole house was. And if he tried to leave . . . He smelled the hot dog. His stomach rumbled. His mouth watered. He grabbed it and ate it in three bites.

Whiskey still cried now and then. Did dogs remember traumatic events? It gave him a hairy lump in the throat. *Stop that*, he told himself. Whiskey was alive. They hadn't killed him.

He still couldn't figure out why they wanted him. Except that it couldn't be anything besides his dad, and his dad's work.

He knew more than he'd ever let on around his folks. He knew they didn't want to talk about too much in front of him.

What do you do, Dad?

That usually got either a shrug or a brush-off. Once it had gotten a bit of truth: 'I keep people out of trouble.'

When his dad said that, his mom had looked across the room with concern. Seth got the feeling they had some secret deal not to tell him about his dad's work, and that his dad had just violated it.

Like Dad was a criminal. And Seth was a baby.

'Your dad's home nowadays,' his mom had said.

Mostly, Seth had thought. His dad didn't have overseas deployments anymore, but he still went on business trips. Seth would see him packing his passport in his jacket pocket.

I keep people out of trouble. But now Seth was in trouble, and it was because of his dad. Where *was* his dad? Did he know about this? It had been six days. Seth might keep losing track of time, but he knew that much. Six bowls of Rice Krispies. Six Hot Pockets. Now six hot dogs. Later he'd drink a bottle of Gatorade and then it would get dark and the house would get locked down tight and he would feel the fear because the men were *out there*.

He had heard them talking, when they grabbed him in the park. The human hot dog told the man with acne

100

that security was going to be useless. 'The returns are going to be *huge*. Through the roof.'

How long was this going to go on? When was his dad going to get here?

Because he would. Seth knew it. He knew it like he knew the way home through the park in the dark. Like he knew the entire back catalogue of the Foo Fighters and the guitar riff for 'The Pretender.' Dad would get here. The men might have threatened him, told him if he didn't behave he'd never see his dad again, but he didn't believe them. No matter how scared he got of his dad – and he did, because he knew his dad wasn't like other fathers, didn't install electrical wiring in apartment buildings or put braces on people's teeth. He kept people out of trouble.

Seth was in trouble. His dad would help. Seth could count on that. He could tell his dad anything, no matter how hard it was – even this. He just had to be patient. But for now, right now, he had to get out of here.

'This the place?'

Ian Kanan looked up from his phone. The taxi was crawling west along Crissy Field Avenue. The field was empty. Nobody was out. The cabbie eyed him in the mirror.

'Hang on,' Kanan said.

He couldn't go home. They'd be watching the house, twenty-four/seven. And they'd be trying to trace his location via cell phone triangulation. He went into the phone's menu, deep down, and set it to Nontransmit. Airplane mode – he could leave the phone powered up, take photos, retrieve all the information stored in it, but his handset would not transmit or receive. It didn't check in with any cell towers. And nobody could find him.

In a submenu, he configured the phone to activate the transmit mode at ten P.M. Friday night.

He saw the writing on his right arm. *Severe memory loss. I cannot form new memories.* No kidding. He didn't remember telling the cabbie to come to Crissy Field. He didn't remember getting in the taxi.

He was in trouble. He didn't have his backpack, his computer, anything besides his phone. His head was leaking memories like air from a punctured scuba tank. He was alone, by the bay in San Francisco, and he was aiming to lay low. The plan, obviously, was blown.

He had to go to his fallback.

'Let me out here,' he said.

'You sure, buddy?'

'Positive.' He buttoned his denim shirt over the Fade to Clear T-shirt. It was going to be cold out. 'Do you have a pen and paper I could have? I'll buy them from you.'

That got him another look in the mirror. The cabbie turned, heavy in the seat, and handed him a ballpoint pen and a chunk of Post-it notes.

'Thanks.' Kanan paid him, stuck the pen and paper in his shirt pocket, and got out.

The wind slapped him side-on. The cab drove away, heading for someplace that wasn't deserted.

The plan was blown. He had to go to the fallback. That thought blew through him harder than the March wind. He turned up his shirt collar and snugged his arms to his sides. Seth's Fade to Clear shirt could help keep the chill out. He told himself to hang on to that thought.

For a second, he saw Seth, all elbows and skinny legs, glasses sliding down his nose, face deadly serious as he played his guitar. The school talent show, an audience of loopy fourteen-year-olds cheering for his kid's band. Misty standing by his side, face bright. She had leaned against him, almost laughing with pride. In the din, he leaned down, pulled her hair back, and murmured in her ear, 'He's all you, babe. Talent and passion.'

Now he hoped that Seth had inherited enough of Misty's grit. His son would desperately need it.

Kanan had never felt so alone. He wanted to see his family more than anything, but he couldn't, not until this thing was done. He fought to keep his focus. He couldn't let his mind wander. He had to do the job.

I cannot form new memories. And he realized that from now on, all he might have of his family were memories.

He needed a plan. It had to be simple.

Get a vehicle. Get weapons. Track Alec, then the others.

He scanned the road, the steel-gray bay, and the towering Golden Gate Bridge. The bridge approach loomed high overhead on the hillside, through eucalyptus trees and pines bent to the wind. He put his head down and walked into the wilderness of the Presidio.

Late that afternoon, Jo got through to Misty Kanan. Ian's wife didn't like the idea of being interviewed.

'Ian's lost and sick. Why aren't you out on the street

103

looking for him instead of giving me the third degree?' she said.

'We'll have a better chance of finding him if we talk to the people who know him best. And that's you.'

Misty paused. 'Fine. Five P.M.'

At four thirty, Lieutenant Tang pulled up in front of Jo's house in an unmarked car. She honked like an impatient teenager. Jo hopped in and Tang peeled away from the curb.

'Got a plan to tackle this psychological non-autopsy?' Tang said.

'The groundwork's the same for evaluating Kanan's situation as for a case of equivocal death. Build a personality profile of the subject.'

Tang headed downhill. Jo braced herself against the incline. They passed a woman in her seventies out walking her beagle, chugging up the sidewalk like Tenzing ascending Everest.

'I'll evaluate him using the NASH rubric,' Jo said. 'Try to determine whether his brain injury is natural, accidental, or a case of attempted suicide or homicide.'

In conducting a psychological autopsy, Jo normally reviewed police and accident reports along with the victim's medical, psychological, and educational history. She interviewed a victim's family, friends, and colleagues. Reactions by friends and relatives to a person's death were particularly pertinent. So were early warning signs of suicide and any indication that somebody had intended harm. She looked at things the victim had written, learned about his hobbies, reading habits, taste in music. About his fantasies, fears, and phobias. She tried to find out whether he had enemies.

She explained to Tang. 'I'll build a timeline of events leading up to Kanan's injury. Maybe that'll help us find out what happened to him.'

'Fine. You play the good shrink. I'll strip the bark off of Misty Kanan.'

'You think she needs it?'

'If Kanan's involved in a bungled heist, how likely is it that his wife's oblivious?'

Jo considered that. She had her doubts. 'Let's get the lay of the land. Build up to that slowly.' She glanced at Tang. 'This is still somewhat unofficial on your part, isn't it? Let me take the lead.'

They beat Misty Kanan to her house, a flat-topped postwar stucco home in the Richmond District north of Golden Gate Park. The houses were packed together like shoeboxes, the street a vista of asphalt, concrete, and overhead electrical wires. But cherry trees were in bloom. Bright fistfuls of blossoms had turned the curbsides an aggressive pink, brightening the view. In many cities, the neighborhood would have been considered the tough end of middle-class. But in San Francisco, if you dropped a burger wrapper on the sidewalk and gave it a street number, it was worth $500,000. The Kanans were doing well.

They parked at the curb. The rain had stopped. The clouds were broken, and along the western horizon the sun was a screaming orange. Tang huddled into her coat, chewing gum and biting her thumbnail.

Jo said, 'Are you fighting the urge for a nicotine fix? Because that would be good.'

'I'm on pins and needles, praying my dream date asks me to the prom.'

'Neato. I hear this year's prom theme is *Carrie*.'

Tang hunched in her jacket. Jo backed off and shut up.

Down at the south end of the street, a midnight-blue Chevy Tahoe turned the corner from Fulton. It was tricked out with hunting lights and a bull bar. Misty Kanan was behind the wheel. She cruised up the street and turned into the driveway.

Jo and Tang got out and walked over. The Tahoe idled on the driveway as the garage door went up. Misty put down her window.

'Let me go in and turn off the burglar alarm. I'll come around and open the front door,' she said.

She drove into the garage. The brake lights glowed hot red, exhaust swirling around them. Jo and Tang went to the front door and waited in a blustering wind. After several cold minutes, Misty let them in.

'Sorry. I checked the bedrooms and the utility room. I was hoping Ian might . . .' She shrugged.

'Has he been here?' Jo said.

'No.' She spread her arms and let them drop to her sides. 'I can't believe he ran from the hospital.'

'You have any idea why he ran?' Tang said.

'Because he's . . . off the wall, mentally.'

Shrugging again, Misty led them along the front hall and through the kitchen. The house was compact and modern, floored with blond wood. Dishes were stacked in the sink, a bottle of ketchup open on the counter. The fridge was covered with magnets and a high school schedule. A dog bowl sat in the corner, full of food.

Jo said, 'Mrs Kanan, the police have asked me to evaluate Ian's mental state. I need to ask some direct questions if we're going to find your husband and figure out what has caused this –'

'Disaster,' Misty said.

'Yes.'

'I'm a pretty tough cookie. You can be direct.'

Misty headed to the living room. It had been decorated via Target, with a cheap-and-cheerful chic. A stack of newspapers slumped across the coffee table. A hamper of laundry sat on the floor, and in the corner the ironing board was set up, iron propped up, ready to go. Misty, though, had seemingly been stopped in her tracks.

Maybe she was a tough cookie, but she looked exhausted and on edge. She sat in an easy chair, hands clenched on her knees.

Jo sat across from her on the sofa. 'Has Ian phoned you since he left the hospital?'

'No.'

'Could I listen to the messages he left after his flight landed?'

'I erased them,' Misty said.

Damn it. Jo kept her expression neutral. 'Why?'

'Forty-nine messages? "Misty, I just landed." "Misty, I'm on my way." "Misty, please pick up." Same tone, same confusion. It was, like, *replay.*' She scraped her fingernails over her tartan skirt as if she had a dreadful itch. 'I couldn't take it.'

Tang pricked up her ears, like a Jack Russell terrier that had heard a squirrel in the bushes. 'Mrs Kanan, after you left the hospital your husband assaulted Dr Beckett.'

'What are you talking about?' Misty said.

'He dragged her into an elevator, pulled a knife, and pinned her to the wall.'

Misty gaped at Jo. Her anger was immediate and hot. 'He pinned you? That makes no sense. I don't believe it.'

'And he made threats,' Tang said. 'Against what I'm assuming is a list of people.'

'That's not possible.' She glanced back and forth between Tang and Jo. 'Where are you coming up with this? Threats? Ian is severely *ill*.'

Jo clasped her hands in her lap. 'I know. Ian may have been contaminated with a substance that has caused his brain injury.'

'Contaminated? Where'd you get that?' Misty said.

'From your husband. Do you have any idea how he could have been poisoned?'

'No.'

Tang took out her notebook. 'He was on a business trip to the Middle East and Africa. What was he doing?'

'What he always does. Corporate security.'

'Specifically?'

'Ian doesn't discuss his work with me. It's a matter of corporate confidentiality.'

'Is Ian's job dangerous?' Jo said.

'No.'

'Overseas security for a high-tech firm? Never?'

'He makes sure that the people he escorts *don't* get into trouble. He keeps them miles away from dangerous situations.'

'What does Chira-Sayf do?' Jo said.

'Materials research.' Misty tried leaving it there, but Jo and Tang both stared at her until she added, 'Nanotechnology.'

Jo nodded blandly. But in the back of her mind, a red flag went up. 'What's his background and training?'

'Why?' Misty said.

'I need to gather as much information as I can.'

Misty crossed her knees. Her foot jittered in the chunky boot. 'Ten years in the army. Came out and found a career where his skills were valued.'

'Which skills?'

Misty eyed her closely. 'You been in the military?'

'No. Why?'

'Some civilians just think: army. Shoot 'em up. Camouflage and *yessir, nosir*. There are dozens of specialties within the armed forces. Ian was in reconnaissance.'

Tang wrote it down. In the quiet of the house, her pen strokes were audible.

Jo glanced at a framed photo on a bookshelf. 'Is that your son?'

'Seth,' Misty said.

The boy in the photo had Kanan's coppery hair and frosty blue eyes behind his glasses. His smile had a cocky

109

edge chipped into it. *The joke's on them*. The smile reeked of adolescence but seemed impish rather than sarcastic. Seth was sitting cross-legged on the lawn, playing a guitar. A big dog, with an Irish setter's coloring and a Labrador's goofy hopefulness, was poking his nose against his shoulder.

'Nice-looking boy. How old is he?'

'Fourteen.'

Jo waited for her to say more. In this situation some people would ask her questions or blurt emotional revelations. Others clenched everything in, defending their preconceptions, their hopes or myths about their loved ones. She waited to see whether Misty would say anything about her son. She didn't.

'Have you told him?' Jo said.

'Not yet.' Misty's foot continued jittering.

Jo wanted to ask, *Everything all right with the family*? But *tough cookie* was turning out to mean stubborn, defiant, defensive. So she played it in a lower key.

'The psychological evaluation requires me to map the victim's life. I investigate the victim's entire history, meaning medical, psychological, and emotional – family, relationships, marriage . . .'

The blush started at the base of Misty's neck and rose up her cheeks. 'You want me to talk about our sex life?'

Jo put up a hand. 'I'm just saying, relationships are something I ask about.'

Misty licked her lips. 'No, it's fine. Ian and I are close. We always have been. It was chemistry at first sight.'

The blush was so hot it was practically pulsing. Jo thought

110

that if they turned off the lights, it might bathe the room in a scarlet glow.

'He's my soul mate. I could forget myself in him. I could . . .' She stopped, realizing she'd used the word *forget*. Her eyes looked flash-bulb hot. 'Great, a Freudian slip.'

Maybe so.

'I didn't mean anything by it.'

'Psychiatrists note things like that, Misty. But we don't judge.'

Misty worked her jaw back and forth, as though saying, *Sure*. 'We're happy in bed. How's that?'

'That's fine.'

Misty's foot continued jittering. She looked at the floor. When she looked up again, her eyes were bright with tears.

'What's he going to be like from now on? Is he going to forget me?'

Jo paused, working out how much she could say and with what certainty.

'I'm his wife. And I'm a school nurse. You can tell me anything.'

'His memories before the injury should remain intact,' Jo said.

'So there's no way he's going to forget his own name, where he grew up, what he does for a living, that kind of thing.'

'No.'

'How about our marriage?'

'He'll remember. His amnesia isn't the kind you see

portrayed in most movies. Anterograde amnesia means he can't form *new* memories.'

'So when he sees me, he'll know who I am. He'll come home and know this is our house.'

'Yes.'

Misty's knuckles, clutching her knee, were white. 'And over time, he'll improve?'

'We don't know for certain, but it's unlikely.'

Misty's eyes flashed like a strobe, white and cold. Just as quick, the look was gone. 'You don't really know what happens to the brain, do you? You're a shrink. You deal with emotions, not medicine. Breakthroughs happen every week.'

And she was a *nurse*? 'Not with this, I'm afraid.'

Misty looked at Jo as though taking her photo with a crime scene camera. 'Let me tell you one thing for certain. This is a lock. Ian and I love each other. From the day I first set eyes on him I knew he was the man I wanted. I still know it, and I'm not going to let him slip away. I will fight to help him.'

Her stare lost its chill and seemed to throb, as though she were daring Jo to contradict her. It was as if she'd let a crack open in her armor and had poured out words she had kept dammed inside for so long that they had nearly turned to rust.

Tang said, 'Why would he bring back two daggers and a scimitar from the Middle East?'

Misty's eyes lit briefly, a dull flash, as if from the weird steel of the knife Jo had seen hanging from Kanan's hand. 'He works for some strange and egocentric people. They

112

probably want to hang that stuff on their walls like trophies.'

Her cheeks were mottled with white patches. Jo took it as a sign of stress. It was the pale pepper of humiliation.

'These guys at Chira-Sayf, they're all about who swings the biggest dick. But did they get those swords themselves? No, they had Ian do it.' Her face was sour. 'They're a bunch of empty jockstraps.'

'We need to speak to his boss,' Jo said. 'Which empty jockstrap would that be?'

Misty stood up. 'Riva Calder. I'll get you the phone number.'

She walked to the kitchen island, tore off a piece of scratch paper, wrote down a number, and gave it to Jo.

Tang scooted forward on the sofa. 'Who's Alec?'

Misty nearly did a double take, like they'd head-faked her. 'Alec?'

Tang looked up. 'Yes.'

Misty hesitated. 'Maybe it's Alec Shepard. He's the CEO of Chira-Sayf.'

Tang wrote it down. 'Does Ian have a beef with Shepard?'

'No. Of course not. What are you getting at?'

'When your husband attacked Dr Beckett, she saw a list of names written on his arm, including "Alec."' Tang underlined a word in her notebook. 'And "They die."'

Misty stood stone still. Her face paled to the color of potato paste. 'Hold on. You think he wrote a hit list on his own arm? No way.'

Tang clicked her pen. 'Can you offer another explanation?'

113

Misty put up a hand, like a traffic cop. 'Why are you attacking Ian like this? What are you trying to prove?'

'We're trying to find out what he's doing,' Tang said.

'You have an agenda, and it isn't to help him.' Her voice rose. 'You think he's on a vendetta? That's paranoid. It's ridiculous.'

Jo said, 'If you know what else it could be, please tell us.'

'I have no idea. Maybe Ian's worried about those people. Or desperate to contact them.'

'But not to contact you?'

Jo might have slapped her. She winced. 'Why are you attacking me? My God, Ian has a memory problem. Of course he wrote things down.'

'"They die"?'

'Jesus, I don't believe this. He's in trouble. He's sick. The longer he's missing the more danger he's in. And you come here and tell me he's the problem?'

Tang clicked her pen. 'Who has he gone out to kill?'

'He hasn't.'

'Do you know that for certain?' Tang said.

Misty clenched her fists. 'How dare you? You think you can get inside Ian's head deeper than I can?' She turned to Jo. 'You think you can know him better than me? Why – because he pinned you against a wall for five seconds?'

Tang said, 'Is Ian happy at work?'

'Very.'

'Have you heard anything about thefts from the company?'

'Now you're insinuating that he's a thief?' Misty's gaze didn't heat so much as distill to a clean, frozen sheet of glass. 'Ian is an honest man. He would never steal from anybody. Never. And I'm done talking to you.'

Tang held on a moment, as though considering whether to press her weight. Then she closed her notebook and stood up. 'We're trying to get at the truth, Mrs Kanan. We'll talk again.'

Jo followed Tang to the door. Misty held it open. She didn't say a word to the lieutenant, but as Jo passed by, she put a hand on her arm.

'All I want is Ian.' Her tears looked hot. 'Find him.'

At the curb, in the damp wind of sunset, Tang pulled out her cigarettes. 'Playing good shrink, bad cop with you is a blast. That was illuminating.'

'That was painful,' Jo said.

'She knows more than she's telling. Even odds her husband is crooked, and she's covering for him.' She lit a cigarette, inhaled, and squinted at Jo. 'We need to find out what he stole, and from who. Add it to your to-do list.'

115

10

Ron Gingrich carried the last two bags of crushed ice to the aluminum bucket on the terrace near the pool. He split them open and dumped them in.

From the house, Jared called, 'Don't forget to light the tiki torches.'

Gingrich sent him a salute. Since getting off the flight from London he hadn't had two minutes to himself. He strolled to the garage, flip-flops slapping, got a case of Stella Artois from the stack, and schlepped it back to the terrace. His ponytail batted in the wind. The clouds had blown off and the evening was chilly and sparkling clear.

He pushed his fists into the small of his back. And he wondered yet again how he'd ended up working as a gofer for a twenty-six-year-old kid, a boy genius computer game designer who considered himself a rock star for the twenty-first century.

Ron shoved beer bottles into the ice in the king-size

bucket. The previous day and a half seemed like a blur. Jet lag really was a bitch, especially at his age. Sure, he knew how to make things happen on the road and off. He'd managed tours for heavy metal bands for twenty years, gone on the road once with the Grateful Dead, before coming over to Jared's Silicon Valley start-up as a jack-of-all-trades, the get-it-done guy. Buy the boss twenty black T-shirts, and the right brand saggy jeans, and Crocs to match whatever color the cool CEOs were wearing down the road in Sunnyvale.

He was willing to put up with plenty of shit. He wasn't too proud to work hard, he liked to tell people.

He gazed past the pool and down the hill past the cypresses, toward the bay. From up here in this ten-million-dollar neighborhood, the water was an iridescent gray-blue in the sunset. The Sausalito ferry chugged for harbor. He could see planes taking off from SFO. From this distance they looked like silver ants crawling the sky.

What was he supposed to be doing?

He looked at his hands. He was holding two warm beers.

Ice bucket. The party. Right. He stuck the beers in the pail.

From the house came voices. People were arriving. Young tech hipsters – the guest list was mostly game designers, overgrown teenage boys who'd hit the jackpot and found a way to rake in the bucks playing video games. Plus some of the venture capitalists who funded them. And a few people from the CGI end of the film industry. Maybe even one or two folks from Industrial Light & Magic.

Jared stuck his head out the patio door. 'Ron, the tiki torches. And get rid of that stack of tools by the pool shed. Somebody might trip over it, and I have lawyers coming.'

'Sure, boss.'

'And don't call me boss.'

'Sure.' *Ass.*

Jared shouldn't mind being called boss. Jerry Garcia hadn't minded when Ron called *him* boss. God, he missed the Dead.

He took his iPod from his pocket, stuck in the earbuds, and scrolled through his playlist. When 'Attics of My Life' rolled into his ears, he smiled.

He got his lighter and lit the tiki torches around the pool. A chilly wind was blowing, but the boss wanted atmosphere. His gaze wandered and he saw jets taking off from SFO.

That guy going nuts on the flight from London – talk about a freak-out. When the man ran up the aisle to the emergency exit, Gingrich thought for a second that the plane was on fire. But the flames were only in the dude's head. Gingrich had watched him, thinking, *WTF?* Then he and Jared looked at each other and knew that if they didn't do something, it wouldn't get done. They jumped up and wrestled the wacko away from the emergency exit.

He rubbed the cut on his arm where the man's belt buckle had scratched him in the scuffle.

'Ron?'

* * *

Jared sounded perplexed. Gingrich turned.

The sun was down, the tiki torches flickering on the terrace. The noise from the party was bombastic.

'Where have you been?' Jared said.

'Going to put away those tools, like you asked.'

Jared looked at him cockeyed. 'And lock up the pool shed. The electricians didn't finish with the pool lights. There's live wiring going to the pool. We have to keep the power off. I don't want anybody accidentally mistaking the garden lighting switches for the pool.'

'Sure.'

Jared continued looking at him strangely. 'You all right, Ron?'

'Tired. The London trip kicked my butt.'

Jared nodded, let his gaze linger a bit longer, and headed back to his guests.

Gingrich wasn't tired. He was bloody exhausted, as the Brits would say. His legs felt stiff, as if he'd been standing there by the side of the house for hours. For . . . crap, he was cold. When had the sun gone down?

He glanced at his watch. 'Whoa.'

Eight P.M. How had an hour slipped away?

He ran a hand over his goatee and slapped his cheeks to wake himself up. The pool shed. Get the tools inside. Yes, boss. Then he could finally go home and hit the sack. He walked around the side of the garage.

The pool shed was toasty inside. Jared kept the pool heated like a hot spring, because he had grown up in some dusty house by the freeway in Daly City and hated dirt and loved the clean, chlorinated smell of pool water.

Jared swam every day, wallowing in his wealth and just maybe, Gingrich thought, washing off the stench that stuck to him from his computer games. Stuff designed for people who were bored with Grand Theft Auto and needed something a bit more stimulating. Marketed to eighth grade kids, too.

Gingrich turned on the light. It was harsh, a single bulb overhead. Moths flew around his head. The heater and pumps and filter motors chugged away.

That flight from London – what had been wrong with the wack job? The shrink who came aboard didn't think the guy was crazy. Gingrich had seen him on the floor after the cop Tasered him, in some sort of trance, turning like he was being spit-roasted. The memory made him shudder.

He could hear noise behind him at the party. Fifty party-hearty, greedy, talented, demanding guests, drinking beer and talking deals and celebrating the release of Jared's new game. It was so hot in this shed. He stared at the circuit breakers on the wall.

The pumps hummed almost hypnotically. He blinked.

Man, his legs felt stiff. He felt like he'd been standing forever. He looked at his watch. It was nine thirty P.M. People would want to swim. He should go light the tiki torches. Get some beers from the garage and pack them in ice in that big aluminum pail.

Jared would want the pool perfect. He always swam, every day. Gingrich looked at the machinery in the shed. The door had swung shut behind him. It was damned

120

hot and musty in here. He heard the humming of the pumps, and 'Brokedown Palace' in his earphones.

Why was he standing in the pool shed? He didn't remember coming in. Obviously he had a reason, but . . .

The circuit breaker box was open. That was weird.

He looked inside at the switches. Four of them, three for the circuits on the gaudy garden lights that illuminated the gardenias and rhododendrons, and one in the center for the underwater pool lights. That breaker was flipped to off.

Jared must have asked him to come in and flip it on. Jared must want to go swimming. What time was it?

He looked at his watch. 'Shit.'

Ten o'clock? Man, he was so tired he was completely losing track of time. Jared must want to swim in his beautiful pool in the dark, pretending he was a dolphin swimming in the deep. Maybe Jared even had a date. And the guy couldn't manage to come flip the switch himself.

He reached out for the breaker box. Stopped himself.

Something felt wrong.

Jared. Lazy genius. Grew up in a heated shack near 280 and was now too precious to turn the lights on in his own pool. Was that it?

His hand lingered in the air. Man, he needed a new job.

Then he shook himself. He was being ridiculous. This was work. He was just jet-lagged. He had a cushy job. He was in the cream.

Jared wasn't a bad kid. Gingrich had, if anything,

encouraged the guy to let him take care of everything. How else did you make yourself indispensable?

He turned on his iPod. The Who, that was the ticket. 'Teenage Wasteland' – he hadn't heard it in ages.

He flipped the big breaker. Wiped his forehead. It was hot in this shed, stuffier than hell. Moths were flying around. The pumps were so noisy, really annoying.

He shut the breaker box, turned off the light, stepped outside, and shut the door. It was fully dark outside. The night was loud. The music pounded in his ears, Daltrey wailing. The party was really hopping. Some of that new music the younger generation liked – what did they call it, emo? Screamo. That was it. Heart-rending teenage songs, overlaid with a pouty singer screaming into the mike. And around the corner by the pool, it seemed like Jared's friends were singing along.

He didn't get that music. It wasn't like the Dead, not classic stuff. The night was cool, but he felt like he'd been standing next to a dusty furnace for hours. He wiped sweat from his brow.

The people at the party, the game designers and screamo fans, they weren't his people. He needed to get home and crash. And tonight he needed it bad, with this unbelievable jet lag. By the pool the lights were off, but in the light of the tiki torches everybody was running around. Jared was having another crazy party. These kids. Playing tag around the pool even though they were adults. But he guessed that was what you did when you sold games for a living.

He walked around the side of the house. His flip-flops

slapped on the sidewalk. He had a beer in his hand. He popped the top and drank. Ah, that was better.

He decided not to interrupt the party. He didn't need to say goodbye. He just needed to get home. The boss would understand.

He unlatched the gate and walked out to the driveway and ambled on down to the street. In the night, the stars were pinpoint-clear. He stretched his hands over his head and glanced back at the house. The front door was open. He saw people inside, racing around. They were yelling, running in and out, some of them in swimsuits. One of them sprinted past him down the street, shouting at the top of his lungs.

Gamers. Playing capture the flag, maybe. He looked to see where the guy was going.

What do you know? A fire truck was screaming up the street.

Blue and red lights lit up the hillside, and the sirens blared. More people ran out of Jared's house. It was a regular circus.

11

A rattling wind woke Jo. She opened her eyes to see an acrylic blue sky flying high above the skylight. It was six A.M.

In her teens, Jo would have sold her baby sister to a traveling carnival for an extra hour of sleep in the morning. But medical school had reset her body clock. By her second year, she'd been able to ride across the Stanford campus in the dark, with her lab notes in one hand and a coffee mug in the other. She'd done it once at five thirty A.M., in a white coat and pajamas. Now she rarely slept past seven.

For a minute she hunkered beneath the covers. Her bedroom was full of hot colors that fought against the city's chilly weather. The bed had a lacquered black Japanese frame and a red comforter. Gold and orange pillows were heaped around her. Coral-colored orchids were blooming on the dresser.

She wondered where Ian Kanan was – in a hotel, or huddled in a downtown doorway, or wandering the streets. She wondered whether Misty Kanan had told their son that Ian was injured and missing. Misty struck her as defensive, quick to see her and Amy Tang as threats. Maybe Tang was right and Misty was covering up Ian's part in a botched heist. Something about the mood in the Kanans' home certainly seemed off balance. Or maybe, faced with catastrophe, Misty was simply trying to protect her own sanity.

Jo also wondered about Chira-Sayf's nanotechnology work. For all its promise, nanotech had a spooky edge. If Kanan had been poisoned, nanoparticle contamination rated investigation.

It was too early to reach anybody at Chira-Sayf. She'd left multiple messages for Kanan's boss, Riva Calder, and would try again at a civilized hour, but right then she was wide awake and buzzing. She threw back the covers, put on workout gear, and drove to the climbing gym.

Mission Cliffs filled a converted warehouse in the Mission District. The gym was a maze of artificial rock walls that soared to the ceiling, an indoor playground for grown-ups. Jo signed the lead climbers' log, stretched, and put on her climbing shoes, harness, and chalk bag. Another early bird offered to be her belay partner. She took out her lead rope and approached the head wall. It was fifty feet high, the color of the rocks in Monument Valley, studded with artificial holds in Play-Doh colors. And, in the early morning sunshine coming through the skylights, it was all hers.

Nothing topped the purity and challenge of rock climbing to pump her up, clear her head, make her feel alive. Except for sex, on a good day. On a pitch, it was all physics and courage: thinking through the route to the top; judging force, leverage, angles, and her limits. It came down to guts and gravity.

Climbing the wall took about two minutes. She did laps up and down via different routes. She finished above it all, in the air. With nothing but a thin rope and her own strength holding her to the wall, surrounded by space and light, she felt exhilarated.

Why would anybody want to fly in an aircraft, strapped in an aluminum can, when they could climb?

When she left the gym, the city was gleaming. In San Francisco, daylight shines white. It reflects from the walls of Victorian houses that cover the hills like cards. It tingles from dissipating mist and leaps like fish off white-caps on the bay. Jo put on her sunglasses and drove up the road to find coffee.

After a block she changed her mind and headed to Noe Valley.

Gabe's 4Runner was parked outside a craftsman house overhung with live oaks. He answered the door barefoot in jeans and a USF T-shirt. His hair was confused. His bronze skin shone in the sun.

Who needed caffeine? 'Morning, Sergeant.'

He paused a beat. Usually he'd reply with 'Doctor Beckett' or 'Ms Deadshrinker,' but he just stepped aside and let her in. 'You look revved up.'

'I wondered if you've gotten a line on Ian Kanan's background.'

'That brought you here at seven thirty A.M.?'

'Yes.' She smiled. 'No.'

She pushed him against the wall and kissed him.

His eyes widened. 'You switch from orange juice to high-octane today?'

'Got a match?'

From the kitchen, a child called, 'Dad, the eggs are burning.'

For a second Jo held him there. She heard a sizzle from a pan in the kitchen and the morning news on the television. Gabe's face turned rueful.

'Take it off the burner, honey,' he called.

Jo exhaled and stepped back. Gabe's nine-year-old daughter, Sophie, poked her head around the kitchen doorway.

'Hey, Jo.'

'Hey, kiddo.'

Sophie had a bashful smile and a long braid the color of Hershey's Kisses. She was wearing a blue and gray parochial school uniform.

'We're learning about ancient Egypt in history. Did you know King Tut was buried without his brain?' she said.

'That's the way they did it back then.'

'Gross. But cool. I'm hungry.' She twirled like a ballerina and disappeared into the kitchen.

Gabe lowered his voice. 'She catches the school bus at eight. I have to get rolling.'

Jo swiped her hair back from her face. 'Never mind. It'll take me longer than that to stop thinking about Catholic school uniforms.'

He raised his hands. 'No. Don't put that image in my head – I do not picture you in a parochial uniform.'

'But I remember wearing one, and now all I can hear is Sister Dominica leading the girls' choir in "Holy Virgin, by God's Decree."' She brushed a fingertip across his lips. 'I gotta go.'

'About Kanan – I have a call in to an air force buddy. He knows the people who should know.'

'Great. You know how to find me.'

'It's my job, girl.'

Still smiling, she turned toward the door. In the kitchen, the local news came on.

'. . . have not released the names of the victims, but witnesses confirm that fire and rescue units were called to the home of Jared Ely, CEO of the computer gaming company Elyctrica, and that Ely may be one of the three people killed in this bizarre accident.'

Jo had her hand on the door. She stopped.

'Accident investigators declined to comment on how the swimming pool came to be electrified, but there is speculation that wiring from repair work may inadvertently have been live.'

Jo dug in her satchel for her phone. By the time she found it, it was ringing.

Lieutenant Amy Tang turned, phone to her ear, and surveyed the terrace outside Jared Ely's home. It overlooked the bay from a hillside near the Presidio. The house was fabulous and cool and the tiny swimming

128

pool, which had probably added a hundred grand to the price of the place, was now empty of bodies.

'Beckett?' she said. 'You know how I wasn't officially involved in your memory man's case? I am now.'

Jo stepped outside so Sophie wouldn't hear. 'Jared Ely's dead?'

'Along with two of his guests. Somehow, last night's cocktail hour turned into an electrocution.'

'What happened?'

'From what I can sift out of the panic and confusion, apparently one of his employees flipped a switch he shouldn't have. An unshielded cable went live and turned the swimming pool into a deep fryer. I presume the name Ron Gingrich will ring a bell.'

Jo seemed to have tunnel vision. Her fingers felt cold. 'Is this a courtesy call?'

'No. You need to talk to Gingrich and find out why he seems to have no memory of the event.'

Traffic on Lincoln Boulevard rushed past Ian Kanan, anonymous, fast, sunlight winking off car windshields. He walked uphill in the bike lane. Below him, surf pounded the sand on China Beach. He had a piece of paper in his hand.

Car, it said.

An urban forest of Monterey pines and peeling eucalyptus trees towered along the eastern flank of the road. This corner of San Francisco was a boondocks of green shadow and damp chill. The Presidio had once been a plum posting in the U.S. Army. The decommissioned base was now part of the Golden Gate National Recreation Area. It was a ghost place, beautiful and empty. Get away from the road, cross a deep gully or two, and the sounds of traffic faded; the land filled with the smell of pine needles and deep grass and dirt.

The Presidio was a fourteen-hundred-acre wilderness on the shoulder of a big city. And it was pocked with abandoned buildings, such as the crumbling barracks where he had spent the night.

He knew he'd slept in the barracks because he had a photo of the building on his phone. He didn't remember it. Now he was walking toward a neighborhood of multi-million-dollar homes atop a cliff in the distance. He was on a hunt. The rules were simple. Get a vehicle. Get weapons. Find Alec. Then the others.

On his left forearm, where his cuff was rolled up, the end of the message was visible. Written with the black ink of a Sharpie, the words seemed to shout at him.

They die.

The day was cold. The wind was scattering the mist, but the morning sunlight did nothing to warm him. He felt as if he had been sliced open with the knife known as fear, and grief, and finality.

He was tired and needed a shower. He ran a hand over his face. And a shave. He felt as though he'd spent a week in the back row of a jumbo jet. He felt lost. But above all, he felt empty.

He wanted to see his family but couldn't unless he got

this thing done. He couldn't go home. They were watching his house. He wanted his life back, but that wasn't going to happen. Too much had gone wrong.

Everything had been stolen, including his recent memories. He remembered Africa. He remembered the river, remembered the flask. He saw the scabby gouges on his forearm and remembered the bald panic on Chuck Lesniak's face.

He remembered nothing since.

But he knew the job was blown. He was out here in the cold, on his own, empty-handed. He had not delivered the stuff. He'd been screwed six ways from Sunday, starting when Lesniak decided to cut, run, and sell the stuff to a higher bidder. Now, to finish the job, Kanan had to go to his fallback plan.

At the thought of confronting Alec, dread filled him like wet sand.

Kanan forced the thought away and tried to focus. He was aware that when he let his mind wander, things simply . . . faded. And when he tried to remember what he'd been thinking of, he lost touch with what he was supposed to be doing. He couldn't form new memories; he could barely keep track of where he was. He couldn't let himself get distracted. He had to focus on the goal.

But without volition, he seemed to hear Misty laughing. He saw her sweep through the living room, jerk a thumb over her shoulder, and tell Seth, 'Put down your ax and do your homework, sport.'

Seth had looked at her with surprise. 'Mom, where'd you learn to call a guitar an ax?'

131

Misty nodded like a head banger and gave him the heavy-metal devil horns.

Seth put his hands to his forehead and moaned, 'I have no mother.'

Kanan had laughed out loud. The things kids didn't know about their parents.

Now he fought not to cry.

He looked up. To his surprise, he was hiking through the Presidio along Lincoln Boulevard, heading for the expensive homes above China Beach. He was holding a piece of paper in his right hand.

Car, it said.

First get transportation, then weapons, then go down the list. He saw their names written on his arm, and *They die*.

That was a no-shit plan.

When he climbed the hill into the neighborhood, the sun had burned the mist away. Though the homes screamed of wealth, the streets were quiet. The occasional BMW hushed its way along the manicured roads, but apart from him nobody was out. This time of morning, the only people on foot around here were maids walking to work from the bus stop.

He strolled up the street, casually, hands in his jeans pockets. Ahead, parked in the driveway of a Spanish-style mansion, was a Ford Navigator, the color of dried blood, tricked out as if the owner were planning an expedition across the surface of Mars. Bull bar, hunting lights, luggage rack. Tinted windows. Everything but a .50-caliber machine gun mounted on the roof.

Kanan sauntered toward it, checking the front windows of the house in his peripheral vision. The house was dark and still.

He walked up the driveway, staying close to the flank of the Navigator. By the front wheel he crouched down and ran his hand under the lip of the wheel well. He felt around and – what do you know. He found the magnetized case holding the spare key. The wheel well was an old-school hiding place and on the surface not such a bright idea. But it was good luck for him. In the case were a key and a fob with a remote for the alarm/immobilizer. Kanan knew that he couldn't just stick this key in the lock or even punch the remote and then slide the key in the ignition. There was a special sequence for this particular vehicle. Get it wrong, and you were hosed, LoJacked, flat on the road with your legs spread and your hands locked behind your head and the barrel of a cop's weapon pointing at your center of mass.

Kanan slid the key halfway into the door lock, carefully, until he felt a tiny click. He flicked the remote and saw the lights flash. He eased the key the rest of the way in, flicked the remote again. The Navigator chirped.

He opened the driver's door, climbed in, and fired up the engine. The heater and radio came on, full blast. REM, 'Everybody Hurts.' He could have predicted it. The irony felt as thick as bile in his mouth. *Everybody hurts* . . . Not the man who owned this house, drove this SUV, lived this insulated, charmed life. He reached over and turned down the stereo.

When he did, he saw the writing on his arm.

For a moment he sat helpless, as though his throat had been sliced through. He opened his mouth but could draw no air.

All across the city, people were getting ready for the day. Kids were eating breakfast and packing their school lunches. They were waving good-bye to their dads. But not Seth. Wives were kissing their husbands before heading to work. But not Misty.

He couldn't inhale. What if he never saw them again? What if he saw them again but couldn't remember? He put down the window, but even with the wind and blue sky and the endless ocean right there, he couldn't get a breath.

He couldn't go home, couldn't call, couldn't reach them. Did his family think he had abandoned them?

'Stop it. Focus,' he whispered.

He put the Navigator in reverse and whipped out of the driveway. He jammed it into drive and drove into the morning sun. He knew who he had to find. *Alec.* Shepard was target number one. The others were down the line. But even if he killed the others, even if he tortured them before he executed them, Alec would be the worst, because when Kanan found him, they'd be confronted with the inescapable truth of his betrayal.

A new song rolled from the stereo. 'Breakdown.' Tom Petty and the Heartbreakers, cold and sinuous. *Break down, go ahead and give it to me . . .*

That was more like it.

12

'Forget the coffee. Get in the garage. Now.'

Murdock opened the door and jerked a thumb at Ken and Vance. Ken lumbered through the doorway. His shirt stretched over the fat around his waist and across the veined flesh of his bulging arms. His acne seemed more inflamed than ever.

'I told you Kanan was a wild card,' he said. 'He's gone off the rails and he's going to take us with him.'

'Hold it together,' Murdock said.

The garage was cold and the bare bulb gave off unfriendly light. Vance jittered in a circle around them. 'Are we screwed?'

He sniffled and tugged on his belt buckle to keep his jeans up. Or maybe to check whether his package had slunk away overnight without him knowing.

Murdock shook his shaven head. 'Focus on the big

picture. We hold the winning hand. Kanan is going to close the deal.'

Vance wiped his nose. ''Cause if we're screwed, I want to get out of here. Get things over with. I'm sick of waiting. And bored out of my skull.'

Murdock glanced at Ken. 'Explain to your cousin what we need to do.'

Ken sucked his teeth. 'We're going to stake out places Kanan is likely to show. You're going to watch his house.'

Vance adjusted the blue bandanna that was tied over his hair as a do-rag. 'This was supposed to be a sure thing.'

Ken glowered at him.

Ken may have been a pessimist, but he was a pro. Vance, though, was an incurable amateur. He was supposed to be Ken's apprentice in the art of specialist theft, but Murdock saw that even Ken had doubts about his cousin's potential. And this was a job on which they couldn't afford any more mistakes.

'Eyes on the prize,' he said. 'That lab in South Africa made bottled magic, and Kanan got it.'

'So how come he ain't delivered?' Vance said.

'Stop fidgeting.' He stepped toward Vance. 'Do you realize what a huge advantage we have, obtaining this stuff? This isn't like trafficking firearms or C4 overseas. The logistics are astounding. We don't need a Ryder truck or a shipping container. This stuff can be carried in your pocket. It's the score of a lifetime.'

Ken rubbed his nose. *Yeah, yeah*, Murdock thought – the stuff was incredibly tricky, too. But that was what made it so incredibly valuable.

He pointed a finger at Vance. 'This is going to turn you into a badass beyond your wildest, gun-toting, ho-and-bitch-filled dreams. This stuff is the real deal. It's a superstar. And we're about to be the world's sole suppliers.'

Vance shrugged his shoulders and wiped his nose again. 'Yeah. Cool.'

Murdock nodded at Ken. 'Call Sales. There's no need to postpone the auction. One way or another, Kanan's going to deliver today.'

He spread his arms. 'We're going to be the lords of fear.'

Amy Tang was waiting outside Ron Gingrich's apartment building on a side street in the Haight, talking on the phone. The breeze lifted Jo's hair from her collar and spun it around her face. She buttoned her peacoat and jogged across the street to the magenta-painted building.

Tang, repudiating the neighborhood's Day-Glo color scheme, was wearing black jeans, a black sweater, black boots. She looked like she'd shopped at Baby Gap for Goths.

She put away her phone. 'I told Gingrich his boss is dead. He's upstairs bawling like a baby. I need you to tell me if he's faking.'

Behind Tang on the corner, three grimy teenagers slouched on the sidewalk, panhandling. One of the girls held out her right hand for money and talked on a cell phone with her left. The cardboard sign at her feet said, AT LEAST I'M NOT A HOOKER.

Jo and Tang walked up creaking stairs to the third-floor

apartment where Ron Gingrich lived with his girlfriend. A uniformed SFPD officer was standing outside the door. The apartment was small and haphazardly friendly. Batik sheets covered the sagging sofa. Spider plants decorated the television and bookshelf. Hendrix and Grateful Dead posters decorated the walls. The kitchen smelled like bacon and fried eggs.

Gingrich's girlfriend, Clare, was thin and nervous. So were the three Chihuahuas jumping around her feet like grease in a frying pan.

'You're a shrink?' she said. 'Please tell me what's wrong with him.'

Gingrich was sitting in a beanbag chair by the bay window in the living room, wearing gym shorts and a Metallica T-shirt. His ponytail was greasy. His eyes, watching pro wrestling on the television, were bright.

Clare and the dogs approached him. 'Ron, sweetie, the doctor's here to see you.'

Gingrich looked up pleasantly. 'Hey, it's the shrink from the plane.' He stood. 'Man, that was weird. Did you end up sectioning the guy?' He offered his hand to Tang. 'I'm Ron.'

Tang's mouth tightened. 'We met a few minutes ago.'

A dust bunny of confusion scooted across Gingrich's face. 'Sure. You guys here to interview me about the fight on the plane?'

'No,' Jo said. 'About Jared.'

'Just give him a call. He'll be happy to talk. He's rich and all, but you don't need to go through me. He's approachable.'

138

Tang shifted uncomfortably and cut her eyes at Jo.

'Want coffee? Clare, baby, we got some of that Colombian?' Gingrich smiled and headed into the kitchen. 'We haven't eaten – you gals want to stay for breakfast?'

Clare's face was frozen. 'He ate three eggs, toast, and bacon half an hour ago. He ate three more eggs fifteen minutes ago.'

Whistling, Gingrich pulled out a skillet and turned on the stove. 'How you like 'em, ladies?'

Jo avoided Tang's scowl and walked into the kitchen. 'Ron, hold on a second.'

'No eggs for you?'

'I need to ask you about Jared.'

'Sure, but why so serious?' His eyes were red but untroubled. 'What's going on?'

'It's about the party at his house last night.'

'Last night?' He smiled, but his expression was vague. 'I don't think so.'

'Did you flip the electrical switch in the pool shed?' Jo said.

'Doctor, I think you're confused. I just got back from London.'

'Ron, Jared's dead.'

He stopped cold, holding an egg in his hand. For a moment, it looked like he'd taken a two-by-four between the eyes. Then he sagged back against the stove. He groped for balance and crushed the egg against the counter.

'No. How did it . . . ? Oh, Christ.' He looked at his girlfriend. 'Clare – Jared's . . . oh, God.'

139

Gingrich slid down the counter into a wretched crouch and burst into tears.

Jo saw the red slice on his forearm. It looked like it had been gouged with a dull nail.

'Ron?' she said.

He thrust his head into his hands.

Jo turned to Clare. 'He needs to get to the hospital.'

She took out her phone and called neurologist Rick Simioni.

Kanan swung the maroon Navigator into the marina. The bay was stippled with whitecaps. Alcatraz shimmered in the morning haze. He cruised toward the forest of sailboat masts, scanning for threats.

He was operating on a simple principle: To stay alive, assume the worst. Expect an ambush. He'd once seen a sign tacked to the door at a U.S. Marine firebase: HAVE A PLAN TO KILL EVERYBODY YOU MEET TODAY. It was pertinent advice.

He cruised along, checking for vehicles or people who seemed out of place. Two Post-it notes were stuck to the dashboard. The first read: *Vehicle, Weps, Alec, THEM.* The word *vehicle* was crossed out. He was driving it. The second note said, *Somebody's Baby.*

The voice of the GPS system said, 'Make a U-turn.'

He looked up. He was at the San Francisco marina, staring out the windshield at the Golden Gate Bridge.

He turned around, drove back to the boats, parked, and got out. The sky was a happy, mocking blue, but the pines shuddered in a melancholy wind. He pulled up the collar of his denim shirt and walked toward the mooring slip.

He felt the dagger jammed in his boot. Felt a rock where his heart should be, dense and so heated that for a moment he could barely inhale.

Suck it up, he told himself. Go past the betrayal, finish the job, and get them.

The marina looked full – only a few sails were visible on the bay. The people who moored their boats here were at work in the financial district or Silicon Valley, humping sixteen-hour days to pay for their hundred-thousand-dollar toys.

Ahead he saw *Somebody's Baby*. Her fiberglass hull gleamed in the sunshine. He hopped aboard, descended the stairs, and jimmied the lock on the cabin door.

Ken Meiring sat in the black van and watched the Navigator cruise past him, twice, three times – Jesus, how many times was this guy going to circle the parking lot? Finally the Navigator U-turned and drove back. Ian Kanan got out and headed for the boats.

Meiring got out and followed.

Inside *Somebody's Baby*, the cabin was sleek and quiet. Nobody was aboard. Kanan went to the galley, got a set of keys, and unlocked a cabinet built into the bench seat along the cabin wall.

'Damn it.'

No weapons. No handgun, no shotgun, not even the

boat's flare gun. Someone had taken them. He stared in dismay.

The boat rocked and shoes squeaked on the deck above.

Quietly, Kanan retreated to the galley. He pulled its half door partway closed and crouched behind it. The squeaking shoes came down the stairs. They sounded heavy, like rubber-soled boots. They stopped.

Kanan peered around the half door. A man stood, his back turned, in the center of the cabin. He was in his late thirties, white, built like a freezer. Fat circled his waist like sculpted shortening. His neck was inflamed with the grotesque acne that resulted from steroid abuse. His right hand held an HK automatic pistol.

Kanan's skin prickled with adrenaline. A stranger with a gun. One of *them*?

He estimated his chances. The man looked slow. He had turned his back without first searching the galley. If he was a pro, he was not at the top of his game.

But neither was Kanan. This block of lard had been lying in wait, and he hadn't spotted him.

The man was three steps and half a second away, confined in a narrow space. Kanan bunched, threw the door back, and sprang.

The man heard him and began to turn. Kanan swept the man's left knee with his right leg and hit him in the spine flat-handed between the shoulder blades. The man pitched forward. His head cracked the edge of the bench seat and he hit the floor like a pot roast. Kanan stomped on his right hand and took the gun.

He dropped a knee onto the man's back and put the barrel to his skull. 'Who are you?'

Sounding shocked, the man said, 'This is my boat.'

'It isn't. What do you want?'

The man gave up the pretense. Through clenched teeth, his voice roughened. 'You're in trouble. You haven't delivered and the deadline's coming.'

Kanan slid his knee up to the back of the man's neck and pressed his weight against it. 'Where are they?'

The man's face grew red. 'Deliver the stuff.'

'You want to walk out of this alive? Tell me.'

'The stuff. Or go fuck yourself.' The man raised a hand to his throat. 'Air . . . get off.'

Kanan pulled his arm back like a batter winding up and swung the pistol across the man's forehead. The man's skin split and his eyes unfocused. A skid mark of blood pulsed from the cut. His head flopped against the floor.

Kanan rifled the man's pockets. He found a driver's license and cell phone. The man's name was Ken Meiring. He scrolled through the phone's call register.

Murdock.

Vance.

A 650 number.

Kanan stopped. He knew that number. What the hell?

He scrolled further. The number appeared again, and again, and again.

'Oh, God,' he said. He had wondered who was behind everything. But not . . . 'Christ.'

Beneath him Meiring bunched and groaned. Drool

slipped from his mouth. Kanan pressed the weight of his knee against Meiring's neck. As he did, his hand hit the phone's camera function. A stored photo popped on-screen.

It was a snapshot of Seth.

Kanan gaped at it. A snapshot of Seth on his bike, riding to school.

The dense rock in his chest seemed to burn. 'You stalked my son? You brought him into this?'

Meiring struggled beneath him, lips pulled back, groaning and trying to squirm away. 'We can all still go home winners. Don't fuck this up.'

Seth. His boy. Kanan could barely see. His voice cracked like a ruined china bowl. 'Tell me where they are. Or I will kill you.'

Meiring kicked out and tried to grab Kanan's arm. 'Kill me and you're screwed.'

Kanan pressed the barrel of the pistol against Meiring's temple. 'Forget going home a winner. You want to go home? *Tell me.*'

Meiring's eyes flicked to the pistol's safety, which was off, and the trigger, which had Kanan's finger on it.

'Don't – Christ, okay, I'll . . . they're down the peninsula.'

'Where?'

'I'll take you.'

'Where?'

'No way.'

Like a bell had begun ringing, Kanan made the connection. The familiar number in Meiring's cell phone. Down the peninsula. Jesus Christ.

'Off San Antonio Road in Mountain View,' he said flatly.

Meiring's eyes widened.

Shit. That was the address. An old ranch house, supposedly used as a rental – but these people were using it for a safe house. That's where everything began and ended.

A terrible urgency filled him. He had to get there. And he had to write it down before he forgot it.

'San Antonio Road in Mountain View. San Antonio Road . . .'

He looked around for something to write with. He stretched and reached for a drawer. Beneath him Meiring roared. Bucking like an animal, he threw him off balance. Kanan fell against the bench. Meiring rolled and began punching like a madman. Kanan wrestled him onto his back, wrapped his thighs around the man's head, and squeezed him in a crazed wrestling lock.

'San Antonio Road Mountain View,' he said.

He pulled out a drawer. Junk poured across the floor. He grabbed a marker with his left hand. Meiring grunted and fought for purchase with his feet. Kanan squeezed his legs around Meiring's neck and pulled off the cap of the pen with his teeth. Meiring groaned, dug his heels into the floor, and arched his back. His fists windmilled, batting at Kanan's legs.

Kanan pressed the marker to the fiberglass floor. Wrote *San An* –

With a strangled roar, Meiring broke free from the headlock. Kanan brought up the gun but Meiring elbowed him in the face and thumped to his feet and fled up the stairs.

145

Hold on to the words, hold on – Christ, he needed Meiring, alive and talking, because he would forget. Meiring knew everything and he was getting away.

Kanan scrambled to his feet. Up top, Meiring stuttered across the deck. His foot clipped a cleat. He lost his balance. Lurching for the edge, he tried to jump for the dock. He missed.

With a shout, he fell from sight.

Kanan heard a splash. He stared out the cabin door at the empty deck and the blue sky. The sunlight stung his eyes. Gulls shrieked overhead. He put a hand against the cabin wall for balance.

Where was he?

He held still and oriented himself. He was aboard *Somebody's Baby*.

He had an HK pistol in his hand. The cabin door was jimmied open and a drawer had been dumped on the floor. He was out of breath and his shoulder hurt, maybe from breaking open the door. He didn't recognize the pistol, but if it had been in the drawer, it would do. He ejected the magazine. It was full. He inserted it again and cleared the chamber.

He heard splashing outside, and a fearful cry.

He ran up the stairs to the deck. Bending over the rail, he saw a man in the water below, desperation on his face.

The guy was heavyset, and his forehead was bleeding. He struggled to the boat and slapped the hull, trying to get purchase. He sank under the surface and came up spitting.

Like goddamned Chuck Lesniak in the Zambezi River, clawing to get back aboard the jet boat.

'Hang on,' Kanan said.

He hesitated, then pulled off his denim shirt, stuck the HK and his phone in the sleeves, and set it on the deck. He knelt, reached down, and snagged the collar of the man's shirt.

'Calm down. I got you.'

To his shock, the man shouted, grabbed his arm with both hands, and pulled him overboard.

Kanan hit face-first and plunged into water so cold that it burned. He came up gasping and saw the man's face. It looked like an out-of-control freight train.

The man was one of them.

He grabbed Kanan's hair and scythed his elbow around Kanan's neck like a wrecking crane swinging its claw arm. They went down together.

Knees, elbows, fingers, enormous strength quickening around Kanan's windpipe. They sank and twisted, legs locking. The man's grip was crushing.

The light dimmed. Below the surface the water was the color of coal slag. His lungs and bones and skin screamed at him. *Air*.

He fought the panic, brought up his knee, and reached into the side of his boot. His arm felt sluggish in the water. The night came at him from the edges of his world, gray and then black around the corners of his eyes, a tunnel, telescoping to a single point at the center of the big man's belly. He pulled the dagger from his boot.

147

He drove his arm forward, at the last gray point of daylight in the center of his vision.

The blade struck through cloth and skin, through fat and fascia and muscle, to the core. With a gush, the water warmed around Kanan's hand. The fat man relinquished his grip around his throat.

Warmth spread in the water. Kanan pulled the knife out and pushed the man away and kicked for the surface. The sun above was a dim pinprick.

The pain in his lungs was intense. Unable to fight it any longer, he breathed. And his lips, his nose, his eyes crested the surface. Gasping, he sank back beneath the water. Kicked. This time he came up and stayed up, gulping oxygen. The slate gray hole at the end of the tunnel brightened and expanded to dark water and the gleaming white hull of the boat. He grabbed the mooring line.

A plume of blood was muddying the water.

No bubbles. The breath had already been expelled from the man's lungs and rolled upward to rejoin the atmosphere.

Kanan hung on the line. The blood spread around him in luxuriant swirls. He needed to get away.

Letting go of the mooring line, he swam through the frigid water to the far side of the sailboat. He dunked himself, again and again, washing off the fat man's blood. He climbed up the fixed ladder. On the deck he found his denim shirt. His phone and a pistol were wrapped inside.

He put on the shirt and stuck his phone in the shirt

pocket. He worked the gun into the small of his back. He slid the knife back into the edge of his boot.

He hopped to the dock and walked, shivering, away from the sailboat. In the parking lot he saw a red Navigator. He had a set of keys in his pocket, and they opened the doors.

Teeth chattering, he stood by the Navigator and pulled off his denim shirt and the soaked Fade to Clear T-shirt beneath. His arms were covered with writing. Some of the ink had run. He found a Sharpie in the glove compartment and copied over every letter, slowly, until each word and name was vivid and sharp and black.

D. i. e.

He stared at the word. If he ever saw his family again, would they understand? Would 'I did this for you' keep him from being ruined in their eyes?

He had a vehicle. He had a knife and a handgun. He wished to fuck he had any information.

He got in the Navigator and started the engine.

13

Phone to her ear, Jo paced the hallway in the radiology department at San Francisco General. Tang paced the other way, chewing her thumbnail. Ron Gingrich's girl-friend, Clare, leaned against the wall and watched them go back and forth like dots in a game of Pong.

Jo hung up her phone. 'Still can't get hold of anybody knowledgeable at Chira-Sayf. I'm going down there.'

Tang's face looked like a closed fist. 'Take it to them. Find out what they're cooking up in their lab and whether Kanan is sprinkling it around. Don't take no for an answer. Attack, attack, attack.'

'If you get any news about the MRI, call me.'

Clare clutched herself tightly, like a little kid. 'What's wrong with Ron?'

'I can't say for certain. Let's hope it's nothing serious,' Jo said.

She left, feeling like a liar.

Forty minutes later she pulled the Tacoma into the headquarters of Chira-Sayf Incorporated. The company occupied a quad of sandstone-and-smoked-glass buildings in a Santa Clara business park. The birches were just beginning to leaf out. The parking lot was full of sleek new cars. CHIRA-SAYF was chiseled in a block of stone on the landscaped lawn. That spoke of permanence, or of a CEO with hubris and excess cash on hand.

Inside the main building, the atmosphere was cool, quiet, and minimalist. The receptionist told her to wait.

Jo looked around. No chairs, no place to sit. No plants, just an esoterically arranged rock garden. The only thing that offered hospitality was a rack of brochures: stiff, glossy promotional material about the company. Her Chinese acquaintances would have a field day with the feng shui of the place.

Jo paced. The air-conditioning hummed like a mantra. After ten minutes, she took a brochure from the display. Maybe she could fold origami while she waited. Create a paper menagerie of swans and field mice and nanobots.

'Dr Beckett.'

At the sound of clicking heels, Jo looked up. A woman in her forties walked into the lobby, hands clasped. She had a square face, square figure, flyaway blond hair. And a look in her eyes like a beachcomber watching a rogue wave roll toward her.

Jo knew that when she told people, 'Hi, I'm performing a psychiatric evaluation on your employee who's wanted by the police,' it went down like a glass of nails. She smiled and extended her hand.

151

'Ms Calder?'

The woman shook, briefly, with just her fingers. 'I believe my admin told you to speak to our H.R. representative.'

Calder's voice sounded thin in person, and Jo caught the undertone of a Southern drawl. Jo put a note of bright certainty into her reply.

'It's better to go straight to the source, and Misty Kanan assures me you're it. I can talk to H.R. later.'

Calder paused, seemingly baffled that she hadn't shooed Jo off. She cleared her throat. 'Right.' To the receptionist, she said, 'She's with me, Jenny. Sign her in. No calls.'

The receptionist eyed Calder sharply. Jo clipped a visitor's badge to her blue blouse and followed Calder down the hallway to a conference room. Calder closed the door and gestured for Jo to take a seat at the conference table.

'Ian Kanan isn't employed by Chira-Sayf,' she said.

'Excuse me?'

Calder sat across from Jo and laid her hands flat on the mahogany tabletop. 'He's an independent contractor. Chira-Sayf uses his services on a per-diem basis. Technically, he's self-employed.'

The zipping noise in her head, Jo thought, was the sound of Calder pulling on a fireproof suit. One that would cover her ass.

'Ms Calder, I'm not here to interrogate you. Ian Kanan is missing and critically ill. I'm trying to find him.'

'You're working for the police. I presume you're gathering information to use if you testify in court.'

Against the company, she meant. She was skittish about liability, bad publicity, or something worse.

'And even if he were an employee, privacy laws forbid me from releasing personnel records without a subpoena,' Calder said.

'I don't need his personnel records. I need to talk to people who know him and find out where he may have gone.'

'The police warned us that Kanan might be violent. We're having to institute new security protocols, bring in protection for the office and senior executives.' Her eyes were narrow in her square face. She wouldn't quite look at Jo. 'We don't know what Kanan might do. People are afraid.'

'I understand. But I'm on your side. I'm trying to get Kanan off the street.'

Calder pressed her hands against the tabletop and stared at the air around Jo's head as if seeing a halo or fluttering wings. 'I don't think anyone's going to talk to you.'

'No? Then let's talk about the company.' Jo opened the corporate brochure. 'What kind of nanotechnology work does Chira-Sayf do?'

'I don't see how that's relevant.'

'Chip design? Medical applications?'

She flipped through the brochure. There were photos of techs in clean-suits working in sterile manufacturing conditions. Scientists in white coats. The CEO, Alec Shepard, posing on the corner of his desk. He was an expansively sized man in his late forties, with a penetrating gaze, a red beard going gray, and a master-of-the-universe smile.

The next page showed a laboratory someplace – red dirt, hot climate. Lions. Jo frowned.

Calder said, 'I'm sorry, I can't reveal proprietary information.'

Jo looked up casually. 'Ian may have been poisoned. I need to know if he could have been contaminated in the course of his work for Chira-Sayf.'

'Contaminated? He couldn't – that's not possible. Not because of work. He hasn't been in the office for almost two weeks.'

'I know. He's been on a business trip to the Middle East and Africa. And I'm trying to retrace his steps to find out where and how he came in contact with a poisonous substance.'

'But that could be anywhere. The world is dangerous. People want to steal our intellectual property. They want to steal the very materials we work with. One of our labs, people broke in and ripped the copper wiring out of the walls. Just hacked away at the dry wall with crow-bars and tore out the phone lines.'

'Was that the lab in South Africa – this one?' She turned the brochure. 'Have there been other thefts?'

Calder stared wide-eyed at the brochure. Jo kept a pleasant expression on her face, wondering what had set Calder clicking like a Geiger counter.

'It's irrelevant. That brochure's out of date.' Calder held out her hand. 'Here, I'll take it and get you some more current information.'

'That's all right.' Jo put it in her satchel. 'Is Ian happy here at Chira-Sayf? Has he had any problems?'

Calder looked at the satchel like Gollum eyeing the Precious. 'I'm sorry. I just can't tell you anything. Ian's unexceptional. I don't see him that often.'

'I thought you were his supervisor.'

Calder frowned as though she'd just tripped over a crack in the pavement. 'Not his direct supervisor. As I explained, he's an independent contractor. He doesn't fit into our corporate structure.'

'He's a lone wolf.'

Her cheek twitched. 'Kind of.'

'Who did he work for before he came to Chira-Sayf?'

'I'd have to look that up.'

Jo felt her blood pressure rising. 'Ms Calder. Did Ian's trip to South Africa last week put him in any dangerous situations?'

'I can't tell you anything about that. I don't supervise his trips overseas.'

'Who does? Who should I speak to? The travel department? Engineering?'

'I'm sorry. I can't help you.'

Jo lay her hands flat on the table and counted to ten, slowly. 'In that case, I'd like to speak to Alec Shepard.'

Calder stood up like she'd been goosed. 'That's not possible. He's out of the office.'

'Then I'll wait for him to get in.'

'Dr Beckett, you're wasting your time. You need to talk to Ian's friends and family to figure out what's . . . made him unbalanced. There's nothing more I can help you with.' She walked to the door and opened it. 'I'm sorry.'

'Me too.'

Calder escorted Jo out. When she got in the truck, Jo looked back at the building. Behind the blue glass Calder stood gripping her hands tightly in front of her, like a funeral director.

Jo found her phone and punched a number.

'Chira-Sayf,' the receptionist said.

'Alec Shepard, please.'

The receptionist transferred the call. Shepard's secretary picked up. Jo identified herself and asked to speak to him.

'He isn't in the office today. May I ask what this is regarding?'

'It's an emergency. I'm conducting a psychiatric evaluation for the San Francisco Police Department. It's about Ian Kanan.'

Pause. 'Let me transfer you to our legal department.'

Snap. Jo heard the sound of another Chira-Sayf employee wriggling into a girdle of flame-resistant, ass-covering spandex.

'Tell Mr Shepard I'm investigating whether Kanan might try to kill him. Have him call me.'

Longer pause. The secretary took Jo's number.

'Thank you.'

She hung up, put her hand on the ignition, and hesitated, staring at the company's chic buildings. From her satchel she took the Chira-Sayf brochure.

She flipped through it, wondering why Riva Calder

156

had gotten so nervous about her reading it. The brochure was blurby. Nanotechnology is our future. Buckyballs of the world unite. There were photos of happy, smiling Chira-Sayf employees, industrious people at work, building the magic of the twenty-first century.

She stopped, staring at a photo of several people. Their names were listed from left to right. 'Damn it.'

The heat of anger climbed up her chest. She got her phone again. This time, when she phoned Chira-Sayf, she got Calder's voice mail. She hung up and called back.

'Ruth Fischer, please,' she said.

The call was transferred and a woman picked up. 'This is Ruth Fischer.'

Jo heard her Southern accent. 'It's Jo Beckett. Here are your choices. I can go back to the lobby and request to see your boss, or you can wait for me to bring the cops to talk to you, or you can meet me up the road in the shopping center. There's a Taco Bell.'

After a stricken pause, Fischer said, 'Taco Bell.'

Maybe they'd serve crow. In sizzling, red-hot portions.

Kanan stared out the Navigator's windshield at Chira-Sayf's headquarters. Parked a block away, he had a good view of the entrance. The birches on the lawn were coming into leaf, spring green in the sunshine.

He was achy and bruised. He felt as though he had been in a fight. He touched his lip. It was split, but he didn't remember being hit in the mouth. He was wearing brand-new clothes – a jean jacket, gray flannel shirt, T-shirt, jeans, boxers, socks. His old clothes were on the floor in a bag from Target, soaking wet, like his boots. On the passenger seat, in another Target bag, were Post-its, indelible markers, disposable cameras. He didn't remember shopping at Target.

Among the Post-it notes stuck to the dashboard, one read, *Find Alec*.

Obviously he was deep in Fuckupistan. He hadn't delivered the stuff. He couldn't, because he didn't have it. So he was working the fallback plan, going after Alec.

He checked his watch. Ten thirty A.M. That was news to him.

He knew he had a problem. He couldn't rely on himself to know how much time had passed. He realized that he was forgetting almost everything. Having this memory glitch felt like being detached from time, existing in a bubble that floated from moment to moment. The world was vivid, but he had no sense of past or future, only a sense of now. He felt wide awake, extremely clear, and yet adrift.

He scratched at the scabbed-over gouges on his arm. On his skin, in fresh black marker, he saw his own handwriting.

His heart took a stumbling beat and his stomach clenched. He opened the glove compartment. A pair of binoculars was inside. He put them to his eyes and focused on the Chira-Sayf buildings.

There should be a silver Benz parked near the entrance. Not too close, not too far away. Just the right distance to let the worker bees feel that the boss hadn't lost touch with the hive. Alec should be in the office, holding court. People came to see him, right? He didn't need to go out. Except for meeting with Pentagon types in D.C. Or sailing that boat of his, *Somebody's Baby*. Or flying to Johannesburg when Chira-Sayf pulled the plug on the research.

Kanan didn't see the car.

And what in hell was he going to say to Alec when he found him? Would it turn into a grief-fest, a screaming match about betrayal? Would anything be rectified?

The stuttering heart tripped him up again. His family. His beautiful, feisty Misty. His big-hearted Seth. He had been poisoned, and with it his whole life.

His eyes stung. He let the tears well. He felt, hot against his leg, the steel of the blade.

At Chira-Sayf, a woman walked out of the main building. She was young, dressed down, had loose brown curls that swirled in the wind. He looked at the dash-board. Beside the Post-it notes, a laminated photo I.D. was clipped to a heater vent. He checked. It was the same woman. JOHANNA BECKETT, M.D.

The doctor got in a Toyota pickup, pulled out, and drove past him. He followed.

Across the Formica-topped table, the woman who had called herself Riva Calder grabbed a taco and bit down. The tortilla shell snapped and crumbled. Ground meat and cheese and lettuce spewed out.

'Anytime,' Jo said.

She wiped her mouth. 'She would have fired me. Thrown my ass out.'

'Are you saying that's why you lied to me, Ms Fischer?'

The woman killed the rest of her taco, grabbed a box

159

of popcorn chicken, and popped three bites in her mouth. She washed them down with a swig of Diet Pepsi and eyed Jo.

'You don't act surprised. Or is that your shrink demeanor?' she said.

'I'm not surprised. I'm seriously pissed off.'

Fischer looked down. 'I don't know why I went along with it. It was stupid. As soon as I saw you with the brochure I knew it wouldn't work.'

She dug into the popcorn chicken as though it was aspirin. Or Valium. Jo let her worry.

'Things are about to go very badly for you, workwise at a minimum. Copwise at maximum. I recommend that you tell me everything,' Jo said.

Fischer sighed so hard her entire body sagged. 'Yeah. Fine.'

'What were you trying to accomplish?' Jo said.

'To give you the brush-off, obviously.'

'Why wouldn't Riva Calder actually see me?'

'I don't know. She isn't even in the office. Hasn't been in for days. She phoned and asked me to do it.'

'Why?'

'Why did she ask me to impersonate her? I'm a temp.' She spread her hands. 'Look at me. Who's the slowest, fattest target?' She slumped. 'And now she's going to can my sorry butt.'

'Go through it from the beginning.'

'I was at my desk when Riva's secretary came running down the hall. I mean *running*. She put me through to Riva, who said I had to do this thing.'

'What did she want you to do? Particularly?'

'Placate you. Keep it vague, make you think there was nothing to find out. Get you to go away.'

Jo felt a thorny anger poking at her. She felt insulted. And irate. And, possibly, willing to restrain herself from throwing an entire burrito supreme at Ruth Fischer, depending on what the woman told her now.

'Why the ruse?' Jo said.

'Riva said she couldn't meet with you in person. She said it was impossible. But you needed to think you were talking to her.'

'Didn't that sound weak to you?'

'It sounded off the wall.'

'What does she look like?' Jo said.

'Skinny. Young, of course. Pretty, I guess, in a sharp way. Tense.'

'Chicana, Asian, African-American?'

'No, white as meringue. Dresses like *Vogue*. The Corporate Harpies issue.'

'What did you tell her?'

'I got flustered. It was just so weird. I didn't know if I could pull it off. She said if I didn't want to do it, she'd find somebody else. Somebody who wanted to keep their job.'

'Did Riva give you instructions?'

'Play along. Don't mention my name, or hers. Said you'd presume I was her. I didn't have to lie. And that's what happened. I never confirmed for you who I was. You just assumed.'

Still a lie. 'What were you supposed to tell me?'

'That we couldn't release Kanan's confidential employment history. That we didn't know where he was. That there was nothing we could help you with.'

'And what's the truth?'

Fischer gripped her Pepsi cup as though she wanted to throttle it. 'Ian Kanan is a scary guy. A ghost who slips in and out of the office. Doesn't talk to people. Doesn't do meetings or the company picnic.'

'And what does he do?'

'At Chira-Sayf there's computer security, and there's building security – rent-a-cops, same as the rest of the business park. And then there's Ian Kanan. He's off the charts. He is not a guy I want to run up against.'

'Why did he go to South Africa last week?' Jo said.

'I don't know. But he wasn't going in to prep for a bigwigs' summit this time.'

'Chira-Sayf has a lab in South Africa, doesn't it?'

Fischer shook her head. 'Did. They shut it down.'

Jo took out a notebook and pen. 'What did the lab do?'

Fischer pushed her cup away. 'Experimental. It was offshore to avoid U.S. law.'

'What were they working on?' Jo said.

'It was over my head. Research. Government contracts, good works. You know, helping African business. But . . .' She looked around the restaurant and back at Jo. 'They shut it down real suddenly.'

'Why?'

'No idea. But folks were upset. Around the office, people's auras got real spiky.'

162

Jo's pen was poised above the notebook. She set it down. 'Sure.'

Fischer fanned herself with her hands. 'I'm probably throwing off sparks. If you could see my aura, you'd get a fire extinguisher.' She attempted a smile. 'Yours is light purple.'

'Okay.'

Fischer took her napkin and blew her nose. 'People with lighter shades of purple are refining their spiritual nature. Are you actively working on that?'

'Ms Fischer –'

'Ruth. Please.'

'Ruth, what happened when Chira-Sayf shut down the South African lab?'

'Chaotic auras from some of the people. The engineers were ticked off. The execs got dark. You know, tense.'

'Riva?'

'Red flares.' Her narrow eyes briefly widened. 'She's a soul sucker.'

'How do you mean?'

'Her essence is askew. She disrespects people. She always thinks people are out to get her. Typical Silicon Valley. She's a queen bee, but she's jealous and empty. She wants to suck the spirit out of other people because she's empty herself.' Fischer leaned across the table. 'I'll tell you something else. She's way too interested in Ian Kanan.'

'How so?'

'He's got a yellow aura, by the way. It flares above him.'

163

'Don't worry about describing his aura.'

'But it's different from everybody else's. Chira-Sayf executives, they think they're so hot. Real self-important. And paranoid. As if Hewlett-Packard is going to send a death squad crashing through the windows.'

'But?'

'But Ian, his aura is serious. He carries himself like he's the real deal. Like he knows about life and death in the real world.' She picked at the chicken. 'I don't think I've ever seen him smile.'

'Why do you say Calder is too interested in him?' Jo said.

'Always making sure she gets to talk to him. Leaving her office door open when she knows he's around. Wearing perfume. Which goes *badly* with her crimson aura, let me tell you.'

'She's interested in him romantically?' Jo said.

'Maybe. Maybe she's just trying to keep him on her side. I don't know what power struggles go on in the corporate hierarchy. Except' – she glanced around again – 'maybe she figured if she couldn't have the cute one, she'd get the powerful one.'

'Hold on. Are you saying Kanan turned down her advances, so she had an affair with one of the top executives?'

Fischer shrugged. 'Maybe.'

Jo wrote in her notebook. When she looked up, Fischer's face was pale.

'What?' Jo said.

'I'm sorry. I feel like a real clod for leading you on.'

'Thanks.'

Fischer's puffy eyes narrowed further, like coin slots in a vending machine. 'There's something else, about the Johannesburg lab. Nobody's supposed to talk about it. But one of our employees is missing.'

Jo's eyebrows rose. 'Who?'

'Chuck Lesniak. He left Johannesburg but hasn't come home.'

'When did this happen?'

'His last e-mail was a good-bye from the Jo'burg office a week ago. Said he was heading to London for R&R, and that he'd see us all back in Santa Clara this week. Except he didn't show up. He missed his flight from London.'

'What's the company say?'

'Nothing. Zero.'

Jo clicked her pen. 'How do you spell his name?'

'L-E-S-N-I-A-K. You think this relates to Ian's disappearance? I mean, two guys from the same company. In one week.'

'It may be coincidence. But I have my doubts.'

Jo's phone rang. It was Rick Simioni, the neurologist.

'I've got Ron Gingrich's MRI results. You need to see them.'

'On my way.'

165

14

The hallway of the ranch house was musty and dim. The men pulled the woman by the arms toward the darkened bedroom doorway. She dug her heels into the shiny carpet.

'Stop it,' the big one said.

But the panic corkscrewed through her again. 'Let me go.'

The big man, Murdock, was bald, with no neck and sloping shoulders. His palm was clammy. Gold bracelets nestled among black hairs on his thick arms.

She tried to squirm free. 'Let me go and I'll pay you. Take me to the bank. I'll empty my account.'

They reached the bedroom door. Inside was a bed with a ratty mattress and a pillow covered with brown stains. The windows were boarded over. She clamped her teeth and pressed her hands against the doorjamb. The thought of going back in there for one more hour, much less one more day, was intolerable.

'Give it up, or I'll have to cuff your hands behind your back again.' Murdock's voice sounded wet. He had tiny teeth and glistening pink gums. 'If you fight or even scream, you know who'll pay. So save your breath. It won't get you out, just get your family hurt.'

The young man, the one called Vance, stuck his nose in her face. 'Yeah. This is baby Gitmo, bitch. Consider yourself an enemy combatant.'

In the kitchen, rap music pounded from the stereo, and the dog barked. The sound of both was deep and angry. Vance pried her fingers loose from the jamb and shoved her through the door with a hard slap on the butt.

She spun, fists up, ready to fight if Vance came at her, if he tried to throw her down on the bed. He stood silhouetted in the doorway.

'Frisk her,' Murdock said. 'Make sure she didn't hide the phone on her.'

Vance swaggered into the bedroom with the exaggerated, rolling gait of a gangbanger. Why this skinny white boy thought he was starring in *8 Mile* she didn't know, but the phrase *desperately overcompensating* popped into her head.

He spun her around. 'Spread 'em.'

She put her hands against the wall, spread her feet, and bit back her revulsion as Vance ran his hands up her legs. They'd done this every time they brought her back to the room, and each time Vance let his hands wander farther across her. His fingers lingered for a second on her crotch before moving on. Her face heated.

Finally he backed away. 'She's clean.'

'Behave,' Murdock said. He pointed to a brown paper bag on the floor in the corner. 'And get changed. What you're wearing doesn't smell too fresh anymore.'

'And that ain't ladylike,' Vance said.

They slammed the door and locked it from the outside. She sagged against the wall, head back.

None of this made sense. Why had they taken her?

'Stop kidding yourself,' she muttered.

It made perfect sense. She was here because of Chira-Sayf, and Alec, and the work the company was doing in South Africa. She was here because of Ian and the overseas trip he'd taken the previous week.

She was being held as a pawn in some corporate battle that had gone beyond sales projections and industrial espionage. This was about Slick.

A knot the size of a golf ball lodged in her throat. Tears welled in her eyes. She'd seen their faces and heard their names. That was a bad omen for her future.

Then she breathed. She couldn't fall apart. Fall apart and she was sure to lose whatever game they were playing with her. She had to hold it together and think of a way out of here. Now that they'd finally uncuffed her, she finally had a chance.

But how? The door to the room was cheap and hollow. Given enough time, she could probably kick a hole in it. But if she did, Murdock would carry out his threat to harm her family.

'Parents, kids, pets, all fair game,' he had warned her.

She didn't know where she was. When they grabbed her, they'd bound her hands with plastic handcuffs and blindfolded her. But she knew they'd driven south, and now at frequent intervals she could hear a locomotive. It had to be the Caltrain, which meant they were on the Peninsula.

The room was close and smelled of mold and damp. This place was a cheap old tract house, with cheap old windows built high into the walls. What kind of architectural dumbass had decided, back in the sixties, that it would be stylish to put the windows in a kid's bedroom five feet off the ground? It made the room feel like . . .

Like a cell.

She laughed bitterly. *Focus, will you?*

She climbed on the bed and pushed aside the venetian blinds. The window was boarded up from the outside. The glass was cracked in a cheap aluminum frame. She unlatched it. The frame stuck and complained, but she managed to slide the window open about two feet. Wide enough to slip through, if she could get the plywood off.

She pressed her palms to the wood. It was dry and warm. She pushed but it didn't budge.

She steadied herself on the creaking springs of the bed frame and shoved again. No luck. Unless she managed to beam a claw hammer into the room, she'd never get the board off.

'Wouldn't that be slick,' she muttered.

Slick.

Ian had told her about it. Even though he wasn't supposed to be so clued in about Chira-Sayf's big project,

169

much less to talk about it, even in the parking lot outside the company's H.Q.

'Alec's worried,' he'd said.

But if Alec had been worried, Ian had been livid. His face had set in blank rage, pale behind the freckles and chilly blue eyes.

'Something backfired. Slick doesn't work as advertised. Alec's shutting the project down.' He looked at her. 'This doesn't leave this car.'

'Of course not,' she said, feeling alarmed. Ian Kanan did not take his work outside the office, ever. Did not talk to others at Chira-Sayf about office scuttlebutt or product development or anything except Raiders football and close personal protection. He compartmentalized.

But he knew that something had gone haywire with Slick. Chira-Sayf's killer app had somehow turned on the company.

'Alec's pulling the plug. The military's never going to get it.' He stared out the windshield. 'There's a fight brewing.'

'Between?' she said. 'Are they dragging you into it?'

'If they do, they'll regret it. Because I'll take care of things.'

And when Ian took care of things, the results weren't pretty.

The nails in the boards wouldn't budge. She wiped her palms on her pants. Maybe she could split the plywood. It was dry and brittle. She ran her fingers over the board until she found a chip in the wood, about a quarter of an inch wide.

The window faced the street. Maybe she could shove something through the chip in the wood and send a message. Wave a flag. Somehow.

How could she alert a passerby? She didn't have any I.D. They'd taken her purse, cell phone, car and house keys. They'd taken her jewelry. Even her wedding ring, the thieving bastards. And they'd shoved her in this stinking bedroom.

She turned to the brown paper bag. Inside were the clothes Murdock had provided in his strange burst of generosity – a turtleneck sweater, wool slacks, blouse, a designer sweatshirt. She got the sweatshirt from the stack. She could pull the string from the hood and use it somehow.

Wait. She turned up the hem of the sweatshirt. There was a dry cleaning label inside.

CALDER.

Her heart rate bumped up. Talk about waving a flag.

Then a weird suspicion came over her. She got the slacks and looked inside the waistband. Again she saw the dry cleaning label. She got the blouse. Same.

These clothes virtually begged for somebody to identify her. Somebody, for instance, dragging a body out of the mud flats on the bay.

'Holy shit,' she whispered.

She sat down on the edge of the bed and tore the hem of the blouse with her teeth. She ripped out the tag on a long strip of fabric, like a nurse preparing a field dressing, and got to work.

*　　*　　*

Jo walked into radiology feeling that something was on her heels, waiting for the opportunity to bite her. Lieutenant Tang was in the hallway talking on the phone, looking unsettled and grim. She jerked her head at a doorway and murmured, 'Go on in.'

The room was cool and hushed, illuminated by X-rays in light boxes and MRI images on the radiologist's computer screen. Bone art. Soul stripped bare, to neurons and gray matter. Rick Simioni was standing by the desk, wearing his white coat over a dress shirt of Egyptian cotton as rich as cream.

'Rick,' she said.

When he looked at her, the light from the computer screen gave his face an eerie, hollow look.

Dr Chakrabarti, the radiologist, gave Jo a prim nod and pointed at the screen with a pen. 'Mr Gingrich's MRI.'

The images on the screen were repetitive and disconcerting, like Warhol's grayscale death montages. The three of them stared.

What *was* that?

Jo slowed her breathing. Training and experience had taught her to hold part of herself back when seeing the evidence of a catastrophic diagnosis. She pulled her emotions safely off the ground, tucked them away, close enough for empathy but not so close that she'd get sucked into the patient's tragedy.

And nothing that happened to the human body could surprise her.

So she thought. But though she stood rooted to the

172

floor in front of the computer screen, she wanted to run away.

The same black threads that had chewed through Ian Kanan's brain were advancing through Ron Gingrich's, doing – what? Growing, or eating their way through his medial temporal lobes.

'You're sure it's not an imaging artifact?' Jo said.

The fluorescent tubes in the light boxes hummed like bug zappers. Simioni crossed his arms and stared at the screen. Chakrabarti hadn't looked away. It was as if the Warhol images were hypnotizing him.

'It's not an imaging error,' Chakrabarti said. 'The same thing emerges on both sets of MRIs. I don't know what it is.'

Jo looked at Simioni. 'Rick?'

Simioni focused on the screen. 'A natural neurotoxin? A tropical parasite? Something they both came in contact with on the airplane?'

'An industrial pollutant?' she said. 'A contaminant from high-tech manufacturing?'

'That's an interesting possibility.'

'Kanan works for a nanotechnology company.'

Both men turned to her. Simioni said, 'Really?'

'Really.'

With a knock, Amy Tang opened the door and stuck her head in. 'Got something going on at the marina. It may relate. I'm heading over.'

Jo nodded, and Tang disappeared. Jo turned back to the MRI images.

'Thoughts?' she said.

Simioni turned pensive. 'Nanotech is being investigated as a treatment for brain tumors. Treating brain cancers is notoriously difficult, because many anticancer drugs consist of molecules too large to cross the blood-brain barrier and reach the tumor site. The barrier keeps most agents out. Only very small substances can breach it.'

'Are nanoparticles small enough?'

'Some are. But nanoparticle chemotherapy is problematic. If the wrong agents cross the barrier they can cause serious brain infections, which are tenacious and difficult to treat. And some nanoparticles deliver anticancer drugs but don't target only tumors – they accumulate in surrounding healthy tissue.'

'You're saying nanoparticles can be a Trojan horse,' Jo said. 'They could slip past the brain's natural defenses and cause havoc.'

'Precisely.'

All three of them stared at the images on the screen. Simioni pointed at the images of Gingrich's brain. 'What could cross the blood-brain barrier and lodge so specifically in this one area, I'm not sure.'

'Where's Mr Gingrich now?' Jo asked.

'Upstairs. We admitted him.' Simioni continued gazing at the screen.

'Is it contagious?' Jo said.

He looked at her. 'I hope not.'

15

Standing aboard the crowded AirTrain, Stef Nivesen watched the clouds above the coastal mountains. They were so bright they seemed to amplify the sunlight. They looked like klieg lights in the sky.

The AirTrain rattled along the elevated track toward the terminal at San Francisco International Airport. Stef was stuffed in a corner, holding the handle of her roller case. She kept her balance as the train rounded a curve. She pretended to ignore the looks from men on the train. She knew her red Virgin Atlantic uniform fit her to perfection. She was twenty-six, she worked out, she wore heels that made her legs look great. The Virgin uniforms were retro-styled, giving off the aura of jet-set glamour. And she knew she could take down any of these guys in a judo bout. She flew the SFO-Heathrow route, and she loved her job. Loved flying to London, loved British men, and knew they regarded a long-haul flight as a twelve-hour party with an open bar. At times she wished the 747 carried a fire hose, so she could blast sloshed and grabby passengers straight back to their seats.

She scratched her arm. The train was hot. She felt tired but wide awake.

The train stopped, doors opened, and people streamed out. Stef looked around in surprise. What was she doing at the car rental stop? She'd been going the other way, from the garage to the international terminal.

How had she missed her stop?

She checked her watch and relaxed. She had plenty of time.

People streamed aboard, hauling luggage, and the train pulled out. Stef stared at the clouds in the sky above the coastal mountains. They were as bright as klieg lights.

At least it was sunny today. Not like yesterday when her flight came in with the lunatic on board. *That* had been weird. She scratched her arm again. She was glad those two men had stopped the nutball before he opened the emergency exit. She'd been strapped in her jump seat forty feet away. She would have had a hell of a time reaching him, much less stopping him.

Why had Berserko tried to open the door? Did he need air? She sure did. The train was hot and close. And bright. Everybody seemed exceptionally bright and sharply defined.

'Miss? Are you all right?'

Stef blinked at the man standing in front of her. Forty-Niners cap and forty-nine pounds of pudge around his waist.

'Excuse me?' she said.

'Are you all right? You were turning around, like something was pushing you.'

'I'm fine.' What a weird thing for the man to say.

The train stopped and the doors opened. Crap, this was the international terminal. She rushed out as the doors closed.

She took the crew lane through security and headed straight for the gate. It was already crowded with passengers waiting to board. She checked her watch.

Alarm rang through her. Thirty minutes to departure. Holy crap, how had it gotten so late?

She picked up her pace. Her cell phone rang. She checked the display. It was Charlotte Thorne, one of her British colleagues.

Stef answered in a rush. 'I'm on my way.'

'You said that an hour ago. Where are you?'

'I'm coming down the concourse. What do you mean, I said that?'

Charlotte exhaled with annoyance. 'Are you really here this time? You sure you haven't been skiving with your boyfriend?'

'Don't be ridiculous. I can see the gate.'

She hung up, irked. Why would Charlotte claim she'd lied? She hadn't spoken to Charlotte an hour ago. She hadn't spoken to her since their last flight together. How daft, as Charlotte would put it.

She reached the gate. Throwing her shoulders back, she smiled and walked toward the plane.

*　　*　　*

177

Jo dropped her satchel on the kitchen table, turned on the coffeepot, and opened the French doors to the patio. It was chilly, but after seeing Ron Gingrich's MRI she wanted fresh air.

She got out her notes and checked e-mail. A message confirmed that Kanan had customs papers on the daggers and sword he'd brought back. They were classed as museum pieces, purchased from an antiquities dealer in Jordan, destined for display. Kanan was transporting them on behalf of Chira-Sayf Inc.

Chira-Sayf. Where did that name come from?

Chira wasn't in her dictionary, but *chiral* was a chemistry term, relating to molecular structure and atomic mirror-imaging. *Sayf* was the transliterated spelling of the Arabic word for *sword*. Photos showed ancient scimitars whose blades shone with the luster of the knife Ian Kanan had flashed near her face.

She stared at the screen. Out back on the lawn, black wings fluttered and she heard a sharp *caw*.

Two crows were pecking at an object on the grass. She went outside, clapping her hands to shoo the birds away. They bustled into flight, leaving their prey limp and dismembered on the lawn.

She looked at it, puzzled.

They'd been tearing apart a little stuffed animal. It was a floppy emerald-green bear, about eight inches long. Its eyes hung by threads. The fabric was stained and slimy. Jo nudged it with the toe of her shoe. It looked as though it had been probed by aliens, with their most thorough tools and lubricants.

She heard the doorbell. Leaving the bear, she jogged inside to answer it. She opened the door and lowered her gaze six inches. Amy Tang looked like she had bitten into a sour green apple.

She handed Jo a photo. 'From a CCTV camera at the marina.'

It showed a man, sopping wet, unlocking the door of an SUV.

Jo's shoulders tightened. 'It's Kanan.'

'Thank you for the I.D. Now I can apply to a judge for a murder warrant.'

Jo looked up sharply. 'Come in. Tell me.'

'A white male was found floating in the marina beside a yacht called *Somebody's Baby*. Passerby saw a slick of bloody water, thought it was *Jaws*, and called in the cavalry. Only the victim didn't have shark bites. He had a major abdominal stab wound.'

Jo led Tang down the hall to the living room. 'What makes you think Kanan is involved?'

'"Involved"? As in, stuck the victim like a pig?'

'Yes. As in.'

'Witness saw a man fitting Kanan's description walking away from the slip, dressed in street clothes, soaking wet. He climbed into a red Navigator and pulled out like his hair was on fire.'

'Fitting Kanan's description?' Jo said.

Tang handed her another photo. It showed Kanan standing at the open door of the SUV, bare-chested, tossing his wet shirt into the vehicle.

'And no,' Tang said, 'I have no proof that Kanan

179

stabbed the victim. But when a man walks away after a knife fight, it generally means he's the winner.'

Jo examined the photo. Kanan looked strong and alert.

Tang glanced around the living room. 'Nice digs.'

'Thanks. I inherited it.'

'Lucky you.'

'Tell it to my in-laws. The house was in Daniel's family for a hundred years.'

Tang panned the room, taking in the red Egyptian rug, the Japanese watercolors, and the *Sopranos* box sets on the bookshelf.

'You have a Mafia fetish?'

'Psychiatrists all watch *The Sopranos*. It's the shrink's dream show.' Jo continued examining the photos of Kanan.

Tang arched an eyebrow. 'You don't believe Kanan could kill somebody? Want to see the body to compare the wound dimensions with the blade Kanan pulled on you?'

'I don't need to see the body.'

'Right, you don't do blood and guts. You just rip the lid off the psyche and catch the screaming meemies that fly out.'

'Didn't catch these, apparently.'

Tang took the photos back. 'Don't feel morose. You're a doctor. You're trained to see him as a sick man, not a killer.'

Jo didn't feel morose. She felt a liquid silver fear that seemed to roll across her skin like mercury. 'I believe it. But I want to know what's behind it. That might help us pinpoint his targets and shut him down.' She brushed her hair back from her forehead. 'Have you identified the victim?'

Tang took out her notepad. 'Ken Meiring.'

180

'Who was he?'

'We don't know his connection to Kanan, but he has a record. Fraud, receiving stolen goods, and illegal weapons sales.' Tang's expression was astringent. 'He was a thief and a lowlife thug. And he was Kanan's first target. Shall we connect the dots?'

'Was it his boat?'

'I doubt it. According to the records for the marina, *Somebody's Baby* is owned by Chira-Sayf Inc.'

'What?'

'Yes. Curiouser and curiouser. It's –' Tang looked out the bay window. 'Isn't that your neighbor?'

On the sidewalk outside, waving at them, stood Ferd.

Jo raised a hand in lukewarm response. 'Don't make any sudden moves. He'll take it as an invitation and appear on the porch.'

'His monkey is more debonair than I imagined,' Tang said.

Mr Peebles stood beside Ferd. He was wearing a tiny lampshade on his head like a fez.

'If I were you, I'd move. Leave everything in the house and go,' Tang said.

'Like any other neighborhood in this town would have fewer eccentrics?'

Ferd pointed at Jo's front door and hustled toward it.

'Shoot. Hang on,' she said. When Ferd knocked, she opened the door just wide enough to see his face. 'Hi. Sorry, I can't talk right now.'

'I have a few quick questions about the monkey virus,' he said.

'Can I give you a call later?'

He rubbed his throat. 'I'm worried. Could I catch it?'

'Dude, Mr Peebles doesn't have Congolese monkey virus. So, no.'

With a little shriek, the monkey darted between Ferd's legs and through the doorway past Jo.

'Ferd, get him.'

Jo ran after the creature into the kitchen, with Ferd and Tang following. Mr Peebles sprang onto the table, scattering her notes. He pulled open her satchel and began rooting through it.

Tang walked calmly to the table and nabbed him with a tube of lipstick in his hands. 'You little larcenist.'

Ferd collected Jo's notes from the floor. 'You see how antsy he is?'

Mr Peebles twisted the lipstick and ran it madly around his mouth. Tang tried to take it. He swiped it at her like a pale-pink switchblade.

'Look at him – he's just not himself,' Ferd said.

'He's exactly himself,' Jo said. 'Ferd, he's fine. You're fine.'

Tang pried the lipstick from his fingers and held it out to Jo.

'Not even with tongs.' She got the wastebasket.

Tang tossed the lipstick inside and held Mr Peebles out to his master, but Ferd had looked away. He was staring at Jo's notes.

'Are you planning to invest in Chira-Sayf?' he said.

Jo took the notes from him. 'No. And sorry, but that's out of bounds.'

'You're curious about the company's name?' He pushed his glasses up his nose. '*Chirality* refers to the way sheets of carbon nanotubes can be folded.'

'Ah. Got it.'

'They're grown at high temperatures, and depending on how, carbon nanotubes can be folded over, or rolled, or bent tip to tip. It's like they have a certain spin or twist.'

'Thanks.' She thought about it. 'Do you know anything about the company?'

'Not much. It handles a mix of civilian and military projects. Blue-sky stuff.' He tapped his fingertip against the printout, like a woodpecker. '*Sayf* is an Arabic word for *sword*.'

Tang stepped closer. 'Arabic? Strange choice for a Silicon Valley firm.' She eyed Jo. 'No offense.'

'Don't even start,' Jo said.

Tang enjoyed ribbing Jo about her pan-global heritage. Jo's paternal grandfather was an Egyptian Christian. Her maternal grandmother was an army bride from Osaka. The rest of the family was Irish, loud, and argumentative. Sit everybody down for Christmas dinner, add pepper, and watch them blow. And while Jo loved her family, she didn't want to get into a snarking match about the Middle East.

She knew too well that in the U.S., all things Arabic – even the language – could be seen as suspect. She saw no point in telling Tang that Copts in Cairo may have spoken Arabic for fourteen hundred years, but some Coptic Egyptians didn't even regard themselves as having an Arabic heritage. They still referred to the Arab conquest of Egypt in the seventh century.

She let it go. 'I'm a doctor, not a fighter. Let's skip this.'

'Like I'd ever want to get on your bad side,' Tang said.

Ferd tapped the printout again. 'The point is, *sayf* is a play on words here.'

'What do you mean?' Tang frowned at him, as if to say *Who appointed you the expert?* Mr Peebles grabbed her collar and peeked down her sweater. She slapped his little hands.

Ferd held up the printout. 'Damascus steel. It's an ancient form of steel. Thousands of years old.'

'How do you know that?'

'My master's is in computer programming, but my bachelor's is in structural engineering. The thing is, Damascus steel isn't made today. Because nobody knows how to do it.'

'What?' Jo said.

'Damascus steel is unusually strong, light, and supple. And it wasn't made in Damascus, just crafted there. It originally came from India. Nobody knows how it was made. In hand-built furnaces, probably, and hammered out by craftsmen. It has a high carbon content.'

'Like a *katana*,' Jo said.

Ferd nodded. 'But here's the freaky thing. Damascus steel contains carbon nanotubes.'

'Seriously?' Jo said.

Tang looked skeptical. 'Aren't carbon nanotubes created under exotic laboratory conditions?'

'Yes. But electron microscopy shows that swords made from Damascus steel contain them. Nobody knows why. Maybe it had to do with the charcoal in the furnaces. Or the heat at which the steel was hammered out as it cooled.'

Tang stared at his Compurama name tag. *Hi, I'm Ferd.* 'How do you know so much?'

He spread his hands. 'Hobby. Message boards. World of Warcraft gamers discussions. I like this stuff.' He turned to Jo. 'The point is, *chira* relates to nanotech. And *sayf* is obviously meant to indicate things *are* safe. Secure.'

'You're saying Chira-Sayf's business involves security,' Jo said.

Ferd nodded enthusiastically.

Jo took Mr Peebles from Tang and handed him to Ferd. The monkey eyed her from under his tiny fez like an assassin in the souk.

'Thanks, Ferd. You've filled in some gaps in my understanding,' she said.

He beamed. 'My pleasure.'

She nudged him out the door. When she returned to the kitchen, Tang's brow crinkled.

'What else is bugging you?' Tang said.

'Chira-Sayf isn't simply into security. They must have chosen *sayf* because their business involves weaponry.'

'Swords?'

'No. The Damascus saber and the daggers may be for display or may have been purchased to see if the steel could be reverse-engineered. The point is, Chira-Sayf just shut down a research facility in South Africa. Its nanotech work is weapons-related, and something's gone wrong with it. And maybe because of that, Ian Kanan is on the street killing people.'

'You're worried that Kanan was contaminated with some kind of experimental nanogunk.'

'It's my number-one suspicion. As for Damascus steel, the real point is that scientists don't understand everything about how carbon nanotubes behave.'

'Maybe nanogunk is what Kanan stole from Chira-Sayf's South African lab. But the robbery went wrong, and he was contaminated.' Tang quieted for a moment. 'What are you most afraid of?'

'That Kanan's going to kill more people. With a knife, or a gun, or even with a touch. And I don't think we have much time to stop him.'

She looked again at the CCTV photo of Kanan standing barechested by the open door of the Navigator. His face looked strained. She could see the writing that ran up his arms.

There were more words on his arms than she remembered seeing.

'Hang on. I think he's written new messages on his skin.'

The photo was low resolution and the print was small. Jo got a magnifying glass and looked closer.

Her bright little fear grew claws and teeth. 'Oh, no.'

Tang leaned in to see. 'Christ.'

On Kanan's left arm, the message Jo had seen only part of was now visible in its entirety.

Saturday they die.

'He's got a countdown,' she said.

She looked at the clock on the wall. Saturday was less than twelve hours away.

16

Stef Nivesen heard the bell over the 747's P.A. system. She unhooked her five-point seat belt and stood up.

'Stef?' Charlotte had a perplexed look on her face. 'Where are you going?'

'To set up for the beverage service.'

'Are you barmy? We'll be getting takeoff clearance any second.'

Stef glanced out the window in the exit door. They were on the taxiway, in line to take off.

Charlotte put a hand on Stef's arm. 'I know the pinstriped drunk sitting in twelve-B keeps pushing the call button, but he'll have to wait for his Jim Beam until we reach cruising altitude.'

Stef could hear the British banker in row twelve, talking loudly to his seatmate.

'Sit down, pet. Let Allen deal with him,' Charlotte said.

Stef's colleague Allen was strapped into the jump seat by the forward door. He was eyeing the sloshed passenger with prissy disdain. He caught Stef's glance and rolled his eyes.

Stef sat back down. The klieg-light sky looked so bright it was nauseating. She lowered the window shade and buckled up.

The captain came over the P.A. 'Flight attendants, prepare for takeoff.'

The engines cycled up to full thrust and the big jet began to accelerate down the runway. The cabin rattled. Stef closed her eyes.

Stef heard a bell ring. She sighed and unhooked her seat belt.

Charlotte tugged on her arm. 'What's wrong? We've only been airborne ten seconds.'

'I thought . . .'

'Twelve-B pushed the call button again. We're at a thousand feet. Stef, are you quite all right?'

Twelve-B? What did Charlotte mean, 'again'? The floor was pitched at a steep angle and the engines were roaring, still near takeoff thrust. Why had she unbuckled?

She was hot. The air-conditioning seemed to be blasting, but the plane felt stifling. She lay her head back against the bulkhead.

'Are you feeling unwell?' Charlotte said.

'Not so great, to tell the truth.' They lurched. 'Kick-ass turbulence.'

But turbulence generally never bothered her. It could

189

freak out the passengers, though. Sometimes they begged to get off the flight. Sometimes while airborne.

The crazy passenger on the flight in from London – what had made him rush for the exit? The heat in the airliner? The lack of oxygen? She tugged at the scarf that was tied stylishly around her neck. She hated the stale, germ-laden air in jetliners. The wild man, Kanan, had been desperate to get off the plane. She understood how he felt.

She pulled off the scarf. 'So damned hot.'

And she was itching. She scratched at her arm. Actually, it was itching at the spot where Kanan had put his hand on her during the scuffle. She felt a twinge of alarm.

She looked around the cabin. The walls were curved at a parabolic angle. Sunlight etched the faces of the passengers so sharply that she could see every thread in the seams of their clothing, every hair on their heads. The turbulence jostled them in their seats. The passenger in 12B was leaning into the aisle and waving to her colleague Allen like a bar patron summoning a cocktail waitress.

Why didn't somebody turn on the air conditioner? The cabin felt – God, it felt choking. There wasn't any air at all. Somebody should do something. Lack of oxygen could kill airplane passengers and crew.

She recalled the training. Anoxia can kill silently, quickly, and invisibly. Depressurization at high altitude asphyxiates, and the plane's emergency oxygen system – those masks she'd demonstrated a thousand times – delivers only ten minutes of air. If there's an explosive decompression the pilots must descend below fifteen thousand feet immediately. Otherwise, everybody aboard passes out.

But a window blowing out isn't the only thing that can choke off the plane's oxygen supply. The cabin can also fill with deadly fumes.

The 747 kept climbing. The five-point restraint was crushing her lungs. She really couldn't breathe there, next to Charlotte. Charlotte was taking all the oxygen. Everything looked cramped and crystal-clear in the cabin – as though they were in a vacuum, with no air to haze the view. The man in 12B unbuckled and staggered to his feet. He looked drunk already, maybe some British banker who got sauced in the upper-class lounge before boarding. He tottered down the aisle toward the lavatory.

She had to breathe. Across the plane, by the other main door, the jump seats were empty. Stef unhooked her seat belt, lurched to her feet, and headed across the galley to sit down.

'Stef?' Charlotte said.

'Need air,' she said.

She pressed her hand against the bulkhead for balance and pulled down the jump seat. The jet bounced. Outside the little window the horizon zigged up and down. She pulled down the window shade and pressed her head back against the flimsy bulkhead wall. The air still felt close and hot.

Really hot. She let her eyes flicker open. Everybody but the drunken banker was seated. The plane was pitched nose-up in a climb.

Her arm itched where the wild man had scratched her. She looked at it.

The man had kept wiping his hands on his jeans during the flight. She remembered now. The man in row 39 – handsome guy who hadn't shaved, looked exhausted, stared at the seat in front of him like he was burning holes in it. Those eyes, like a blue star, so pale.

He had long, deep scratches on his left arm. During the scuffle with the other passengers, the scratches had been pulled open. They'd bled.

Had she told anybody? She didn't think so. She should have told that doctor.

The fuselage creaked.

God, she was hot. Like she was in an oven. The cabin felt roasting. She could barely draw breath.

Blue Eyes, sitting back in row 39. Maybe he couldn't breathe either.

The plane rocked. Blue Eyes – maybe he understood. When it was an emergency, you had to take action right away. Evacuate this monster of a jet in ninety seconds. Three hundred fifty people it had taken forty minutes to load – get them out in a minute and a half.

Blue Eyes wanted to open the emergency exit.

She felt as though the cabin were at one hundred twenty degrees. Or hotter. And the air was just not there.

No, it wasn't a hundred twenty degrees. It was a hundred forty. Fifty, maybe. More. It was the intense heat of a sauna.

Outside the lav, the banker was trying to pull open the door. Allen was coming down the aisle to usher him back to his seat. But the banker probably wanted to splash water on his face because he was just as damn hot as she was.

She yanked at the collar of her blouse. Two buttons chattered loose and bounced, clicking, off the door. Only one thing could be making the cabin so hot.

In an emergency, when the plane is at low altitude, and there's – Christ. Heat. This much heat meant there had to be a fire. Fire meant smoke. That's why she felt so hot and couldn't breathe. She couldn't see it, though she could see everything else with laser-etched clarity. Fire meant smoke – or, more accurately, combustible gases. And gases could be invisible.

In such an emergency, when passengers and the crew aren't able to breathe, and the supplementary oxygen system hasn't deployed, it's imperative to clear the smoke from the cabin.

Her eyes widened. There was only one way to do that. And it had to be done at low altitude, because above ten thousand feet, the jet became too highly pressurized and it wouldn't work.

'Oh, my God,' she said.

Blue Eyes had felt it, too. The heat, the lack of oxygen. He knew what had to be done. He'd tried to do it.

You had to do it quick. Before the plane reached the critical altitude.

She was suffocating. The temperature was heading toward boiling. Toward baking. How much more before it reached ignition point?

Those two men in the main cabin had wrestled Blue Eyes to the floor. Blue Eyes kept shouting that they were crazy, but they wouldn't listen. He writhed and threw them off, but by then his path was blocked.

The 747 was nose-up. It hit an air pocket and dropped, a swooping, silent dip through the bounding atmosphere. She clutched her knees. She hadn't heard any signals from the flight deck. None of the other cabin crew seemed to notice. Allen was arguing with the drunken banker, and Charlotte was focused on the argument.

Everything looked clearer than fresh snow. If she didn't do something *now*, they wouldn't make it. Even if the pilots were wearing oxygen masks, the heat was intolerable. And it would do no good for the pilots to land the jet safely if everybody back here in the main cabin was dead. Carbon monoxide was colorless. And a by-product of incomplete combustion.

The goddamned 747 was on fire. Blue Eyes had seen it and had tried to warn everybody. He had been trying to save the plane, and she'd ignored it, and those two bullies back in economy, those two crazies, had kept Blue Eyes from saving them all.

She tried to inhale but her lungs wouldn't expand. The air around her was clear and roasting. Tears of panic filled her eyes.

Nobody was aware. The gas was affecting them already. Blue Eyes was out of action. She had to act.

She was terrified, but she had trained for this. She could do it.

She stood up and disarmed the door.

Across the airliner, Charlotte cried, 'Stef? What are you doing?'

She had to do this before the 747 reached ten thousand feet, or the pressure inside the cabin would jam the door into the opening.

'Stef, *no*!'

She pulled the lever to open the door.

With a blast of noise and a wind like God sweeping down to smite them, the door retracted. An inch, two, six. The air in the cabin turned to frozen mist and as Charlotte screamed, everything that wasn't nailed down sought the exit as if magnetized, as if fleeing a little box of hell. The door moved with rugged determination, inward and upward. The jet turned freezing. Outside, all was air. Beautiful, cool, plentiful air. Stef inhaled. Seven inches. Eight. Twelve. The banker howled and lifted off his feet. Coffeepots and magazines and eyeglasses and a man's jacket screamed past Stef through the widening aperture.

She flew out to join them.

17

After Tang left, Jo tried to reach Misty Kanan. She left messages on Misty's cell and the Kanans' home phone.

Feeling increasingly frustrated, Jo called Chira-Sayf and left new messages for Alec Shepard and Riva Calder. She felt that everybody involved in this case was playing hide-and-seek. And she was It, stumbling after them blindfolded.

In the backyard, the green leaves of the magnolia tree flickered in the wind like a revivalist congregation shaking their hands in the air. She set her cell phone on the kitchen table. It rang.

The ringtone jangled through the room: Incubus, 'Sick Sad Little World.' She jumped at it like a soldier diving on a live grenade.

'Got some information on Ian Kanan,' Gabe said.

'Great, give it to me. Rock my world.'

'Sounds like your day's going well.'

'Like a P.J. who forgot to pack his chute for a mission.'

'You should hear the information in person. I'm heading for Noe Valley – have you eaten lunch?'

'I'll meet you at Ti Couz.' She grabbed her keys and headed for the door. 'Give me the basics. Five words or less.'

'Regarding Ian Kanan? Bang-bang.'

A minute later she was jogging along the sidewalk toward the truck, which was parked around the corner and across the cable car tracks in parking space *numero quince*, when the phone rang again.

'Dr Beckett? Alec Shepard.'

The Chira-Sayf CEO's voice was worn and dry, like a splintery wooden stake. Jo's pulse kicked up.

'Thank you for returning my call,' she said.

'You certainly saw to it that I would. My pilot gave me the message that Ian wants to kill me.'

'Can we meet?'

'We'd better. I just left the San Jose airport. I'm on 101 heading for the city.'

'You know the Mission? There's a restaurant on Sixteenth. Ti Couz.'

'I'll find it.'

This time when Murdock and Vance hauled her through the door into the cold garage, they seemed on the verge of losing it. Murdock shoved her hard toward the chair that sat on the concrete beneath the bare bulb.

'Sit.'

She lowered herself slowly into the chair and swept her

hair over her shoulder. They had total physical control over her, but she could try to maintain emotional control, at least over her self-respect. Murdock ripped the duct tape from her mouth. He positioned himself in front of her, bent over, and put his hands on his knees so his wet gums and shining bald head were at eye level with her.

'Where's Ian?' he said.

'I don't know.'

'He tells you everything that goes on at the company. He'd tell you where he's going.'

'No.'

Vance strutted up. 'You want me to break out the enhanced interrogation techniques, bitch?'

He grabbed his crotch. The spit stuck in her throat. Murdock swatted him back as if he were a fly, and Vance retreated to the far side of the garage with a sneer, adjusting his saggy jeans.

'Who's Ian after?' Murdock said.

'I don't know.'

'How do we find him?'

Murdock was right in her face, breathing the words on her. But she heard what he wasn't saying: *How do we find Ian before he finds us?*

They were scared and getting desperate. Something had happened. The third man, the one with extreme acne, wasn't around anymore. Something had screwed up their plans. Something, maybe, named Ian Kanan.

'Are they dragging you into it?' she had asked him.

'If they do, they'll regret it. Because I'll take care of things.'

198

And the results were not pretty. Inside her heart of dark hearts, she rejoiced.

Murdock leaned closer and nuzzled her hair with his nose. His words sounded moist. 'Play nice, remember?'

Just so they didn't tell her to play dress-up in the warm clothes they'd brought along, the ones that would shout 'Riva Calder.' What was that line Dave Grohl sang? About the face you see, mirroring your stare?

'Where's Ian?' Murdock said.

That song had another line. *I'm the enemy.* The one who will bring a foe to his knees.

She swallowed her fear and stared him in the eye. 'What'll you give me if I tell you?'

Murdock's gaze went flat. 'Wrong question. What'll I give you if you don't?'

Jo had a clear view of Sixteenth Street through the front windows of Ti Couz. The restaurant was short on decoration and long on atmosphere, with high ceilings, glossy paint, wobbly tables. Great food. Plates clattered and waiters shouted good-naturedly at the cooks in the kitchen. At the next table a burly, bearded couple held hands. They looked like grizzlies in button-down shirts.

Watching for Shepard, Jo leafed distractedly through a copy of the *Bay Guardian*. It was like browsing a time portal, absorbing the latest manifesto from the Summer of Rage. The Man, no surprise, was bent on oppressing the people.

Her phone chirped with a text message from Gabe. *10 min. out.*

Through the plate-glass windows she saw Alec Shepard stride along the sidewalk. He was the only man on the block wearing a suit. Not just any suit, but one the color of a stealth fighter, sleek and tailored, with a crisp white shirt and an electric-blue tie that hung on his chest like a broadsword. He was built to substantial dimensions, with the broad head and chest of a bison. His gray hair and salt-and-copper beard were clipped close. His stride was confident. He stepped through the door, took off his sunglasses, and gave the room the same bottomless stare that Ian Kanan had given her aboard the 747. Maybe it was a patented Chira-Sayf glare.

She waved. He strode to the table and shook her hand.

'I can only stay a few minutes. The police called me. Apparently, someone stole my new Navigator from the driveway this morning.' He sat down across from her. 'It's turning out to be quite a day.'

Shepard didn't hesitate to put his back to the windows. Even though Jo had warned him that Kanan was after him, the idea of a deadly threat seemed not to fit with his mental landscape.

'Please explain this melodramatic message you left with my secretary,' he said.

'Ian Kanan may be planning to kill you.'

'Absurd.'

Jo held his gaze, trying to judge his tone, his attitude, whether he was nervous or frightened. He was stone.

'Why do you think it's absurd?' she said.

He put his sunglasses on the table. 'I think, in the circumstances, you're the one who owes me an explanation.'

'Haven't you spoken to the police?'

'About the auto theft. I just flew in from Montreal. If there's anything else, the captain didn't get it over the radio.'

Jo leaned back. 'Have you heard anything in the past thirty hours? Kanan has suffered a brain injury that's caused short-term memory loss.'

His mouth twitched, like a fishhook had caught in his lip. 'I heard. I want to talk to the neurologist about that. I'd like you to stick to evaluating Ian's psyche. Tell me why you've reached this bizarre conclusion that he's become a homicidal maniac.'

'Mr Shepard –'

'Alec.'

'Alec, strange things are going on at Chira-Sayf. One of your employees is missing. Another lied to me two hours ago about her identity. Yesterday Ian assaulted me. He thinks he's been poisoned. He has a list of names written on his arm, starting with yours, and a declarative sentence ending in "they die." And I think his injury originated in the theft of materials from your nanotech lab in Johannesburg.'

Shepard's eyes were the pale gray of dirty quartz. He peered at her a long moment, assessing her the way she'd assessed him.

Jo's face heated. This wasn't psychoanalysis. She couldn't afford to sit there like an analyst waiting for defenses to fall, connections to click, insights to light the room. She generally avoided pushing people to respond to her questions. When their memories and impressions unrolled without her prompting, she got more honest answers. But Shepard was stonewalling.

'Who sent Ian to Africa?' she said.

'When?'

'Last week. South Africa, Zimbabwe, Zambia. That's where he arrived home from yesterday.'

'I didn't know he was in Africa.'

'No?' Jo put her hands flat on the table. 'Why did Chira-Sayf shut down the Johannesburg lab?'

'That's not within your purview.'

'What nanotech projects did the lab work on?'

'I thought you wanted to talk about Ian.'

'I do. Tell me about your relationship with him. Start at the beginning and don't leave anything out. Explain whether you think he could be involved in a theft from the lab, whether your nano project could have poisoned him, and why he was seen walking away from the scene of a murder at the marina this morning.'

That got him to drop the mask for a second. Shock lit his gaze. 'Murder?'

'Alec, SFPD detectives have been trying to reach you. A man was found floating dead in the water next to *Somebody's Baby*. He'd been stabbed to death. Ian was seen leaving the marina immediately afterward.'

'That's . . .' He shut his eyes.

'Alec?'

Ignoring her, he took out his phone, dialed, and put it to his ear. 'Jenny? Put me through to legal.'

Shepard rubbed his forehead. His face had turned as red as a radish. Behind him, outside on the street, the sunlight jangled off passing vehicles. Jo realized she was clenching her jaw.

'Bill? Alec. We have a hell of a problem. Why didn't you contact me?'

Beyond the parade of vehicles on Sixteenth Street, Jo saw the shine of maroon paint. Her eyes refocused. A red SUV was parked across the street from the restaurant. Her mind clicked back to the CCTV photo of Kanan taken at the marina.

'Alec – the car that was stolen from your driveway. A Navigator?'

He looked up, irritated at the interruption.

She leaned forward. 'Is it a red Navigator?'

'Yes.'

She nodded out the window. 'That one?'

Ian Kanan stared through the Navigator's tinted window at the little restaurant on Sixteenth. He saw Alec sitting at a table inside. A woman was sitting across from him, in the gunfighter's seat. Young, dark hair, good-looking, leaning toward Alec with an intense expression on her face.

He scanned the dashboard. Next to a bunch of Post-it notes, a photo I.D. was clipped to the heating vent. JOHANNA BECKETT, M.D. Same gal.

So Beckett was in this, connected somehow. He held up his phone and snapped a photo of the two of them.

He looked at Alec, and his stomach went hollow. His mind, the bright bubble of *now* where he existed, filled with the word *betrayal*.

203

He took the gun from the small of his back. It was an HK semiautomatic. He checked the magazine and racked the slide to chamber a round.

Shepard craned his head toward the window, phone to his ear. His annoyance turned to puzzlement, then surprise.

He ended the call. 'That's my Cal sticker in the back window. I'll be damned. Son of a bitch – what are the odds?'

He pushed his chair back. Jo reached across the table and put a hand on his arm.

The Navigator's windows were tinted. The wintry sunlight bleached the glass a cold yellow. They couldn't see the driver.

'Ian could have taken it,' he said.

'How? He has a key?'

His brows furrowed. 'No. But he knows the procedure to disarm the alarm, and where I keep a spare key. He set up the security system for our fleet of corporate vehicles.'

He moved again to stand. Jo tightened her grip on his forearm.

'Why hasn't he come in? Alec? What's going to happen if we walk outside?'

'Nothing good.' He stared out the window. His splintery voice seemed to scratch the air. 'Are you going to call the police?'

So he did think Kanan was dangerous. 'Yeah. After we get out of his line of sight.'

She waited until a waiter swept past, arms laden with thick white dinner plates. He stopped at the burly gay

204

couple's table and began unloading them, blocking the view through the window. She grabbed her satchel and slid from her seat, keeping a hand on Alec's arm.

'Follow me. Don't look around. Don't draw attention to yourself.'

He stood up. She led him back through the restaurant and pushed through the kitchen door. The cooks looked up but she hurried past and led Shepard out the back door into an alley.

She glanced around. 'We need to move away from here, as fast as possible. Where'd you park?'

'Across from the restaurant.'

'In sight of the Navigator?'

'Unfortunately.'

Jo knew the neighborhood, but not well. The Mission police station was several blocks away, and to reach it they'd have to cross Sixteenth. The alley ran only the length of that block, meaning they would have to cross Sixteenth in sight of the Navigator.

She dug her phone from the satchel and dialed Gabe.

He answered brightly. 'Be right there.'

'Are you in the FourRunner?'

'Negative. On foot.'

'Damn it.'

Gabe walked along the busy sidewalk, a block from Ti Couz. 'What's wrong?'

'Ian Kanan's sitting in a red Navigator across the street from the restaurant. I just went out the back. Where'd you park?'

205

His radar spun up. 'On Guerrero.'

He scanned the street. Eighty yards ahead, he saw the red Navigator, parked facing away from him.

'Jo, I have it. Twelve o'clock.'

The driver's door opened and a man stepped out. He was lean, had rusty hair, and moved as smoothly as a snake. He checked for traffic and walked across the street, headed for the door of the restaurant. Outside the plate-glass windows he stopped. Peered in, standing absolutely still. He touched the small of his back and pulled down his gray flannel shirt over his waistband.

Gabe's pinging radar turned to a solid droning tone. His vision tunneled. 'He's armed.'

'Jesus. Gabe –'

'Stay on the line.'

Abruptly Kanan turned and ran back across the street to the SUV.

'He knows you split out the back,' Gabe said.

Kanan jumped in the Navigator, fired up the engine, and peeled away from the curb.

'Jo, he's coming.'

'Which way?'

'Around the east side of the block. Head west.' Gabe turned and dodged back toward Guerrero Street. 'Hang on. I'm coming to get you.'

Running flat out, he hung up and redialed 911.

Clutching the phone, Jo nodded up the alley in the direction of Albion Street. 'Go.'

Shepard glanced around. Jo grabbed his arm again.

'Come on.'

She pulled him up the alley. Lagging a second, Shepard broke into a heavy jog.

'Why does Kanan want to hurt you?' she said.

'I don't know.'

She looked at him sharply. 'Don't, Alec. Now I'm in this with you. Tell me.'

The alley was narrow, lined with garbage cans and Dumpsters. The concrete drain along its center was wet from the previous day's rain. Noise from other restaurants came and went as they ran by. Kitchen sounds, pans and cutlery and people calling out in Spanish and Cantonese.

Shepard shook his head. 'It makes no sense. It has to be the head injury.'

'He has no beefs with you?'

'No.'

'He's not a disgruntled employee? Or a thief?'

Shepard moved like a lumbering buffalo. His breath whistled from his lungs. 'For God's sake, no.'

Her phone rang. *Sick sad little world* . . . She put it to her ear. 'Gabe?'

'Cops are on their way. I'm getting the FourRunner. Keep heading west and watch out for Kanan.'

'Alec Shepard's with me. He's –'

Behind her, tires crunched on broken glass. She looked over her shoulder.

The red Navigator was turning into the alley.

Her pulse rang like an alarm bell. 'Run.'

Shepard glanced back, doubt in his eyes. She dug her nails into his arm.

'Now.'

The Navigator revved and accelerated at them down the alley. In its wake, trash and old newspapers swirled into the air. Jo broke into a sprint.

A second later, as though he still didn't grasp that he was in a situation where split seconds mattered, Shepard did too.

'Gabe —'

'I'm two blocks from my truck. Keep running.'

'Am.'

Jo's Doc Martens felt like cement on her feet. Her satchel swung from her shoulder like a paving stone. Behind them the groan of the engine grew louder. Metal clanged as the Navigator ran into trash cans and kept going with the mindless inertia of a bowling ball. The end of the alley, where it emptied onto Albion, was a hundred yards straight ahead.

Straight ahead wasn't going to work.

Past a cluster of overflowing trash cans, Jo saw an open door. 'This way.'

She heard Shepard breathing hard behind her and the heels of his expensive oxfords scuffing on the concrete. And the engine rising in pitch.

She jammed through the doorway. Found herself in the back hall of a clothing store. Kept running and heard the Navigator screech to a stop. Then she heard the door of the store slam. She looked back. Shepard had shut it and was fighting with a dead bolt lock.

He looked at her. 'Keep going.'

Outside, the Navigator revved. Its tires screeched as

it pulled away. Shepard threw the dead bolt and lumbered toward her. She put out her hands.

'No. He expects us to bolt out the front door and dash for your car. He's coming around the block. We need to go out the back.'

Shepard skidded to a stop on the slick tile floor. 'You're guessing.'

'We have to guess. Mine is that he'll think we're too panicked to double back.'

'What if he's stopped ten yards up the alley, waiting for us?' He glanced at the back door and then out the front windows. 'We could stay here. Sit tight.'

'Plate glass? We'd be sitting ducks. He's armed. We have to lose him.'

She ran to the back exit and put her ear near the door. Heard no engine.

She thought, *Am I a good gambler?* If this were a dime edge of rock, two hundred feet above a valley floor, and she had to decide whether to throw herself sideways for the next hold or retreat down the pitch, what would she do? Her heart was ringing, cymbals, timer bells, cuckoo clock.

Just breathe. She shut her eyes, held still, and listened. She heard customers in the store, and a cash register, but no big-block engine.

'Let's go.'

She threw the lock, opened the door, and leaned out. The alley was empty.

She ran out the door. Across the alley, past a flattened trash can that had spewed its contents like a gutted fish, the back door to another business was propped open with a brick.

'This way.' She put her phone to her ear. 'Gabe – you there?'

'I'm nearly at the FourRunner,' he said, breathing hard.

'We're heading into a store that's on Fifteenth Street. I'm listening for sirens.'

Shepard put an arm out. 'No police.'

She turned her head sharply. 'What?'

'Call them off.'

Fear and anger whipped a stripe across her back. 'No way.'

She ran through the propped-open door and along a dim hallway. Shepard pounded behind her, each breath echoing off the walls.

'Call off the police,' Shepard said. 'You don't understand.'

'Don't understand what? Kanan is dangerous, he's armed, and he's after us.'

She emerged from the hallway into the back of a dry cleaner's. Clothes hung in plastic bags on a mechanized track on the ceiling. The eye-watering pong of cleaning chemicals filled the air. On the far side of a partition, a bored clerk sat on a stool, reading a magazine.

The plate-glass window out front was covered with red lettering. The street was quiet, a few parked cars, motorcycles lined up perpendicular to the curb across the road.

She lowered her voice. 'Kanan's after you, but I'm after *him*. We need to get him back in custody, and I'm damned well leaving that to the police.'

Shepard was wheezing. Sweat glistened on his forehead and splotched the fabric of his shirt. His gray eyes were brimming with pain and confusion that she couldn't decipher.

'Is it true that in five minutes he'll forget he ever saw us?' he said.

'Yes. But that hardly means he'll give up tracking you. He may circle the block for hours. He may hide the SUV and lie in wait. Don't expect him to wander away. He won't,' she said. 'He's on a mission. A mission that will never end for him, even if he's successful.'

Shepard didn't actually shiver, but he looked as though an invisible hand had just slapped him hard across the face.

'I can't turn him in to the police,' he said hoarsely.

'Why not? Tell me why you don't want the cops involved.'

Shepard's jaw and shoulders were taut. He looked as though all his energy was being drained by an invisible power cable.

'I can't turn him in. He's my brother.'

18

Kanan drove south on Albion. He was gripping the wheel like he wanted to wring its neck. The turn-signal indicator was flashing. He reached the intersection with Sixteenth. Following the instructions of Alec's car, he turned left. The big SUV heaved around the corner.

His pulse was pinging. He was simply driving in midday traffic but was breathing rapidly. Something was up. Something big. He looked at the Post-it note on the dashboard.

Alec in Benz.

He scanned the road ahead as he cruised along in traffic on Sixteenth. The day seemed extraordinarily clear. Sunlight lit the clouds to prism brightness. The overhead electric wires looked so sharply defined that he felt if he really concentrated, he would be able to see the current flowing through them. He saw the traffic on the street and felt that he could count the cars, the trucks, the buses, figure the ratio among them, and work out the speed at which they were moving, just by watching how quickly they passed between two telephone poles. The street scene seemed to glide by in slow motion compared to the speed at which his mind was racing.

He looked again at the dashboard. Next to the Post-it note about Alec was another one. *Doctor – blue Tacoma.* With a license number written below it. He didn't know what that was about, so he continued looking for Alec, who must be around here someplace – because he had no reason to come to the Mission District, except to find his brother.

He braked. There, parked at the curb, was the Benz. Nobody was inside. He swept the street – no sign of Alec.

The car behind him honked. Kanan accelerated and drove to the corner. He would search for Alec in a radial pattern with the Benz as a center point. He slowed and turned left onto the cross street.

Jo stared at Alec Shepard. At once, the pain and confusion in Shepard's eyes looked comprehensible.

'Your brother,' she said.

'Yes. And I refuse to submit him to arrest.' He took her elbow. 'Let's get out of here.'

She pulled loose and retreated behind the hanging garden of dry-cleaned clothing. 'Okay, big bro – what's he more likely to do? Drive in a straight line away from where he lost sight of us, or circle the block?'

'You said he'll forget he saw us here.'

213

'He will. He can't form new permanent memories. But he can certainly rely on training, instinct, and the problem-solving skills he's honed over the course of his lifetime. He's gotten this far so he must have figured out a system of some kind. So tell me – what's he like, Mr Shepard?'

She hit the last name sharply.

'I'll explain everything.' Again he took her elbow.

Jo didn't want him controlling her. She pulled free from his grip. 'Why didn't you disclose your relationship right away? Because unless you cough up a big dose of honesty, immediately, I'm not following you past the door of this store.'

'I didn't know if I could trust you. And the fact that you didn't already know we were brothers disinclined me to confide in you.'

And, *damn*, Jo thought – why hadn't Misty Kanan told her? Why had she held that back?

'What's the deal? Half brother? Stepbrother? Foster child?' she said.

'We're full brothers. Our father died when Ian was a baby. Our mother remarried when he was six and I was a senior in high school. Her husband adopted Ian and gave him his name.'

She peered around the forest of plastic-shrouded clothes at the front window. The street was quiet. 'Best guess. Gut instinct. Brotherly mojo. Which way are we least likely to run into him?'

'He's unpredictable. That's his genius and his problem.'

A hard nasal voice cut through the shop. 'What the hell are you doing back here?'

In the hallway stood the owner of the dry cleaner's. He was small, puffy, and wrinkled, like a beige comforter that had been squashed by the spin cycle of a washing machine.

'We're being chased by a car. We ducked in here until the police arrive,' Jo said.

'Bullshit. Get out.'

Shepard put up a hand. 'If you'll let me explain –'

The man reached behind him and pulled out a baseball bat.

Jo spread her hands placatingly and backed toward the counter. 'Two minutes.'

'Get out of my shop.' He raised the bat like Mickey Mantle stepping to the plate. 'And keep your hands where I can see them.'

Jo ducked around the counter and cast a glance out the front window. Cruising up the street toward them was the red Navigator.

'Alec,' she said.

The owner lunged toward Shepard and pulled back the bat, winding up to take a swing. '*Out*, I said.'

Shepard backed away from him. 'I'll give you fifty dollars to let us stay.'

He chased Shepard around the counter. 'Out, goddamn it.'

Shepard reached for his wallet. 'A hundred dollars.'

The red Navigator was approaching. Shepard thundered toward Jo. Close on his heels, the wrinkled little owner swung the bat. It swished the air. *Crap*. He swung again. Strike two missed Shepard's head by inches.

The owner wound up again, his eye on Jo's face like she had *Rawlings* printed on her forehead. She opened the door.

The store's bell rang. Without looking up from his copy of *Guitar Player*, the cashier said, 'Have a good one.'

Jo stumbled onto the sidewalk with Shepard hard behind her just as the Navigator drove past. She turned her face away from the street but heard tires scorch the asphalt.

'Run,' she said.

They took off. Jo looked for cover, but the building next to the dry cleaner had barred windows and a locked door. Beyond that, the apartment building on the corner was sequestered behind a security gate. A strangling sensation crept into her throat. She rounded the corner onto Valencia. Glanced back. Shepard was lumbering in her wake, tie and suit jacket flapping. Behind him, Kanan was skidding the Navigator through a hard U-turn in the middle of the block. The front wheels were locked, the back end swinging around, gray smoke boiling off the tires. He pulled a one-eighty, straightened it, and gunned it up the block toward them.

'Faster. Sixteenth Street,' she said. 'Your car.'

Sweat was rolling down Shepard's face into his salt-and-copper beard. 'That puts us back at square one.'

But surrounded by a solid German frame and four hundred horse-power. She pounded along the sidewalk. This street offered no cover, just locked apartment buildings and glass-fronted businesses and budding trees along the curb. Ahead at the intersection with Sixteenth, the light was green. Horns honked behind them.

Jo looked back. The Navigator was stuck at the corner, blocked by cross traffic.

She pumped her arms. Ahead at the intersection, the light turned yellow. Pedestrians in the crosswalk jogged for the curbs.

'Go for it,' she said.

They ran into the crosswalk as the light turned red. Another horn honked, loud, in her ear, and Shepard danced out of the path of a rusty Honda Civic.

Jo belted across the street to the sidewalk. Up the block the Navigator was weaving through traffic, heading for the red light. She and Shepard had about thirty seconds to get out of his sight.

'Where's your car?' she said.

Shepard shook his head. 'No. Split up.'

'Alec —'

'He'll follow me.'

He cast a look at her, hot and determined and somehow ruthless. Then he ran out into the middle of Valencia Street. He stopped in the crosswalk and turned to face the Navigator.

He spread his arms. She couldn't tell whether the gesture meant surrender, *Come and get me*, or *Just try it, man*. The Navigator's engine revved. Shepard turned and fled toward the far side of the street.

Jo stood rooted to the sidewalk. The Navigator approached the red light. With barely a pause, Kanan put the pedal down and accelerated toward the intersection, toward cross traffic, straight at her.

19

The Navigator's engine swelled in Jo's ears. Its red paint flashed in the bright sunlight as the SUV veered toward her. Cars in the intersection and people on the sidewalk swerved like crazed fish scattering at the approach of a shark. She turned and ran.

She crashed into a cluster of trash cans by the curb. She went down amid a clatter like steel drums falling over, hands out, and pitched to the sidewalk.

'Look out,' a woman shouted.

Over the shining barrel of the trash can, Jo saw the Navigator bearing down on her.

Get your butt up off this sidewalk, Beckett. She scrambled to her feet and aimed for the door of a Chinese restaurant. All around her on the sidewalk, she saw fleeing backs. She heard distant sirens. Through the window of the restaurant, people stared at her with alarm, eyes wide, chopsticks frozen halfway to their mouths.

A cry escaped her throat. If she ran into the restaurant, the Navigator would ram the window.

She jinked left and pitched along the sidewalk at a flat, crazed sprint. Her hands were clenched, her hair falling from the claw clip into her face. Behind her the engine revved. The street streamed by, trees and cars and shops painted with throbbing murals in rain forest colors.

She needed a cement wall to dive over. A bank with an open vault. A crack. A dime edge, a fire escape, a drainpipe to climb. Her feet pounded the sidewalk.

Ahead she saw a parking garage. She pinned her gaze to it. Reinforced concrete, tight turns, and a hundred metal chassis she could put between her and the Navigator – she aimed for the entrance.

In her peripheral vision she saw a black vehicle on the street ahead. It was barreling in her direction. She heard the Navigator, seemingly right between her shoulders. She swerved into the entrance of the parking garage, toward the ticket machine.

On the street, tires squealed. She heard the Navigator's brakes engage, hard. She glanced back.

Gabe's black 4Runner had skidded to a stop, half askew, blocking the entrance to the garage. The Navigator was stopped in the street beyond it. Kanan honked, a solid insistent blast. The 4Runner didn't move. The sirens grew louder.

Kanan spun the wheel. With sunlight flashing off his tinted windows, he roared away.

Jo stood for a second. She couldn't seem to move,

could barely inhale. The world was throbbing in sync with her heartbeat.

Gabe climbed out of the 4Runner and strode toward her. She ran and threw herself against him. Without breaking stride he swept an arm around her shoulder and shepherded her toward the 4Runner.

'You okay?' he said.

She nodded tightly.

Eyes sweeping the street, he led her to the passenger side and opened the door. She jumped in. He jogged around, hopped behind the wheel, and pulled sharply back into traffic.

'How did . . . ?' She grabbed his shoulder. 'Thank you.' Her hand was shaking. 'How did you find me?'

'The phone. You never hung up. I heard you tell Shepard to head for Sixteenth Street.' He checked the mirrors and panned the street. His face was grim. 'You hurt?'

She fumbled her seat belt into the buckle and scraped her hair back from her forehead. 'Fine, Sergeant.'

He looked at her palms. They were scraped and black with grit from her fall over the trash cans. As she stared at them, the shaking in her hand spread up her arms and across her shoulders. Then her whole body began chattering.

'Shit, that was scary.'

He took her hand and held on tight. Anxiety fizzed behind her eyes, bright and bubbly. No – it was tears. She blinked and they fell to her cheeks. She wiped them roughly away.

She couldn't believe she had admitted her fear to him. She could only recall confessing fear to her parents when she was five, and once to Daniel when they were four hundred feet above the valley floor in Yosemite, and to her sister Tina one desperate empty night after Daniel died. But it had just poured out of her mouth to Gabe. Yet she didn't feel embarrassed or weak for having done it. Maybe she was in shock.

She looked around the street. 'Did you see which way Kanan went?'

'South, out of sight. And no way are we going hunting for him.' He gripped the steering wheel. 'My number one priority is to protect you. My other number one priority is to protect Sophie – she needs a father, not a hero.'

He slowed for the light at Sixteenth and signaled left.

'I'm unarmed and in no position to take the fight to Kanan. We talk to the police and get you home safe,' he said.

The sun was tipping toward the west. Lengthening shadows etched the road. She heard anger in his voice. He didn't want her to think he was running from a confrontation.

As if. She touched his face. The light changed and he turned onto Sixteenth. Ahead, outside Ti Couz, an SFPD black-and-white was stopped, lights flashing. Gabe drove toward it.

Hearing a glass note in her own voice, she said, 'What did you find out about Kanan?'

Another sidelong glance. Gabe didn't speak, just put a hand on her arm, half to reassure her, half to see if she was clammy and about to hyperventilate. P.J.s. What could you do?

'He wasn't a security contractor?' she said.

'It's worse.'

20

Seth Kanan was scared. He was tired and felt alone, because nobody would tell him anything. But mostly he was scared.

Everybody wanted to keep him in the dark, it seemed – in such absolute night that he couldn't tell whether his eyes worked anymore. He couldn't sleep. He couldn't talk to his parents. Even though he was all by himself, he felt absolutely controlled. He couldn't do anything except worry.

He kept waiting for his dad to walk through the front door, but he hadn't. It had been another night without him. And the men were out there.

Seth pressed the Scotch tape around the bridge of his glasses to hold them together. He'd seen the men today. He tried to keep them distant in his mind, to put them in a corner of his memory like cockroaches, but they just swelled back up and took over his thoughts. Sneering, making wet sounds, jeering, threatening him. He had a feeling that something had happened today. Vance, the rapper wannabe, had followed him around. Vance had been edgy, like he had bees swarming around him.

'You're safe,' Vance had said. 'You want to stay that way, you play nice. You say *please* and *thank you, sir*.'

Safe. What did that mean? Safe as in protected? Safe as in everything else was dangerous? Seth had the feeling that bad things had happened in Vance's world today. And the way the guy looked at him, it was like Vance thought his dad was the one behind it all, putting Seth in danger. That made no sense. That made his stomach burn.

And Murdock had stood behind Vance, staring over his shoulder at Seth like burning holes with his eyes would make Ian Kanan appear on the spot.

'Play nice,' Vance had said. 'Keep quiet so Mommy doesn't hear any complaints from you. Otherwise her and your dog could find theirselves getting the torture treatment at baby Gitmo.' Then he made pathetic barking, whimpering sounds.

Seth had turned his back on him.

Yeah, something had gone wrong for Vance and Murdock. They were all of a sudden in a big hurry. And he was a pawn they would be only too happy to sacrifice to get whatever it was they wanted.

He needed a weapon.

Something sly, something unexpected. He turned to the bed. He scooted the mattress back from the edge of the frame. He began working on the spring, bending it back and forth, back and forth.

He didn't know how long it would take. But he did know that not all metal was the same. He knew that from shop class and chem class. And from his dad and Uncle Alec telling him about sword-making, metallurgy, scimitars and daggers. And about Damascus steel.

He kept working, back and forth. This spring wasn't Damascus steel. But it was galvanized, and when it broke, it would be brittle and sharp.

Jo locked her front door behind her and followed Gabe down the hallway to the living room. He walked like Mr Kicked Back, a guy without a worry in the world. But his gaze swept the living room, the hall, the stairs, the kitchen, and the view of the back yard. She turned on a table lamp, crossed to the bay window, and closed the shutters.

They had talked to the police at the scene outside Ti Couz. But Kanan had disappeared, and so had Alec Shepard. His Mercedes remained outside the restaurant and he wasn't returning her messages.

And Gabe had held his counsel while he drove her home. She turned and faced him.

'Tell me, or forget about it and kiss me, but open your mouth, Quintana.'

His gaze finished its slow sweep of the house. He looked at her, fierce and quiet, as cool and centered as a stone in the middle of a flowing stream.

'Ian Kanan served ten years on active duty in the army. I don't have official confirmation, but my air force contact told me some things that jibe with my own impression. Kanan was Special Forces.'

'"Impression"? Does that mean rumor or hard facts?' she said.

'Off-the-record verification. Plus your description of Kanan. Lean and whippy, that's how the Special Forces like 'em.'

If Kanan had been in special ops, his service record would be buried in a hole. 'Honorable discharge?'

'Far as I know. Contact military records – maybe Amy Tang can shove through the request. You might get some information in a couple of weeks.'

She put her hands in the back pockets of her jeans. 'And after he left the army?'

'He went to work for a private security contractor.'

'Blackwater?'

'Another outfit, similar deal. Cobra.'

'Because *Daisy Hill Security* wouldn't instill esprit de corps.'

'Or fear,' Gabe said. 'Kanan spent four years with them. Baghdad, Ramadi, and two tours in Afghanistan.'

'So he's a soldier of fortune.'

'Contractors earn their keep, and the military loves them for it. They handle security and logistics, they take the heat, and they take the pressure off the army.'

'They're mercenaries who double as chauffeurs and event planners.'

'And bodyguards, marshals, private Secret Service. They even handle security at the Iraqi parliament.'

'So they're the bigwigs behind the scenes,' she said.

'And until recently, they've had immunity from prosecution. There's been absolutely no way to hold them accountable for things they do wrong.'

'What did Kanan do for Cobra?' Jo said.

'Kept visitors to Kabul alive. From the moment they touched down at the airport to the moment they were wheels-up again, he was in charge of security. At their hotels, on the road, in meetings with government and NGOs – he isn't anything close to just a corporate babysitter.'

'Why is it worse than you thought?'

'Guy I know who was active, served in the Afghan theater, remembers a run-in with Cobra in Kabul.'

'Between U.S. air force personnel and private security?'

'Over nothing. A traffic jam. Everybody honking at some chaotic downtown intersection. The Cobra people pulled their weapons on the airmen.'

'Kanan did? Your guy saw him?' she said.

'No, but the Cobra people were Kanan's men. Either he was there or they were following his rules of engagement.'

'So Kanan possibly has a temper and poor impulse control.'

'Jo, he's a mercenary. He's a full-on pro. He's armed at the very least with a knife. If he doesn't have guns at home, he knows plenty of people in the Bay Area who can supply him.'

'If he can remember to contact them.'

'If he assembles a posse, he won't need to. They'll remember for him.'

*　　*　　*

The traffic light in front of Kanan turned green. His right turn signal was blinking. The street sign swinging from the traffic standard said DOLORES. He put his foot on the gas and turned right. He was in the Mission District in San Francisco. The radio was playing. The sun was fading toward the west. A car coming the other way flashed its lights at him. He turned on his headlights.

What was he doing here?

The street was busy. On the radio a chirpy deejay said, 'Welcome to Friday drive time.'

Kanan reached to turn up the radio, and as he stretched, he saw letters written on his arm. His throat caught.

He blinked and tried to breathe normally. *Holy mother of God*. Was he really doing this?

Yes. He was alone, and this was Alec's Navigator. It was Friday, and evening was coming on.

He pulled over. Post-it notes were stuck to the dashboard. *Check phone pics*. He took out his cell and scrolled through the photos he figured he must have taken. They looked like this neighborhood, but earlier – with the sun high in the sky. A restaurant, Ti Couz.

He looked out the window. The restaurant was right across the street. As he peered through its windows, a waiter in a white apron opened the door, stepped outside, and stood staring at him.

His skin cooled. He could think of no reason for the waiter to do that, unless he'd been driving around the block, or stopping in front of the restaurant, for a while. Maybe all afternoon. Either that, or people were looking for him.

He was running out of time. Panic rilled through him, a feeling that everything was fading, sliding out of his control. On his right arm he saw the words *Memory loss*.

He needed help.

He thought about it for a moment and punched a search query into the GPS unit. The answer popped up within seconds. Thank God.

He got a Post-it, wrote *Diaz*, and stuck it to the dashboard.

Nico Diaz had been in his unit. He was the man who'd introduced him to the people who ran Cobra.

Diaz ran a sporting goods store. Friends of Diaz knew that his inventory extended beyond the basketballs and fishing rods on the shelves. He had been a scout sniper in the army. Diaz was a useful friend to have.

The GPS unit pinged. An arrow pointed straight ahead. An address in Potrero Hill popped up. Diaz's store.

Kanan drove toward it. Get Diaz on board – Diaz would be able to hold everything in his head at once. Diaz wouldn't forget what was going on.

Diaz would ride shotgun when he went after Alec.

21

Jo stood for a second, facing Gabe, tension winding her up like an alarm clock. 'I need to call Amy Tang. She can start digging up the names of Kanan's contacts in the Bay Area.'

'You okay?' he said.

'Hundred percent.'

'That means no.'

They were four feet apart. She thought if she moved, she might spring like a jack-in-the-box and hit the ceiling.

'This case is driving me nuts. I can't put it together. Kanan. The brain injury. What poisoned him? Was it a nanoparticle? Did he steal it from Chira-Sayf? Did it also contaminate Ron Gingrich? And what's going on with his family, and that freaking company?'

Gabe shook his head. 'Let it go. Let your mind work on it at another level. The answers will come to you.'

'I can't. Kanan's got a hit list and a deadline written

on his arm. And I'm missing a huge part of the puzzle. Something is tearing Kanan up.'

'Yeah. Greed. And a lust for revenge.'

'No. Something deeper.' She ran her hands through her hair.

She got her phone, called Tang, left a message. Pacing in a circle, she called Alec Shepard and got voice mail.

'He's not answering.' She found the television remote control. 'Maybe there's something on the news.'

She turned on the T.V. A cartoon bloomed on the screen, yellow sea creatures with eyes bugging on stalks. She switched channels. Gabe came up behind her. He put his arms around her waist, pulled her back against him, and bent his head to her ear.

'Let it go,' he said.

She leaned her head back against his cheek. He took the remote from her and set it on the coffee table. She held on a second longer, and then, centimeter by centimeter, eased her shoulders down. Eased herself against him, tried to soften.

'I'm not usually like this,' she said.

'Define *usually*,' he said. 'And *this*.'

'Are you saying I'm mercurial?'

'I mean I'm still figuring you out.'

'Ditto, dude.'

'Me?' There was real surprise in his voice. 'I'm a simple guy who likes kids and jumping out of airplanes. And a certain forensic psychiatrist.'

'Don't give me simple. Two dozen jump missions for the air national guard? "Moral Theology, a Contemporary

231

Catholic Approach"? And God knows what those Jesuits at USF have put in your head about women.'

'You want to disabuse me of my misconceptions?'

Despite herself, she felt a smile forming. 'It might be necessary.'

Her shoulders dropped another inch. Outside, the sun was gold and sharp, etching cool shadows across her garden beneath the blue sky.

She turned around and laced her fingers with his. 'What you did this afternoon was incredible.'

The light in the living room was low. His eyes were dark. And hot, like a slow-burning fire. She didn't know how to read his look.

He turned her hand and examined the abrasion on her palm. 'Let's get that cleaned up. Where do you keep your first aid kit?'

A red line of heat rolled down her chest. 'Upstairs.'

Holding loosely to his hand, she led him up the stairs.

They had been taking things slow. She believed he was giving her time to adjust to the idea of a new relationship, her first since she'd buried Daniel. But Gabe was a P.J. He might look like a cool drink of water, but pararescuemen – like rock climbers – were adrenaline junkies. They hated running in first gear. If he was throttling down, it was because he was keeping his natural instincts in check for her sake.

But she didn't know for certain. He was enigmatic. She wondered what really went on in his heart. And she couldn't shake the feeling that something was eating at

232

him. She wondered what he was holding back, and why.

His hand was cool against her palm. At the top of the stairs she turned into her bedroom, led him to the bathroom, and got the first aid kit from the cabinet.

'I could do this myself, you know,' she said.

He took the kit from her. 'But you know what they say.'

'Yes. Hello, doctor. Meet your patient, the fool.'

They stood side by side at the sink. He cleaned the abrasions and carefully bandaged her hand. His work was thorough and economical.

He set down the medical tape. 'That'll hold for a few days.'

She wrapped her arms around his shoulders. 'Thank you.'

His hands slid around her waist. He leaned down and kissed her.

And kissed her again. He drew her close and held her, with an assurance and ease that seemed more than hope, that seemed like being home. She held there a second, eyes on his. Taking his hand, she led him to the bedroom.

Outside, sunlight skidded across rooftops. She put a hand to his chest. His heartbeat came back at her, strong and regular and fast.

This was new, and not. Her first time, and not. Familiar, and strange. A man she wanted, but not the man she had moved into this house with, into this bedroom with.

Just breathe.

She slipped her fingers under his unbuttoned work

shirt and began easing it off his shoulders, slowly. He let go of her and did it faster. Then he pulled her sweater over her head. She walked into his arms and ran her fingers into his hair, kissed him, hard, wrapped her arms around his neck, felt his hands untucking her T-shirt from her jeans.

Lips still close to his, breathless, she said, 'Shoes. Hold on.'

She tried to get the left one off by stepping on the heel with her right foot but lost her balance. Gabe pulled the T-shirt up to her shoulders. She turned in a circle and bent and fumbled with her shoelace. Her arm was stuck in her sleeve. Gabe hoisted her off her feet and swung her toward the bed. She wrapped her legs around his waist and they toppled as one onto the thick red comforter.

He rolled on top of her and kissed her mouth, her cheek, her neck, the hollow at the base of her throat where her pulse throbbed. She grabbed for his T-shirt but he was pressed against her. She felt the planes of his back and shoulders, lean and strong and smooth. His hands were warm. Her skin felt hotter.

She felt like a gong that had been rung. She held on to him, holding back some part of herself. She was afraid if she let everything go, she would uncoil like a whip and begin to scream, or sing, or bite.

This was what happened when it had been too long. Tears stung her eyes. She squeezed her eyes shut so he couldn't see. She didn't want to think, or remember, or see. She wanted to feel.

She told herself: *Shut up, brain.*

She worked her hands to his waist and fought with the top button on his jeans. He got to his knees and pulled his T-shirt over his head. He wrestled her T-shirt up off her and pounced on her again. Skin against skin, they grappled on the bed. Every inch of her felt electric, so charged that she thought she might short-circuit.

He was ripped, he was intense, very intense, *really* focused. The only sounds in the room were their breathing and her own heart, thundering in her ears.

They fumbled for buttons. On his jeans, her jeans. Their fingers were fast and awkward and if this had been a rock ledge high above a valley floor, or a triage case where dexterity was necessary, they'd have been in big trouble.

Big trouble . . . 'Gabe, do you have . . .'

He pulled his wallet from his back pocket. He dug through it and a twenty and a supermarket receipt fell out, and then he pulled out a foil packet. Jo was yanking her socks off as though they were on fire. She looked up, waiting for him to tear the foil. And she saw his scars.

They rode the curve of his right hip, white and smooth. Old scars, half a dozen at least. They were the marks of violence. Something sharp, or explosive, had ripped through him.

She reached to touch them and stopped. Gabe tore open the condom foil with his teeth. She looked up at him. Eagerly, he looked back.

He wasn't smiling, but he was happy, in a crazed way,

and then in a fraction of a second he readjusted. He saw something on her face. Her surprise. Her brakes-on, *What-the-hell-is-that?* look.

Her fingers hovered near his hip. Her eyes asked the question.

'Old news,' he said.

'Gabe?'

'I mended.'

These scars hadn't come from tripping over a trash can. They weren't surgical or superficial. They had gone messy and deep. They had gone with a trainload of pain.

'What happened?' she said.

Every now and then, Jo would experience a moment when she managed to stand outside herself and see a situation from an unobstructed vantage point.

This was one of those moments. She saw herself, shocked and concerned and inherently nosy. She saw Gabe, hot and damned annoyed. The look in his eyes said, *Not now, for God's sake.*

She blinked. 'Sorry.'

She grabbed him by the waistband of his jeans and hauled him back down on top of her. He looked at her, half . . . what? Angry? For being interrupted? For being distracted? For being *reminded*?

Pain had risen in his eyes, a heat like a burning cigarette, red and concentrated. He wasn't kissing her. He was lying on top of her, breathing hard.

Waiting, perhaps, to see if she would keep picking at the wound. She shook her head. She put her fingers to her own lips, indicating that she was going to keep her

236

mouth shut. Then she touched his lips in return, smoothed her thumb across his mouth, and said, 'Come here.'

He held back for half a beat.

It was long enough for the phone to ring.

Jo didn't break from his gaze, didn't look at the phone, didn't reach to answer it. It rang.

'They'll call back,' she said.

As though a warm breeze had crossed the room, his gaze cleared. He lowered himself against her again and kissed her. The phone kept ringing. She took the condom package from him and ripped the foil wide open.

The phone clicked to voice mail. Clear and loud from downstairs in the hallway, Amy Tang's voice cut through the sound of their breathing.

'Beckett, you're there. I know you are, so pick up.'

Jo ignored her.

'You called me fifteen minutes ago. I'm calling back at your request.' Loudly: '*Beckett.*'

Gabe glanced out the bedroom door, as though Tang was in the house, about to come upon them in flagrante delicto. Jo turned his head back.

'She'll still be stewing in –'

'Three minutes?' he said.

She broke into a ridiculous smile. 'Race you to the finish?'

Finally he smiled back. 'Go.'

They grabbed at the remaining articles of each other's clothing, trying to pull them off.

'Beckett,' Tang said. 'Pick up. A flight made an

237

emergency landing at SFO today. One of the flight attendants opened a door at ten thousand feet.'

Jo and Gabe stopped simultaneously, hands on hooks and buttons. They looked in the direction of the answering machine.

'It was the young woman you spoke to when you boarded Ian Kanan's flight – Stef Nivesen. She was sucked straight out the door,' Tang said. 'Beckett, people who were on Kanan's flight are going crazy.'

Jo was already running to pick up the call.

The sporting goods store had a CLOSED sign on the door. From the Navigator Kanan could see Nico Diaz inside, shutting down for the night. Kanan drove up the street, found a parking spot in the next block, and walked back.

When he knocked on the door, Diaz looked up agreeably. He saw Kanan and stilled.

Nikita Diaz was a second-generation Venezuelan immigrant with a love for baseball, women, and the USA. He stood five foot seven and wore dreadlocks in a ponytail long enough to serve as a kite tail. Tie a string around him, Kanan thought, wait for a stiff wind, and watch him set sail for the sky. And every inch of the man was sinew and muscle. He was fast-twitch, dead quiet, perfect aim. His eyes locked on Kanan for two full seconds. He shut the cash register, pocketed the key, and strolled to the door.

When he opened it, his face was impassive but his gaze was bright. His gaze, Kanan thought, was eager.

'Sarge,' he said. 'What brings you here?'

238

'I need your help,' Kanan said.

The eagerness distilled. Diaz pulled the door open. 'Let's talk in the back.'

'Two fatalities,' Tang said. 'It could have been much worse. There were two hundred forty-seven people aboard.'

Jo stood in the front hall, phone to her ear, trying to zip her jeans with one hand. She had one arm in the sleeve of a blouse. A bra strap was hanging off her shoulder. Gabe jogged barefoot down the stairs. His belt clinked as he buckled it. Beyond him in the living room, the television was still on. The screen flashed bright. BREAKING NEWS.

On-screen Jo saw a 747 sitting on the runway at San Francisco airport, surrounded by fire trucks. The front and back cabin doors were open. So was a door along the middle of the fuselage. Emergency slides were deployed like huge yellow tongues. Gabe got the remote and turned up the sound.

Jo pulled up her bra strap. 'No chance it was an accident?'

'No. Another flight attendant watched Nivesen stand and open one of the main doors, almost two miles up. Then, *whoosh* – straight out into the sky without a parachute.'

The thought made Jo queasy. She tucked her hair behind her ear. 'Have the police talked to the passengers and crew?'

'SFPD Airport Division is interviewing people. NTSB has a go team on the way.'

'Did Nivesen say anything before she opened the door?'

'Haven't heard.'

'What do you know about her? Drug or alcohol problems? History of psychiatric disorder?'

'You're doing a psychological autopsy on her in your own head. We don't know squat – except she did it deliberately.'

A thin drip of worry, like a chilled trickle of water, scored its way down Jo's back. 'After the pool electrocution, now –'

'First, French fried game designers. Now stewardesses turning themselves into sky-high confetti.'

'You need to contact everybody who was aboard Kanan's flight from London.'

'Working on it. See you in ten.'

Hanging up, Jo stood quietly in the hallway, her bare feet cold on the hardwood floor.

'You going to the airport?' Gabe said.

'Tang's swinging by to get me.' She put a hand on his chest. 'Rain check?'

'I'm picking you up for dinner at eight. And tonight's weather forecast is for clear skies.' Though his tone was light, his gaze turned solemn. 'You copacetic about going to SFO to deal with an air accident scenario?'

'Rock solid.'

'That's the attitude.'

His concern touched her. His belief in her strength touched her more. But what remained unspoken, uncertain, and buried worried her most of all.

22

In the fading March light, Jo and Tang slipped quietly into the back of the room in a remote operations area at the San Francisco airport. Airline officials and police officers stood toward the back. The NTSB go team, three investigators in polo shirts and khakis, sat at a table talking to flight attendant Charlotte Thorne.

Thorne's hair had been whipped into a mess. Her uniform jacket was torn, and she had a bruise across one cheek.

She looked haunted. 'Stef seemed disorientated. Yes.'

'How so? Can you describe it?' asked one of the NTSB investigators.

'Twice she stood up to begin the beverage service. Once while we were still taxiing into takeoff position, the second time when we'd only been airborne for ten seconds. Both times she seemed baffled when I asked her to sit down.'

Jo looked across the tarmac toward the bay. The 747 had been towed to a hangar on the far side of the runway and sat empty in the sunset. The jet, so sleek and powerful, looked strangely chilling.

Tang leaned toward her and whispered, 'It's not going to come after you.'

Jo gave her a look.

Tang thought she was phobic about flying. She wasn't. She simply hated it. She wouldn't even keep a copy of *Top Gun* in the house.

Copacetic, Beckett. Gabe understood the source of her hatred. He had been the P.J. on the scene the day of the air accident that killed Daniel.

Thorne dabbed at her eyes with a tissue. 'Then Stef said she was hot and needed air. She tore off her restraints and rushed to the far side of the airplane. It was like she couldn't breathe. Like she felt trapped.' Thorne had a hitch in her voice. 'When the door opened she was gone just like that. The passenger from twelve-B, Mr Pankhurst, he went straight after her.'

Jo and Tang listened to the NTSB investigators question Thorne for several minutes. Jo knew they might continue for hours. She raised her hand, identified herself, and said, 'Two questions.'

'Dr Beckett, yes, I remember you,' Thorne said.

'You said Ms Nivesen seemed disoriented. Do you mean she seemed confused – as in, she couldn't string her thoughts together? Or did she seem coherent, but forgetful?'

Thorne exhaled. 'Forgetful. She couldn't seem to remember where we were. Even before the flight, she was late – I rang her repeatedly, and each time she sounded surprised to hear from me. Insisted I hadn't spoken to her.'

'Second question.' Jo glanced out the window at the 747. 'On the flight from London yesterday, did Ms Nivesen have physical contact with Ian Kanan?'

The cops, the airline people, and the NTSB investigators turned toward her.

Thorne's voice was rocky. 'Yes. Stef helped hold him down, and afterward she had scratches and blood on her hands.'

'Thank you,' Jo said.

She led Tang out of the room and strode along the hall. 'Contact public health. Everybody who had physical contact with Kanan aboard the flight yesterday needs to be examined ASAP.'

'You had contact with him.'

'No broken skin, no contact with bodily fluids.'

She glanced at Tang and saw concern in her eyes. She inhaled and felt it turn into a gulp.

'I know. We have fuck-all information about what's contaminating people and how it's transmitted,' she said.

'We'll pull Alec Shepard and the entire workforce at Chira-Sayf in for questioning. Raid the business if we have to.'

Passing a window, Jo glanced again at the 747, gleaming red with the light of sunset. 'Do that. But I think the horse has already bolted from the barn. Something has escaped from Chira-Sayf's lab, and it's on the verge of getting out of control.'

*   *   *

243

Nico Diaz leaned against a shelf in the back room at the sporting goods store, arms crossed, his expression poised between anger and disbelief.

'You're moving fine, talking sense. You sure about this memory thing?' Diaz said.

'Ask me in five minutes if I remember this conversation.'

'How long till it improves?'

'I'm not counting on it.'

The orange light of sunset filtered through the frosted glass window at the back of the stockroom. Diaz stewed. Kanan had seen that look on the man's face before, when a mission had taken a random turn into ambush or death.

Diaz was a man of few words and long silences. He was also a man of minimal bravado. He didn't swagger or clothe himself with machismo. He didn't care about visible projections of power. He moved without wasted motion, without wasted emotion, with no display. He looked like a mellow dude with dreads, and people sometimes mistook him for sleepy, or even lazy. But Kanan knew that inside, Diaz wasn't so cool, that under the correct circumstances a seam of temper could ignite. People who underestimated Nico Diaz often made a fatal mistake.

Kanan set his phone and wallet and a cluster of Post-it notes on the desk. Diaz sauntered over.

'What's all this?'

'My memories. My collection,' Kanan said. 'Go through them. Put them in chronological order. Help me organize a plan.'

Diaz leafed through them. Kanan took off his jean jacket and flannel shirt and pulled his T-shirt over his head.

Diaz looked up. He stared. 'Boss. Man.'

Kanan's arms and chest were covered with writing. He raised his left arm and made a fist. The words inked on his skin stood out. Diaz's expression hardened.

His gaze scrolled up Kanan's body. *Find Alec. Get Slick.*

I cannot make new memories. Write it down.

'Brief me,' Diaz said.

'I went to Africa to get the product. It went wrong. Guy from the company tried to steal it behind our back. But now I'm home, and I don't have it. And the only way to get it now is from my brother.'

'Boss, this thing . . . Misty, have you –'

'No. Pray she'll understand why I'm doing this.'

Diaz nodded.

'Alec has access to the last existing sample of Slick. He'll never give it to me. And if he finds out I'm after it, he'll destroy it. We have to get to him before he does.'

'Time frame?'

Kanan held up his left arm and made a fist. *Saturday they die.*

'Right.' Diaz sorted through the Post-its. 'While I organize this stuff, you think you should go back to the hospital?'

Kanan didn't remember going to any hospital. 'No time.'

'Okay. Anybody you've told about this?'

245

'Don't know.'

Diaz held up the phone. 'Names in here? Intel? Targets? Opposition?'

'You have to tell me.'

'Has it been turned on the whole time?'

'I don't know. Diaz, I can't remember where I've been since I landed at SFO. Double-check that I set the phone on airplane mode, so it won't transmit or receive.' He ran his hands over his face. He felt damned tired. 'If I followed my own procedures, I programmed the phone to activate at a particular hour but not before. It's the system I set up for Chira-Sayf. That way when execs go overseas nobody can hack their calls or track their location.'

Diaz fiddled with the phone. 'It's scheduled to activate at ten P.M. tonight. You expecting them to call?'

'I guess I must be.'

'Who's looking for you?'

'Presume everybody. Police, the targets. Chira-Sayf.'

Diaz held up a laminated hospital photo I.D. 'Johanna Beckett?'

Kanan gazed at it with curiosity. For an instant he seemed to smell a woman's perfume, like incense. Seemed to feel his hand around the hilt of a knife.

What the hell was wrong with him?

Diaz scrolled through the cell phone photos. He showed one to Kanan. Shot through the window of a restaurant, it showed the woman in the hospital I.D. photo, sitting at a table with his brother. It was labeled 'Doc and Alec.'

'She's involved,' Kanan said.

'How?'

'I don't know.' The admission felt like being splashed with paint stripper. 'She could be chasing me. I could be chasing her. I don't know whose side she's on.'

'But you think she can point you to Alec?'

'I must.'

'And you can't find Alec at any of his usual haunts?'

'No.'

Diaz paused. 'This isn't payback. You know that, right?'

Kanan didn't answer that question. 'What gear do you have here that we can use?'

'What are you looking for?'

Kanan reached behind his back and removed the HK pistol from the waistband of his jeans.

'What kind of ammo, and how many magazines do you want?' Diaz said.

'How many you got?'

The SFPD patrol car rolled past the elementary school and the little city park. The street was busy with Friday rush-hour traffic. The sun was heading down, headlights coming on. Officer Frank Liu drove halfway past the red Navigator before he noticed it parked at the curb.

At the corner he U-turned and cruised back. He pulled over behind the vehicle.

He checked the BOLO. Be on the lookout for a red, late-model Navigator, stolen that morning. He checked the license plate. Called it in.

*　　*　　*

Tang stopped the unmarked car on the street outside Jo's house. In the vanishing light, the forested hills of the Presidio had darkened to black.

Jo opened the door of the car and got out. Tang leaned across.

'Beckett, this is unspooling fast. And two hundred eighty-three people were on Kanan's flight yesterday.'

Jo held on to the door. 'I know. We can't determine how quickly the next strike is coming, but we have to presume it's already inbound.'

'Find him. Dig into Kanan's worm-eaten psyche and figure out where he is, before more people get dead.' She gave Jo an unblinking look. 'Get yourself checked out, too.'

Jo nodded, feeling the gulp rise in her throat again, and began to shut the door. Tang lowered her voice.

'And your blouse is buttoned incorrectly.'

Jo looked down. She turned hot. She shut the car door and jogged up her front steps fumbling with her buttons.

When she opened the door, Tina leaned out the kitchen doorway.

'Hey, sis. Get changed or we'll be late.'

Tina had a sunny smile on her face and a leftover doughnut in her hand. She was wearing black workout pants and a red tank top. She stuffed the doughnut in her mouth and licked sugar from her thumb.

Jo kissed her on the cheek. 'I know, girls' night out. I can't.'

Tina's shoulders dropped. 'Don't do this.'

'It's an emergency. I'm sorry.' Jo handed Tina her phone

and swept past her to the kitchen. 'And please get rid of the "Sick Sad Little World" ringtone.'

'Fine, I'll give you something cheery from the Killers. And I'll tell you what we're doing tonight.' Tina set the phone down and picked up her backpack. She took out a filmy turquoise scarf to which were sewn four dozen cheap silver coins. She shook it. The coins jingled and winked in the light.

'Are you loony?' Jo said. 'Belly dancing?'

Tina tied it around her hips. 'I told you – it's cultural.'

'Our culture? You and me and Nefertiti? Hon, I will never tie that scarf around myself and shimmy around a dance floor. I have no equipment to shimmy *with*.'

'You promised,' she said.

'I know. But I can't.' Jo shook her head, consternated and amused at her sister's enthusiasms. 'You like shiny things, Tina. Disco balls, cheap coins . . .'

Tina turned toward the French doors. 'What was that?'

In the back yard, in the dusk, a small dark shape had plunged to the ground.

'I don't know,' Jo said.

She went to the doors. As she peered at the lawn, another object hit the grass like a lawn dart falling to earth. She looked next door at the dark second-story windows of Ferd's rent-a-mansion.

'I don't like this.'

She opened the French doors and went outside. On the grass lay a plush toy squid and a small floppy tiger. They were ragged and pathetic.

Tina walked up beside her. 'Beanie Babies.' She bent

down. 'They look . . . oh, yee-eww. Why would your neighbor mangle stuffed animals and throw them at your lawn?'

In reply, another one plunged through the air like a doomed sky-diver and crashed at Jo's feet.

'He wouldn't,' Jo said. 'It's not Ferd. It's his alter-id, Mr Peebles.'

'His pet's a bunny-basher?' Tina peered at the darkened mansion. 'What are you going to do?'

'Not a thing. Ferd can retrieve this stuff when he gets home.'

'Aren't you going to stop him?'

Jo headed for the house. 'I ain't the monkey police. And unfortunately, I have bigger problems to attend to.'

Tina looked at the limp bunny again. 'They've still got the tags on, covered by tag protectors. Jo – they're mint-condition collectibles.'

'Not anymore.'

'Uh-oh.' Tina crouched down. 'It's scorched.'

'Forget about it. Ferd will have to deal with this.'

'No, *freshly* scorched. I can smell it.' She glanced at Jo and up at the darkened window. Gingerly she put a fingertip on the toy's smushed little face. 'It's still hot.'

Jo came back and picked up the ragged bunny. It smelled of burned polyester. Even in the dusk, she could see a blackened patch between its ears. A little flame of alarm crackled inside her. She looked at the window and saw a flare of yellow light inside the black frame.

'Oh, crap.'

The light disappeared. Then it bloomed again and flickered. And vanished.

'He's got a lighter,' she said.

She ran inside her kitchen with Tina on her heels. She opened a cabinet door and grabbed a set of keys from the rack inside.

'Ferd works at Compurama on Geary. Call and tell him to come home.'

The shortest distance to Ferd's house was straight over the fence. Jo rushed out the kitchen door and across the grass, launched herself at the wood, grabbed the crossbeam, and scrambled over. She landed on Ferd's lawn with a thump and ran toward his back door, sorting keys. As she charged up his back steps, she saw another toy rocket from the upstairs window. It was a vividly colored bird. And this one either had a bright gleam in its eye, or it was alight.

Damn it. Molotov cockatoo.

Jo turned the key in the lock and raced through Ferd's dimly lit kitchen to the stairs. She ran up two at a time.

Upstairs was dark. She stopped at the top of the stairs and fumbled along the wall for a light switch. Ahead was the partially opened door to the Beanie Baby launch site.

She knew from trial and error – better known as failure – that when confronting a nimble, pea-brained adversary with opposable thumbs, the first task was to confine him. Which meant shutting him in a room with the door and window locked.

But she couldn't simply close the door down the hall.

251

Do that, and Mr Peebles could still burn the house down. She had to get in there and grab the lighter before he climbed out the window and ran off to stuff burning Beanies through her neighbors' mail slots.

Maybe Ferd was right. Maybe a monkey virus did exist.

And was making *her* crazy.

Quietly she approached the door. In the dark beyond it she heard cooing sounds and the click of the lighter wheel. A bobby pin was jammed into the lock on the door. The little sociopath had figured out how to jimmy it.

She slipped inside the room and shut the door behind her.

Mr Peebles was crouched on a desk in front of the open window. His tiny fingers were working the wheel of the lighter. His next sacrificial victim, a floppy hound dog, lay splayed on the desktop in front of him. When the door clicked shut, his febrile hands went still and his head swiveled. His eyes, glaring at Jo in the dark, reflected the gleam of distant streetlights.

He sat as still as an idol. A tiny, hairy, manic idol that may or may not have been vaccinated for rabies. Jo crept toward him.

With a screech he threw the lighter out the window, like a busted dealer dumping his junk. He grabbed the floppy hound and leaped onto a floor lamp. Jo crossed the room and slammed the window. Mr Peebles sprang to a bookshelf, clutching the puppy to his chest.

On the floor in the corner of the room, a plastic container tub was tipped over. The lid had been pried off and dozens of Beanie Babies spilled onto the floor. Some were ripped apart. Others had been –

'Oh, you nasty monkey.'

They'd been . . . loved to death. A terrible sound rose in her head. Barry White, singing 'Can't Get Enough of Your Love, Babe.'

On an easy chair was a larger, thoroughly debauched collectible. And if Tickle Me Elmo wanted a cigarette to celebrate his night with Mr Peebles, he was out of luck. The lighter was gone.

'Couldn't you just pee in his shoes like a normal pet?' she said.

Ferd was either in denial or too oblivious to see that what ailed his helper monkey wasn't viral but hormonal. She glanced around the room. There were no World of Warcraft stickers, nor a Klingon dictionary. The bookshelf contained coffee table books about Italy. This office didn't belong to Ferd, but to the owners of the house. So, probably, did the collectibles.

Mr Peebles chuffed and glared at her. She reached for him and he nearly flew into her arms. He curled against her shoulder, clutching her sweater with three prehensile extremities and the toy hound with the fourth.

'Where's your crate?'

The one strewn with copies of *Plush Toy Monthly* and *Monkey Hustler* magazine.

Holding him tightly, she headed up the hall. Two doors down, in Ferd's office, was a six-by-six-foot crate with a climbing tree and comfy bedding. She peeled Mr Peebles's fingers and toes from her shirt, turned him smartly around, and set him inside. She latched the door and turned to the desk, looking for something to seal it with. Her hand bumped the computer mouse and Ferd's screen woke up.

She inhaled. A vein began throbbing in her temple.

On-screen was a Technicolor image downloaded from an episode of *Star Trek*. She recognized the sexy Borg woman wearing a silver bodysuit slicked to her skin like spray paint. Her hip was thrust out. She was hoisting a weapon the size of a whaling harpoon.

Jo's head had been Photoshopped onto her body.

In the crate, Mr Peebles screeched and jumped on the bars. She gaped at the screen.

Seven of Jo. She didn't know whether to rip out the computer's guts or laugh her head off.

Out the window, movement caught her eye from next door. She looked across the fence and down into her brightly lit kitchen. Froze.

A man was inside.

Fear lit her up like lightning. From the sharp upstairs angle, she could see only his legs. He was slight and nimble, wore jeans with a blue bandanna hanging from the back pocket. He walked across the kitchen and turned, slowly, looking around.

Where was Tina?

She stuck her hand in her jeans pocket for her phone. Came up empty.

Shit. Her phone was on her kitchen table. She picked up the phone on Ferd's desk and punched 911.

She couldn't see Tina anywhere. The living room

looked empty. Upstairs, the lights were off. The man turned to the kitchen table and opened her laptop.

'Nine-one-one emergency.'

'There's an intruder in my house.' She gave the dispatcher the address. Her voice sounded chipped. 'My sister's in there. Hurry.'

'Stay on the line, ma'am,' the dispatcher said. 'I'm sending a police car.'

As the intruder's hands moved across her keyboard, a second man's set of legs strolled into the kitchen, holding her satchel. He dumped it out on the kitchen table.

She tried to catch her breath and couldn't. 'There's another one.'

Where was Tina?

The second man, stockier than the first, picked up Jo's notebook and flipped it open.

What was in the notebook?

What wasn't? Ruth Fischer's name and number. Snarky notes on Riva Calder. A mention that Alec Shepard was Ian Kanan's brother.

Misty Kanan's home phone number and address.

'Get the cops here. The intruders are going through my computer and my notes on a missing person case and murder investigation. They're going to find the address of the missing man's wife and son. Get somebody over to her house, too.' She gave the dispatcher Misty Kanan's name and address.

Sounds of typing and background chatter. 'Officers are on their way, ma'am. Stay on the line.'

On their way wasn't good enough. 'My sister's in there. I'm going to find some neighbors and go get her.'

The dispatcher's voice hopped up half an octave. 'Ma'am, sit tight. Do not confront the intruders. Stay where you are –'

Jo dropped the phone on the desk and ran for the stairs. She wanted a weapon. She wanted her *katana*.

In Ferd's kitchen she pulled open a drawer. Silverware rattled. She moved to the next. Knives. She grabbed a serrated bread knife with a twelve-inch blade. She hefted it. It was heavy, well-balanced, and looked wicked. The stainless steel blade glinted when she turned it.

She looked out Ferd's back door. Two intruders were in her house. Were more of them outside, waiting in a car or hiding in the park across the street?

Palms tingling, she ran quietly out the back door and down the steps. What did the men want? Was it Kanan and his posse? She bent low, keeping her head below the top of the fence. Holding the knife along her leg, she ran to the corner of the mansion. She peeked around at the darkened sidewalk that led along the side of the house to the street.

Shadows faded to darkness. She couldn't tell whether anyone was hiding there. Holding her breath, she began tiptoeing along the sidewalk.

From the far side of the fence came a man's voice. 'Back door's open. What's out here?'

Feet stepped onto her patio. 'What's all this crap on the lawn?'

She heard a jangling sound. She slowed. A whisper passed her on the air and a hand grabbed her shoulder. She spun, bringing up the knife, and found herself

256

staring into Tina's wide and frightened eyes. Tina's jaw fell open and she inhaled, about to scream. Jo threw a hand across her sister's mouth and pressed her against the fence. The coins on Tina's hip scarf clicked like nickels pouring from a slot machine.

'You hear that?' said one of the men.

Jo held Tina tight against the fence. Tina's gaze kinked back and forth. She was shaking like a Chihuahua.

'Forget it. Get inside,' said the second man.

Jo took Tina's elbow and ran with her up the steps and back inside Ferd's dim kitchen.

'What's going on?' Tina hissed.

Jo clasped her sister hard, shaking, knowing she was about to cry. 'What are you doing here? How did you get out?'

'I called the computer store and left a message for Ferd and then I wondered if you'd caught the monkey,' Tina said in a blistering whisper. 'So I followed you out the back door and I heard men in the house, and it scared the shit out of me, so I climbed over the fence like you did and . . . and . . .' Eyes down. 'Knife? Who? Jo . . .'

'You have a cell phone?'

When Tina nodded, Jo pulled Alec Shepard's business card from her jeans pocket. 'Call.'

Tina dialed, waited, said, 'Voice mail.' She handed Jo the phone.

'Alec, watch out. Two men have broken into my house. I'm worried they may go after your sister-in-law and nephew. If they're carrying out a vendetta, one side takes out somebody from the other side. Even family. Call me.'

257

She found a basket of keys on the kitchen counter. She grabbed it and pulled Tina toward the door to the garage.

'Where are you going?' Tina said.

'We're going.' She opened the door and flipped the light switch. Fluorescents buzzed, flickered, and lit the garage. In the corner a motorcycle was parked under a tarp.

'Come on,' Jo said.

They hauled the tarp off. The bike was a Ducati, sleek and gleaming.

Jo nodded at a pegboard on the wall. 'Get those helmets.'

She set the knife on a workbench and fumbled through the keys. Her hands were still shaking. Tina handed her a helmet. She put it on, swung a leg over the seat, and stuck the key in the bike's ignition. She kicked the kickstand back.

'Hit the door opener. And pray those assholes didn't bring friends.'

Putting on a helmet, Tina ran and pushed the switch. The door began rumbling up. Jo turned the ignition.

The bike growled to full-throated life. Exhaust shot from the pipes. The door opened, exposing the driveway.

Tina jumped on and wrapped her arms around Jo's waist. 'I didn't know you could drive a motorcycle.'

'Me neither.'

She twisted the throttle and gunned the bike out of the garage.

23

Chilly fog was descending on the Kanans' neighborhood. Jo's hands were bone-cold on the handlebars of the bike. Streetlights glowed from within the mist like dandelion fuzz. So did the flashing lights of the police car parked outside the Kanans' home.

The lights spun lazily, red and blue, sweeping across the female officer who stood knocking on the front door. Jo pulled into the driveway, killed the bike's engine, and climbed off.

The officer approached her. 'Mrs Kanan?'

She pulled off her helmet. 'Jo Beckett. I phoned nine-one-one.'

Tina took off her helmet and immediately made a phone call. Jo's legs felt wobbly after the rattling ride on the bike.

'Nobody's home. House looks secure,' the officer said.

Jo felt a glimmer of relief. 'I don't have my cell phone

or Mrs Kanan's number. Let's leave her a note telling her to get in touch.'

The officer handed Jo a notepad. Jo scribbled a note to Misty and stuck it in the doorjamb like a writ.

Turning to the officer, she said, 'Two men broke into my house. Can you find out whether they've been apprehended?'

'Of course.'

The cop walked to the patrol car and picked up the radio. Tina climbed off the Ducati and walked over.

'Dokie's on his way,' Tina said. 'He'll be here in two minutes.'

Dokie was this week's boyfriend. Tina collected guys like charms on a bracelet.

She hugged herself, shivering. 'I'm an icicle.'

Jo put an arm around her and rubbed her shoulder.

The cop looked up. 'No word yet, Dr Beckett.'

'I'm not going home until I know those men are in jail,' Jo said.

The cop spread her hands. She couldn't offer Jo any certainty. Jo sighed.

In rock climbing, uncertainty provided the kick. On a difficult pitch, uncertainty – that you could reach the next hold or power your way over an overhang – was inspiring. It was called a challenge. But uncertainty as to whether the two home invaders had been captured caused nothing but a cramp in her stomach.

'You have someplace to go?' the cop said. 'I'll have the department call you.'

Jo gave her Tina's number. The officer got back in

the patrol car, turned off the flashing lights, and drove away into the thickening fog. As her taillights faded, a rustbucket Nissan came toward them up the street, its headlights blurry in the mist. Waving, Tina stepped to the curb. Dokie pulled up and got out, all fawn's eyes and silver facial piercings and gleaming zippers on his leather jacket. He was Tina's latest shiny thing. He kissed her.

Tina turned to Jo. 'Let's get coffee and go to my place.'

At the end of the street, another vehicle turned the corner from Fulton. From the sound of the motor and the height of the lights, it was an SUV. Jo's anxiety zinged and she tried to see whether it was the red Navigator. Misty Kanan's Chevy Tahoe materialized from the fog.

Jo glanced at Tina. 'I'll catch up. I need to talk to this gal first.'

'You sure?'

'Positive. Twenty minutes, tops.'

Tina turned to go, and turned back. 'At Ferd's house . . .' She half laughed and blinked back emotion. 'You were going to rescue me with that humongous knife? Awesome.'

Jo squeezed her hand. She felt herself smile.

Tina grabbed her in a rabid hug. 'I was so scared.'

'So was I.'

'Thanks.'

Jo smiled. 'I love you, too.'

Tina shot her a winsome grin and ran to the car. In a cloud of white exhaust, Dokie pulled away.

The Chevy Tahoe slowed, engine rumbling, and turned into the driveway. The driver's window came down.

Misty Kanan's eyes were wide and wary. 'Is it Ian? Have you found him?'

'Afraid not. I came to warn you. Two men broke into my house and rifled my files. They may have obtained your name and address.'

Misty turned off the engine and climbed out. Her face was tight. 'You mean they grabbed the information you've gathered on Ian?'

'Possibly. And I don't know if they've been caught.'

Misty gave her a strong look, unblinking. 'You presume this break-in has something to do with Ian. With me. Us.'

'I can think of no other reason two men would invade my house and rummage through my case notes and computer files.'

Misty stormed to the porch. She unlocked the door, headed in ahead of Jo, and flipped on a light.

'Why do you have it in for us?' she said.

Jo stepped back mentally. She recognized a paranoid question when she heard one.

'I'm here to alert you, not to grill you. Some dangerous people may have obtained your name and address. I think you should get out. Take Seth and go someplace safe until these men are under arrest.'

The house was cold. Only the single hall light was on. Misty stood between Jo and the rest of her home, arms crossed, keys clenched in her fist. Perhaps she was drawing into a shell to protect herself psychologically from chaos and fear. But with every second that passed, Jo grew more suspicious.

'I know you're terribly worried about Ian. But people are dying.'

'Dying? Who?'

'Two people who were aboard his flight yesterday have been killed, and at least one other passenger has the same brain damage as Ian. Whatever injured your husband may be contagious.'

Misty drew back, frowning in disbelief. 'No.'

'And a man was stabbed to death in the marina this morning. They found him floating beside *Somebody's Baby*.'

'What?'

'The police have issued a warrant for Ian's arrest.'

'The police think Ian killed a man? No – that's . . . but he's sick. He can't be held responsible for his actions.'

Wow, Jo thought. Misty didn't deny that her husband might have stabbed a man to death. She didn't even try to deny the possibility.

'If it was him,' Jo said.

'Yeah. If it was him.'

The odor of sour milk wafted from the kitchen. Misty's attitude smelled every bit as bad.

'Who was the victim?' Misty said.

'Man named Ken Meiring. Ring any bells?'

Misty stared blankly for a moment. She blinked and tilted her head to one side as though trying to crack a balky vertebra. 'No idea who that is.'

'Really?' Jo said. 'You sure? Ian stole his brother's

Navigator this morning. It was spotted at the marina after that. And he chased me with it this afternoon.'

Misty's bearing changed. For a second Jo thought she was going to lunge at her.

'You saw Ian this afternoon?' she said.

'I saw the car he stole, coming at me down Valencia Street. Then he took off after Alec.'

A flash of heat in Misty's eyes. 'What does he want with you?'

'I don't know. Misty, the situation is critical and deteriorating. More people could die. Please help me. Tell me anything you know.'

'Where did Ian go? Why didn't you tell me this right away?'

'I'm telling you now.'

'Where's Alec?' Misty said.

'I don't know – we got separated. I can't get him on his cell or at the office or home. Do you have another way to reach him?'

'No. Wait.' She put up a hand. 'Let me think.'

Whatever Misty was hiding, she was doing a lousy job of it. The cold of the house sank through Jo's clothes.

'Why didn't you tell me Alec is Ian's brother?'

'You should have told me you saw Ian. You should have called me.' Misty's tone was icy.

'I did. Check your voice mail.'

Outside the kitchen window, the mist was roiling into a heavy fog. The streetlights had dimmed to cotton. Jo's nerves were still throwing off sparks from the shock of seeing the intruders in her house. And if a police consultant had shown up on her doorstep and warned her to take her kid and get the hell to safety, she wouldn't have stood around the front hall complaining about the visit. She would have hauled ass.

'Misty, you're a wreck. Something's killing you. Tell me what's going on.'

Misty began kneading a pendant that hung from a gold chain around her neck. Two gold dolphins leaping around a blue sapphire.

From the first, Misty's reactions had perplexed Jo. At the E.R. she had seemed devastated by the news of her husband's condition. But instead of staying with him, she'd left in a panic. Jo had thought she was fleeing from the bad news – trying literally to outrun Kanan's diagnosis. But now she thought something else entirely had driven Misty to flee. She didn't know what – simply that everything about Misty Kanan was out of kilter.

'I just want him home. He's everything to me,' Misty said.

'Of course,' Jo said.

Kneading the dolphin pendant, she turned and headed for the living room. Jo followed.

'Why would Ian hunt down his brother?' Jo said.

'I don't know.'

'Frankly, I think you do.'

Misty turned on a table lamp. The Ikea furniture looked forlorn in the dim light. The laundry lay crumpled in the basket beside the easy chair. The iron was still sitting at attention on the ironing board in the corner, patiently waiting. Misty had revved into the red zone

265

with worry about her husband, but the rest of her life had ground to a stop.

Misty picked up a yellow throw pillow. She fluffed it and threw it on the couch.

'Is somebody putting pressure on you?' Jo said.

'No.'

'Chira-Sayf?'

Misty gave her a scornful look. 'Don't be ridiculous.' She bustled around the living room, picking up last week's newspapers and putting them into a pile on the coffee table.

Jo put out her hands in a calming gesture. 'Hold still for one minute.'

Misty picked up the television remote and tossed it on the newspapers. The remote skidded across the topmost and sent them all sliding to the floor again.

Jo put out a hand. 'Sit down.'

Misty grabbed her wedding ring and began twirling it. 'Nobody's pressuring me. And I don't know what's going on.' Her voice was brittle. 'Alec and Ian have a difficult relationship. But that doesn't mean Ian wants to kill his brother.'

The wedding ring matched the necklace. Dolphins circling a sapphire.

Seeing Jo's gaze on it, Misty stopped. From the laundry basket she took a T-shirt. Russell Athletic, gray, a man's shirt. She smoothed it and stared at it, seemingly with fondness.

'Misty?' Jo said. 'Where's Seth?'

Confusion briefly creased Misty's brow. She put the

shirt against her chest as though protecting it. 'At a friend's.'

'Does he know what's going on?'

'Excuse me, but that's none of your business.'

Jo tried to keep her expression neutral. Misty's jaw tightened and her shoulders inched up.

She dropped the shirt back in the laundry basket. 'Excuse me.'

She headed to the kitchen. Jo heard her open a cabinet and get out a glass. A second later the faucet turned on.

Jo sat listening to a clock tick. It had now been three minutes since she warned Misty to grab her son and scram. Either Misty was too stupid to feel frightened, or she was in on things.

Jo wasn't going to get any more useful information from Misty. Amy Tang needed to turn on the bad dog attitude. She stood up.

Newspaper sections lay scattered at her feet. Inserts had fallen out, glossy advertisements and coupon sections, and had slid partway beneath the sofa. But one of the glossy pages wasn't from the newspaper. It was the corner of an eight-by-ten photograph. Jo bent and picked it up.

It was a wedding photograph, embossed at the bottom with *Misty & Ian, together forever*. It must have fallen from the bookshelf and slipped beneath the sofa.

The Kanans had married in a park. Ian looked young, fit, and handsome in his blue suit. His ice-chip gaze was worldly. Even at twenty he'd possessed a preternatural ability to see straight through people. He looked almost defiantly relaxed. He had his arm around Misty.

She was smiling, bending against his side, holding a bouquet of gardenias. She was wearing a wispy wedding dress, and she was bare-foot. She had baby's breath in her hair. She looked about eighteen.

She was not the woman in the kitchen.

Heart knocking, Jo pored over the photo. She must be making a mistake.

She wasn't.

The woman in the wedding photo looked much like the woman calling herself Misty. Amazingly like her, in fact. Same sylphlike figure, same creamy skin and sleek caramel hair. And the same pendant hanging around her neck: two dolphins leaping around a sapphire. But the woman in the photo had warm eyes and a gregarious smile, not the chill and resentfulness of the woman Jo had been speaking to. And in the photo Misty had a Celtic tattoo on her right arm.

Outside the windows, the fog had thickened. Jo's thoughts sharpened to a single word: *imposter*.

She began seeing clearly – the fact that the house was always cold and dark, and Misty rarely around. The hesitation about details of the family's life. The woman's lack of interest in how Seth would cope with everything.

Because the woman didn't care about Seth.

Jo's breathing accelerated. The police had gone. Tina and her boyfriend had gone. She was on her own.

She quietly folded the photo in half, slid it under her sweater, and tucked it in the waistband of her jeans. She stood and turned around.

The imposter was standing six feet from her. She had the iron in her hand.

Steam hissed from it. The woman raised her arm and roared across the living room at Jo.

Hot. The thing was blazing hot. Jo jumped onto the coffee table and leaped toward the easy chair. The woman was between her and the front door, and *shit,* a hot iron would brand her, melt her face off. The woman spun, swinging the iron in her hand like a bowling ball. Its long insulated cord swished behind her, the heavy plug chittering against the floor like the rattler on a diamond-back.

Jo jumped back. Behind her was a bookshelf and the wall. She needed a shield. Something big or – *damn*! The iron swept within a few inches of her. It smashed the lamp and sent it flying to the floor. The light in the room turned bald and glaring.

Jo grabbed a book from the shelf, an atlas. The iron came at her. She held the atlas in front of her and took the blow with it. She heard a crisping sound and smelled burning. Her fingertips, wrapped around the edges of the book, felt a dry impossible heat.

The woman was thinking brutally, not clearly, but she was bound to figure it out – she didn't need to burn Jo straightaway. If she brained her with the iron, she could knock her out, lay her flat, and ablate her entire dermis from her body, till she was pressed and creased and dead.

With a yell, Jo shoved the book at her. The woman stepped back, off balance. Jo took a wild swing and slammed her hard in the chin. The woman stumbled back, stunned. Jo ducked sideways, trying to get around her, and the woman charged at her again. *Shit*. She saw the woman's eyes, dead but wild, and the iron, looming near. In desperation she grabbed the woman's arm, threw herself backward, and rolled to the floor, as though peeling off a rock face and landing in a back somersault.

The woman flailed, head up, and her face hit the corner of the wall where it met the hallway. Jo heard the crack. The woman's head snapped back and she flopped heavily on top of Jo. The iron fell.

No – Jesus, hot . . . Jo shrank from it, felt it sizzle against the sleeve of her shirt, fought down a yelp. The iron thunked to the hardwood floor.

The woman's forehead fell against it. She came alert with a shriek.

Jo shoved the woman aside, skittered to her hands and knees, and crawled away. A hand grabbed her ankle.

Jo tried to pull free. The woman reached for the iron. Jo grabbed the electrical cord and cracked it like a whip. The iron battered its way along the floor. The woman slapped her free hand down to stop it but missed.

Jo kicked loose and stumbled to her feet. Hanging on to the cord, she ran through the living room and into the kitchen. She heard a low growl behind her. With her free arm she swept dishes onto the floor. And a two-liter bottle of olive oil. It shattered and she heard a glugging sound.

The front door was straight ahead. She heard footsteps behind her. The electrical cord went taut as the woman grabbed the iron again.

Then she heard the long gritty swoop of a shoe sliding across oil and shards of glass. With a thump, the woman went down. Jo glanced back.

The woman was splayed on her back, grimacing. She fumbled for the cabinets and countertop, trying to sit up. She was woozy but not neutralized. And she was surrounded by cutlery.

Jo figured she had thirty seconds. She ran for the door.

24

Jo crashed out the front door into fog the color of concrete. She ran toward the Ducati, struggling to pull the keys from her pocket.

What was *that*?

Goddamn it – the woman inside the house was not Misty Kanan. Jo jumped on the Ducati. With a shaking hand she jammed the key in the ignition. She looked back at the gaping front door.

The woman stumbled into view. She bumped the door-frame and lurched outside. Jo kicked the bike into life. She didn't have the helmet. She didn't care. The woman staggered to the Tahoe and opened the door. She reached inside and came out fumbling with something.

A gun. *Shit.* She was struggling with the safety.

Like she was spurring a wild horse, Jo jammed her feet against the pedals and swung the bike toward the street and took off.

She swiped at the controls until she found the headlight. It turned the air in front of her into a white fiberglass wall.

She had to get to the corner. If she could turn onto Fulton, she'd be lost from the woman's line of sight. Get to Fulton and she could stop, run around, strip naked, and scream, which she really felt like doing, at least the screaming part.

The fog bit at her hands and face. It numbed the air, muffling other sounds. Her eyes streamed. Where was the corner? She had to call Amy Tang. Who the hell was that woman?

A black shape swelled in front of her, low, sleek, big – *car.*

She braked. The vehicle materialized, parking lights like yellow canines, engine muted by the fog. Her back tire locked. The car was rolling slowly but was *right there . . .*

She hit it almost head-on and vaulted straight over the handlebars. *Ball up*, she told herself. She slammed against the hood with a metallic thud and slid into the windshield.

The car shrieked to a stop. She rolled and lay still.

The hood was warm. The engine thrummed. Adrenaline lit her up like an electrical storm. She was too shocked to feel pain yet. She raised her head and looked through the windshield at the horrified face of Alec Shepard.

Shepard jumped out of the Mercedes. 'Dr Beckett?'

She rolled over on the hood of the car, hearing a hum in her head, seeing him through the fog. His dress shirt and blue tie and salt-and-copper beard seemed to pulse.

He rushed to her. 'Christ, you came out of nowhere.'

She slid off the hood. 'We gotta move.'

Her feet hit the ground. Her legs held. The Ducati lay revving near the curb. Its headlight glared blindly into the fog, illuminating their legs. The mist ate their shadows.

He put a hand under her elbow. 'Let me turn on the flashers.'

'No, we have to get out of here.'

'You're in no condition to go anywhere. We need to stay here and call the police and file an accident report.'

'Woman in Ian's house has a gun. *Come on.*'

His brow puckered. 'Did you hit your head?'

Her fight-or-flight reflex was zooming like the bike's engine. She put her hands against his chest and shoved him toward the driver's door.

'She wants to kill me. *Go.*'

He hesitated only a second longer. She lurched to the car and got in. He jumped back behind the wheel and put the car in gear.

Jo could see nothing but fog. 'Turn around and get off this street. Come on, get out of here so I can call the police.'

She said *police* with the same vehemence she might have said *rip your nuts off.* It did the trick. He pulled a U-turn and gunned the car down the street toward Fulton.

She fumbled for her seat belt. She was trembling. She could tell that her ribs had taken the brunt of the impact.

'What are you doing here?' she said.

'I got your message about the break-in at your house. I came to check on Misty and Seth. I called your cell phone.'

274

'My phone's at home.' She held out a tremulous hand. 'Give me yours.'

He took it from his jacket and handed it to her. She dialed Amy Tang's cell. Shepard stopped at the corner, signaled, and turned onto Fulton. Jo glanced over her shoulder to see if the imposter was on their tail, but the night was a solid white wall.

'Where have you been since Ian chased us this afternoon?' she said.

'Staying out of sight.' He cut his eyes at her. 'I wasn't sure whether he found me by following you to the restaurant.'

'Me neither.'

Amy answered the phone, crisp and rushed. 'Tang.'

'It's Jo. Send a unit back to Ian Kanan's house.'

'What's wrong?'

'The woman we thought was Misty Kanan is an imposter. She just tried to kill me.'

'Beckett?'

'Putting you on speaker.'

Jo set the phone on the center console and, trying to compose herself, told Tang and Shepard the short form. The Mercedes rolled east on Fulton. Golden Gate Park scrolled past on their right. The trees were a depthless black that absorbed even the fog.

'You in one piece?' Tang said.

'Yeah, but never ask me to take part in an extreme ironing competition.'

'You got it.' Tang's voice was as sharp as a diamond. 'Why is another woman impersonating Kanan's wife?'

Shepard looked at her. Behind the salt-and-cinnamon beard, his face was taut.

'Is the fake working with Kanan?' Tang said.

'Maybe. Maybe she's working against him – for the people he's hunting. And . . .' A thought rose in Jo's head like clear air. 'Kanan knows her.'

Shepard looked at her sharply. 'What are you talking about?'

'Your brother knows the imposter. In the E.R. at San Francisco General, she walked right up to him.'

Jo recalled it clearly – the woman's attitude, her familiarity, her *close* familiarity. 'He put his hand on her shoulder. He knows her well.'

Tang said, 'So she's on his team.'

'Maybe.' Jo swept her hair off her face, thinking about it. 'But that feels wrong.'

What had happened between Kanan and the imposter in the E.R.?

She turned to Shepard. 'Where's Misty?'

'I don't know.'

'When did you last see her?'

He raised his shoulders. 'Maybe six weeks ago.'

'How's Ian and Misty's marriage?' Jo said.

'Solid. Totally.'

'Does Misty wear a white jacket? Tartan skirt with chunky boots?'

'Yeah.'

'Drive a Chevy Tahoe?'

Worry creased his face. 'Yeah.'

'The imposter has her car, her clothes, her keys, her

276

house. So where's Misty?' She raised her voice, making sure Tang heard. 'The house has been shut. Nobody's been there for days. Where's the dog? Where's Seth?'

The Mercedes thrummed along the street, smothered in fog.

'Jo?' Tang said.

'God.'

She remembered Kanan holding her against the wall in the elevator, telling her to listen to him. She remembered his every word, all his threats. But they weren't threats.

'Amy, something bad has happened to Kanan's family. They're gone.'

25

'The Kanan family is gone? Where?' Tang said.

Shepard stared out the windshield at the fog. In the dim interior of the car, his face was etched with the frosty blue lights of the dashboard instruments. A red streak reflected in his eyes.

'Something has happened to them,' Jo said. 'Damn it, we've been looking at everything backward.'

'Explain,' Tang said.

'Before Kanan fled the hospital, when he cornered me in the elevator, he interrogated me. Said, "Who are you working for?" and "Do you have it?"'

Shepard glanced at her from the corner of his eye.

'What set him off was seeing Misty's scarf. He pinned me to the wall, demanding to know how I got it. I said she'd been in the E.R. He got angry and said, "Bullshit."'

'He has no memory. Why was that so strange?' Tang said.

'Because any other happy husband who ends up in the E.R. and hears that his wife's around the corner says, "Which way did she go?" and runs to find her. Kanan didn't. Because he thought it was impossible that Misty could be there.'

'What are you implying?'

The cold, kept at bay inside the car, crept again along her skin. 'Goddamn. He told me. He told me flat-out, and I didn't understand. He said, "I will get them."'

'The people who poisoned him.'

'No.' In her mind's eye Jo saw the grief on Kanan's face; the determination, his desperation. '"I will get them." He didn't mean get revenge against bad guys. He meant he was going to get his family. He meant he was going to get them *back*.'

'Seth and Misty . . .'

'They've been grabbed. Somebody's holding them hostage.'

Misty Kanan pressed her ear to the locked bedroom door. Through the cheap laminate she heard echoes from the rest of the house.

The television. A loose screen on a window, clacking against the wall in the wind. She exhaled and focused everything into listening. For thirty seconds she held still, eyes closed, fighting her hopes and her dread.

She didn't hear the men.

Usually Vance and Murdock clumped around the house and talked, flushed the toilet, threw bottles in the trash. But for the past hour the house had been quiet.

They could come back at any minute. It was a risk. She took a breath: No guts, no glory.

She pulled her sweater over her head.

When the men grabbed her and dumped her here in this house, they had taken everything – from her cell phone to her dolphin necklace and wedding ring. They'd patted her down, run their hands all over her body. They'd locked her in a room that was stripped to four walls and a stained mattress.

The thugs who'd grabbed her had taken almost everything. But they'd left her with her lingerie.

She pulled out the underwiring from her brassiere. Over the past day she had bitten a hole in the bra's stitching and worked the wire loose from the fabric. The metal was slim but tough. Tough enough, she hoped, to work as a screwdriver and a lock-picking tool.

Misty thought of herself as a good mom and a good school nurse, a woman who enjoyed reading Dr Seuss to feverish first graders while they waited for their parents to pick them up from school. But she was also the wife of an ex-Special Forces soldier. She listened when he talked and believed him when he said, 'You never know when you might need to use this trick to get out of a tight situation.'

She needed it now.

She had been abducted because of Ian's work. She was desperate to escape – for him, for Seth. And she knew that Seth would be worried to death, and Ian would be going out of his mind trying to find her. But she couldn't wait for him to bust down the door and rescue her.

Use what you have at hand, Ian would say. Turn whatever you can into a tool or a weapon.

In the dim light, Misty set to work. Carefully she bent the wire in half. She slid the folded end into the slots in the flathead screws in the doorknob assembly. The door was old and cheap. If she could unscrew the assembly and gain access to its inner workings, she might be able to use the wiring as a probe and flip the lock.

But she had to work fast. The kidnappers were getting ready to dump her again – and not in another room. Not anywhere above-ground. They'd stopped feeding her. They were getting ready to dump her wherever dead bodies were likely to be found.

'Hostage?' Tang said. 'Beckett, are you dropping acid?'

'No, and I have no proof. But Jesus, Amy, I'd bet the farm on this.' She swallowed. 'We can't afford *not* to bet on this.'

With Shepard's Mercedes rolling along Fulton Street through the foggy night, Jo shut her eyes and brought up the memory. The hospital elevator. Kanan pressing her back to the wall. The blade of the dagger shimmering near her face.

'He asked who I was working for. He said, "Do you have it?"'

'"It"?' Tang said.

Beside her, Shepard drew in a breath.

'Ian said, "I'm on the job. I'm doing it." And he said, "Where are they?"'

'His wife and son.'

281

'"I'm going to get them." It wasn't a threat. It was a promise.' A hitch crept into her voice. 'It was a vow.'

'But why were they taken?' Tang said.

Jo turned to Shepard. 'Alec? What's going on?'

For a few more seconds he held the wheel straight. A traffic light slowly bloomed from the mist, thick green. An intersection materialized. He spun the wheel and veered around the corner into Golden Gate Park. Jo lurched against her shoulder belt. The streetlights faded into the fog and the trees loomed spectrally around them. He pulled over.

He dropped his hands from the wheel. 'Christ.'

'Ian isn't trying to hunt you down because he thinks you cheated him or poisoned him, is he?' she said.

'No.'

'Ian isn't on a vendetta or a killing spree. He's being forced to do something. He's been told he has to get something to save his family.' She turned to him. 'He's trying to raise the ransom.'

Shepard stared at the fog. His lips pulled back, as though he was working to keep his emotions under wraps.

Abruptly, in her mind's eye, Jo saw the writing on Kanan's forearm. And she understood why Kanan had seemed not just angry, not just confused, but frenzied with fear and urgency.

'Saturday they die,' she said.

'Jesus,' Tang said.

'It's not a hit list – it's a deadline.'

Shepard looked bereft. 'If they've been taken, the kidnappers must have given Ian until then, or they'll . . .'

282

His voice trailed off.

'Or they'll kill Misty and Seth. What do the kidnappers want?' Jo said.

He looked anxiously at the cell phone, and then at Jo, holding back.

Her face heated. 'When Ian grabbed me, he said he'd been poisoned in Africa. He asked if I wanted to know why. And he said, "Slick. Really. Slick." Does that mean anything to you?'

He said nothing. Outside, the fog enveloped the car.

Tang broke the silence. 'I need to get on this. I'll get a patrol unit and forensics to the Kanans' house. We know what the imposter looks like. And, Jo, you fought with her.'

'Yeah. The house is full of forensic evidence. Fingerprints, face prints, DNA from blood and saliva – I did my bit for the investigation.'

'She's blown, sky-high. The house is a treasure trove of evidence. We'll I.D. her, and then we'll get after her.'

Shepard leaned toward the cell phone. 'Lieutenant, I don't know if I can help, but . . .'

'You have any idea who might have taken your sister-in-law and nephew?'

'No. But I'll think about it.'

The answer was weak, and Tang let an accusatory silence hang in the air for several seconds. 'Do that. Think hard. Jo, you all right?'

Shepard looked at her. 'Shall I take you home? Or to the E.R.?'

'I got my bell rung, but I'm okay.'

She wasn't, exactly, but didn't want to say so. She was running on adrenaline – and it, like gasoline, would eventually run out.

'We need to solve this. Get going. I'll pass out later,' she said.

'Where will you be?' Tang said.

Jo had spent nearly two days trying to pin Alec Shepard down and get answers from him. He held the key to what was going on, and to locating Kanan. Now that she'd found Shepard, she wasn't letting him out of her sight.

'I'm with Mr Shepard. On this number.' She caught his eye. 'You and other people from Chira-Sayf know more about Ian than I ever will. You have the knowledge and resources to track him.'

'Of course,' he said.

Tang spoke up. 'Jo, if we're right, and Kanan's family has been taken to force him to do something for the bad guys . . . exposing the imposter has just upset their plans.'

'You're saying things have become more dangerous?'

'Without a doubt.'

Jo ran her hands into her hair. The engine of the Mercedes thrummed with the numbing constancy of a drill.

'Let me get things up and running. I'll call you back,' Tang said.

Shepard ended the call and put the phone in his pocket.

Quietly, Jo said, 'Now you can tell me what you weren't willing to reveal to the police. What do the kidnappers want? And why is Ian the one they want it from?'

Shepard stared blankly at the dashboard. Finally, his eyes closed and his head dropped. 'Slick.'

'It's Chira-Sayf's nanotech project, isn't it?'

'Yes. And they can't get it.'

'Why not?'

'Because I had it destroyed.'

26

In the heated cocoon of Alec Shepard's Mercedes, Jo tried to keep cool. 'You had Slick destroyed because it proved dangerous, didn't you? It's so dangerous, you didn't just shelve the project – you closed your lab in Johannesburg.'

His eyes widened. 'Who have you been talking to?'

'Nobody. I did basic open-source research. Stop looking at me like I'm an industrial spy.' She turned sideways in the seat. 'Is Slick what poisoned your brother?'

He looked away, as though he was preparing to hedge his answer.

'I saw his MRI, Alec. And the MRI of another passenger who came in contact with him. It's poisoning other people who were on his flight from London.'

His expression, in the weird dashboard light, turned stark.

'Sayf, S-A-Y-F. Transliterated from the Arabic word

for *sword*. So either your company's cutting shawarma with a big knife, or it's pulling a play on words, because you're updating an ancient form of technology. Damascus steel. Carbon nanotubes.'

His gaze broke from hers. 'I'm not accusing you of industrial espionage. Somebody's trying to steal our product. But they don't want the formula or lab notes. They want the real thing. Christ. What a clusterfuck.'

'Talk. Your brother is in desperate straits, and he's not the only one.'

Shepard's face looked bleak. He took out his phone. 'We need backup.'

'Who are you calling?'

'My right-hand man.' He didn't smile, but she saw an acerbic light in his eyes. He pressed the phone to his ear. 'I want to triple-check our lab security. And get Ian's travel and expense records.'

'Money trail.'

'Exactly.' He glanced at her again, as though surprised that she'd thought of it.

'Trace the airline ticket,' she said. 'Maybe Ian charged it to a Chira-Sayf credit card. Maybe somebody else paid for it. Find out who.'

He nodded.

'Who sent your brother to Johannesburg?'

'That's one thing I'm going to have the company look into.' He listened. 'Voice mail.' His tone became curt. 'We have a crisis. Meet me at . . .' He looked around. 'Golden Gate Park, outside the Japanese Tea Garden. Pronto. I'll explain when you get here.'

He snapped the phone shut. 'We'll get this figured out.'

'You trust your right-hand guy?' Jo said.

'Implicitly.' He put the Mercedes in gear and pulled away from the curb.

'Tell me why somebody would want to steal Slick.'

'It's valuable. And I'd decided to destroy it rather than let it be put to use.'

'Would Ian steal it? Sell it? Hurt you?'

'Never. He knows its potential, and I simply cannot believe that he would ever want it used in the real world. He was a soldier.' He shook his head. 'No, he'd only agree to obtain it to save Seth and Misty. He also knows I'd never agree to give it to him. It means he's at the edge of despair.'

Shepard crept along the curving road through the park. His demeanor had become locked-down and tense. His gaze swept between the rearview mirror and the wing mirrors. With each yard they drove away from Fulton Street, the chrysanthemum glow of streetlights and apartment windows faded. The trees swallowed what little light could penetrate the fog. They moved in a bubble, able to see only the inside of the car, neither behind nor ahead.

'Slick was an experimental nanotech project,' he said. 'Its official designation was C-S/219.'

'Military?'

'Chira-Sayf doesn't manufacture weapons. It was DOD-funded, but it was supposed to neutralize IEDs.'

'It was a bomb-killer?'

'It was supposed to save lives.'

'Is Slick the substance that contaminated your brother?' she said.

The silence was thicker this time, dry, like dust. 'It shouldn't be possible. We destroyed it.'

'Why?'

'It was supposed to deactivate roadside bombs. It didn't.' His expression turned bleaker. 'You're a doctor – have you seen blast wounds? Afghanistan, Iraq, the London tube . . .'

'Yes. Ghastly.'

'Body armor will protect soldiers' vital organs, but their arms get blown off. A suicide bomber's rib gets embedded in a soldier's femur. Shrapnel, nails, ball bearings get sprayed into some little girl's face.'

Abruptly, Jo thought of Gabe's scars. *I mended.* A knot formed in her throat.

'Carbon nanotubes are tiny machines,' Shepard said. 'They're simple, stupid bots. They work at a molecular level via chemical interactions. Ours was supposed to bond with compounds found in commonly deployed IEDs and neutralize them.'

'But?'

'It had the opposite effect. It made explosives even more unstable.'

'Jesus,' Jo said.

Shepard's shoulders were tight. His gray eyes were piercing, like his brother's. 'When we tested it, bombs went off prematurely. When we tried to dispose of them, after removing the detonator, they ignited. It was a disastrous result.'

'So you shut the project down,' Jo said.

'Slick was unpredictable, unstable, and dangerous. I killed it.'

'Didn't the DOD want it anyway? They're the world's biggest buyer of ka-boom.'

'I authorized the project to save lives. I didn't want to pay for Chira-Sayf's corporate jet by manufacturing munitions.'

'And that's why you shut down the South African operation?'

'Yes, the Jo'burg lab was producing Slick. And Ian must have gone to Africa to get a sample. But he must have failed. Or . . .' He exhaled harshly. 'Or made a mistake and got contaminated. Now he wants to get it from me.'

'So Ian thinks you have Slick? You, personally – or that you have access to it?'

'Yes.'

'But you said it was all destroyed.'

'I thought it was. But if Ian's – affected, then he had to have come in contact with it.'

'Because that's what is destroying his memories?'

'Slick will screw you up if it gets into your bloodstream. It binds with iron. And it's lipophilic,' he said. 'It attaches to fats in the bloodstream – in effect gets coated with them – and then slips past the blood-brain barrier.'

'Slick is a Trojan horse, isn't it?' Jo said.

'Yes,' he said.

It slipped inside other molecules, lipids and iron-ferrying

290

molecules, and fooled the brain into letting it past. Once there, it accumulated, assembled itself into strings, and destroyed the medial temporal lobes.

'That's how it ruins the ability to form new memories,' she said.

'And once it gets past the gates, it starts rewiring the brain.'

'Rewiring – Jesus, what can it do?' she said.

'Carbon nanotubes have low electrical resistance for their size. They could generate low-resistance pathways for neuron formation.'

'You mean they could create new connections in the brain?'

'Yes. Fast ones.' He ran a hand over his beard. 'Does he know he's contaminated?'

'Yes.'

'Will he forget that?'

'I don't know. Why?'

'Because if he does, and he handles Slick, a second dose would overwhelm his neural system and kill him.'

Jo leaned back against the headrest. Her ribs and leg were thumping. The car inched along through the fog.

'Ian must have obtained a sample of Slick from the Jo'burg lab. I see no other way he could have become contaminated by it. But if he's trying to get more from me, he must think I'm the one person at Chira-Sayf who can still provide it to him,' Shepard said.

'Are you?'

He didn't answer that. 'If he's after me, where's the sample he obtained?'

291

'Alec, Ian can't remember. If he got hold of a sample in Africa, he could have stashed it someplace, and he'd never be able to recall where.'

'So he wants to get more from me?'

'Right. And the people who are putting him under duress think you can get it.' She thought for a moment. 'But if he had it in his possession . . .'

He put the car in gear. 'Where is it now? And how long do we have to find it before it comes in contact with a substance that could cause an explosion?'

It was dark in the bedroom, and stuffy. Boards were nailed over the windows and the door was locked. Seth could hear a television playing someplace in the house. He didn't know exactly what time it was, but from the T.V. theme tune, he knew it was early evening.

He wanted to hear the news come on, maybe find out if there was a bulletin asking people to look for him. His photo, description, police telling everybody to be on the lookout. He wished he knew where he was. When the men snatched him from Golden Gate Park, they'd duct-taped his mouth shut, put a pillowcase over his head, taped his hands and feet together for the drive. And all the way, he'd heard Whiskey crying.

The men had wanted Seth not to know where they were going. And they'd done a pretty good job, except he knew they'd driven fast, on a freeway. And they hadn't crossed any of the big bridges. Now, regularly, he heard a train whistle. So they were south of San Francisco.

He tried to see the door lock in the dark. His feet

were tied and his hands bound behind him with plastic handcuffs. The human hot dog, the man called Murdock, had jammed him against the wall and bent his wrists around behind his back to bind them. He'd done it after Vance came in to collect his dinner plate and saw the scratch marks around the lock and found the broken spring from the bed, which Seth had been trying to use to pick the lock.

His hands were going numb. He was going crazy.

The men were gone, he was pretty sure. Nobody was moving around out in the house. He didn't know when they'd be back, just that he felt so, so alone.

He inched himself to the door. 'Whiskey?'

He got no reply.

He couldn't believe they were just going to leave him there. But he had a bad feeling that things had changed and were about to crack in half.

Shepard's Mercedes crept along the road, deeper into the foggy park.

Jo's voice was hot. 'You knew Slick had neurological effects?'

'Not on people. We tested it on animals. They . . . they didn't do well.'

She couldn't keep the edge from her voice. 'But that didn't stop your research.'

'Of course not.' He gave her a look, quick as a jab. 'You want to know why we need to destroy Slick once and for all? It destabilizes hydrocarbon-based substances, turning *them* into bombs. It's odorless, colorless, impossible to spot with metal detectors, X-rays, explosive-sensing machines at airports, bomb-sniffing dogs.'

'Oh, my God.'

It was a bad guy's dream weapon. All the scum of the earth would want it. Plus U.S. and foreign militaries. Intelligence services eager to destroy enemies without leaving a footprint. Organized crime. The Mafia. Mexican narcotraffickers. Islamic Jihad. Al Qaeda.

Shepard glanced edgewise at her. 'Does your silence indicate understanding?'

'Unfortunately.'

'Whatever you're thinking, it's worse than that.'

'How can it be worse than some cocaine lord with his own army deciding to slip an undetectable explosive aboard a Mexicana flight? Or a terrorist painting a children's hospital with Slick and standing back to watch it immolate everybody inside?'

'The lingering effects,' Shepard said. 'As it spreads, it contaminates people it comes in contact with. It's a twenty-first-century dirty bomb. Heat of the explosion can allow conditions for Slick to replicate. That's how it can spread.'

Jo's stomach slithered. 'Where is it? What did your brother do with it?'

'That's what we have to figure out. Before he does himself. And before whoever got to him gets their hands on it.'

27

Kanan heard footsteps ascending wooden stairs behind him. He turned around. He was in the stockroom of a sporting goods store, under bright fluorescent lights, surrounded by shelves stacked with basketballs and baseball cleats. A collection of Post-it notes and printouts from his phone's camera was spread on a desk nearby. His arms were covered with writing. The footsteps drew nearer. He looked toward an open door that led to the basement.

A man appeared at the top of the stairs, dreadlocks swinging from his ponytail, his dark face deceptively serene. He was carrying a rifle with a night scope and three boxes of ammunition.

A wave of hope and relief rolled across Kanan. 'Diaz. Damn, it's good to see you.'

A look crossed Diaz's face like he'd just stepped on a sharp rock. 'Here you go, boss.' He set the rifle on the desk.

'We've got this, plus the HK, the sidearm I'll be carrying, and a Kbar in an ankle sheath.'

Diaz didn't want to look at him. He seemed to be nursing a hurt.

'Have I been here long?' Kanan said.

'Long enough to say hello fifteen times.'

Kanan stared at his arms, then the desk, and understood. 'Sorry.'

Diaz looked up at him. 'You can keep saying hello. And I'll keep you informed of our progress.'

Kanan checked his watch. It was seven forty-five P.M.

'Friday night,' Diaz said.

Kanan ran a hand over his face. He felt grubby and needed a shave. 'Everything I can remember, I see extremely clearly.'

He recalled, with neon intensity, getting the text message saying that his family had been taken hostage. It had started with him sitting on the sunny terrace at the Four Seasons in Amman, drinking thick Arabic coffee from a silver cup, planning to catch his flight home with his trophies – the beautiful Damascus saber and daggers destined for the wall of Alec's office.

Instead, he got a call from Chira-Sayf corporate, alerting him that the materials tech, Chuck Lesniak, had disappeared. So he headed to South Africa to find him.

And when he landed, the text message arrived.

Got them. With photos of Seth and Misty bound and gagged and tied to a chair in a bare garage under a glaring electric bulb.

Get Slick or they die.

More messages had followed. *Don't tell the cops. Don't tell Chira-Sayf. Don't contact Shepard.* Then they'd sent operational information about tracking Lesniak, who had stolen a sample of Slick from the Jo'burg lab and, instead of turning it over to these people and taking his 10 percent commission, had tried to cut his own deal with a higher bidder. Lesniak, the selfish, stupid son of a bitch, had wanted to grab the whole prize. But Lesniak didn't hit the jackpot, because these people figured out they'd been double-crossed. And they figured that the only person who could recover Slick for them was Ian Kanan.

And they knew that the only way Ian Kanan would ever turn Slick over to them was if they threatened to kill his family if he didn't.

He remembered the jet boat and the roaring sound of Victoria Falls. He remembered tightening down the lid of the flask and jamming it in his jeans pocket before he shoved the throttles hard forward and fought the current to safety.

And here he was, in San Francisco, without the flask, gearing up for a hunt. He looked at his arm.

Saturday they die. He closed his eyes so that Diaz wouldn't see him fighting his own desperation.

'Getting Slick from Alec is my fallback plan,' he said, shaking his head. 'I'm betraying him, but I see no other way to save Misty and Seth.'

Diaz put a hand on his shoulder. 'I know.'

Meaning, *You already told me.*

Kanan knew why the kidnappers had insisted that he not contact his brother: because Alec would stop him.

Alec knew how dangerous Slick was. He would worry about national security. If Alec found out what Kanan was doing, he might not help him, but go to the CIA or FBI instead.

And Kanan knew why somebody had written *Find Alec* on his left arm – because Alec was cagy. The kidnappers had to know that he himself was the only one who could track down his brother. He had designed all of Alec's security precautions. He was the only one who knew how to get through them.

And the kidnappers had to know that Alec would never suspect his own brother – he would let Ian get close enough to put him in a helpless position.

Jesus, what a betrayal.

Diaz looked at the weapons laid out on the desk. 'Sarge, I'm with you here, no questions asked, you know that.'

Kanan's smile felt wry. 'So go on and ask your questions.'

'You *sure* Slick is gone – you didn't bring it back?'

'No, I'm not.'

He turned to the messy collection of notes and photos on the desk. 'If I did bring it back, the clues to where it is would be in this stuff.'

Diaz picked up a laminated photo I.D. 'This Johanna Beckett, she's a doctor.'

Kanan shook his head. 'No idea.'

Unexpectedly, the room seemed to sway. He put a hand on the desk.

'Boss, you all right?' Diaz said. 'When's the last time you ate?'

'I have no idea.' He steadied himself. 'Actually, I'm ravenous.'

'Sit tight. There's a Wendy's around the corner. I'll grab us some grub.' Diaz put on a black jacket. He wrote a note and stuck it to the back door of the store before unlocking it. Cold mist blew in from the alley outside. 'You go through that pile of notes. Maybe we can get the stuff without going after your brother. I'll be back.'

Diaz shut the door. Kanan locked it, sat down at the desk, and pressed his fingertips to his eyes. He was damned exhausted.

He opened his eyes. Held still. What was he doing in the stockroom of a sporting goods store?

Shepard's Mercedes curved along the road through Golden Gate Park. Jo gripped the door, hoping Shepard could see well enough to keep from running into another car. Her head was pounding. Her ribs and leg were pounding. The enormous park, eaten by the fog, was a void of white mist.

Golden Gate Park stretched three miles across San Francisco, nearly half the width of the city. In daytime, the rises were green, fields emerald, lakes blue and ruffled by the breeze and by ducks paddling. Monterey pines and stands of eucalyptus turned the center of the city into a forested reserve. The road was wide, and during the day, parked cars usually lined the curbs. Tonight, nobody was around.

'Japanese Tea Garden's going to be closed, and I'm not crazy about meeting your colleague in the dead dark.

299

How about a warm, well-lighted public place, with plenty of people around? The de Young Museum's open on Friday nights.'

Shepard shook his head. 'I'm not putting in a public appearance. The people who want Slick will go to any lengths to get it.' He glanced at her. 'You're safe with me. But I need to be sure nobody can get to me by tracking you. Do you have a pager? BlackBerry? Any communications device? If so, turn it off and remove the battery.'

'I'm clean,' she said.

Out of the fog, trees grasped for clear air. Flower beds full of pink hydrangeas flowed past, dusty gray in the darkness.

He lifted his foot from the accelerator. 'This is it.'

In the distance, rising like arthritic hands, were the sculpted trees outside the tea garden. Shepard pulled to the curb on the left side of the road and parked against traffic. Killing the engine, he put down his window a few inches so he could hear approaching motors. He was scared and smart. The quiet poured in along with the damp chill of the fog.

'Alec, we don't have much time. How can we get hold of Ian? Is there someplace your brother would go? Do you know his friends? His old army buddies? Can you contact him?'

'I've tried. I called him at home, I e-mailed him. No luck. And his phone isn't answering – if I know him, he's set it not to transmit.'

'Does he have any hangouts? A bar? A gym, a church, a storage company where he keeps weapons?'

Shepard shook his head. 'I'm sorry. I really don't know. He runs. He camps and fishes. He spends weekends tinkering on his SUV, or doing things with Seth and Misty.'

Jo tucked her arms against her chest to keep warm. 'How is Slick transported? What form is it in?'

'It's grown – baked, however you want to understand it – as singlewalled carbon nanotubes, at high temperature. But it's put in an oilbased solution, so when it's dispersed, it can be sprayed, fired from a bazooka – we had all kinds of ideas.'

'What does it look like?' she said.

'Slick itself? The nanoparticles are each incredibly small. Basically, they're molecular machines. Very tiny.'

'Why do the kidnappers want the actual nanoparticle?' Jo said. 'Why couldn't they steal the research data or smash a window and grab a hard drive that has all the information? Why do they need the actual product?'

Shepard ran a hand across his forehead. 'It's devilishly hard to duplicate the research and get Slick to grow correctly – it's like baking from scratch. When you bake, you need yeast as a catalyst. If the kidnappers obtain Slick, they can use the actual particle as a catalyst. Under correct conditions another lab could get it to replicate.'

'So this quantity is the seed supply?'

'Yes.'

Shepard killed the engine. They sat for several minutes, listening to the engine tick as it cooled. They could see nothing. Finally Shepard opened his door.

'Where are you going?' Jo said.

'I can't just sit here. I'm going stir-crazy. Come on.'

He closed the door and disappeared into the fog. Reluctantly, Jo followed.

The trees were shadows. The night was utterly quiet, close, and chilly. She hunched into her sweater, feeling how stiff her leg and ribs were growing. By the morning, she would be congealed into a solid bruise. A few hundred yards away, she knew, the park opened into a wide panorama. The de Young Museum was there somewhere, invisible, as was a huge outdoor music pavilion. She saw the slightest glow from the museum buildings.

Beyond the curving sidewalk the smell of pine and damp was thick. The pagodas of the Japanese Tea Garden, with their red lacquered wood and ornate black roofs, were lost to the mist.

Shepard stopped outside a heavy wooden portico. The gates were closed, the calming pathways of the garden locked up.

Jo lowered her voice. 'Alec, how do you neutralize Slick?'

'Acid immersion. It unravels the carbon nanotubes.'

'No other way? Burning? Freezing? Detox? Chemotherapy?'

'X-ray exposure, but only a sustained, high-power burst.' He gave her the briefest glance. 'Carbon nanotubes are resilient things.'

'Resilient machines that can get inside your head and reconfigure your brain.' *Hell*. 'Slick apparently spreads by direct contact with open wounds.'

302

'Yes. Blood-to-blood contact.' He turned his head sharply. 'You examined him?'

The gulp lodged again in her throat. 'Yes. But I avoided touching the lacerations on his arm, and I had no cuts or scratches myself.'

The air felt clammy. She fought a shiver.

Shepard's expression softened. 'You should be fine.'

The shiver sloughed off, and for a second the cold air felt refreshing. She closed her eyes and breathed out. She wanted to smile. Wanted to laugh out loud.

'Thanks.' She did smile, with relief. She breathed in again. 'Can Slick spread in any other ways?'

'Inhalation following an explosion. But of course, in an explosion, it would penetrate any blast wounds via shrapnel.'

'Inhalation puts fire and rescue crews at risk.' A vision of frightening emptiness passed through her mind. An entire street of people whose thoughts would be harvested before they could become memories.

'If it comes to it, hope Slick blows up in somebody's office or car, not outside,' Shepard said.

'How much does it take to cause an explosion?'

'Two ounces would be more than enough.'

Her breath frosted the night. 'Presume Ian got it when he went to Africa. And that he's after you because he no longer has it in his possession.'

'Yes. He must have lost it.'

'Lost it? Or did he forget where it is?'

He turned to her. 'Yes. Damn. Where is it?'

'How would somebody transport it?'

303

'Slick is dispersed in an oily emulsion. It could be liquid.'

'Presume he brought it back from Africa. Would he have checked it in his luggage?'

'He would never have let it out of his sight. Not out of his immediate possession. Never.'

'So where did he get separated from the sample?'

She thought of every place he'd been. South Africa. London. The 747. The airport, the ambulance, the hospital. The city of San Francisco.

'If he had it with him when he boarded the flight from London, he would have kept it on his person or in his carry-on luggage,' she said.

'Without a doubt. If it's . . . oh, Ian.'

'Alec?'

'He doesn't know about proper handling protocols. He's trained in handling people. Not nanoparticles. Christ.'

Jo felt a chill rise through the air. Of course Kanan hadn't handled Slick properly. It seemed self-evident.

'If my conjecture's correct and your man Lesniak stole it from the South African lab – would he have known proper handling protocols?' she said.

'Yes. He's a materials technician. He worked with the stuff.' Shepard stuffed his hands in his pants pockets. 'That doesn't mean he *did* handle it properly. Who knows how he got it out of the lab and transported it.'

'What's scaring you?' Jo said.

'If Ian brought Slick back with him on the plane . . .'

'The cops and the paramedics went through his clothing.

304

The cell phone was all they found.' She thought harder. 'His backpack had a laptop in it, I'm sure. But the cops said they didn't find alcohol or drugs – I didn't get a chance to go through his things.'

Shepard's voice turned weightless, like he had no breath with which to speak. 'Slick is in a liquid suspension. But with current security restrictions, Ian couldn't have brought a large container of liquid into the cabin of the plane. He would have disguised it.' He ran his hand over his forehead again. 'If he put it in any kind of plastic container . . . Slick can corrode it. Break the seal. Leak out.'

'And?' The feeling of alarm rose through her like brackish water. 'Does Slick destabilize ordinary plastics?'

'Yes. And when Slick comes in contact with oxygen, the plastics become volatile. Slick encourages even the most innocuous substances, in the right circumstances, to explode.'

'The hospital will still have his backpack. I'll call.'

In the distance, creeping toward them, came a set of headlights. Jo and Shepard backed against one of the heavy wooden gateposts. The headlights curved along the road. They could hear a quiet motor and the hum of tires on asphalt. Gradually the headlights turned from fuzz to scalpel sharpness.

Through the fog Jo saw a high-profile vehicle pull to the curb and stop. After a few seconds the headlights boomed to high beams.

Shepard exhaled and stepped out from behind the gatepost. 'We're good. That's her.'

'Her? Your right-hand man?'

'Metaphorically. She's my head of finance. Riva Calder.'

Jo put a hand on his arm. 'Hold on. Calder?'

'Riva knows Ian. She can help us find him. Hopefully before he causes a disaster.'

'I met one of your employees today who has only bad things to say about Riva Calder – Ruth Fischer.'

His face soured. 'Ruth Fischer has been fired. Did she critique your moral fiber by analyzing the color of your aura? She's an unreliable judge of character. Forget whatever she told you.'

Jo tried to gauge his face in the fog. She saw annoyance and real worry.

'Riva's the go-to gal in the company,' he said. 'She knows everything and everybody. She'll access Ian's files and records, his contacts, everyplace he's traveled for Chira-Sayf. She can pinpoint where he's hiding. And she'll help keep us away from places and people he's likely to be following.'

'And Ian won't have included Calder in his list of people to follow? He won't be after her?'

'No.'

He said it so imperatively, with a derisive snort, that Jo wondered what lay behind his vehemence. He put a hand against Jo's back and strode with her toward the SUV.

The driver's door opened and a woman got out. 'Alec.'

Shepard waved. 'She's also an old friend of Misty's. She's like family.'

Calder walked around the front of the SUV, shrouded in the fog. Gradually she turned from a silhouette to a

306

three-dimensional woman. Jo halted. The vehicle was a Chevy Tahoe. She saw the woman's chunky boots and white coat. She saw the dried blood on her face.

Shepard sped up. 'Riva. My God, what happened to you?'

Jo saw the wild heat in the woman's eyes. She saw the red imprint of a steam iron on the woman's forehead.

She shouted at Shepard. 'Alec – no!'

The back doors of the Tahoe opened and two men jumped out.

'*Run*,' Jo said.

The men sprinted toward them. Jo broke for the bushes. She got ten feet before Calder threw the steam iron at her, holding on to the end of the cord like she was swinging a battle mace. It hit Jo in the back of the knee. Her leg buckled and she sprawled to the dirt.

Shepard said, 'What the hell?'

Calder dropped onto Jo's back like a hyena. 'Not so much fun when you're the one on the receiving end, is it?'

28

Radio mike in his hand, Officer Frank Liu listened to the dispatcher as she relayed more information about the red Navigator parked by the curb ahead of his patrol car.

'There's a warrant for the arrest of Ian Kanan,' she said. 'He's a suspect in the murder at the marina this morning. He's presumed to be armed and dangerous. Approach with extreme caution.'

Liu scanned the street. The Navigator was empty. Kanan might have dumped it or might still be in the vicinity.

'Officer requests backup,' he said. 'I'm going to patrol the street on foot.'

He put the mike down and got out.

Jo kicked, struggling to knock Calder off her back. Calder pressed a hand to Jo's neck and pushed her into the dirt. Jo tried to scream but could only cough.

Shepard cried, 'Riva, what's going on?'

'Shut up, Alec,' Calder said.

He approached. 'This is Dr Beckett. She's –'

'I know who the hell she is.' Calder pointed at her own face. 'She did this to me.'

Shepard frowned. 'She . . .'

Don't say it, Jo thought. *Just get it. Get it fast, and help me.*

Calder turned to the men. 'Get her up.'

She climbed off Jo's back and the men wrestled Jo to her feet. Jo's ribs and knee throbbed, but she knew she could run. She had to go and take Shepard with her, into the trees and fog. She shook her hair out of her eyes and got a good look at the men who were holding her.

They didn't look like they'd been hired for their grasp of theoretical physics.

One had a shaved head and the well-packed physique of a kielbasa sausage. How the gold chain stayed around his head she didn't know, because his shoulders sloped and he had no neck. His eyes were the temperature of coals on a barbecue grill. The second man was as slight as a whip of licorice but had a grip like a pair of garden shears. He was bug-eyed and jumpy. Jo wondered if he had a thyroid condition. Or a methamphetamine condition. He had dressed for a desperate attempt to impress Snoop Dogg. A blue bandanna hung from the back pocket of his saggy jeans.

They were the men who had broken into her house.

Calder stepped up, sneering, and slapped Jo in the face.

Her cheek stung like wild. The kielbasa's lips retracted with a wet sound and his gums gleamed in the headlights.

Shepard gasped. 'Riva, what are you doing?'

She spun on him. 'Shut *up*.'

He shut up. Jo couldn't tell whether he was dumbfounded or plotting behind the façade of dumbfoundedness.

'Where's Ian?' Calder said.

'I don't know.'

'Don't treat me like your gofer. Where is he?'

'I have no idea. If I did, I'd get him and take him to the hospital.'

In the fizzing headlights, Calder's forehead looked an angry red. The burn from the iron had blistered in the jutting shape of a ship's prow. Her eye was twitching.

'Where's the last sample of Slick?' she said.

'Ian has it.'

'He does not. I asked him in the E.R.'

Jo said, 'In the E.R., Ian was confused.'

'He wouldn't lie to me.'

'He couldn't remember. He may have brought Slick back with him and forgotten entirely.' Jo's face throbbed where Calder had slapped her. She took a chance. 'Let's go to San Francisco General and look for it.'

'Forget it. I searched his luggage.'

'Not all Ian's belongings were in the room when you came.'

'Shut your mouth.'

Calder rubbed the ring on her left hand. It was Misty's – the double dolphins, bound by a sapphire. Eye still twitching, she turned to Shepard. 'You're going to get Slick and turn it over.' She gestured to the men. 'Put them in the Tahoe.'

The kielbasa grabbed Shepard's arm. He and the licorice whip hauled him and Jo to the SUV, shoved them in the back seat, and slammed the doors.

Shepard looked stunned and furious. 'I can't believe this.'

The men walked around to the front of the SUV, lit up like clowns by the headlights, and stood talking to Calder. Shepard pointed at the kielbasa.

'I've seen him before. He applied for the security position at Chira-Sayf.' He still looked flabbergasted. 'Ex-cop or something. Had problems with his background check.'

'Riva apparently saved his résumé,' Jo said. 'You said she knows the Kanans?'

'For fifteen years. She was Misty's sorority sister.' He shook his head. 'Unbelievable.'

'She's in love with Ian, isn't she?' Jo said.

He looked at her sharply, as if thinking, *How did you know?* 'Yes.'

'Ruth Fischer told me Riva's too interested in your brother. And you said Ian would never follow her – like he wants to keep as far from Riva as possible.'

And watching Calder twirl Misty's wedding ring had given Jo a hot kick in the brain.

'Riva impersonated Misty to get inside dope – from me, the police, the hospital – but it's more than that, and it's dangerous,' she said.

The licorice whip walked to the Tahoe and climbed in the front passenger seat. He shut the door, sniffing and squirming beneath his jacket. Calder continued talking to the kielbasa and got on the phone.

On the road in the distance, the headlights of another car appeared like dandelion fuzz. Calder nodded the kielbasa away from the Tahoe. After ten feet they faded into revenants.

Jo was sitting behind the empty driver's seat. She punched the button to lower the window. Nothing happened. The licorice whip turned.

'Childproof lock. Doors won't open from the inside, neither, so don't bother.'

Letting his self-satisfied sneer linger for a moment, he reached behind his back. When he leaned forward Jo saw a tattoo on the back of his neck, in Gothic typeface. VANCE. He took out a pistol.

Jo's stomach coiled. He set the gun on his lap and crossed his arms, pouting at her like he was an extra in a Tupac video. The guy was a dumb criminal, writing his name in 156-point type on his own skin, but that didn't make him any less dangerous.

The dandelion headlights turned into a Toyota Camry and hummed past before vanishing into the mist. Shepard watched the car disappear. Jo sensed anger radiating from him. She saw Calder and the kielbasa, vague in the fog.

Her fear was increasing by the second. Riva was wearing Misty's clothes, her necklace, her wedding ring – and Jo might have taken all that for an elaborate effort at pulling off the impersonation, but Calder continually massaged the ring and clutched the dolphin pendant as if doing so might conjure Ian Kanan by her side. Calder had erased Ian's phone messages to Misty because she 'couldn't take it.' She'd told Jo, '*He's my soul mate*' and blushed about the idea of their sex life. And she had clutched Ian's T-shirt from the laundry basket with the same yearning Jo had seen when Mr Peebles held the Beanie Baby to his chest. Longing, craving, *owning*.

Calder didn't want to play the role of Kanan's wife. She wanted to take the place of his wife.

Jo looked at Shepard and spoke in a murmur. 'This is bad. She's obsessed. She told me, "All I want is Ian."'

Shepard frowned.

'Think about the implications,' she said.

Vance turned again. 'Shut it.'

Jo held Shepard's gaze, hoping he saw it the way she did. Riva wanted Slick. Not as the starter dish for her own lab, and not so she could sell it to Chira-Sayf's commercial rivals. Kidnapping and thuggery weren't the way business was conducted in Silicon Valley.

No, Riva planned to sell Slick on the black market. Murdock, Vance, and the late Ken Meiring were probably her partners, waiting for the product to arrive. And they thought she'd had the delivery lined up. But now she was about to default on the contract. Her big score was turning to sand between her fingers, and Jo doubted these men were the type who would react by deleting her from their Christmas card list.

And Jo realized how the words *Saturday they die* had

come to be written on Kanan's arm. Calder had written them, while she was alone with him in the E.R.

That was the only possible reason Ian Kanan would have taken on this brutal hunt for his own brother. Shepard would never agree to turn Slick loose to the bad guys. He would have to be forced. And the only way they could force Kanan to attack his own brother was by threatening to kill his wife and son.

She swallowed to put some spit in her mouth, so she wouldn't sound as impossibly frightened as she felt. She leaned toward Vance. 'Did she tell Kanan the exchange is tonight? Slick for Seth and Misty?'

'None of your business.'

'She'd better do it. Breaking her word to Kanan will cause you major grief.'

He eyed her as if she were a sorceress for knowing Riva's plans. 'Sit back and keep your mouth shut.'

Jo leaned back. Worry hardened in her chest like a chunk of wood.

Did Riva have any intention of letting Misty Kanan return home to Ian? Would she let Seth go alive? Jo glanced at Shepard. His bearded face was pale and fraught. The look he gave her said *Time's running out.*

Ahead, Riva and the kielbasa had receded to gray outlines in the fog. After twenty feet, the mist took everything.

Jo thought, *If they can disappear into the fog, so can I.*

In the front passenger seat, Vance wiped his nose with the back of his hand. Beside her, Shepard was breathing hard and shifting like a caged bull.

314

He held his left hand by his knees and signaled to her. Two fingers – him and her. One finger – the man in the seat in front of him. Two against one.

Could Shepard see that Vance had a pistol? The gun was two and a half feet from her right hand, resting on Vance's knees. At such close quarters, that made it two against however many bullets were in the magazine.

'What you looking at?' Vance said.

She deliberately held his gaze for a moment. 'Poor odds.'

The engine of the SUV guttered, rumbling awkwardly from being left in park. Vance glanced at the dashboard.

Shepard lunged at him.

He swept his arms around either side of the front seat, grabbed Vance's sweatshirt, and hauled him back against the seat. Whipping his arm around Vance's neck, he locked his hands together and pulled back with all the force behind his bulk, strangling Vance against the headrest.

Vance kicked and clawed at Shepard's arm. Jo thought: *Dynamic.* She brought up her right knee and got the sole of her Doc Marten clear of the center console. The gun was bouncing on Vance's lap.

She kicked him square in the side of the head.

He snapped sideways. Jo heard his teeth click. His hands flailed and grabbed and clawed at Shepard's arm.

'Go,' Shepard shouted.

Go meant over the center console and past Vance. Her heart was thundering. She couldn't stop now. Stop and he'd shoot her. This was as far from uncertainty as a situation could get. Fight or die.

Jo kicked furiously, hysterically – at his head, at his arm, at the pistol. Vance thrashed and made choking sounds.

And got hold of the gun. He brought it up and squeezed the trigger.

The magazine fell out.

For a bizarre second Vance froze, she froze, they stared, and the gun hung useless in midair.

Then Vance swung it, beating the barrel against Shepard's hands. Jo scrambled over the center console into the driver's seat.

She didn't hear the driver's door open. She felt a cold swish of air. Heavy hands grabbed her around the waist and hauled her backward out of the Tahoe. The kielbasa whipped her around and carried her away from the vehicle.

Calder stalked to the door. 'Fuck you, Alec.'

Jo kicked and thrashed, but their chance was blown. Shepard continued fighting Vance. He had lost focus. He didn't remember that Riva had a gun herself.

She raised it and aimed it into the Tahoe.

'Don't!' Jo said.

Calder turned. 'Why not?'

'Because I know how to get hold of Ian.'

It was the only thing she could think to say. Riva shook her head.

'Murdock,' she said, pointing at the kielbasa. 'Hold the little bitch still.'

'So, the sales department plays hardball,' the kielbasa said.

He hugged Jo tight and put a hand beneath her head, holding her jaws closed.

316

Vance threw open his door and cringed from the passenger seat, hand to his neck. Blood was pouring from his nose.

Calder pointed the gun into the Tahoe at Shepard. 'You're going to get the last remaining samples of Slick and give them to me.'

'You're out of luck,' Shepard said.

She jabbed the gun at him. 'Out.'

Vance opened the back door and Shepard climbed from the SUV. Calder shoved him into the shadows.

'I'm the one who made the project possible. I made it happen,' she said.

'Riva, for God's sake –'

'I got the funding. I did the deal to open the Jo'burg lab, so Chira-Sayf could manufacture Slick cheaply and without U.S. government oversight. Me.'

'Is that what this is about? Recognition?' Shepard said.

She slapped him. Hard and poorly aimed, like a furious child. 'Recognition? You promised me money, you bastard, and instead you threw it all down the drain. You're ruining the company and my career. Goddamned backstabber. Right-hand man, my ass. More like I'm shit on your shoe.' She raised the gun. 'Where is it?'

'You're out of luck.'

'No. You are.'

Jo's stomach dropped. *God, don't shoot him –*

Calder scythed the barrel of the gun down Shepard's face. It connected with a dull crack. Shepard went down on the grass like a stunned ox.

Calder turned to Murdock and nodded at Jo. 'Stow Lake's across the road. It should be deep enough.'

She picked up the steam iron from the grass and handed it to him. 'Tie it around her feet.'

Jo screamed, but Murdock's huge hand was clamped to her throat, pressing her jaws shut.

Murdock muscled her toward the curb. Jo dug her feet into the grass. They were going to throw her in the lake. They were going to weight her down with the iron. But the iron weighed only two pounds – it couldn't drag her to the bottom. Tying her feet would tire her, but she had good upper body strength. She could stay above the surface. She'd have to.

Calder walked to the Tahoe, clicked a remote, and popped the tail-gate. 'Tie the cord of the iron to this.'

She began working the spare tire out of the SUV.

29

Calder hoisted the spare tire from the back of the Tahoe. Weighted with a steel inner wheel rim, it bounced heavily when she dropped it. She rolled it toward Vance. Murdock kept his vise grip on Jo, one arm around her chest, the other clamping her neck, and dragged her past Shepard. He lay sprawled on his back, head cocked to one side, moaning.

Jo felt herself unwind like a spring. She kicked, aiming for Murdock's knees with her Doc Martens.

He shied. 'Vance, get her legs.'

Vance grabbed Jo's right leg and the men hauled her into the street, into the fog, with the spare tire rolling alongside them.

How deep was Stow Lake? Probably over her head. If not, the bottom was likely several feet deep with sediment that would suck her down until the water closed above her and the muck swirled around her.

She kicked at Vance with her free leg. She was breathing uncontrollably fast, drawing oxygen.

Vance bent to grab her left foot. She kneed him in the chin.

'Fuck *her*,' he said.

She bucked, unable to get hold of a single thought or a plan beyond *fight*. Through her teeth she said, 'Stop. You need me. I can contact Ian.'

The men lugged her across the road and onto a sloping lawn, carrying her like a rolled-up rug. Murdock was breathing hard and starting to sweat. Vance kicked the spare tire along in front of them.

'I know where the sample of Slick is. It's at San Francisco General Hospital. I can get it. I have access as a physician.'

'Shut up.'

Behind her she heard Calder say to Shepard, 'Sit up. Sit *up*.'

The men tromped across the grass toward the lake. The mist was rising off the water. The tire rolled ahead of them, bouncing on the grass like a puppy ready to play fetch, and gained speed.

Murdock said, 'Get it, Vance, before it goes in the – get it, it's gonna roll in the water . . .'

Vance dropped Jo's legs and pitched after the tire. She twisted in Murdock's grasp. His palm was grimy. She was breathing like she'd run five miles. Vance slid across the lawn, splashed into the water, and grabbed the spare tire. He hauled it back to shore and turned, waiting for her.

She screamed again through clenched jaws. But in the

fog, nobody could see her, much less get to her in time to stop the men.

Gabe knocked on Jo's front door. The lights were on inside the house. Her truck was parked up the street, parking spot *numero tres*, she called it.

He rang the bell and knocked again. 'Jo?'

Eight P.M.; he was positive he'd told her the right time. And positive she wouldn't have forgotten.

Ninety-nine percent certain she wouldn't have forgotten.

Consciously.

And damn it, he was starting to think like a shrink. He tried the knob. The door was locked.

'Quintana?'

At the bottom of the porch steps, Ferd Bismuth stepped into view. His eyes were on the large bunch of gold and white orchids in Gabe's hand. His face was fretful.

Gabe's internal sonar pinged. 'Ferd. What's up?'

'Something's wrong. Jo's sister Tina called me at work and said there was a problem at my house. When I got home, the garage door was up. The homeowners' motorcycle was missing and upstairs, their collectibles are ruined.' He held up a turquoise belly-dancing scarf. 'And I don't even want to know what this was doing on the kitchen floor.'

Gabe banged on the door, hard this time. 'Jo, are you in there?'

No answer. He pulled out his phone.

*   *   *

Officer Frank Liu walked along the sidewalk, one hand on his night-stick, the other loose near his holster. Traffic slurred past. Headlights were turning to fuzz in the fog. He strolled past the stolen red Navigator.

The street was mostly small businesses – an auto parts store, a locksmith, a pawnshop. Most were closed. He glanced across the street. The park was dark. He walked past a sporting goods store. The lights in the front of the store were off, but in the back, behind transom windows, fluorescents were buzzing. Shadows moved around. Somebody was there. Two doors farther down, the lights were also on in a hair salon. He walked to the corner and turned onto the cross street. Down the block, bright signs beckoned people to Burger King and Wendy's.

The unmarked car eased to the curb next to him and the passenger's window came down. 'Officer Liu? Lieutenant Amy Tang.'

Liu got in and shut the door. 'Navigator is parked around the corner and one block up. Street's quiet – mostly small businesses. Everything's shut for the night, but the lights are on in a hair salon and there's activity in the back of a sporting goods store.'

The lieutenant peered out the windshield at traffic. 'Kanan has a head injury that severely affects his memory. I don't know what he can remember, but he's ex-Special Forces. Presume he remembers how to kill people.'

'What do you want to do?' Liu said.

'Lights in the back of a couple businesses, you said?'

She nodded up the street. 'There's an alley halfway up the block. It'll run behind the store. Let's take a stroll.'

Jo felt the mist sink through her clothes and skin as Murdock dragged her toward the lake. The gangsta-flavored licorice stick named Vance was at the shore, holding on to the spare tire.

Jo jammed the heels of her Doc Martens into the grass. 'Kanan's going to call me. I have to be home. He set his cell phone to dial me and if I don't answer, he'll never call back.'

Murdock put his lips against her ear and nuzzled her hair. 'Shut up.'

The panic sank all the way through her. He was enjoying this.

He handed the iron to Vance, who began looping the electrical cord through the inner rim of the wheel.

'We couldn't just take her to the house?' Vance said. 'Do it in the bay when we get the others and –'

Murdock went rigid. 'Shut up.'

'I just –'

'Close your stupid mouth.'

Vance rigged his deadweight. 'All I meant was . . .' He stopped. 'What's that?'

Murdock looked at his shirt. A lively melody was pouring from his pocket. *Coming out of my cage and . . .*

It was the Killers. 'Mr Brightside.' A catchy pop song with mordant lyrics that Tina knew a psychiatrist would appreciate. *And it's all in my head but . . .*

'It's my phone,' Jo said.

323

Murdock stared at his pocket.

'You stole it off my kitchen table when you broke into my house, didn't you?' she said.

Vance straightened up. 'It might be the cops. Throw it in the lake.'

'It might be Kanan. Let me answer,' she said.

The cheery ringtone neared the end of the verse. If it went to voice mail, she was done. Her voice mail recording would be her valedictory speech, her farewell message.

Murdock took it from his pocket and checked the display. '"Gabe."'

Jo felt tears rush toward her eyes. 'He's Kanan's army buddy. Served with him in Afghanistan. Kanan won't call on his own phone – too easy to trace.'

Vance shook his head. 'He's her boyfriend or something. Dump it.'

'For Christ's sake, you want to take the chance?' Jo said. 'Lose your shot at the payoff?'

The ringtone hit the chorus. Murdock shoved the phone into Jo's hands. Then he grabbed her hair, pulled her head back, and put his ear next to hers.

One shot, she thought, and answered. 'Gabe.'

'I'm at your place. We still on for tonight?' he said.

She blinked back her emotions. 'Absolutely. It's now or never. Tell Kanan the exchange is on – the lab sample for his wife and son. These people just need the time and the location.'

Please, Quintana – play along, and get ready to redial the police and triangulate my location from the cell phone signal. The silence stretched.

Vance muttered, 'It's a trick. Throw the phone in the lake.'

Gabe spoke again, his voice measured. 'And if both the sample and the Kanan family are delivered safely, everybody goes away happy.'

'Including me,' Jo said.

Murdock grabbed the phone. 'I want to talk to Kanan. How do you put it on speaker?' He fumbled with the controls and hit the speaker button. 'Put Kanan on.'

A thick silence filled the air. Jo willed Gabe to develop a new voice. She willed her legs to hold her up.

A new voice came on the line. 'This is Kanan. What do you want?'

'For starters, prove it's you,' Murdock said.

Jo's legs weakened. It was Ferd. She felt as though she'd just opened the cockpit door and seen that a stewardess was flying the plane.

'Don't play games with me,' Ferd said. 'We don't have time.'

Murdock snapped his fingers at Vance and jerked a thumb over his shoulder. 'Get Riva and Shepard, quick. They can verify it's him.'

Vance wiped his nose and ran off into the fog to find them.

Murdock said, 'Give me proof, or you don't get the family back. No tickee, no laundry.'

Ferd coughed, hesitating. Jo could barely see straight.

Ferd cleared his throat. 'What kind of proof do you want? The security specs for the Johannesburg lab? Electron microscopy proving that Chira-Sayf accurately

325

predicted the chirality of the carbon nanotubes? Or do you just want me to take the Damascus saber and shove it down your blowhole?'

Murdock breathed heavily.

'Well, jerkwad?' Ferd said.

Jo thought: *Keep the Seven of Jo photo on your computer, Ferd. Make yourself a calendar.* She leaned toward the phone. 'Ian, put Gabe back on.'

Murdock said, 'We don't need to talk to his pal.'

She glanced at him. 'Gabe has to arrange the rendezvous. Ian can't hang on to new information – he has a brain injury. If you talk to him, he'll just forget everything.'

'Yeah?' To the phone, loudly, Murdock said, 'What happened to you, Kanan? And where?'

There was a heavy pause. 'Southern Africa. Monkey virus.'

Murdock looked at Jo. 'That so?'

She shut her eyes and tried to stop her heart from stammer-stepping. 'There's been an outbreak in the Congo. It's transmissible to humans. Go online from my phone – the World Veterinary Association will confirm it.'

Gabe came back on the line. 'Just so we understand – Ian brings the lab sample, you bring Jo and the Kanan family.'

Jo piped in. 'And, Gabe – when Ian transports Slick, make sure he handles it with extreme caution. After this much time, it's likely to be extremely volatile.'

In the distance, she heard voices. Vance was coming back with Calder and Shepard.

'Hold on. I need to confer with my associates,' Murdock said.

'We can't wait while you hold a tea party. We have to get the stuff and bring it to you within the hour,' Gabe said.

'Why?' Murdock said.

'That's how long I figure Kanan and I can stay ahead of the police. You want the stuff, you meet us. Sixty minutes or nothing.'

Jo knew Gabe was cool, but she didn't know he was such a gambler.

'Public place,' Gabe said. 'Open ground. You dig?'

'Fine,' Murdock said. 'You leave the stuff in a locker at –'

'No. Simultaneous exchange. We see Jo and the Kanans, or you get nothing.'

Murdock breathed. 'Someplace where the cops can't blend in with the crowd.'

Gabe paused a beat. 'The Stanford campus.'

The voices approached. Murdock hesitated.

'Top of the quad,' Gabe said. 'It's neutral ground. Wide open for hundreds of yards in all directions. No way for you to ambush us.'

Murdock stared at the fog, looking for Vance and Calder.

'Sixty minutes,' Gabe said. 'Jo, hang in there. And, assholes – they'd all better be in tip-top shape. You get it?'

'Yeah. And so'd the stuff.'

Jo said, 'Get going. I'll talk to you in an hour.'

'See you there.' Gabe cut off the call.

'Shit.' Murdock grabbed the phone, but Gabe was gone. 'If he's lying, you'll pay.'

Gabe turned to Ferd. 'You did good.'

'Did I?'

'*Huevos* like brass bowling balls.' He called directory assistance and told the operator, 'I need the number for the SFPD Northern Station. Connect me.'

Ferd stood beneath the porch light and scratched roughly at his face. 'What do we do now?'

'We get the police to triangulate Jo's location from her cell signal.' Gabe glanced at Ferd. 'Where'd you learn to talk trash to thugs?'

Ferd scratched his arms and chest. 'Dealing with psycho über-geeks at Compurama.'

The operator connected Gabe to the police station. He said, 'I need to speak to Lieutenant Tang about the Kanan investigation. It's an emergency.'

The desk officer said, 'Please hold.'

Ferd took his glasses off. 'What are you going to do about Jo?'

Gabe looked at him. 'I'm going after her. That's what I do. I find people and get them back.'

30

Amy Tang and Officer Frank Liu walked up the sidewalk. The fog was twisting its way between buildings. Tang pointed at the cross street where the stolen red Navigator was parked.

'You take the street. I'll take the alley,' she said. 'Nice and casual. We'll meet at the other end of the block.'

'Yes, ma'am.'

'Don't call me ma'am.'

'Yes, Lieutenant.'

Liu headed around the corner. Tang walked to the alley's entrance. About sixty yards in, light leaked from a window, shining on the water that trickled along the concrete gully in the alley's center. She unbuttoned her black peacoat and popped the snap on her holster.

Silently she walked into the darkness. She smelled wet cardboard and garbage. She scanned doorways and unlit windows. Swung her gaze up to the rooftops.

She heard the hum of a ventilation system coming from a building to her left. The noise of traffic echoed off the walls, dimming with every step she took. She neared the beauty salon. Upstairs, the windows were lit. Shadows crossed the ceiling. She crept along. Forty feet farther on was the window of the sporting goods store. It was frosted glass, crosshatched with reinforcing wire. Beyond it a metal door was painted a peeling red. She walked past.

Inside, a figure moved around.

She kept walking. Two feet past the door, she looked back. The figure inside the window was pacing back and forth. With the frosted glass, it was impossible to tell whether the figure was Kanan. She crossed to the far side of the alley and backed into the shadows, watching.

Her phone vibrated. She grabbed it, backed farther away from the window, and answered in a murmur. 'Tang.'

The desk officer from the station said, 'A Gabe Quintana for you. Says it's an emergency.'

'Put him through.'

The phone clicked. Gabe came on. 'Lieutenant, we have a critical situation. Jo's been taken hostage.'

She stilled almost involuntarily. 'Holy Christ.'

He relayed his conversation with Jo. 'At least two men are involved. I set the rendezvous for an hour from now.'

Across the alley, the figure behind the frosted glass window hoisted something.

'But they'll be on the move and you can track Jo's cell phone signal. They'll –'

'Hang on.'

Tang couldn't tell for certain, but the object in the figure's hands seemed to have the long barrel of a rifle.

'Gabe, I'll call you back. Text me the details of the rendezvous. I'll take point on this and coordinate the response.'

She rattled off her cell number for him and hung up. She pulled back her jacket and took her weapon from the holster. She held it low, came out of the shadows, and crept down the alley.

Vance ran out of the fog toward Jo and Murdock. Thirty feet behind him came Shepard, bleeding and stumbling. Calder was prodding him along with the gun.

Out of breath, Vance said, 'Got them.'

Murdock held up Jo's phone. 'Too late.'

He threw the phone to Vance the way he'd discard a piece of trash. Without hesitating, Vance turned and lobbed it into the lake.

Murdock shouted, 'No –'

They heard the phone splash in the darkness.

'Idiot,' Murdock said.

Vance looked at him with confusion. 'I thought you wanted me to dump it.' He pointed at Jo. 'I told you, you can't trust her.'

Shoving Shepard ahead of her, Calder ran up to them. 'You're damned right you can't trust her.'

Shepard looked dazed and ill. His forehead was split where Calder had pistol-whipped him. A dark flow of blood covered his face and spattered his dress shirt.

He needed help. But one step at a time. Continuing to breathe was a victory. Getting out of the park would be the next.

Jo turned to Calder. 'Kanan's going to be at the rendezvous in fifty-nine minutes. You really want to hang around here?'

Jo understood why Gabe had chosen the Stanford campus. He knew it, from the air – the 129th had choppered patients to Stanford Medical Center more than once. He also knew that she could navigate it blindfolded and half-asleep. And, despite what he'd told Murdock, the top of the quad offered at least a dozen places for him to set an ambush.

But she could think of only one reason why Murdock had agreed to rendezvous so far down the Peninsula, and so soon: Misty and Seth were in that area. Gabe had just narrowed the search radius considerably.

Murdock nodded at Jo. 'She has to come with us. Price of the deal.'

Calder frowned. 'Fine.' She turned to Shepard. 'Last chance. You want to hand over the sample?'

'I can't.'

Calder pointed toward the road. 'Put Beckett in the Tahoe.'

Jo's spirits soared. Murdock locked his hand around her arm and began leading her up the grassy slope. Calder put up a hand.

'Wait. As insurance, to make sure she's telling the truth, we'll leave a marker here.'

'What do you mean?' Murdock said.

She kicked the spare tire. 'Tie it to Alec's feet. The bridge to the island's over that way. He should be strong enough to tread water for an hour. If we get Slick, we'll tell Ian where to find his brother.'

'No,' Shepard said. 'Wait. You can't –'

The gun swiveled and stopped between his eyes. 'Don't tell me what I can't do. You're not putting anything over on me ever again, cocksucker.'

She hawked out the word as if it had been festering in her throat for months. Shepard recoiled.

'*Move*,' she barked.

Vance pushed the tire along the shoreline and Calder prodded Shepard in the back with the pistol. They faded into the night.

Murdock hauled Jo up the lawn toward the Tahoe. From the depths of the fog she heard Shepard's voice.

'Don't. For God's sake, Riva, please –'

Then she heard a splash.

Gabe wrote a text message to Tang as he ran down Jo's front steps.

Ferd trundled alongside him, scratching his arms and neck. 'Are we going to Stanford?'

'I am.' Gabe looked him up and down. 'You're going to the urgent care center. You're covered with hives.'

'What?' Ferd held his hands out. 'God almighty.'

'It's not Congolese monkey virus. It's the aftermath of courage.'

'I don't want to leave you to handle this –'

'I know what Jo looks like. I can recognize Shepard

333

and Kanan, if it comes to it. Somebody needs to point them out to the cops on the scene.' He slapped Ferd on the back. 'Get to the doctor. Take it from a paramedic.'

He sent the text to Tang and sprinted toward his 4Runner.

Ian Kanan blinked the fatigue from his eyes. He was standing beside a desk in the stockroom of a sporting goods store. A mess of Post-it notes and photos was spread across the desk. So were three pistols, a Kbar knife, an ankle sheath, and several boxes of custom ammunition. He was holding a night-scoped rifle in his hands.

It was a Remington, tactical model, one of the most popular American bolt-action rifles. It had an adjustable trigger and detachable box magazine. It would do.

He set it on the desk and saw a photo from his wallet – him with Misty and Seth at the beach, Whiskey with a Frisbee in his mouth. He ran his fingers over the snapshot.

'Please, understand,' he murmured.

Outside the frosted glass window, he saw movement in the alley. It was just a shift in the darkness, but he stepped to the door and put his back against it.

The darkness outside flowed as insubstantially as smoke, but he saw movement. Somebody was there.

The door was dead-bolted and a note was taped to it. *Gone to Wendy's. Back in 10. STAY HERE.*

Quietly he unlocked the dead bolt and opened the door. He stepped into the mist in the alley.

Ten feet ahead was a figure in a black peacoat. The light from the frosted window shone on the barrel of the pistol held close to the figure's leg.

One of *them*.

He wasn't silent, but with traffic passing by on the street, he didn't have to be. He took three running steps, bringing his fists up. The figure was tiny, with spiky black hair – turning to look at the window, and turning faster, hearing him approach. He saw an East Asian profile.

It was a woman. He chopped his fists down. He measured the blow, hitting her on either side of the neck, at the base where it met her shoulders. She went lights-out and collapsed like a ventriloquist's dummy into his arms.

He threw her over his shoulder and carried her inside.

31

'Wake up.'

Kanan tapped the woman's cheek again, harder this time. Her head swerved up and knocked back against the support pole. Her eyes struggled open.

She focused. Saw him squatting in front of her, balanced on the balls of his feet, forearms resting on his knees. She jerked and found that her hands were bound behind the beam with athletic tape. Her mouth was gagged with a small rubber ball.

'When I remove the gag you can scream until you turn purple, but nobody can hear you down here,' he said.

She glared at him, then looked around. The basement of the sporting goods store was cold and bare.

He pushed on her cheeks and popped the rubber ball out of her mouth. She turned her head and spit at the floor.

'I'm a police officer, and you're under arrest,' she said.

'I found your badge, Lieutenant.' He nodded off to

one side. Her badge, weapon, and phone were laid out on the concrete floor. 'Apologies for disrupting your evening. But before I let you head back to the station, we need to talk. How did you find me?'

'Detective work. Ian, we know your family has been taken hostage. We're working to rescue them.'

His skin went hot. 'You – rescue them?'

'We know they were taken to force you to obtain nanotech samples from Chira-Sayf. We want to help. Let me go. We don't have any time.'

'Where are they?' he said.

'I don't know. The kidnappers are going to bring them to a rendezvous. But we have to arrange for law enforcement to get there first. Cut this tape.'

She looked like a wild hedgehog – tiny, tough, and ready to bite him.

'Are you alone?' he said.

She jerked against the athletic tape. 'Of course not. Ian, you can't dick around. Your family is running out of time.'

He didn't know whether she was lying. He picked up her phone.

One new message.

'What's this?' he said.

Exchange: Kanan's wife and son for Slick. Stanford quad. Top of oval 9 pm.

He stood up, his heart racing. He read it again.

'Who sent you this?' he said.

'Ian, I have to alert the authorities. We don't have a second to waste.'

He held out the phone so she could see the display. 'Who sent this?'

Upstairs, somebody pounded on the back door to the store. He glanced up the stairs.

'Please, Ian. This is your chance to get your family back. You have to –'

He grabbed her nose, pinched it, and pushed her mouth open. He stuffed the rubber ball back inside to gag her. Hanging on to the phone, he ran up the stairs into a stockroom. She mumbled through the gag, trying to get him to come back. He closed the basement door and the sound disappeared.

He paused, looking around. He saw sports equipment, plus a scoped rifle and handguns on a desk. Somebody banged on the door again.

'Boss, let me in.'

Relief and excitement filled him. He set the phone on the desk, crossed to the door, and flipped the dead bolt. When he opened the door, light fell on the welcome sight of Nico Diaz's face.

'Good to see you, Nico.'

Diaz came in, shivering. 'Lock the door.'

Kanan threw the lock. He nodded at the weapons on the desk. 'Yours?'

'Yours.' He handed Kanan a bulging sack from Wendy's. 'This too. Eat up. You need the fuel.'

As soon as he opened the sack, voracious hunger overcame Kanan. How long had it been since he'd eaten? He pulled out a cheeseburger and dug into it. He'd never tasted anything so good.

Diaz caught his eye. 'Boss, I've been thinking. You may have left the sample at San Francisco General. We should check.'

'Good. Yeah – Diaz, absolutely.'

He had no memory of going by San Francisco General Hospital, but if Diaz said so, he believed him.

He tore into the burger. Dumped out the sack on the desk, grabbed a fistful of fries, and stuffed them in his mouth. He didn't think he'd ever felt so hungry. He pulled the lid off the large coffee Diaz had brought and drank it down.

'Thanks, bro,' he said. 'Need this.'

Diaz looked at the desk. 'Where'd this phone come from?'

Kanan looked at the phone. 'No idea.' He patted his jean jacket. 'Pocket, maybe.'

Diaz picked it up and read the display. 'Christ. Boss – look at this.'

Kanan wiped his hands and took it. His vision sparked white. 'Jesus.'

He and Diaz looked at each other.

Diaz grabbed the rifle. 'My truck's out back.'

Kanan strapped on the ankle sheath and slid the Kbar into it. He finished the coffee and jammed two pistols in the small of his back.

'Let's go get them,' he said.

The Chevy Tahoe rolled along Palm Drive, heading toward the center of the Stanford campus. Jo gazed out the window. Palm trees picket-fenced either side of the road. Beyond the palms, the landscape darkened to chaparral and live oaks and towering eucalyptus groves. The huge campus had originally been a farm, and much of it was still undeveloped.

'Speed limit,' Calder said.

Vance lifted his foot from the accelerator. He was a restless driver and tended to speed up without provocation. They'd gotten from San Francisco to campus in record time.

Traffic on Palm Drive was light. It was a Friday night. Most students were elsewhere on campus – studying, partying, losing their virginity, inventing fabulous new tiny technologies that could blow up the world or the inside of your head. Nobody was paying attention to a single blue Chevy Tahoe heading for the quad.

In the front passenger seat, Calder couldn't stop sighing and squirming, peering at other vehicles and turning to check on Jo over her shoulder. In the blue light of the phone display, Calder's fashion-forward face was drawn. Her nerves and eagerness were getting the better of her. She finger-combed her sleek hair and put on fresh lipstick.

Too bad Ian Kanan would notice the nasty Sta-Prest burn on her forehead, Jo thought.

Vance stopped at the intersection with Campus Drive. Half a mile ahead, through the palms, was the quad. Its sandstone arches were warmly lit. The mosaic on the façade of Memorial Church glimmered under spotlights.

Riva punched in a phone number and put the phone to her ear. She raised a finger, demanding silence.

Murdock, sitting across the back seat from Jo, simply looked her way and adjusted the barrel of the gun to point in her general vicinity.

'New schedule,' Riva said. 'The bidding is now open.'

She was silent for a minute, listening. Without saying good-bye, she put the phone away.

'Slow down,' she said to Vance. 'Campuses are speed traps. The cops are always out to get you.' She turned on him. 'I said slow down, you stupid son of a bitch.'

Shrugging away from her like a scolded dog, Vance slowed again. They drove toward the end of Palm Drive. The trees gave way and the vista opened wide. The road split into a loop that curved up to the front steps of the quad and circled back. The landscaped lawns and flower beds in the oval's center were black in the night.

Vance crept along. There were parking slots along either curb, mostly empty this time of night. Just off the right edge of the road, a curtain of oaks camouflaged academic buildings.

'Slow,' Calder said, leaning forward and peering out. 'This is reconnaissance.'

Jo glanced at her watch. Nineteen minutes to the rendezvous. She thought of Alec Shepard, struggling to stay above the surface of Stow Lake. She thought of his strength ebbing with every breath.

'Please, call in a rescue for Alec. You can't possibly count on him treading water for an hour with just his arms. Find a pay phone and do it anonymously.'

'No,' Calder said.

Jo clenched and unclenched her hands. She saw no

sign of the police. And they were running out of time to pick up Misty and Seth.

'Make a loop,' Calder said.

'What's Ian going to do when he sees you?' Jo said.

She threw out the question as bait. Information, especially information that included unconscious self-revelation, was power. She needed to learn as much as she could. Calder could not rationally imagine that she was about to win Kanan's love. But when it came to Kanan, Calder was not rational.

'What's Kanan going to do?' she said again.

'What makes you think he's even going to see me here?' Calder said.

'He doesn't know you're behind all this, does he?' Jo said.

'You're a nosy bitch, you know?'

'You say that like it's a bad thing.'

Calder snorted. Jo decided it was as much respect as she'd ever get from the woman.

'How did you do it?' Jo said. 'Did Murdock and Vance deliver the threat to him? Text, video, digital photos of Seth and Misty held prisoner? Did you talk to him at all before he took off to get Slick back and bring it to you?'

'None of your business.'

Calder had stayed in the background, Jo thought. Delivered the threats via proxy.

'Who are these guys, anyway? Your cousins? Your puppets?' Jo said.

No reply.

'Who was Ken Meiring?' Jo said.

342

Around her, they all squirmed.

'How do you plan to conduct the exchange? I need to know, so I don't blow it or scare you into doing something rash. When Ian arrives with the stuff, do we just get out?'

'You get to climb out when Murdock has the stuff in his hands. You get out when I see Ian with my own eyes. None of this bullshit about talking to this Gabe person.'

Murdock eyed her. 'Why did you even have Gabe's first name in your phone?'

'I'm a psychiatrist. I have to protect the privacy of clients and contacts. I never put people's last names in my phone. Ever.'

And she thought, *wow, that was a good idea.* She should implement it.

'When are we going to get Misty and Seth?' she said.

'Don't worry about them.'

'Isn't it time to pick them up?'

'No.' Calder glanced at her. 'I'm renegotiating the terms of the exchange. If you and the folks on the phone were telling the truth, and Ian's really bringing Slick to the rendezvous, we'll go get them. If not . . .'

Oh, shit. Dread coursed through her. Calder had no intention of bringing the Kanans here.

Calder made a looping motion with her hand. 'Go around again.' She glanced back at Jo. 'You can't trust anybody.'

Officer Frank Liu circled the block and returned to the lieutenant's unmarked car. She wasn't there. She hadn't been at their meeting point or at his patrol car, either. He walked back to the alley. There was no sign of her. He got on the radio.

The clerk behind the lost and found counter handed Kanan his backpack. 'Here you go, sir.'

'Thanks.'

He signed for it, slung it over his shoulder, and turned to go. Nico Diaz was standing there.

He smiled. Diaz – large as life, out of the blue, and just the man he needed.

He clapped a hand on Diaz's shoulder and together they strode along a hallway.

'Glad the pack was here all along,' Diaz said. 'You obviously got separated from your belongings when you came in. Good thing nobody else took it home with them.'

Diaz was cool as an ice rink, but Kanan's nerves ginned up. They crossed a quiet lobby and walked out a set of automatic doors. It was a foggy night. Kanan looked back. The sign over the doors said SAN FRANCISCO GENERAL HOSPITAL.

Diaz had parked his pickup truck in the ten-minute zone. The dashboard was cluttered with cheap plastic toys and religious memorabilia. They got in and Diaz fired up the engine.

'What are we doing?' Kanan said.

Diaz reached over and pulled up Kanan's sleeve, showing him the words *Saturday they die*.

'We're going to the meet. Is the stuff in the backpack?' he said.

344

Kanan unzipped the pack and took out the battery from his laptop computer.

'That's it?' Diaz said.

To casual examination, the battery looked completely normal. But in Zambia, he had disassembled it and junked the actual battery. Then he had filled the plastic battery casing with the gel from the flask, screwed its two halves back together, and sealed the joints with superglue. The plastic felt warm in his hands, and there was some softening near the seal. It was holding but wouldn't forever.

But the kidnappers could deal with that. Fuck 'em.

'You cool with what we're doing?' Diaz said.

Kanan looked at him. 'This memory thing freaking you out?'

'I'm past it now.'

'I don't matter, Nico. Only Seth and Misty.'

Diaz gave him a slow nod. He glanced at the battery. 'That stuff's valuable?'

'It's my family's freedom. It's priceless.' Kanan pointed at the road. 'Drive.'

32

Gabe crept through the trees toward the Oval, treading carefully so his feet wouldn't crunch on fallen oak leaves. He had a crowbar in his hand. He had a folded Buck knife in his back pocket. His 4Runner was parked two hundred yards back, on a cross road, aimed straight at Palm Drive so that he could cut off any vehicles leaving the Oval. In the chilly air, the quad was gloriously lit. The road was quiet. The lawn and garden in the center of the Oval were dark and empty, except for a lone cyclist pedaling furiously toward the chemistry department.

Keeping to the trees, he ran counterclockwise up the right side of the Oval, in the same direction as the one-way traffic around the loop. He stopped at a vantage point seventy yards before the pickup zone, which was near the plaza and steps leading to the quad at the top of the loop. That put him behind anybody who stopped there. And people who stopped in the pickup zone would likely be busy looking ahead or toward the quad, not watching their backs. He ducked behind the trunk of a live oak and blended into the shifting shadows.

He checked the time. The illuminated blue dial of his diver's watch read eight forty-five P.M.

Jo knew Stanford inside and out. After four years at the medical school, she could probably scramble from one side of campus to the other via rooftops and steam tunnels. He knew the campus too, but not nearly as well. And he didn't know what kind of vehicle the hostage-takers were driving.

He checked his phone. No messages from Tang. No sign of any law enforcement. He didn't know whether the lieutenant was sending the Stanford Police, Palo Alto P.D., Santa Clara County SWAT, or a combination of the three.

But he wanted her to send somebody, and now. She had told him she was taking point on this, and he believed her – but he also wanted confirmation. He called her cell phone and got voice mail.

He clicked off and redialed the SFPD Northern Station. He kept his voice to a murmur.

'This is Gabe Quintana from the One twenty-ninth Rescue Wing at Moffet Field. I phoned forty-five minutes ago with an emergency message for Lieutenant Tang. I'm calling to verify that she's coordinating the police response to a hostage situation on the Stanford campus.'

The desk officer's voice perked up. 'Let me check, Mr Quintana.'

He saw an SUV cruise up Palm Drive and begin to

347

circle the Oval. It was a blue Chevy Tahoe, driving slowly. He put the phone against his leg and peered around the tree trunk.

Diaz rolled along University Avenue at exactly twenty-five miles per hour. The cops in genteel, leafy Palo Alto didn't have much crime to clean up, so they came down on speeders like a bunch of gorillas. Ahead, University became Palm Drive and cut through the campus to the central quad.

The GPS on the dashboard showed the road layout of the rendezvous site: Palm Drive aimed straight for the quad, but instead of dead-ending, it turned into a one-way loop, an oval about a quarter-mile long. At the top of the oval, closest to the quad, was the rendezvous. At the base of the oval was a cross road where they might be able to set an ambush.

'Let's scout it,' Kanan said.

'Fucking-A,' Diaz said.

Kanan took the computer battery from his backpack and the Kbar from the ankle sheath. He carefully stuck the tip of the knife between the two screwed-down, super-glued halves of the battery casing. As delicately as possible, he pushed the blade through the seal a few millimeters. Most of the way.

Diaz eyed him with calm interest. 'Boss?'

'A researcher at Chira-Sayf told me what this stuff can do.' He pulled out the knife and examined the seal. 'Slick will eventually eat through any petrochemical-based container. Give it a week and it'll pretty much destroy it.'

'So?'

'So now that I've slit it, Slick will also eat through this seal, in about an hour if I'm right. Then it'll get a taste of oxygen. At that point it gets dangerous.' He looked at Diaz. 'Don't worry, I'm just priming it. When it's time, I'll puncture it the rest of the way.'

'What happens when it breaks through the seal?' Diaz said.

'Within a few minutes, whoever's holding it will get a nasty surprise. Though they won't live long enough to appreciate it.' He slapped some athletic tape across the stab mark in the seal. 'It's not as reliable as C-4, but it's as effective.'

Diaz watched him put the container back in the back-pack. 'So we need to make sure Seth and Misty are out of range by then.'

'I won't puncture the seal unless they're safe.'

Diaz drove with one hand and set a timer on his watch for fifty minutes in the future. 'Yours too.'

Kanan turned the outer ring on his diver's watch. 'Set.'

Calder held up a hand, gesturing for Vance to slow the Tahoe. 'Okay, nice and easy. Take us to the top of the Oval and pull over in the pickup zone.'

They cruised again around the right side of the Oval, past parked cars, oaks, and bushes, past the darkened buildings of the chemistry and computer science depart-ments, toward the golden stone of the quad and the Technicolor gleam of the mosaic on the façade of Memorial Church. Jo felt like she had a clamp around her chest.

Calder peered out the windshield. 'Now it's time for proof. We see if you're lying, or whether Ian's coming.'

Jo wasn't about to tell her he wasn't.

Or that the police were.

She dug her fingernails into her palms. It was nine P.M. In one minute, maybe two, Calder and her goons would be in custody and she would be free. Rescue would be on its way to Alec Shepard.

If things went right.

She was terrified. Riva had a gun. Murdock had a gun. Alec was drowning. Time was running out, and she was in a vehicle with an armed paranoid in the front seat, an angry narcissist at the wheel, and a psychopath beside her.

And the police needed to take them alive and get them to confess where Seth and Misty were being held.

Jo breathed, trying to make sure her voice didn't shake. 'Ian doesn't know you're behind it, Riva. He'll come after this vehicle without hesitation.'

'No,' Calder said. 'If he sees me he'll think I'm innocent.'

'Wrong. If he sees this SUV, and if he sees me get hurt, he's going to think just one thing. *Bad guys inside.* He'll take this vehicle apart. You don't think he has weapons by now? He told us on the phone at the lake – he sees his family *and* me, unhurt.'

None of them replied. The Tahoe crept around the Oval. Calder took out her phone again and read an incoming message. She was as fidgety as a cat facing a bath. She was trying to set something up, Jo thought – a sale, or a getaway.

With her impersonation of Misty blown, she was working on borrowed time.

'Ian will never simply walk up to a darkened vehicle and drop his lab sample on the sidewalk. He's going to need proof of life. At a minimum, he'll need to see me,' Jo said.

Murdock said, 'Don't try to pull anything on us. You're trying to save your own skin.'

'Of course I am.'

'You think we're about to let you out of this vehicle?'

'We'll all live longer, and you'll get away, if you let me convince Ian this is an intermediate stop, not a double-cross. He and his buddy Gabe and their armory will be out there.'

And the cops. Please, Christ.

They neared the top of the Oval. Riva put up a hand. 'Okay, this is it. Get ready.'

Gabe checked his watch again. Five minutes had passed. Sticking to the shadows, he crept closer to the pickup zone at the top of the Oval.

He was still on hold with the San Francisco P.D. Still saw no sign of any police presence. It made him feel goosey.

When the police took down the kidnappers, he didn't want to get in the way. And he didn't want to be mistaken for an unfriendly. But he also didn't want the entire campus P.D. showing up with lights blazing – not yet.

He pressed himself to the trunk of a tree, crouched down, and listened. His breath frosted the air. Around

351

him, the night was quiet. In the far distance, beyond the brightly lit arches of the quad, a group of people strolled between buildings. Their laughter echoed off the sandstone walls.

He heard a vehicle coming up the Oval from Palm Drive. It wasn't the police. It was a blue Chevy Tahoe. Maybe the same blue Tahoe that had circled the Oval a few minutes earlier. Its headlights swept across the trees and brushed past the oak he was hiding behind.

They kept going and illuminated the silhouette of a man in the shadows ten yards from him.

They glinted off the pistol in the man's hand.

Gabe's reflexes went into overdrive. The man was standing still and alert, watching the Tahoe circle the Oval. He was trying to see who was driving. And whether to shoot.

The man was dressed in civvies, not uniform, not tactical gear. He had dreadlocks. That big mother of a weapon in his hand didn't look like departmental issue.

He wasn't a cop. That left bad guy, wild card, or crazy mofo – armed and lying in wait.

Gabe charged at him. Two steps, three, sweeping the crowbar low, and he wasn't quiet, didn't even try to be, just covered the ground between them. Fast.

The man was aiming the gun at the car.

Gabe had the drop on him. He hooked the crowbar around the man's ankle and yanked back; at the same time he smashed the guy with the flat of his palm just above the small of his back.

The man flipped forward and went down hard. The

gun was knocked from his hand. Gabe shoved a foot down on his back, grabbed his collar, and pulled up, arching the man's back so he could barely breathe, much less maneuver.

'Show me a badge or I'll kill you,' he said.

The man struggled, stunned, beneath him. He was a little springy black guy with an infuriated look in his eyes. He reached for the gun. Gabe struck his arm with the crowbar and hauled up harder on his collar.

'I'm Gabe Quintana. I'm the one who called the cops about the rendezvous. Show me a badge or I break your neck. In four. Three. Two.'

'I'm Nico Diaz,' the guy choked out. 'I'm with Kanan. We're – fuck, man, we're here to get his family back.'

The Tahoe stopped in the pickup zone at the top of the Oval. Vance put it in park and left the engine running.

Calder turned to Jo. 'Okay, this is it. Murdock, let her out.'

'What? She'll run.'

'Not if we point our guns at her head.'

'She'll still run.'

Calder sighed in annoyance. 'Tie her up. The back of the car's full of camping and fishing gear. Find something. And one of your plastic zip ties.'

Murdock kneeled on the seat and leaned into the far back of the Tahoe. He grunted and came back with a coil of white nylon rope.

'Put your hands up,' he said to Jo.

She raised them in the air. He looped the rope around

her waist. Then he took a heavy-duty zip tie from his jacket pocket, the kind police officers used for plastic handcuffs. He ran it around both halves of the rope and pulled it tight, cinching the rope around the outside of her sweater. He reached down and tied the ends of the rope to the support struts for the front passenger seat.

'Set,' he said.

Calder looked at Jo. 'Get out. Stand on the sidewalk in front of the car. Hands up. Call Ian's name and let's see what happens.'

Murdock opened his door. Anxiously Jo climbed over him and hopped out into the cold night air. The engine was rumbling. Exhaust poured from the pipe and swirled around her feet.

Murdock stared at her through the door. 'If you try to run, one of two things will happen. You'll be shot, or Vance will put the car in gear and we'll drag you to death.'

Slowly, hands up, Jo walked toward the front of the vehicle. Murdock played out the rope like a fishing line. She was the lure.

Pinned to the ground beneath Gabe's foot, the man called Diaz spoke through gritted teeth. 'You called the cops?'

'Kanan's here?' Gabe said. 'How the hell –'

'Text message. It listed the time and place for the rendezvous.'

A chill came over Gabe as fast as if he'd jumped into a freezing ocean. He said, '"Exchange: Kanan's wife and son for Slick. Stanford quad. Top of oval 9 pm."'

'Yes.'

'Goddamn it. God –' He stepped off the man's back. 'Who'd you get the message from?'

Diaz sat up, hand to his throat. 'The sarge found it on . . . fuck, man, who did you send the message to?'

Gabe pulled out his phone. He had three messages from the SFPD. He called the station. 'It's Quintana.'

He looked past the trees. The Tahoe had stopped at the top of the Oval.

'Mr Quintana, yes – we've been trying to reach you. Lieutenant Tang isn't responding and we have no report of a hostage situation at Stanford.'

The chill washed over him like a wave. He glanced at Diaz. 'The cops never got the message. Goddamn it.'

He hung up and dialed 911.

Diaz got to his feet. He pointed at the top of the Oval. 'Look.'

In front of the Tahoe they saw Jo standing in the glare of the headlights, hands up.

'We have to do something. Fast. Come on,' Gabe said. 'Where's Kanan?'

'In my truck, parked back in the brush on the far side of the Oval.'

'Can you call him?'

'No, his phone is set to activate at ten P.M. What are you planning to do?'

'Improvise. We have to get the cops. And we can't let that Tahoe drive away before they show up.'

They took off through the shadows, circling toward the Tahoe. The emergency operator came on the line.

'What is the nature of your emergency?'

'I'm at the top of the Oval at Stanford and I hear a woman screaming for help. Somebody's being attacked,' Gabe said. 'Hurry.'

He ran with Diaz through the trees.

Jo stood in front of the rumbling Tahoe, hands in the air, rope leading from her waist to the open back door of the vehicle. In the blaring headlights, her shadow stretched across the ground before her like a black scarecrow. The vast campus, the inviting warm stone of the quad, the gleaming promise of the church, the landscaped flower beds in the center of the Oval all dimmed. Her world seemed circumscribed by the glare of the headlights.

'Ian,' she called.

She heard no response. Of course she didn't.

She took a breath. 'Ian Kanan.'

Ahead in the distance, from the night, a man appeared. He gradually separated from the heavy darkness of the live oaks and walked toward her. She held still, fighting to see beyond the lights.

From the Tahoe, Calder said, 'Is it him? Ian?'

'What does he look like?' Vance said.

The man emerged from the shadows and walked toward her. His pace was measured. He spread his arms at his sides, showing he wasn't carrying a weapon. He grew clearer. He walked with the self-possession of a big cat.

It was Gabe.

356

Her heart ramped up. What was he doing? Where were the cops?

Oh, shit. There were no cops.

Gabe walked to the edge of the headlights, thirty yards from her, and stopped. Her teeth were chattering. She felt a swell of fear for him. She bit down to keep from breaking into tears.

It was Sophie's dad, coming unarmed to rescue her. If she hadn't loved him before, in that moment she did.

'It's time. Let's do it,' he said.

Jo heard a window going down in the Tahoe. Calder hissed at her. 'Ask him where Ian is.'

'Where's Ian?' Jo said.

'He'll exchange the stuff when he sees Seth and Misty,' Gabe said.

His eyes shone in the headlights. He held her gaze. He had to have a plan. Had to be trying to tell her something.

'Seth and Misty aren't here,' Jo said.

'Tell him why,' Calder said.

'Riva Calder's in the Tahoe. She wants to see Kanan, and the sample of Slick, before she brings his family to an exchange.'

'If Ian doesn't show himself and prove he has the stuff, the deal is off,' Calder said.

'Did you hear that?' Jo said.

'I heard.' Gabe shielded his eyes from the headlights and called out to the people in the Tahoe. 'Let's swap. Me for Dr Beckett. I'll take you to Kanan.'

'What the hell is this?' Calder said.

Vance shouted, 'He's lying.'

'Let Jo go,' Gabe said. 'Take me instead.'

In the distance, floating like a treble note on the air, Jo heard sirens. Vance shouted, 'Hear that?'

Murdock said, 'It's a trap.'

Gabe didn't move. 'This is your last chance. If you drive off now, you'll never get what you're after. Let Jo go and I'll take you to Kanan.'

Vance shouted, 'He's a liar. Let's go.'

The sirens grew louder. Jo held on to Gabe's shining gaze. Vance yelled, 'Come on,' and hit the high beams.

Behind Gabe, she saw a man walking out of the trees. He moved like a gunslinger, swift and sure. The headlights caught the gun barrel that glinted in his hand. The headlights caught his eyes. They shone like blue ice.

33

Ian Kanan advanced toward Gabe from behind, raising the gun in his hand. And the night turned to havoc.

Jo threw her hands out. 'No. Gabe, look out.'

Gabe spun. Kanan shouted, 'Where are they?'

Through the trees, past the bottom of the Oval on Palm Drive, the flashing lights of a police car spun toward them. Vance jammed the Tahoe into drive.

'The cops,' he yelled. 'The cops –'

Kanan swung the barrel of the gun toward Jo.

From the dark by the Tahoe, a man said, 'Boss, *no*.'

The siren and flashing lights swelled. Calder began shouting. Vance let loose with a stream of incomprehensible drivel, spun the wheel, and jammed his foot on the pedal.

'Fuck, no,' Jo said.

She leaped out of the headlights, grabbed the rope around her waist, and threw herself toward the Tahoe.

Vance swerved right and bounced onto the curb. Calder shouted at him to stop. He braked, looked toward the cops and back at the man with the gun charging at him through the high beams. And at the dark eyes of the man with dreadlocks who appeared from nowhere outside the driver's window. He jammed the pedal down again.

And ran into a mailbox.

'Drive, no – stop, Christ, what are you doing?' Calder yelled.

The back passenger door was still open, swinging like a fan. Vance put the Tahoe in reverse. He spun the wheels backing up, and the door flew wide.

Jo held on to the rope. She had to get loose or get back in the vehicle.

Gabe came running. In his right hand he held a huge, sharp Buck knife. He launched himself at Jo, left hand out to grab the rope.

Vance put the Tahoe in drive. Calder yelled, 'What the hell are you doing? That's Ian!'

Gabe grabbed the rope and swung the knife at it. The vehicle bounced off the curb and accelerated, yanking the rope from Gabe's hand before he could cut it. Jo grabbed the swinging door and held on to it, running alongside the Tahoe. Gabe ran behind her. The Tahoe accelerated. It swerved to the opposite side of the road and sideswiped a parked car.

Through the door Jo saw Murdock. His face was suffused with anger.

'Stop the car,' he said.

'Like hell,' Vance wailed.

360

The police car reached the Oval and began driving toward them.

'Stop,' Murdock said. 'Let her go.'

But Vance kept his foot down. Murdock seemed to be the only one who realized that if they didn't cut Jo loose, they'd have to stop in a minute to detach her broken body from under the wheels. She held on to the door, feet windmilling and beginning to drag. She couldn't keep up. Vance bounced across the road and over the opposite curb into the grass in the center of the Oval. Jo clung to the swinging door and jumped, getting her feet back in the vehicle. Five feet away, Gabe sprinted alongside the Tahoe.

'They're everywhere,' Vance shouted.

Jo knew that if she fell, she'd die under the wheels or be dragged to death. If Gabe held on to her and fell, they might both die.

He got his fingers on the door. But he couldn't possibly keep up with the acceleration of the SUV. And at this speed, he couldn't cut her loose.

Hanging on to the door, swinging wildly, Jo looked at him. 'Get away. Get help. Alec – Stow Lake, he's in the water by the bridge.'

The Tahoe swerved and roared off the grass, bounced onto the road again.

Gabe hung on to the frame with one hand. 'Jo . . .'

'Gabe,' she said.

The Tahoe roared forward with a huge surge of power. Gabe's hand was ripped loose from the door frame. She watched him recede from her view.

He kept running, eyes on her. He pointed. To her, to himself. *Gonna get you.*

Then he veered in another direction, sprinting flat-out for the trees.

Jo pulled herself into the chaotic interior of the vehicle. Vance was hunched over the wheel, racing like a frightened weasel for the exit from campus. Calder was hanging out the passenger window, looking back for Kanan.

'Did you see him?' Vance said. 'This black dude popped up right outside my window with a fucking *gun*, the piece was bigger than my head, and – shit, did you see him, he was like the Predator or something, all dreadlocks and crazy eyes and *fuck* that gun was big. Did you see him?'

Murdock sat fuming in the back seat, breathing hard, looking like he knew he was screwed.

Jo pulled the door closed. Murdock glared at her.

Do not cry, she thought. *Do not cover your mouth or indicate that you have a single weakness.*

She breathed. 'Now do you goddamn believe me?'

Vance roared down Palm Drive. A cop car raced past them in the opposite direction. Ahead, more flashing lights spun off the treetops. A stop sign flashed past, and horns smeared in her ears. Vance swerved around the corner onto Campus Drive and headed toward the football stadium, seeking an exit from the campus. Jo held tight to the door handle.

'Without me, you'll never get away with this. It's me plus Misty and Seth – alive and safe – or you don't get Slick,' she said. 'I'm your ticket.'

*   *   *

362

Gabe ran toward the cross road where he'd parked the 4Runner. The blue Tahoe receded down Palm Drive. All the air in his lungs seemed to go with it. A police car blew past him heading the other way, toward the top of the Oval, lights and siren bawling. He looked back.

So that was Ian Kanan.

Gabe held on to the Buck knife. He saw Diaz running across the Oval. Off to the right, a pickup truck flipped on its headlights.

'Boss,' Diaz yelled. 'Wait.'

The pickup spun its tires and gunned down an access road through the trees after the fleeing Tahoe. Diaz watched it streak away.

He threw his hands in the air. Then he hollered at Gabe, pointing at the pickup. 'Quintana, that's Kanan, in my truck. We have to catch him.'

The pickup roared down Palm Drive, taillights scoping to red pinpricks. Diaz angled across the grass, caught up with Gabe, and ran alongside him, breathing hard.

'Kanan doesn't know he left you here, does he?' Gabe said.

'No. He can't hold anything in his head for more than about five minutes. He only knows he has to get his family back.'

Diaz's pickup turned right onto Campus Drive and disappeared from view.

'Can you call him?' Gabe said.

'Not yet, and even if I could, he wouldn't listen to me. He won't break off chasing the Tahoe. He doesn't want to lose sight of the kidnappers.'

'That's smart.'

'That's his only chance. If he gets distracted, even for a split second, facts just fade out of his head. It's like the great beyond collects all his thoughts and burns them.'

They cut through a copse of live oaks. Gabe took out his keys and flicked the alarm remote. Ahead, the parking lights of the 4Runner flashed.

'I thought I had the hostage-takers,' Diaz said. 'But the driver of the Tahoe saw me in the wing mirror and hit the gas.'

'When does Kanan's phone activate?' Gabe said.

'Ten P.M., but we can't wait till then. If he loses sight of the Tahoe for too long, he'll forget he ever saw it. He'll keep driving and we'll never find him again.'

'He found you once.'

'That's not the point now.'

'What is? What's the rush?' Gabe said.

'He's got a container that's volatile. The nano lab sample, it's in his computer battery. He armed it. It won't stay stable even for forty-five minutes.'

'And then?'

'It'll explode.'

Gabe felt anger and futility well inside him. 'And Kanan won't dispose of it?'

'By now he doesn't even remember that he has it. He can't possibly know it's a ticking bomb.'

They jumped into the 4Runner and Gabe peeled out.

'Does Kanan know who's behind this whole thing?' Gabe said.

'No.'

'Jo said somebody named Riva Calder was in the Tahoe.'

'Calder? She's an exec at Chira-Sayf.' Diaz braced himself against the door. 'She arranged for Misty and Seth to get snatched?'

'Looks like it.'

'She knows them. She was Misty's sorority sister. This is bad, man. She spooks Ian.'

'How?'

'She has a major thing for him. Always has.'

Gabe tossed him a look, disbelieving. 'That's crazy-making trouble for Kanan and for his wife.'

'You ain't kidding.'

Racing down Palm Drive, Gabe steered with one hand and dialed 911 with the other.

'Calder will probably have Ian's cell phone number,' Diaz said.

'So when his phone goes live at ten P.M., she'll contact him and pretend to play innocent.'

He swept out from under the trees, turned onto Campus Drive, and sped in the direction of the football stadium. The stadium's field lights bleached the night above them, turning the trees black and white.

'Nine-one-one emergency,' said the dispatcher.

'A woman's been abducted. Men hauled her into a Chevy Tahoe and took off.' He gave the dispatcher a fast rundown of what was going on and turned to Diaz. 'What's your truck's license number?'

Diaz held silent.

'What is it?' Gabe said.

'It's not exactly loaded with Girl Scout cookies, you dig?'

Gabe's anger heated. 'It's a rolling bomb. What's the plate number?'

'Shit.' Shoulders slumping, Diaz rattled it off.

Gabe repeated it to the dispatcher. 'And send police and fire units to Stow Lake in Golden Gate Park. Man named Alec Shepard's in trouble near the bridge.'

He hung up, ran the stop sign, turned left onto Galvez Street, fishtailed, and straightened out. He floored it toward the exit from campus.

'Kanan was messing around with the nano sample in the pickup, while you were with him?' Gabe said.

Diaz shot him a look. 'Why?'

Gabe exhaled.

He raced past huge stands of eucalyptus trees. The stadium loomed on the right, a hulking mother ship that filled the night with deathly white light. Several hundred yards ahead, at the intersection with El Camino Real, he saw the exit from campus. They heard a siren. In his rearview mirror Gabe saw flashing lights.

'Don't stop,' Diaz said.

The cop's headlights inflated in the mirror. Behind them, another black-and-white zoomed into view and joined the pursuit.

'If you stop, it all goes to shit,' Diaz said. 'The thing is to get Misty and Seth back.'

'Without blowing anybody up.' Gabe looked at him. 'Or is that your plan?'

'Nobody you should worry about.'

366

The sirens drew nearer. At the intersection of Galvez and El Camino, the light was green.

'The doc – you care about her?' Diaz said.

The flashing lights grew brighter in the mirror.

'Like crazy,' Gabe said.

They raced toward the intersection. Gabe tightened his hands on the wheel. Then he stomped on the brake, pulled the handbrake, and spun the wheel hard over. The back end of the 4Runner squealed around in a half circle and lurched to a stop.

'Hell you doing?' Diaz said.

'Get out,' Gabe said.

Directly in front of him the police cars laid rubber, red and blue lights wheeling, and braked to a halt.

'They'll arrest you,' Diaz said.

'Playing Lone Ranger won't cut it here. We need a helo searching for Kanan. We need to get you to hazmat decontamination, because you may have been exposed to Slick.' He opened his door. 'And I need the whole state of California hunting for Jo.'

He climbed out with his hands locked behind his head and dropped to his knees in the road.

34

Misty Kanan wiped the sweat from her eyes. Her fingers were numb and bleeding. The paperclip-size screwdriver she'd fashioned from underwiring was bent and cracked, succumbing to metal fatigue. Inside the bedroom it was full dark. She had removed three of the four screws that held the locking mechanism and knob in the door. She felt the lock assembly again for the fourth screw, fumbling like a woman trying to read Braille.

She ran a finger over the screw, found the groove, and inserted her handmade screwdriver. Her fingers slipped. The screwdriver popped from her fingers. She heard it *ping* against the floor and bounce into the darkness.

'Damn it.'

She sank against the door. Her shoulders jerked.

Whiskey padded to her side and nuzzled her shoulder. He whimpered. The sound was feeble. He was hungry and dehydrated.

She balled her fists and pressed them against her eyes. Screw these bastards, who'd let a dog die of thirst.

'It's okay, boy. I'll get us out of here.'

She got to her knees and felt along the floor.

Whatever's at hand, use it, Ian would say. 'A fork, a pen, a light-bulb. Nothing's ever just what it seems.'

'I'm just a school nurse,' she'd told him.

'No, you're not. Not "just." Not ever.' And he took her hand. 'You can't be. That's not the way the world works. And I won't always be here.'

Be prepared. The man was half-psychic, half-Boy Scout, all threat repulsion.

The bedroom was cold, but she was damned if she'd put on any of Riva's expensive clothing. Do that, and she'd be begging people to take one look at her – her long sleek hair and the figure she worked her ass off to keep – and say, sadly, 'Yes, that was Riva Calder.'

Looking like Riva had been great, back when they were in college. Borrowing Riva's I.D. so she could buy beer or fool dumb bouncers at local clubs – that had felt harmless. But now the idea of swapping identities didn't seem so festive.

Karma was remorseless.

She pressed her fingers along the floor in the dark. Her hand brushed the wire. She wiped her fingers on her blouse, picked up the screwdriver, and felt for the slot in the screw. Whiskey whimpered again and pushed his nose under her chin.

'It's okay, boy. I'm going to get you home to a big bowl of water. And a T-bone steak. And Seth.'

Saying her son's name, her voice cracked. She turned the screwdriver and felt the screw loosen. *Yes.* She spun the screwdriver and the screw fell out. She got to her knees and worked the doorknob loose.

Now came the tricky part. She bent the wire into a hook and began probing the innards of the lock. Ian had taught her this one, too.

She whispered to Whiskey, 'Finally, I get the profits of his misspent youth.'

And Riva had sniped that if she married Ian, the sex would be hot but there wouldn't be any profit-sharing. Soldiers made no money.

With a click, the lock turned. Half-disbelieving, she stood and opened the door.

It creaked open to reveal the living room. The lights were off and it was dark outside. She held in the doorway, listening for the men. The house was quiet. It smelled rank. Outside the living room window she saw overflowing trash cans and weeds.

And headlights.

They swept the yard and a vehicle pulled into the driveway.

'Oh, shit. Whiskey!'

She ran across the living room toward the cramped and filthy kitchen. Whiskey bolted by her, passed the kitchen, and ran down a hallway where the rest of the bedrooms were located. He rounded a corner, claws ticking on the parquet floor.

She clapped her hands. 'Whiskey.'

The kitchen door was locked. Outside, the vehicle

idled on the driveway. She heard the garage door going up.

She heard Whiskey put his paws on another door. He barked and began scratching wildly. She whistled, flipped the dead bolt, and threw open the back door. Whiskey barked, pawing the door down the hall like he was going to dig a hole through it. She heard a thumping sound. She froze.

She wasn't alone. Somebody else was locked up in the house.

From the back seat of the Tahoe, Jo watched the garage door drone up. They were at a run-down ranch house in Mountain View, not far from San Antonio Road. The lawn was ratty with weeds. Trash cans overflowed next to the porch.

The garage door opened. The Tahoe's headlights shone on a single chair inside, sitting on the concrete under a bare lightbulb. Murdock hopped out and jogged into the garage to move it.

'Nice place you've got here, Riva,' Jo said. 'Didn't know you were a slumlord.'

Calder shot her a look, half *Who told you?* and half *What are you trying to pull?* Sarcasm, Jo thought, had its uses.

Vance eased the SUV inside the garage and the door began cranking down again. He opened the door to get out.

'Wait,' Calder said. 'Swap seats with Beckett. She's going to drive.'

For a second, it seemed that Vance would protest. But even he appeared to know his driving skills at the rendezvous had been piss poor.

'Tie her to the steering wheel,' Calder said.

Vance opened the back door. Jo climbed out and got in the driver's seat. Her ribs were throbbing and it hurt to draw a deep breath.

Calder got back on the phone. 'Larry, it's Riva Calder. Yes, confirming the flight. There'll be three passengers.'

Murdock went to a cabinet in the garage and came back with a handful of plastic zip ties. He leaned into the SUV and cinched Jo's hands to the wheel. Then he nodded to Vance and the two of them headed into the house.

The SFPD officer walked toward Stow Lake. The beam of his flashlight swung back and forth but found only fog. The bridge remained elusive.

Then, from the soup, he heard splashing. He sped up. A weak cry curled through the mist. He broke into a jog and saw the brickwork of the bridge.

The splashing continued, feebly, like a piece of cloth lapping against the side of a bathtub. He ran onto the bridge and aimed his flashlight at the lake.

He saw an arm batting at the water and a waxlike face sinking beneath the surface.

'Hang on, buddy,' he said. 'I'm coming.'

Misty froze with her hand on the kitchen door. Down the hall, Whiskey was moaning like his foot was caught in a wolf trap.

She felt like she'd grabbed a live wire. Whiskey would only go mad like that for one person.

She heard the SUV pull into the garage. The engine revved and the garage door began going down. Whiskey let out a mournful howl.

She ran down the hall and around the corner. Whiskey was pawing a bedroom door. She flipped the lock and threw the door wide.

'Seth,' she said.

Her son lay on the floor, hands and feet bound by plastic handcuffs. He'd been kicking the door. A sock was stuffed in his mouth, tied with a rag. His eyes popped.

The windows were boarded up. And if Seth couldn't run, they were trapped.

Misty dashed back to the kitchen, grabbed a pair of scissors from the knife rack, and raced down the hall again. She heard the door from the garage bang open. She hurried inside and shut the bedroom door.

Whiskey was wagging his tail, licking Seth in the face and moaning so wildly he was practically singing. Misty knelt and began sawing at the plastic handcuffs that bound Seth's feet. They were zip ties, thick and incredibly tough. Hands shaking, she snapped them clean through.

'Get up,' she said breathlessly.

Seth scrambled to his feet. Out in the house, men's voices filled the living room. Keys dropped on a table.

Across the house, a man said, 'Hey, the door. Murdock, the knob on the wife's door is . . .'

Misty grabbed Seth, ran out the door and straight

373

across the hall into another bedroom. This one had curtains on the window, not boards. She jammed the scissors in the back pocket of her cords. She climbed on the bed, opened the window, and punched the screen out.

'Climb. I'll boost you,' she whispered.

Seth couldn't talk with the gag. He looked terrified. But he nodded to her and mumbled what she knew meant 'You first.'

'No. Go, Seth.'

He turned to the window and put his bound hands on the sill. The door burst open behind them.

Misty spun. Murdock filled the doorway. A pistol hung in his hand.

'Seth, go!' she shouted.

But she saw Seth's face, and her heart sank. Scared though he was, he looked torn, desperate not leave her there.

Murdock let his wet gums and little teeth show. 'Seth, don't go.'

Vance appeared in the doorway, out of breath. He adjusted his do-rag. 'Shit, the kid got his feet loose again.'

Misty felt a watery moment of panic. Then, slowly, she pulled her blouse down over the back pocket of her cords.

Murdock grabbed Whiskey by the collar and simply put the barrel of the gun against the dog's head. His eyes looked like a shark's, blank and avid. His mouth stretched. Revoltingly, he was smiling.

'Your mom will be second,' he said to Seth. 'And you couldn't live with your mom getting killed all because of you.'

Seth climbed down.

Jo twisted her wrists against the plastic handcuffs, trying to loosen them. She couldn't. Her hands were bound to the steering wheel at ten and two, like she was about to have a lesson at the Dick Cheney School of Driving and Interrogation. In the passenger seat, Calder tucked her hair behind her ear and sent another text message. Her tough-cookie face looked strained and drawn. And blistered.

The door from the house opened. Murdock and Vance came through, leading a woman and a boy in his early teens. Vance kicked at a big shaggy dog. The dog jumped and circled, head low, ears pulled back. It immediately put itself between the kidnappers and the boy.

What kind of people took a boy *and* his dog?

Seth's mouth was gagged and his hands bound with plastic handcuffs. He blinked as though the garage light hurt his eyes. His T-shirt hung loose from coat-hanger shoulders. He had a head of coppery hair and his father's ice-chip eyes. He looked at his mom.

Misty Kanan was Riva Calder's doppelganger. She was compact and lithe. Her caramel hair fell across her face in a sheet. Though she looked wrung out, her eyes were large, dark, and brimming with alarm. She seemed to have a kind of crazed determination. Her gaze swept the garage. She was looking for an out, for an escape.

And she was keeping herself between the kidnappers and her son.

Murdock shoved her toward the Tahoe. She shrugged him away with disgust on her face, as if his hand were slimy. Then she registered that the SUV was her own car. She saw Calder in the passenger seat, face bruised and burned.

Compassion and worry overtook her. 'Oh, no.'

Misty's gaze turned to Jo. Her eyes seemed to record Jo's every feature, for a police Identi-Kit drawing or for future revenge. A Beanie Baby could have read the message in her stare. *Die, bitch.*

Murdock pulled Misty toward the back of the Tahoe. Seth deliberately bumped into him, throwing a shoulder like a power forward driving downcourt. He was trying to get Murdock away from his mom. Jo felt a hitch in her breathing. Brave, reckless boy.

Murdock shoved him. Misty practically spit at him. 'Don't touch my son.'

Brave, reckless woman.

The men opened the tailgate of the Tahoe and bundled the Kanans inside. Vance kicked the dog away from the vehicle and swung the gun at him.

Seth screamed behind his gag and lunged at Vance.

'No, Seth.' Misty scrambled out of the Tahoe.

Murdock picked her up and tossed her back in. He shook his head at Vance. 'Don't, dumbshit. No gunfire.'

Vance was holding the gun sideways, like he was a character in a movie. He lowered it reluctantly. Then he kicked viciously at the dog. Jo heard his boot connect with the dog's ribs. The dog yelped and ducked away from him, stumbling toward the corner of the garage.

'Stop being stupid,' Murdock said. 'Put the gun on the wife.'

Sullenly Vance stood outside the tailgate while Murdock grabbed rags and zip ties from the garage cabinet.

Misty turned toward Calder. 'Riva, are you okay? God, what's going on? How did they get you . . .' Her gaze bounced toward Jo. She saw the plastic handcuffs tying Jo's hands to the wheel. 'What . . . Riva, what's –'

'Shut up, Misty.'

Misty's eyes went electric with shock. Murdock brought the zip ties and rags, grabbed her, gagged her and bound her hands, and shut the tailgate.

The men got in the back seat. Vance turned his gun on the Kanans. Calder leaned across Jo and hit the power lock, making sure neither the doors nor the tailgate could be opened from the inside. She pushed the remote and the garage door began whining up. She put the Tahoe in reverse.

'Drive,' she said.

Jo backed down the driveway into the street. She looked at the dashboard clock. It was ten P.M.

'Where are we going?' Jo said.

Calder got on her phone again. She put the SUV in drive. 'San Jose airport.'

377

35

Ian Kanan turned right. His gaze swept the street.

He was in a residential neighborhood. It was full dark. The road signs were in English. His heart was pounding.

Had he just outrun somebody? He checked the road behind him. Nobody was on his tail. Was he chasing somebody? He checked the road ahead. Nobody was making tracks.

A rosary swung from the rearview mirror. On the dashboard was a plastic bobblehead Jesus, wearing shades and holding a soccer ball. Whose truck was this?

He pulled down the sun visor and found the registration. *Nikita Khrushchev Diaz*.

His confidence swelled. Nico had his six. If he was driving Diaz's truck, it meant he'd been gaining ground. But Diaz wasn't here, and neither was his family.

Notes on the dashboard. *Slick's in the backpack*. CHECK YOUR WATCH.

He looked. It was ten o'clock.

The outer band was set for a few minutes ahead. Why?

He unzipped his backpack and saw the battery. He checked the truck. Behind the seats he had an armory. God bless Nikita Khrushchev and all bobblehead messiahs.

A vibration in his pocket startled him. His phone had just gone active.

That had to mean he was on some kind of countdown. The watchband setting might mean he was due to go to an appointment.

He took the phone from his pocket expectantly. Then he saw the display. 'Shit.'

Riva Calder.

She was the last person he wanted to talk to. Dealing with her at work was enough of a strain. During a crisis, especially one he didn't understand – no way.

The phone vibrated again. He hesitated.

Why would she be calling him so late in the evening? Even Riva never phoned him at ten P.M. She was too smart for that. She couldn't hide the crazy lust she harbored for him, but she knew that calling him late on a Friday night would be self-defeating.

Except she was doing it. He didn't get it – but he didn't get Riva. A successful, bright, driven woman, she had a thing for him like an abscess, some wound that went deep and dirty. Some lesion that she liked to dig at, like popping stitches before they could ever heal. She was lucky Misty hadn't taken a baseball bat to her head years back. But Riva never called him after hours on his cell. She knew he wouldn't answer.

Unless something was wrong. He answered. 'Riva?'

'Ian, thank God. I've been trying to get you for hours.'

Her voice came out in a rush, like she'd been running. 'Your house was broken into. Misty and Seth are missing.'

A thought brushed past his mind, thin as smoke. A woman was involved with the kidnapping . . . it was just the shadow of something that had been snatched and stolen. And like that, the thought swirled away again.

'I know. I'm going to get them back,' he said.

'Ian, oh, Christ – we're running out of time.'

'What do you mean?'

'The kidnappers couldn't reach you. Have you had your phone off?'

'Who did they contact?' he said.

'Chira-Sayf. They tried to get Alec and when they couldn't, they sent a crazy message through the switchboard. Security called me.'

He sat up straighter. 'What message?'

'Meet them at ten fifteen.'

'Where?'

'San Jose. Half a mile north of eight-eighty on Coleman Avenue, west of the airport.'

'Did they say anything about my family?'

'"The Kanans will be arriving home from their trip. Pick them up there. And bring the luggage." Ian, did they mean a ransom?'

'Wait.' He grabbed a Sharpie. On the back of his left hand, in big letters, he scrawled, *10:15 p.m. SJC. GO.* He dropped the pen in the center console. 'On my way.'

'Ian, what's –'

He hung up, dropped the phone on the passenger seat, and jammed *Coleman Avenue* into the GPS. A smooth female voice filled the car, sounding as if she had all the time in the world.

'In one hundred yards, turn right.'

A route appeared on the screen, an arrow leading him to his family. He put the truck in gear.

Jo sat behind the wheel of the idling Tahoe, parked in an empty office parking lot just off the 101 in San Jose. Through the windshield she saw Calder hang up her phone. Calder ran across the parking lot and jumped back in the Tahoe.

She put the SUV in drive for Jo. 'Go.'

Calder's cheeks were flushed, her pupils dilated. She looked like she'd just gotten a jolt of sugar. From watching the woman on the phone, and seeing her rub the dolphin necklace, Jo guessed she'd been talking to the intoxicant called Ian Kanan.

Jo pulled back onto the freeway and continued south through San Jose. She couldn't honk, couldn't put down the window and yell at other drivers. She could speed or wreck the Tahoe but knew that if she started swerving, Murdock would turn somebody's face into an exit wound. She stayed in her lane and drove at the speed limit, rolling toward the San Jose airport under the yellow glow of sodium street-lights. In the far back of the SUV, fixed under the barrel of Vance's pistol, Seth and Misty held still.

Two minutes later, Jo saw the airport. The perimeter

381

fence practically abutted the freeway. The end of a runway lay just on the other side of it. Despite everything, she felt a burst of optimism. Heading to the airport had to mean Riva was planning a getaway. And an airport was as stupid a place to kill hostages as Jo could conceive of.

'Take the exit,' Murdock said.

With her wrists cuffed to the steering wheel she couldn't signal. Calder hit the blinker.

Heart drumming, she pulled off the freeway. In the distance she could see the airport terminals, the control tower, and a jet rolling down the runway. She prepared to turn right.

'Go left,' Calder said.

Jo looked at her sharply. 'What? Where are we going?'

'Drive.'

Instead of turning toward the terminals, they went south on Airport Boulevard, around the perimeter fence at the south end of the runways. They passed bristling electronic masts. On her right, a chain-link fence offered glimpses of the tarmac. The runways were black gashes brightened with Christmas-tree lighting. Jo drove past a long, gleaming jet blast deflector. A 737 screamed overhead, lights glaring, engines at high pitch, and touched down.

Ahead, on the far side of the airfield, the private aviation terminals were brightly lit. A phalanx of corporate jets and charter aircraft gleamed under brilliant hangar lights.

Riva made a phone call. 'We'll be there in ten minutes. Be ready to go.'

This was not good. This was, in fact, very bad.

Kanan slowed the pickup and swung around the off-ramp. He scanned the road ahead and turned onto Coleman Avenue, west of the airport. Mineta San Jose International Airport – *International* meant that plenty of airliners lifted off from there and winged away to Mexico, South America, Canada, as well as the U.S. Midwest and East Coast.

He could see over the perimeter fence and across the runways. Jets were lined up at the commercial terminals, hooked to Jetways and fuel hoses like piglets suckling at the teats of a sow. The airfield was a dark expanse between the airliners on the east side of the airport and the private terminals on the west. The runway and taxiway lights shone vividly. Red, yellow, green. He saw them with prism clarity, so clearly that he thought he could pinpoint their exact frequency on the electro-magnetic spectrum.

The thing in his head, the memory eater, was bizarre. It was chopping out most of his world, scooping away his experiences like a combine, collecting all information before he could store it as memory. But this thing wasn't only about recall. It wasn't simply collecting. It was firing inside his head. He felt, when he slowed his breathing and concentrated, that he'd been rewired. He felt like his brain went to eleven.

He could use that to get his family back.

The voice of the GPS purred at him. 'You have reached your destination.'

She had no idea.

'Keep it slow,' Calder said.

At ten fifteen on a Friday night, Coleman Avenue was quiet. It was a major road, but the business parks and warehouses along the road were dark, chilly, and empty. To the west were railroad tracks and, beyond them, Santa Clara University. All the activity was east, beyond a block of industrial parks and aviation businesses, at the airport.

'Turn right,' Calder said.

Jo turned from Coleman onto a side road and headed through a business park toward the airfield. The buildings, the ubiquitous white concrete and blue glass architecture of Silicon Valley, were shut for the weekend. The road ran east for eighty yards, made a left turn, and ran north-south between Coleman and the airport runways. It was absolutely deserted. Jo passed more bristling microwave and radar towers and the entrance to the airport traffic control center.

'Slow down,' Calder said.

Jo slowed the Tahoe to a crawl. At a corner, Calder held up her hand.

'Stop. Pull over.'

Jo pulled to the curb. On the lawn of an office complex, eucalyptus and pines stood cold in the night. To her left, the cross road offered a clear view back toward Coleman. She could see streetlights and, very occasionally, a passing car.

To her right, the cross road narrowed to an access drive. It ended after seventy yards at a gate with a swing arm. Beyond were the private aviation terminals.

There was no guard at the gate, only a card-reading machine and a one-by-four piece of plywood painted black and white. Jo reminded herself yet again that airport security was a game. It was played to placate the flying public and keep security personnel employed and feeding their massive authority complex.

In the sky above, the landing lights of an airliner blared and turbines whined. A jet crossed the runway threshold, flared, and touched down. As it streaked past its thrust reversers howled.

On the airfield apron, parked at varying angles, tail in, tail out, edge on – like a flock of gulls that had circled and landed all askew – were white corporate jets. They were mostly locked up, windows dark. But one jet wasn't tucked in for the night. It was large, with a T-tail and two engines at the back. The door was open and the stairs were down. Inside the lights were aglow. She saw a man walk up the aisle, pass the door, and go into the cockpit.

She wondered if the same crew that had flown Alec Shepard in from Montreal that morning was prepping Chira-Sayf's jet for its flight tonight.

Riva planned to get Slick from Ian Kanan and then fly away. And the only way she could get Slick was by showing Kanan that his wife and son were alive. Jo clutched tight to that thought.

But why exchange them here, instead of at the Valley Fair Mall ten minutes down the freeway? Did Riva plan to put Jo and the Kanans on the plane and fly them someplace where they'd never be seen again – such as the Pacific Ocean?

But that would never work. The pilot would never agree to it. The idea was crazy.

Crazy, however, seemed to be Riva Calder's business plan.

'Cut the lights,' Calder said.

Jo looked at her. 'How?'

Chagrined, Calder reached over and turned off the Tahoe's headlights. Jo sat, hands growing numb from the plastic handcuffs, and watched the pilots moving around inside Chira-Sayf's corporate jet.

Next to her, Calder shifted and her energy swelled. She was looking past Jo out the driver's window, back toward Coleman Avenue.

A truck was stopped at the curb there, lights blazing.

'That's him,' Calder said.

She opened the door and got out. Leaned back in and looked into the back seat. 'I'll call you with instructions.'

Murdock leaned forward. 'Give me your field pass.'

'I'll bring it back.'

She shut the door and jogged across the street. Keeping to the shadows, she headed for the distant truck.

'What do I do now?' Jo said.

Murdock shifted and exhaled. 'You wait.'

Kanan kept the truck idling at the curb and surveilled the area. Traffic on Coleman Avenue was sporadic. Three hundred eighty-five meters to the east, an American Airlines

757 taxied into takeoff position. Two hundred forty-five meters north, in the parking lot of a commercial building, two parked cars sat cold and empty.

A tap on the passenger window startled him.

He turned, and anger washed over him. Then confusion. 'Riva?'

He unlocked the door. She jumped in the cab.

'What happened to you?' he said.

She touched a hand to the blistered red burn mark on her forehead. 'Accident.'

She was breathing fast and her pupils were dilated. She leaned too close and put a hand on his arm.

'This is it.' Her hand was hot. 'I'm scared.'

'It?'

Confusion clouded her face. 'Yes – Ian, I called you. What –'

'The exchange?'

'Yes, of course. I don't –'

'What did the kidnappers say? Just tell me. We get Misty and Seth back, and then I'll explain everything.'

'I don't – Ian, please . . .'

He pulled his arm away from her. 'I don't think we have any time left. What do I need to do?'

She lowered her hand to her lap but kept looking at him like he was a drug, a hit of crack she wanted.

A look of hurt and self-restraint came over her. She got out her phone. 'We tell them we're here.'

Jo was wound like a countersunk screw. The zip ties cut into her wrists. The SUV idled like a disgruntled bear.

387

Murdock's phone rang. He put it to his ear, listened, and said, 'Got it.'

He climbed over the center console, slid his sausage body into the front passenger seat, and pointed ahead. 'Drive up to the next block and cut back over to Coleman.' He put the SUV in gear. 'Slow and steady, chickie.'

She drove slowly up the side street.

Chaos was the world's great leveler. It entered lives with neither forethought nor purpose and cut like a scythe through the dreams and plans of everybody it touched. For years she had convinced herself that this truth must be acknowledged. And now that chaos was here, hell if she was going to accept it.

She knew she couldn't control the chaos. But she could try to control what happened to her and the Kanan family. She could try to get them all out of this.

She glanced in the rearview mirror. She saw Misty's eyes staring back, deeply frightened. And determined.

The red digital clock on the dashboard read 10:17. She drove up a block, turned left, crossed through another darkened business park, and turned left again onto the broad sweep of Coleman Avenue.

'Pull over,' Murdock said.

She stopped at the curb facing south. 'The stuff that Kanan's going to exchange is extremely volatile. Nobody should be around it. And especially not at an airport.'

'Shut it,' Murdock said.

Vance said, 'What if she's telling the truth?'

'I said, shut it. All of you.' Murdock straightened and stared out the windshield. 'Here we go.'

388

Several hundred yards down the road, parked facing them on the other side, was the pickup truck. It sat, headlights bright, idling.

Kanan peered up Coleman Avenue. An SUV had turned this way from a side street and pulled to the curb several hundred meters away. It looked like a Chira-Sayf corporate SUV, one of those brawny vehicles his brother loved and trusted.

He forced his eyes to focus. He forced his mind to concentrate. He forced his heart to still.

The SUV was a blue Chevy Tahoe. Misty's Tahoe. It held his family.

Hold on to that, he told himself. He was seconds away. He could almost touch them, almost feel Misty in his arms, hear Seth calling his name. They were real, they were there, they were coming home. *Hold on to it*.

Riva rustled through his backpack. 'Where is it?'

'The computer battery.'

She took it out, weighed it in her hand. And she smiled. It looked like joy. Like victory.

'Ian,' she said.

He looked at her.

'What did the kidnappers tell you before you went to Africa?' she said.

'That I had till Saturday to get the sample of Slick for them, or my family wouldn't survive.'

'Do you know what day it is?' she said.

He searched, found nothing but blank space. 'No.'

She leaned toward him an inch. 'It's Sunday.'

'What?'

She took a pen from her pocket, a fat black Sharpie, and pulled off the cap.

His pulse soared. 'What are you talking about? If it's Sunday, and I didn't turn Slick over . . .'

She took his arm and pushed his sleeve up. Words were written on his forearm.

Christ. His heart thundered. Riva pressed the Sharpie to his skin and began to write.

The thunder filled his head like water roaring over falls. Those words . . . it wasn't . . . no . . .

He grabbed the pen from Riva and jerked his arm away. He looked again at the Tahoe parked at the curb up the road. It held his family. *Hold on to that thought*.

Wrong, Riva was wrong, *this* was wrong.

A pimped-out Honda rushed past, low-profile tires and mag wheels shining, hip-hop bass booming from the speakers. The smell of the ink was sharp and intoxicating and cleared his head.

He was behind the wheel of a truck. He had a pen in his hand. Words were written on his flesh.

'Ian,' someone said.

He turned his head. Riva Calder was in the passenger seat of Nico Diaz's tricked-out pickup.

'I'm so sorry,' she said.

He looked at his arm. His world crashed down around him.

Saturday they died.

36

Jo watched out the windshield. Her heart was hammering.

Down Coleman Avenue, the pickup truck idled at the curb, headlights glaring. Murdock hung up the phone.

'Riva's all set. Hang on. We do this and everybody goes home. Five minutes.'

But the other car didn't move. Jo's stomach twisted tighter.

All set. That meant Kanan had to have Slick with him.

Jo tried to put it together. Kanan didn't know that Calder was behind everything. She had, until tonight, managed to stay in the background. If he was willing to sit in the pickup talking to her, he must think she was an innocent colleague, helping him out of a desperate situation.

Calder knew her plan was near ruin. Unless she was in denial or remarkably stupid, she would see only one option left: to flee. And she wasn't stupid. She was ruthless. She was going to run. And she wouldn't run without Slick.

And she would want as clean a getaway as possible. Her accomplices, Murdock and Vance, were not top-shelf conspirators. They struck Jo as opportunists and cowards. They didn't strike her as men who would stay silent and go down for Riva Calder. If the police caught them, they would flip for a deal.

Riva had to know that. So what was she going to do about it?

'Oh, my God,' she said.

Calder planned to climb aboard Chira-Sayf's company plane and fly to freedom. She wanted to take two things with her. And those were not Sausage and Scrambled Eggs, mouth-breathing in the Tahoe with Jo. They were Slick and Ian Kanan.

In the pickup truck down the road, Calder had them both.

Her magic getaway carpet was loaded with Jet A and waiting on the far side of the airport perimeter fence. With sickening clarity, Jo heard Riva telling Murdock, *I'll give you the field pass when I come back.*

She didn't plan to come back. She planned to split and cheat her partners out of their share of the profits.

'Murdock, this is bad,' Jo said. 'There's no good reason for Riva to sit there in the pickup. Something's squirrelly.'

'You made a mess of my evening, that's what's squirrelly.'

'She's going to run, and she doesn't want to leave witnesses.' Because she wanted to give herself a head start. Because she hated Misty. 'Put the car in gear. I want to be able to get out of here.'

'Don't be stupid.'

Jo turned to him. 'Murdock, she's going to double-cross you.'

Kanan stared at Riva in the darkened pickup. 'They're not dead.'

Riva was breathing hard. Her eyes were wide. 'Ian, no. I'm sorry to have to tell you this again.'

'Again? What the hell are you talking about?'

'I hate this. It rips the wound open every time.'

'What do you mean, every time?' How many times had she told him this?

No. It wasn't possible.

She put her hand on his. 'Honey, they're gone.'

Honey?

Her palm, resting on his, throbbed with heat. She squeezed his hand and licked her lips as though they were dry.

'Listen carefully,' she said. 'I know it's a blow. But you have to hold it together. We only have a few minutes.'

'What the hell are you saying, Riva?'

'It's okay.'

'It's fucking not.' To him she looked – *frantic* behind those doe eyes. Needy, and . . . cagy, and like she was taking a chance.

'Baby,' she said, 'you can't think about things right now. Just listen to me. We have to grab this opportunity. We'll never get it again.'

He slid his hand out from under hers. 'I'm not your baby. Are you – Christ, Riva. *No*. What are you trying to pull?'

'Ian.' Her hand came up, as if she wanted to reach for him.

He recoiled. 'Where's my wife? Where's my son?'

'I told you. They're dead.'

'And I've hooked up with you instead? You're in fantasy land.'

Her voice sharpened. 'Stop this. We don't have time to mess around.'

Abruptly, self-consciously, she softened and reached to touch his shoulder. The ring on her finger caught the light. He grabbed her hand.

'Why are you wearing Misty's wedding ring?' He looked at her neck. She had on the dolphin necklace. 'I gave those to her. Take them off.'

His fear, his panic and confusion, seemed to fill the air around him like a hiss.

'What's going on? And do *not* tell me I'm sleeping with you. My memory's shot to hell but I know I am not getting between the sheets with you. No way. So stop playing this goddamned game and tell me where my family is.'

Slowly Riva withdrew her hand. When it reached her lap it was a fist. For a moment her lips quivered. Then she swallowed. She snatched the necklace and yanked it off, breaking the chain. She wrenched the ring off her finger. She shoved the jewelry at him, clutched in her fist. She lifted her chin and spoke through her teeth.

'They're dead.' She looked out the windshield. 'And their killers are in your Tahoe.'

Murdock glowered at Jo. 'Stop trying to mind-fuck us. Riva's getting the stuff from Kanan.'

Jo tried to keep her breathing even, but her heart was drumming. The red dashboard clock read 10:24.

'Riva's been in the pickup with Kanan more than five minutes,' she said.

'So?'

'In any five-minute span, Kanan's memory is wiped clean. I'm telling you, she's going to turn on you. This whole setup is wrong.'

Murdock's cell phone rang. He answered it with annoyance in his voice.

'What?' He frowned and sucked his teeth, staring out the windshield at the pickup. He shrugged. 'Sure.'

Hanging up, he turned to Vance. 'Watch them.'

Murdock set his phone on the dashboard and got out of the Tahoe. He stepped clear of the door, raised a hand, and waved.

Riva dropped Misty's necklace and wedding ring into Kanan's palm. The gold felt warm, tainted. He heard, as if through thick walls, Riva on the phone. He looked at her face.

She had been beaten. Her lip was split, her face puffy, and she had a blistered red welt on the side of her forehead that looked like the imprint of an iron. She put the phone away. She was shaking with rage and pain.

395

'What happened to you?' he said.

'I escaped from the kidnappers. Seth and Misty didn't. The police found their bodies,' she said. 'They were beaten to death. Misty was raped.'

The truck, his vision, went white.

'The cops got to their hideout. Misty and Seth were already dead,' she said. 'But the kidnappers don't know that they've been discovered. They still think you're going to hand over the sample of Slick.'

'It's not true,' he said, but without any volition whatsoever, a great cry rolled through him and erupted. He grabbed his head and fell against the window.

He couldn't breathe. He couldn't see.

'Ian,' she said.

He couldn't open his eyes. She grabbed him around the neck with her soft hot fingers.

'Ian, that's him.'

She hit the high beams. He forced himself to look. Up the road, a man was standing next to the Tahoe. Door open, fully exposed. He raised his arm in acknowledgement.

'Two kidnappers,' Riva said. 'Man and a woman. You suspected a woman all along, and you were right.'

He closed his fist around Misty's ring and necklace.

'Ian.' Riva looked like she was about to crack – like she'd had more than she could take. 'I'm with you. Whatever you do. However far you need to take it. But we have to do it now.'

The rifle was behind the seats.

'Take the wheel,' he said.

37

o kept Murdock in her peripheral vision. He stood next
o the Tahoe, signaling to Calder.

The pickup's high beams drilled the street. Behind the
vall of white light she thought she saw a shadow stretch
rom the sunroof of the pickup.

'Oh, hell –'

Murdock pitched backward as though he'd been
lammed in the chest with a wrecking ball. The report
ame as a crack in the air. Murdock fell and lay splayed
n the ground with a dark wet stain spreading across
iis chest.

Aorta, or straight into a ventricle.

'Jesus.' Jo ducked.

The next noise sounded like a marble hitting the wind-
hield at the speed of sound. A small clean hole punched
hrough the glass.

'Hell's happening?' Vance tried to open the back

397

door but the childproof lock stopped him. 'Murdock, what's –'

Crack, another bullet pierced the windshield. It hit the empty passenger seat. Glass dust and upholstery fragments blew around the interior.

'They're shooting at us. Vance, put the car in gear,' Jo yelled.

His face stretched with panic. 'What?'

'Shooting. Put it in gear. *Do it*.'

The pickup roared toward them, eating up the distance down the wide avenue. Another report pinged off the Tahoe's frame. Vance cringed. His face bleached white in the glare of the onrushing headlights.

'Vance!'

Whimpering, he fumbled for the gearshift. Jo yelled, 'Come *on*.'

He yanked the gearshift into reverse and cringed to the floor in the back seat.

Jo floored it.

Crack. A hole powdered the windshield. Vance whimpered. In the mirror, Jo saw Misty work her hands under her butt and pull the gag from her mouth.

'Riva's shooting at us?' Misty shouted.

No, *your husband is*. Jo hunkered down. She needed speed, needed to put distance between her and the shooter, and would never do that in reverse.

She slammed on the brakes. 'Put it in drive.'

They squealed to a stop. Vance's arm flailed for the gearshift. Got it. The SUV jerked into drive.

Jo aimed straight at the headlights. Pedal to the firewall

398

She ducked low and heard a plea in the base of her throat that was mostly terror and some freakish kind of prayer. *Outta my way, motherfucker.*

'What are you doing?' Misty said.

Two hundred yards. One fifty. A hundred.

Above her head, the Tahoe's sunroof shattered. Glass sprayed across the inside of the vehicle. She held the wheel straight.

Airbag wasn't going to protect her below the chest. Her donor card was current.

'Run away!' Vance shrieked.

Fifty yards. She was committed. The high beams were right in her face.

The pickup swerved.

Bam, a hard noise reverberated through the Tahoe. The pickup had clipped the Tahoe's wing mirror clean off. In the rearview mirror, Jo saw the pickup veer, over-correct, and bounce over the curb onto the lawn of an office building. In the far back of the Tahoe she saw Misty bent over Seth, working somehow to free him from the plastic handcuffs.

The pickup's brake lights came on. It fishtailed, kicked up clods of grass, and turned a doughnut on the lawn. Jo saw the dark shape of a man standing on the truck's passenger seat and bracing himself against the sunroof, and he had to have a hell of a big gun. She kept her foot to the floor.

'What's going on?' Misty cried.

'Fuck, oh, fuck oh fuck it fuck it . . . ,' Vance moaned. What's happening?'

'Riva's trying to goddamned kill us. Cut me loose from the cuffs.'

Misty cried, 'Seth, stay down.'

Jo sped south along Coleman. She needed to get to a populated place. She needed a police station. She needed a battle tank and a Stinger missile.

'Call Riva,' Vance cried from the floor. 'Tell her to stop.'

'She won't. We have to get away. Cut me loose.'

In the mirror the pickup's high beams swung around and centered on her again.

Kanan stood on the seat and braced himself against the frame of the sunroof. Riva swerved back into the road and headed south after the fleeing Tahoe. The rifle was steady in his arms.

One down.

One to go. A woman was at the wheel. He couldn't see her from this angle, but he was sure he'd spotted long dark hair, a pale face. Somebody determined to kill them, playing chicken, racing straight at them. No question about it.

The wind raked his face. He squinted at the Tahoe. The pickup's headlights reflected off the tinted glass in its tailgate. He saw movement inside. A person?

'Riva,' he yelled, 'you sure it's just two?'

'Ian, take your shot.'

He bent down and shouted into the pickup. 'Is somebody in the back of the Tahoe?'

'No.'

'You're sure –'

'Misty and Seth are dead. *Shoot.*'

She was practically screaming. He straightened. Through the wind and the night, he raised his weapon.

Jo raced through a red light. Trees and office buildings swept past under the streetlights.

Vance shouted, 'Call Riva and tell her to stop this. Negotiate.'

Talk about denial. 'I can't reach the phone. Cut me loose.'

'How'd she get such good aim?'

'She has a shooter. Cut me loose.'

Misty said, 'Seth, keep your head low.'

Seth piped in. 'Who's shooting? Is Murdock . . . is he . . . where's Dad?'

Jo said, 'Vance, help me or we'll all die.'

The hard marble sound slapped through the Tahoe again.

Vance screamed. 'It's Kanan, isn't it? He's got a gun and he's – Riva warned us about him and . . . ohh, God.'

'It's Ian? Are you nuts?' Misty said.

How nuts, and what kind? 'The live kind, and pray we stay that way,' Jo said.

Above the trees in the sky ahead, a descending jetliner approached the airport perimeter fence, landing lights blazing. More jets were lined up on approach behind it.

Seth said, 'Why is Dad shooting at us?'

Jo knew why. 'He doesn't know you're in the car.'

'He's *shooting* at us?' Seth said.

'He knows you've been kidnapped. He's trying to rescue you.'

Misty gaped at Jo, her mouth slowly opening.

Seth said, 'I knew Dad would come and get us.'

Kanan would never deliberately harm his family. If Jo was certain of anything, it was that. He would put himself on the line for his wife and son. He would kill to defend them.

And he wouldn't riddle their kidnappers with bullets before they told him where his family was. He might kill them, though, if he thought his family had been rescued.

She was never going to outrun Kanan. She might outrun the pickup, but not a high-powered rifle. Through trees and industrial buildings she saw the runways and the blazing lights of the airport's commercial terminals. At the airport were armed San Jose cops and maybe some quick-witted young national guardsmen standing watch. She had to get there.

'Misty. What did Ian do in the army?'

Jo glanced in the mirror. Misty was lying low, trying to hold Seth below the tailgate window.

Her eyes were flinty. 'He was a scout sniper.'

He definitely might kill the kidnappers if he thought his family had been rescued.

Voice rising, Misty cried, 'Seth, keep down.'

With a splintering, liquid *crack*, a bullet hit the back window.

38

The marble sound spit through the Tahoe. The plastic round the stereo splintered, sprayed, and hit Jo's right arm. She flinched but couldn't pull her hands from the wheel.

She was a target in a shooting gallery. Let's play cowboys and psychiatrists.

From the floor behind her came a dribble of curses, Vance's sniveling plea to a stunted and foul little god. When the dust flew through the vehicle, he screamed.

His arm came up, waving his pistol. 'Drive faster, bitch.'

'Then cut me loose,' Jo shouted again.

She raced down Coleman and burned past another car. Maybe they'd call 911. But even if they did, and even if the police responded within a minute, a bullet needed only a second to do its work.

Like a berserk rat, Vance scrambled into the front passenger seat and grabbed for the door handle. His jeans were falling down on his skinny butt. He clawed at the handle. Got it open. The wind rushed in. Then, with a piggy squeal, he launched himself out, kicking off the driver's seat like a swimmer off the blocks, clouting Jo in the face with his shoe.

Her head snapped sideways. Stars flared in her eyes. The Tahoe's back wheels rolled over an obstacle. It felt like hitting a log, or Snoop Clodd.

Misty clambered into the front passenger seat. In her right hand she held a pair of scissors. The blades were long, sharp, and bloody.

'You stabbed him?' Jo said.

'In the ass.'

Affection bubbled in Jo's chest. 'Please, be my best friend.'

Hunching low, Misty reached across the car with the scissors and tried to cut the zip ties that bound Jo to the steering wheel.

'Hold still,' she said.

'Fat chance.'

The Tahoe had power but steered like a fridge-freezer. The shears veered back and forth, dagger points swinging near her wrist.

'Don't watch me, watch the road,' Misty said.

'Mom *warned* me about driving with scissors.'

'I'm a nurse. If I slit your wrist, I'll stick on a Little Mermaid Band-Aid and give you a lollipop.'

'I'm a shrink. If you slit my wrist, I'll have to section myself.'

Calder's headlights swelled in the rearview mirror, blinding white.

'We have to get to the airport main terminal and surround ourselves with cops,' Jo said.

'Freeway. Eight-eighty, entrance is up ahead.'

Jo could see the overpass a quarter-mile down the road. From there, getting to the main terminals by freeway would take five minutes.

'No time.'

Ahead she saw one of the side streets that led to the private aviation terminals. She slammed on the brakes and slid around the corner. Misty lurched against the dashboard.

'Sorry.'

Jo didn't know she could push her foot so hard against the gas pedal. She didn't know if they were going to make it. She boomed past a darkened business park. Misty jammed the scissors under the zip tie around Jo's right wrist, squeezed the grip with both hands, and snapped the plastic.

The gate to the airfield lay dead ahead at the end of the street.

She held the wheel steady. 'Scissors.'

Misty handed them to her.

'Murdock put his phone on the dash. Look on the floor,' Jo said.

Driving with her left hand, Jo worked the blades around the plastic cuff and snapped it. Misty fumbled around and came up with the phone. Peripherally Jo saw her squinting at the display, dialing a number. She was near tears. Ducking low, Misty put the phone to her ear and peered around the seat to look out the back window.

'Ian's not answering.'

In the rearview mirror Jo saw the pickup take the turn onto the side road badly. It overcorrected and ran toward the curb, splashing water from the gutter. Kanan had a rifle in his arms.

'Seth, you okay?' Misty called.

No answer.

Misty raised her head. 'Seth?'

'Mom . . . I'm hurt.'

'Jesus.' Misty scrambled between the seats and dived into the far back.

Jo looked at the speedometer. She was going eighty-five. Her eyes jinked to the mirror, trying to see the boy. All she saw, through a back window peppered with bullet holes, were Calder's headlights.

She looked ahead. The Tahoe swallowed ground, speeding toward the airfield gate. Beyond it were the cherry-red lights of the airfield.

Okay, *now*. 'Hang on.'

She braced herself. The gate was a simple swing-arm, painted red and white, with a control pad on the driver's side to swipe the field pass. She didn't know if it was wood or steel, whether it would splinter when she hit it or come through the windshield at sixty-five miles per hour.

She hit it going ninety. Metal shrieked. The gate clanged out of her way, flinging sparks like a sharpening wheel, and she drove onto the airfield apron.

'Is Seth hit?' she said.

Misty's voice came back, screwed down tight. 'Shoulder, through and through.'

406

Jo hurtled past a corporate aviation terminal, plush and brightly lit. Its plate-glass windows overlooked the runways, but she couldn't see anybody moving around inside. She drove past parked cars and past parked single-engine planes.

Surely Calder wouldn't follow her. She couldn't. Even she wasn't crazy enough to conduct a running gun battle on an active runway at a major metropolitan airport. Jo looked in the mirror.

Kanan saw the Tahoe smash aside the airfield gate like it was a spatula. He held on to the rifle and braced against the sunroof. He felt the pickup slow.

He leaned down and looked at Riva. 'Follow them.'

She looked up in shock. 'No.'

'Go, damn it.'

'Out onto the airfield? That's insane.'

Why was she looking at him like that? Why did she suddenly seem to think everything was screwed? She slowed the truck even further, approaching the broken gate, and looked around.

In the distance, on the tarmac outside a private hangar, he saw the Chira-Sayf corporate jet. The stairs were down, the lights on. It was being prepped for a flight.

He reached behind his back and pulled out the HK pistol jammed in the waistband of his jeans. Left-handed, he aimed it down at Riva's head.

'The people who killed my family are not getting away. Drive.'

*　　*　　*

Staring in the rearview mirror, Jo willed the headlights of the pickup to turn around and disappear. The truck was falling behind. It hadn't come through the gate onto the airfield.

With a burst of speed, it accelerated.

'God, they're following,' she said. 'I can't believe it.'

Kanan wouldn't so recklessly chase people he thought had kidnapped his family, even if he thought they were close to getting away, would he?

No. He would chase people he thought had killed his family.

He would kill them. He would lose himself to avenge Seth and Misty. He would go crazy.

She raced past hangars and private jets along the apron. Obviously, pitifully, there was no security on this side of the airport. She swept by the Chira-Sayf jet. In the distance, across the taxiway, beyond the dark slash of the active runways, were the commercial terminals.

She checked the mirror again. Calder was behind her on the apron and gaining.

Saturday they die. But Ian Kanan had lost the ability to know what day it was.

'Misty, he thinks you're dead.'

'Oh, God,' Misty said. 'We have to do something.'

The airfield was a void between the Tahoe and safety. The runways were more than two miles long. The terminals were almost half a mile away. Attempting to cross to them would knock *How nuts?* out of the park.

The white landing lights of a descending airliner lit the sky. The jet screamed over the runway threshold and touched down. It roared past at well over a hundred miles per hour, thrust reversers roaring.

Behind her, the headlights of the pickup brightened. She inhaled. Throwing the wheel, she cut across an access ramp and toward the west runway.

The pickup followed.

Jo drove straight across the runway. Her hair was standing on end. She crossed the center line, lit to psychedelic primary colors by a trail of green and red lights. She pinned her gaze on the terminals.

Checking in. No ticket, no identification. I didn't pack my bags myself, I'm carrying a full tank of gasoline, a bunch of bullets, and did not put my hair gel or any other shit in a clear plastic bag. Ready or not, here we crazy-ass come.

She cleared the runway and ran onto the dirt. The wheel juddered in her hands. The pickup followed.

She could think of only one more option. 'He'll stop shooting if he knows you're alive.'

In the mirror Misty's face stretched with tension. 'What's wrong with him?'

'He loves you. He's a warrior.'

Misty shook her head. 'Why did you tell Murdock that after five minutes, Ian's memory would be wiped clean?'

'He has a head injury. His memory is affected.'

Misty said nothing, just absorbed it. 'Seth, stay down.'

She got to her knees, spread her arms wide, and pressed her hands against the back window, right in his sights.

The glass in the tailgate was salted with bullet holes.

Jo had no idea whether Kanan could see, much less identify, his wife through the blistered white mess of the rear
window.

Misty pressed her hands to the glass, cruciform, turned
to a silhouette by the white glare of Riva's headlights.

Jesus, what trust. Tears sprang to Jo's eyes. Misty held
her position. The pickup kept coming.

'Mom . . . are you okay?' Seth said.

Ahead, the terminals loomed brighter. Jo bounced
across the dirt. The lights of the east runway grew sharper,
like an electrified fence.

She looked to the right. And saw a jet accelerating
down the runway toward her, halfway through its takeoff
roll.

Kanan leaned forward and snugged the stock of the rifle
against his shoulder. The pickup bounced over the bare
dirt between the runways. Around him he heard the rising
whine of turbofan engines.

The pickup's headlights caught the back window of
the Tahoe and veered away again.

Somebody was in the back.

'Riva,' he shouted into the wind.

The tailgate window was frosted white with bullet
holes, but a woman was kneeling there, both hands
pressed to the glass.

'Shoot her,' Riva yelled.

The noise and wind and mayhem faded away. With a
clarity that made the night vanish like smoke, he saw
the lifeline of a hand he had held for fifteen years. He

410

saw the eyes he looked into at night before he fell asleep.

He swung the barrel of the rifle aside. 'It's Misty.'

'You're seeing things.'

He blinked the wind from his eyes, looked again at the Tahoe, and knew Riva was right. He couldn't identify Misty's palms or a brief gaze from this far away, under these conditions, even with his brain rewired and hyperperceptive.

But he knew that nobody but Misty would step up and put herself in his crosshairs.

'It's her. She's alive. Break off.'

The truck kept barreling onward. What the hell was going on?

'Riva?'

He ducked down inside the cab, bringing the rifle with him.

Riva gave him a crazed look.

'Break off,' he said.

White light swarmed over the cab. He turned. Grabbed the seat belt. He watched the jet roll down the runway.

Holy God, it was a 757.

Jesus, I hate flying. For two years Jo had avoided aircraft at all costs. She had forfeited her frequent-flyer miles. She had thrown out her copy of *Catch Me If You Can*. And still one of the damned things was headed straight for her. She pushed the pedal to the firewall and blew onto the runway. She heard the jet's turbine engines howling.

411

She tore across the runway. The white lights of the jet rotated skyward. The nose lifted. Its landing gear hung below the fuselage like talons. She drove onto the dirt and kept going. The jet howled behind her, wheels lifting off the runway.

'Holy shit,' Seth said.

The 757 growled into the air. In her rearview mirror, the headlights of the pickup reached the runway. Jo bounced onto the taxiway, turned hard, and drove toward a line of airliners parked at the terminal.

'Oh, God,' Misty said.

The pickup raced onto the runway behind the 757. Jet blast hit it, engines at full takeoff thrust.

'No!' Misty cried.

Calder fishtailed. Her headlights went awry, veering like a lighthouse searchlight. The pickup jacked sideways and flipped. In the fury of the jet blast, it caught air and lifted off the ground. Six feet, ten, truly airborne.

It was going so fast that it landed on the dirt, halfway to the taxiway. In the rearview mirror its headlights spun like bulbs in a tumble dryer.

'Ian!' Misty cried.

'Dad!' Seth yelled, and turned to Jo. 'Stop, stop.'

The pickup landed sideways, bounced, and rolled, tires spinning around overhead, dust blowing in a vortex around it. Still traveling immensely fast, it bounced upright and went over again, rolling across the dirt and across the taxiway.

Jo reached the terminal and swerved to a stop behind

the tail of an MD-80. She heard Seth and Misty thud against the side of the Tahoe.

The pickup flipped again and rolled to a stop. Debris was scattered across the tarmac behind it.

'Dad,' Seth cried.

'Let us out,' Misty said.

Jo jumped out, ran to the back of the Tahoe, and raised the tailgate. In the distance, the tarmac was a mess of metal and glass. Steam boiled from the pickup's shattered radiator. The truck lay wrecked on its side against the engine of a 737.

From the windows of the jet, a hundred stunned faces stared out at it.

39

Kanan blinked and cleared his vision. His head was spinning. His chest felt like it had been hit with a sledge-hammer. His right leg throbbed and his right arm responded sluggishly when he moved it. In front of him he saw the shattered windshield of a pickup truck.

He heard tires, horns, his own pulse, and the roar of jet turbines at takeoff thrust. A rifle barrel lay across his shoulder. It was hot.

He heard a woman moaning.

Ambush. Zimbabwe. Slick.

'Ian . . .'

He took hold of the rifle, unbuckled his seat belt, and pushed himself up. The woman's voice sounded familiar. He was bleeding. Through the sunroof he saw a dark sky. They were on an airport tarmac, flipped on their side, urban setting. Major mayhem. *Kabul. IED.* He pulled the stock of his rifle against his shoulder and aimed out the sunroof.

'Ian, get me out of here,' the woman said.

He turned his head. Riva Calder was hanging sideways from her seat belt in the driver's seat. She gave him a long hard look.

'The kidnappers are out there. Shoot,' she said.

Have a plan to kill everybody you meet today. He turned and lowered his eye to the rifle's night scope. His vision was blurry. Blood was running from his scalp across his face.

Across the tarmac, by the tail of an MD-80, three people stood beside a Chevy Tahoe. He saw a woman in Western clothing. She had long dark curls. Another woman. A young man.

'Do it, Ian,' Riva said. 'Your vision's affected. That's them, the kidnappers.'

The dark-haired woman turned and grabbed the hand of the woman standing beside her. They were yelling something, but the roar of jet engines obliterated their words. He blinked again. He had a clear field of fire. He focused on her and drew a breath.

'Shoot, Ian. *Shoot*,' Calder said. 'Look at him – you already shot him once. He's bleeding. Ian, we're trapped here. Don't let them get to us.'

Kanan focused through the night scope. He blinked and looked at the people across the tarmac.

'You really want me to squeeze the trigger?' He raised the HK pistol in his left hand and aimed it at Riva's face. 'Ask me again to fire at my family, and I'll do exactly that.'

* * *

415

Facing the wrecked pickup, Jo, Misty, and Seth held their linked hands aloft. They held there, breathless.

Across the tarmac, Ian Kanan tossed his rifle through the sunroof and crawled from the wreck.

Misty let out a cry of relief.

Seth slumped. 'He's okay.'

Seth's tank finally ran dry, and his legs gave way. Jo and Misty eased him down on the tarmac and leaned him back against the rear wheel of the Tahoe. He was pale and near shock, but his eyes were filled with wonder.

Fire trucks rolled toward them from the distant end of the runway, lights and sirens turning the night to popcorn. Misty was using a strip torn from her sweater as a pressure bandage on Seth's shoulder. She took Jo's hand and pressed it against the wound.

'Keep the pressure on. I'll be back.'

'No.' Jo grabbed her arm. 'Hold on.'

Misty pulled loose. 'Ian's hurt.'

'And contaminated. You can't touch him, or you and Seth could be contaminated too. Wait for the fire crew.'

The fire trucks rumbled up, towering yellow engines blowing diesel fumes. Firefighters jumped out. Jo jogged toward them, waving with both arms.

'I'm a doctor and a San Francisco Police Department liaison. We need hazmat decontamination. We have a blood-borne pathogen. Universal exposure control precautions.'

Kanan pulled himself upright. He threw two pistols on the tarmac beside the rifle and limped toward his family. He was a mess, but the expression suffusing his face, erasing all his pain, was joy.

416

Jo ran halfway to him and held up her hands. 'Stop, an. You've been contaminated with Slick. You can't ouch anybody until you've been cleaned up.'

He halted, swaying, and stretched a hand toward his vife. 'Misty.'

Misty approached Jo's side. Her face looked ready to rumble. 'Ian.'

'Does Riva have a weapon?' Jo said.

He shook his head. 'Negative.'

She felt tension loosen and dissipate into the sky. Inside he terminal, people pressed against the plate-glass vindows, staring and pointing. On the tarmac, ground rew and baggage handlers approached. The driver of a uel tanker opened his door and stepped out onto the unning board. In the loaded 737, passengers jostled to ee what was happening. The captain jogged down the tairs from the Jetway. Cameras flashed.

The scene was chaos, Kanan and Seth were injured, nd behind the swell of jet engines she heard police sirens. he would probably get hauled to jail.

The night felt glorious.

It was over. Jo knew what she was feeling: primal xhilaration. She had survived.

The firefighters pulled on gloves and protective yewear. Jo did likewise, snapping on a pair of latex loves and putting on plastic safety glasses. She said, Favor?' and wangled a coat and stethoscope from them. f she assumed the trappings of authority, she might keep he police off her back temporarily.

Kanan stretched a hand toward Seth. 'Christ – you're

wounded.' He called in distress to the firefighters. 'My son's been hit. Help him. The bastards shot my son.'

Two firefighters grabbed a medical kit and ran to attend to Seth. Another fire truck pulled up by the wrecked pickup and began spraying it with firefighting foam.

Kanan wobbled on his feet, lost his balance, and fell to his knees. Jo followed a firefighter-paramedic to his side.

'Hold still, buddy.' The firefighter began examining Kanan. 'What's this?'

Under his penlight, Jo saw the message written on Kanan's arm. It now read *Saturday they died*.

Kanan stared at it, then looked at Seth, flat on the tarmac, and Misty, standing back, hand pressed to her mouth. He reread the message with horror.

'What the hell's been happening?' he said.

Jo took a gauze pack from the firefighter's medical kit and poured Betadine on it. She knelt at Kanan's side.

'You kept your family alive,' she said.

She rubbed the writing off of Kanan's skin. But though the words disappeared, he continued staring at his arm.

He looked up at her. 'It won't ever go away, will it?'

It broke her heart to know what he meant. 'No.'

He would never know, for more than five minutes at a stretch, that his family was safe. If they were in front of him he would feel elated and wild with relief. If they left his sight he would forget and plunge again into despair.

'Every few minutes, you'll reset to the last thing you recall before your injury,' she said.

418

'I'll always think they're gone and that I'll never get to them in time.'

He would wake up every morning in fear and grief. It would never lessen.

'Did I hunt down the bastards who took them?' he said.

'Yes.'

He nodded, but his satisfaction was short-lived. 'In a few minutes I'll try to hunt them down again, won't I?'

The firefighter touched Jo's shoulder. 'Excuse me, doctor.'

Jo stood and let him get to work. All Kanan's memories – the truth, reality – would be collected, and he would be left only with the unresolved crisis.

The emergency lights danced over the scene, turning it glaring primary colors, red and blue, adding to the white aircraft landing lights. Fourth of July in March. Kanan and Misty looked at each other. Ian's pale eyes were full of tears.

'Woman, you're the best thing I'll ever see.'

'We're okay, hon. Everything's going to be okay.'

Her voice was thready. Jo put an arm around her shoulder. Misty smiled uncertainly at her.

'Ian,' Jo said. 'Do you remember being in contact with Slick?'

'In Zambia.'

'Tonight?'

'No. Why?' And then his eyes said that he knew. 'Second exposure would be fatal, wouldn't it?'

Jo nodded. 'The firefighters are going to take you

through decontamination and then get you to the hospital.'

'Good.'

She turned to Misty. 'Don't let Ian lose eye contact with you. Not even for a minute. Got it?'

Sadness and fear curved across Misty's face. 'Got it.'

Kanan raised a hand. 'Don't worry. I'm never letting them out of my sight again. That's a promise.'

Jo stepped away, took out Murdock's phone, and dialed a number.

It was answered brusquely. 'Quintana.'

She heard Gabe's voice and her throat caught, her spirits soared, straight into a cloud of tears.

'It's me. I'm okay. It's over,' she said.

'Where are you? Where's Kanan?' Gabe said.

'The San Jose airport. Quintana, you don't know how good you sound. Where are you?'

'I just got out of police custody. I'm on the 101 halfway to Moffett. Jo, where's –'

The whoop of a police siren erased his question.

'What did you say, Gabe?' She smiled. She couldn't help it.

'Where's Kanan's backpack?'

'I don't know.' She looked around. She didn't see it by the pickup or in the trail of debris thrown out of the pickup in the crash.

'His computer battery is in the backpack,' Gabe said. 'It's packed with Slick, and it's destabilized. Jo, where is it?'

She walked toward the truck, searching. Heard Riv

ustling around inside the cab, groaning and trying to lither out the sunroof.

'I don't see a backpack,' she said.

'Jo, get the hell out of there. It's a bomb.'

o Beckett, M.D., forensic psychiatrist, was no chump. So she told herself. She knew all the psychological defenses. Denial. Bargaining. Rationalization, projection, isolation, schizoid breaks, binge eating. And she told herself she had a handle on her own defenses, which meant that a crisis couldn't blindside her. Life, and training, and catastrophe had whupped all surprises out of her. When it came to emergencies, she was a sprinter out of the blocks. She had world-class reaction times. Fire a starter's pistol and *pow*, she'd go.

But she stood on the tarmac and felt that Gabe's words had come at her from behind a sheet of glass, like light, and had bounced off.

'What do you mean, a bomb?'

'Kanan's computer battery contains the sample of Slick. It's about to explode. Do you hear me, Jo? Grab your goddamned ass and *run*.'

The noise of the entire world seemed to rush through the glass. And the scene spread out before her, in its shining, tangled horror.

Kanan spent and damaged behind her. Seth bleeding on the tarmac. People in the terminal. People on loaded airliners. Ten, twelve big jets, plus fire, police, paramedics rolling up by the minute. And the truck driver hopping down from the running board to jog over and offer his

421

help. The truck driver from the gleaming jet fuel tanker. Wings. Full of fuel. A fleet of fire waiting to ignite.

'Oh, my God, Gabe – can . . . oh, shit. We need the bomb squad.'

'There's no time. The sample's volatile, it's eating through the container, and when it gets sufficiently oxygenated, it'll explode. Clear the area.'

She looked around. 'We can't.'

'Kanan's army buddy was with him when Kanan armed the device. He gave it seventy minutes maximum before it went up.'

'How long has it been?'

'Ninety-two.'

She seemed to itch, to tingle, to feel like she was rooted to the tarmac. 'Can we contain it?'

'I can't predict how big the explosion will be. The best you can hope is to sequester it inside a fortified steel bunker Jo. It. Is. Going. To. Blow.'

'Stay on the line.'

She jammed the phone in her pocket and sprinted to the nearest police car. If Slick exploded and sent the fuel tanker and jetliners sky-high, the blast would kill everyone on the tarmac and trap hundreds in burning jetliners – bleeding embedded with shrapnel, all impregnated with Slick.

She grabbed a police officer. 'I'm an SFPD liaison. I'm on the phone with the California Air National Guard. There's a bomb in the pickup truck and it's going to explode.'

He searched her face. His gaze hardened. 'You're positive?'

422

'Yes.'

He turned and began waving people back. 'Clear the area.' He called to a fire captain. 'Get people off these planes.'

'What's wrong?'

Jo turned. Kanan was calling to her.

'Ian, your backpack's in the truck. Slick's eating through the seal in your computer battery, and when it does, it's going to explode.'

'When?'

'Any second. It's past the time you estimated.'

'I estimated? Why would I set it to . . .' He turned and stared in horror at the airliners and emergency vehicles. 'We have to get it out of here.'

'How?' Jo said.

He struggled to his feet. 'Drive it away from here. Keep it in an enclosed space.'

'Like an SUV?' She pointed to the Tahoe.

'Yes.' He took a step, patting his pockets. 'Keys.'

'In the ignition.'

The firefighters lifted Seth onto a stretcher and rushed him toward an ambulance. Misty hadn't moved.

Kanan reached into his pocket and pulled out a ring. He looked at it, puzzled.

From inside the wrecked pickup came a whump and an unladylike grunt. Calder had managed to undo her seat belt. She slithered from the wreck covered in fire-fighting foam.

She had the backpack in her hands. Kanan limped toward her.

'No,' Misty said. 'Ian, stop.'

Kanan looked at the rifle he had set on the tarmac, at Seth, and back at his wife. 'How did he get hit?'

Jo and Misty said nothing. He scanned their faces. It sank in.

'I'll be back,' he said.

'Ian, no.' Misty rushed toward him. 'Don't do this. You promised. You said you'd never let us out of your sight. Stop – a second exposure will kill you.'

A cop ran over and ushered her away from the pickup. 'Come on. Move, quick.'

Kanan checked his watch. To Jo he said, 'I have time. I can do it.'

Calder dropped to her knees on the tarmac and pulled the computer battery from the backpack. She looked across the runway, toward the waiting Chira-Sayf corporate jet, as though she might try to crawl to it. Through the firefighting foam, the battery was bubbling.

Misty fought to get loose from the cop. 'Ian, don't leave us. You can't. We need you. For God's sake, don't. You'll be contaminated with a second dose. You'll die. You can't do this to us.'

Kanan looked at her and his face broke. His resolve crumbled.

He turned to Jo. 'I can't.'

A suffocating fear took hold of her. Aboard the 737 she saw people jostling frantically in the aisles. Inside the terminal, pandemonium had erupted. Amid sirens and shouting, firefighters were loading Seth into the ambulance.

Misty battled the cop as he ushered her away. 'Stop. Get your hands off me.'

Kanan watched. With a broken breath, he said, 'Let me forget.'

'What?' Jo said.

'I can do it if I forget all this.' He limped toward her. 'If I forget I have my family back. And forget what will happen if I'm exposed again. Then I can do it.'

Jo stared at him in horror. 'Ian –'

'I caused this. I have to undo it.'

She got control of her voice. 'If you drive too long, you'll forget what's happening. Go too far and you'll keep going. You might head straight back to a populated area.'

He pointed at a patch of dirt a quarter of a mile down the runway. 'Twenty seconds.'

Her heart pounded. 'You sure?'

'Help me. Keep Misty and Seth out of my sight.'

She held his gaze. Then she turned and dashed to the firefighting crew. 'Put Mrs Kanan in the back of the ambulance with Seth and shut the door. I don't have time to explain. Just do it.'

Misty was struggling to get free of the police officer. The firefighters called to him. 'Bring Mrs Kanan to the ambulance. Hurry.'

The cop dragged Misty toward it. She twisted in his grasp.

'What's happening?' She looked at Jo, and then at her husband. 'What are you doing?'

The cop and firefighters lifted her bodily into the ambulance and shut the doors.

Jo turned to Kanan. 'Follow me.'

She led him out of sight of the ambulance. 'Close you eyes.'

He did. Opened them again. 'Wait.'

'There's no time to wait.'

He took her gloved hand and set Misty's wedding ring in her palm. 'Give it to her.'

Jo nodded tightly. 'Close your eyes and count to ten.'

He counted. She breathed along, her chest constricting.

'Ten.'

'Open your eyes.'

He looked at her without recognition.

'Ian, we're at San Jose airport and you have to ge your computer battery from Riva. Don't ask questions just do it. Seth and Misty's lives depend on it. You have ten seconds to grab it and drive your Tahoe to that dir patch at end of the runway.'

Kanan stared at her uncertainly.

'Do it. Riva kidnapped them. Get the battery from her and drive it away from here. This second. Or they'l die.'

For an interminable moment he continued staring a her. Then he turned. Calder sat on the tarmac covered in firefighting foam, clutching the battery. Kanan limped over to her, grabbed her by the arm, and wrestled it free The seal was still bubbling.

She cried out and grabbed his leg. 'Ian. Stay with me.'

He pulled loose and hobbled to the Tahoe. Groaning in pain, he climbed in and started the engine.

Through the back window of the ambulance, Misty

saw him. She ducked past the firefighters, threw the door open, and leaped out. 'Ian, no.'

The path to the runway was clear. He put the Tahoe in gear. Misty bolted toward it. Jo ran and threw herself at her. With a full-body tackle, she brought her down. They fell heavily on the tarmac.

'Misty, you can't.'

'He'll die. Ian!'

Jo clapped a hand over Misty's mouth and held her down. The Tahoe revved. Kanan accelerated around the tail of the jet, around the fire trucks, and raced for the runway.

Gabe hit the traffic jam a mile from the San Jose airport. Nothing but taillights, a bright red river stretching up the freeway as far as he could see. Everybody was slowing to gawk at what was happening at the airfield.

His cell phone was still connected to Jo, but all he heard was fuzz and muffled voices. *Jo, talk to me*, he thought. *Come back.*

Beyond the airport perimeter fence he saw the blue and red pulse of emergency lights flashing off buildings and aircraft.

The explosion was furious and brilliant.

The fireball flashed white. The roar clapped through his 4Runner. The flames spread and fell, yellow, orange, smoke pouring up to obscure them in a black shroud.

'Jo,' he yelled.

He spun the wheel, drove onto the shoulder of the freeway, and floored it toward the perimeter fence.

*　　*　　*

At the distant end of the runway, orange flame consumed the interior of the Chevy Tahoe. The SUV rolled down the concrete and onto the dirt and slowed to a stop. Nobody got out.

Facedown on the tarmac, Jo held on to Misty Kanan. Misty lay suspended in those eerie seconds between the sight of truth and its impact. Jo bit back the tears that were rising in her throat. The door of the ambulance opened and Seth stumbled out.

'Mom.'

Misty crawled away from Jo's grasp, staggered to her feet, and went to him. He fell into her arms and began to cry.

Jo climbed to her feet. Heat rolled over her. Aboard airliners and in the terminal, people stared horrified at the fire. Their faces wore the reflection of flames on glass. She closed her eyes and heard sirens and sobbing. In her clenched hand, she felt the ring.

She turned and walked, head hammering, to Misty's side. Collapsed on the tarmac, Misty held Seth while his hands clawed her shirt and he wept against her shoulder. She raised her head. Jo would remember the look on her face until the day she died.

'Leave,' Misty said.

'He wanted –' Jo's voice caught. 'Asked me to give . . .'

She unfurled her hand. Firelight swam across the gold in Misty's wedding ring.

Misty took it and turned her head away.

Jo stepped back. The heat of the fire was painless in comparison.

Through the spinning emergency lights she saw a man run beneath an airliner, jump and slide across the hood of an aviation tractor, and sprint onto the runway, heading toward the burning hulk of the Tahoe.

She didn't think she had a voice left, but she raised her hands and called out. 'Gabe.'

When he heard her, he turned his head. She was already running. She didn't stop until she reached his arms.

40

The sky flew blue above the park in the morning sun. Under the breeze, Monterey pines trembled and the sage and purple heather bent toward the bay. Gabe stretched his legs and spread his arms across the back of the park bench. On the basketball court, Sophie dribbled toward the hoop and shot a layup. It knocked against the rim and dropped in.

'Two points for Quintana,' Gabe said.

Sophie gave him a shy, pleased smile and retrieved the ball. Strands of brown hair haloed around her face.

Jo paced along the sideline, phone to her ear. Amy Tang sounded cranky.

'You got me involved in this case, Beckett. You owe me a beer. I think I have permanent gluteal damage from sitting on the cement floor in that basement.'

Jo rubbed her eyes and almost laughed. 'I owe you a beer because I got you involved. I owe you a new car for getting me off the hook with the police and TSA.'

She gazed across the park, past her house and across city rooftops, to the Golden Gate Bridge. Beyond it were the windswept green hills of the Marin headlands. Then sky, and forever.

'One question, Amy – how, precisely, did you escape?'

'That support pole my hands were bound behind? It was a couple of feet from the wall, and near the top it had a bracket clamped around it. I crammed my legs underneath me and managed to stand up. Then I put my back to the pole, pressed my feet flat against the wall, and shinnied up. When I got high enough, I sawed the tape back and forth against the bracket. It took me an hour, but I cut it.'

'And?'

She paused. 'That's when Officer Liu and the SWAT team broke down the door.'

'And found you –'

'Seven feet off the floor, feet planted wide against the wall, with my back to the support and a rubber ball in my mouth.'

Jo smiled broadly. 'You pole-danced your way to freedom?'

'If you ever speak of this again –'

'Did SWAT get photos?'

'Beckett . . .'

Jo laughed.

'Any word on Alec Shepard?' Tang said.

'He's in intensive care. When the officer got to him he was hypothermic and had inhaled water. They're calling it a near-drowning. But they're optimistic.'

'You want to sit in when we interrogate Riva Calder?'

431

Jo hesitated. 'I think I've seen enough of Calder.'

'She's going to be a case study.'

'I know. Anterograde amnesia brought on by nano-particle exposure. But I don't think I care to watch her stare out the door, forever hoping Ian Kanan's going to walk through it.'

Tang was quiet a moment. 'You counted how many of your nine lives you used up last night, cat?'

'I'm glad you're okay too, Tang. Get some rest.'

She walked to the park bench, sat down beside Gabe, and gave him back his phone. He handed her a cup of coffee.

'Hope it's not too strong,' he said.

She drank. 'Rocket fuel. That's the ticket.'

He put an arm around her shoulder. She snugged into her sweater and leaned against him.

'Last night at the airport, before the ambulance took Seth to the hospital, I tried to talk to Misty. She wouldn't look at me,' she said.

'She may never forgive you. Harsh, but there's no way around it,' he said. 'But Kanan understood the risk, and he acted of his own free will. He saved his family and God knows how many other people.'

'The needs of the many outweigh the needs of the few? I don't think Misty's going to buy that.'

'Kanan sacrificed himself. But he wasn't simply acting selflessly. He was atoning.'

'For?'

'Killing people. Contaminating others. Bringing ruin to his family.'

432

'He was brave. He loved them,' she said.

He held her tighter. 'You were brave. Helping him took guts.' His voice softened. 'I'm sorry about how it turned out, Jo.'

She brushed the hair back from her forehead. 'Ian knew he would forget they were safe. He knew he was trapped in an endless loop, an eternal present of crisis without resolution.'

'Sounds like hell.'

'Living without memory would be like dying every minute. Forgetting everything as soon as it happens – having your experiences vanish, all the joy, all the tragedy . . . God, what an empty existence.' She watched the trees sway in the wind. 'You only live fully when you bring the past into your life and make it part of you.'

He gazed at her, pensive. 'You hear yourself?'

'I do. We have to embrace both past and present. No matter how painful, or how deep the scars.'

The wind swept her hair into her eyes again. Gabe took an index finger and hooked it behind her ear.

'Thank you. For everything,' she said.

His gaze remained pensive. 'Jo, about me . . .'

She shook her head. 'Don't. Not now. Tell me when you're ready.'

'I know you've been wondering what's bugging me. Why I've been distant. It's not you.'

Shit. 'It's you?'

'I know I've been preoccupied.' He looked at her. 'I may be called up.'

She stilled. 'Called up to active duty?'

433

'It's not a done deal, but that's the rumor.'

Jo's heart clenched. Gabe looked at Sophie.

'Have you told her?' she said.

'No. I don't want her to worry.'

The little girl didn't need to worry. Jo was already doing it for her. *Sophie needs a father, not a hero.* Jo took his hand.

'If I go, it'll be a twelve-months tour,' he said.

'If you go, you know where I'll be. I'm not going anywhere.'

'Yes, you are. Anywhere I am, you're in my thoughts, *chica.*'

Jo leaned in and kissed him. He took her face in his hands and kissed her back.

'You know how I feel?' he said.

'No, but I think you're going to tell me. And even if you don't, I can live with the uncertainty.'

'Then you're tougher than I am. 'Cause I've got to know – if it's clear tonight, do I get to claim that rain check?'

She just smiled.

Sophie bounced the ball under the basket. 'Guys, want to play?'

They looked up. 'Yeah,' Jo said.

She stood and pulled Gabe to his feet. 'You never know what'll happen. You can only wake up and get in the game, every single day.'

His smile was rueful. They headed onto the court.

Gabe clapped his hands. 'Throw me the ball.'

As gripping as Tess Gerritsen – or your money back!

Meg Gardiner's *The Memory Collector* has everything you want from a heart-stopping thriller – psychological suspense, brilliant characters, and page-turning intrigue.

We're so sure about this, that if you don't enjoy it as much as international bestseller Tess Gerritsen we'll give you your money back. All you have to do is return the book to us, along with a copy of your sales receipt and a letter outlining your reasons for returning it to:

Gardiner Money Back Offer
Fiction Marketing
HarperCollins Publishers
77-85 Fulham Palace Road
London
W6 8JB

We'll refund the price you paid for the book, plus 75p to cover your postage costs.

What's next?

Tell us the name of an author you love

Meg Gardiner   Go ▶

and we'll find your next great book.

www.bookarmy.com